The Diamond Palace

By T. M. Kirk

Book Cover by Artscandare Book Cover Design

For Bunny.

This book would not exist without your unending and unwavering support.

Also by T. M. Kirk

The Onyx Palace Series

The Diamond Palace

The Golden Palace

The Don't Bite Me Series

Don't Bite the Director

Don't Bite the Botanist

Magical Mishaps Series

A Fragile Spell

Author's Note

Thank you so much for joining me in Rivella. Rain's journey is not going to be an easy one, and your mental health is important to me. So I want to let everyone know this story does contain some themes that might be difficult for certain readers. There is a decent amount of mental distress in this book, including panic attacks, discussions of mental health medication, and a brief mention of past assault. There is also descriptive yet consensual sexual content, violence, torture, gore, and death, including the death of a parent.

This book is intended solely for readers over the age of 18.

If none of that is concerning to you, then allow me to be the first to say...

Welcome to Rivella.

Prologue

Sweat and blood trickled down the woman's forehead as she tore through the dark woods, ignoring the twisted branches clawing at her face. Heart pounding in her chest, she spared only a single breath to glance at the sleeping infant in her arms. The sopora weed held strong, and she prayed the child would slumber for many hours more.

By the time she arrived at the small structure in the clearing, her burgundy dress was torn and covered in mud, her legs threatening to give out at a moment's notice. She fell to her knees at the door of the ramshackle cottage.

"Caira!" she screamed with the last of her strength.

The icy fingers of fear squeezed tighter around her heart when she heard no movement inside. If the ancient World Walker wasn't home, there was no one left to save her and her daughter. This dark forest would become their tomb.

To her immense relief, the door finally creaked open, and Caira stepped out. It had been nearly a decade since she last laid eyes on the Walker, yet not one of those years showed on the female's face. No wrinkles marred her smooth alabaster skin, and her shoulder-length auburn hair held no traces of white. Her unforgiving slate gray eyes remained sharp as ever as they snapped down to the distraught woman.

Releasing a long-suffering sigh, Caira stretched out a hand. "Come inside, Leeara. You know it's not safe out here."

"No," Leeara wheezed. "There is no time. I need you to send us away now."

The Walker's eyes darted to the trees as the sound of leaves crunching under many boots reached them, growing louder with each passing second. Her lips pursed into a tight line, displeasure making her harsh features appear even more grim.

"Please help us," Leeara begged. "You promised."

Indecision rolled over the Walker's face, and time stood still while Leeara waited for her fate to be determined.

Caira's shoulders sagged in resignation. "Yes, I promised. And so I shall." Grabbing a lantern, she stepped from the crumbling old structure and positioned herself in the clearing just beyond the cottage.

Leeara sagged against the door frame, watching as the Walker began to chant. Soon they would leave this world. Soon they would be safe.

Her relief was short-lived, though. The melodious words abruptly died, taking Leeara's hope for a future along with it.

Caira peered into the dark of the forest around them, then turned to face Leeara, a touch of sadness in those gray eyes.

"They're here. I'm sorry, but I need more time to locate a suitable realm."

Anguish filled Leeara as she studied the sleeping child in her arms, the tattered gray blanket obscuring all but a perfect, tiny face. Her daughter had not yet seen her first year of life. Had not yet spoken her first words.

"You will live," Leeara whispered, running her fingers through the fine tendrils of her daughter's hair. "You will live, you will be happy, and you will never think of this place, not even once."

Summoning her remaining strength, Leeara stood up and strode over to the Walker. "Save Raynella," she pleaded, handing over her only child.

Caira peered at the woman, the shouts of the king's guards growing louder as they closed the distance. "And what will you do?" she asked, raising one perfectly arched eyebrow.

"Find you some more time."

The chanting resumed behind Leeara as she stepped forward to meet the guards emerging from the depths of the ominous woods.

"You will not have her," she spat at them.

"I'm afraid, Leeara, that you are very wrong."

Her body stiffened, but she held her ground. She knew that voice. Remembered how it made her feel like she wasn't alone all the time. Like she would always have someone in her corner, fighting for her. But the words were no longer kind, the voice no longer that of the person she once knew.

She held her ground as the dark-haired male emerged from the shadows, stepped in front of his soldiers, and regarded her with mixed emotions—pity and pride.

Leeara drew herself up, standing tall in defiance opposite the painfully handsome male.

"Bring the child, Leeara, and let us return to the palace," he said. "Let us put this unpleasantness behind us."

"I will never go with you," she hissed. "Do you honestly think me to be so naïve? Do you think I didn't hear all of you talking? I know what will happen, and I will not allow it."

He gave a small sigh as if it was all just a minor inconvenience. "Leeara, there is nothing you can do," he said, stepping closer and placing the tip of his sword at her chest. "This was always to be your fate. And hers. There is no use fighting it."

Leeara searched his face for any sign of the male he used to be, for even a glimmer of his former kindness, but found nothing.

A loud crack of unnatural thunder reverberated through the air, and she knew the time had come—her distraction had worked.

She met his gaze and smiled. "I don't believe in fate." Surging forward, she impaled herself on his sword.

The male let out an agonized roar as gravity took over and Leeara sank further onto the weapon still held between them. He reflexively pulled the sword from her chest, and her life flowed out in thick red rivulets.

Falling to the ground, Leeara twisted her body so she could watch as the Walker slashed a hand through the air and ripped a hole through the very fabric of existence. Staring at that gash in the world, she beheld a narrow pathway ending at a tall building with brightly lit windows, all of them shining like beacons in the dark night.

With a command to grab the child echoing through the clearing, the guards dashed toward the glowing portal.

The Walker was much quicker, though. She spun with ethereal grace, scooped up the child, and slipped through the rift. On the other side, she clutched the infant to her chest and briefly locked eyes with Leeara. She dipped her head in a barely perceptible nod—a promise fulfilled—then waved her hand to close the portal, sealing Raynella away forever.

Chapter One

Breathe.

Just breathe.

I trained for this. I can do it.

My grasp on the wood in my hand tightened. Desperate to calm the turmoil in my mind, I sucked in another labored breath. Time was not on my side, and I had to do something fast. Never show fear or weakness, my instructor had taught me. They can smell it a mile away.

I steadied my hand, loosened my death grip, and let out a slow, calculated exhale. I was ready.

At least I thought I was until I lifted my head to stare into the black depths before me. Eyes glittered in the darkness, narrowing on me, assessing me, forcing me to accept how weak I truly was.

I can't do it.

Sacrificing everything I worked so hard for, I turned and ran.

Pausing only to swoop up the case that lay at the edge of the pit, I kept running until the sweet warmth of daylight kissed my skin.

With the door slamming shut behind me, I fell against the wall to my right, my heavy black braid cushioning the thump of my head against the rough stone.

I slid to the ground, legs splaying out in an un-ladylike fashion, and my head rolled back as I struggled to inhale the filthy, muggy air. I couldn't stop the sharp ragged gasps, couldn't get any oxygen into my lungs.

In a flash of clarity, I remembered the case at my side and began fumbling at the worn silver clasps. My salvation lay within if I could just get it open...

After what felt like an eternity, the final latch released, and I snatched the bottle laying inside. I clawed at the lid to the small container, my airways constricting even further until... A sharp click as the cap gave way. A cascade of pills erupted into the air, raining down onto the lining of the black case. Grabbing one, I swallowed it dry, wincing as it roughly scraped my throat. Sweat-drenched and shaking, I collapsed against the grimy wall while I waited for relief to come.

Five minutes passed. Then ten. People walked by, most not even sparing a glance in my direction. Eventually my breathing slowed, my heart rate returned to normal, and I was left with only the oppressive feeling of despair and failure.

My eyes fixated on the bottle. Orange with a white lid and the printed words:

Rain L. Solis
Klonopin 1 mg
Take as needed for anxiety attacks

I tucked the pills into my pocket, then nestled the delicate wooden instrument into the case. Staring at the violin, I wondered why I had even bothered showing up to the audition.

I secured the object that had consumed nearly half of my life and rose to my feet. With a glance back at the sign for David Geffen Hall, I realized with a sinking feeling that my chance of playing for the New York Philharmonic was likely long gone. Though, if I was being honest with myself, it never really existed to begin with. Not for someone like me.

So I trudged over to the subway entrance and began the miserable trek back to my small apartment in Jersey.

"Honey, I'm home," I snarked bitterly, pushing open the door to my apartment, not actually expecting any response from the sister I shared the space with. I stepped into the entryway, set down my violin, and tossed my braid back over my shoulder as I straightened. On days like this, when depression rode me hard, I was always tempted to cut the damn thing off. What kept the scissors at bay was the knowledge that short hair had never been a good look for me. With my underfed slim body, barely-there breasts, and height just a few inches short of six feet, anytime I tried a shorter style, I inevitably got called "sir" or "bro" at least once a day. Part of that might have to do with the tattered blue hoodie I typically lived in, but I would die before giving up my comfy clothes.

Clothes that I wanted to get back into, so I moved from the tiny hallway into the living room, freezing in my tracks at the devastation before me.

Now, to be fair, no aspect of my apartment is what one would consider luxurious or posh. In fact, it's pretty much exactly what you would expect for a 1960's built, 700-square-foot, two-bedroom unit in one of the more colorful neighborhoods of Jersey. But leaky aluminum windows, chipped paint, and temperamental furnace aside, I could *usually* rely on the place to be clean.

Today the small space looked like a fabric store had exploded. Expansive swaths of colorful velvet covered the old blue couch that filled most of the small living room. Piles of pink and red tulle buried our crappy TV. And the faded brown carpet was blanketed with lavender jersey knit. Three dress forms stood at the back of the room, and it felt like the mannequins were somehow judging me. As if they knew of my failure.

"You're back early," a chipper voice called from inside the first bedroom. I braced myself when a smiling face framed by an untamed mop of red curls popped out from the room.

As she ran over to greet me, I eyed the half-stitched, pink ruffled dress that hung loosely off her curvy frame and the nearly empty package of Oreos clutched tightly in her hand. She tossed the box onto the table and wrapped me in a tight embrace, despite knowing that I was not now, nor would I ever be, a 'hugger.'

Jenn and I might not be biological sisters, but we'd been raised together in St. Philomena's Orphanage until we were eleven and never lost touch as we both spent the next few years bouncing around the foster system. When we turned eighteen, we moved in together, and for the last seven years we'd been practically inseparable.

"Yeah, I'm back," I mumbled, unable to summon any false cheer.

She pulled away enough to look me in the eye, the previous excitement fading to wary concern.

"It happened again, didn't it?"

My response lodged itself in my throat. I wanted to say that of course it didn't happen. This had been the biggest audition of my life, so there was no way I would let anything ruin my chance to play for The Phil. Not even my broken brain.

But there was no point in lying to Jenn. She'd see right through it.

"Yeah," I whispered, looking away. "It did."

I tried to stop the tear that formed in the corner of my eye. I hated crying. Hated feeling like a broken toy that never worked quite right. I had been able to keep my emotions in check the entire subway trip home, but here, with Jenn, I couldn't hold it back anymore. The tear slipped free and rolled down my cheek, the only evidence of how deeply destroyed I felt inside.

Grabbing my arm, Jenn dragged me over to the couch and plopped us down, crushing a stack of fuchsia velvet squares. She leaned back against the faded cushions and drew my head down to her shoulder.

I don't know how long we sat there, me letting a few tears escape and her just being... her. My safe space.

"It's okay," I said with a shaky resolution. "I'm fine."

I turned to look at her, mentally preparing myself for the potential onslaught of pity and useless attempts to cheer me up. Instead, I only saw genuine concern on her face.

"You don't have to be fine, Rain. Not with me."

She had said those same words so many times, but I never took them to heart. Nobody actually wanted a mess for a sister. As often as people said stuff like,

"I'm always here if you need to talk," or "you can tell me anything," they didn't really mean it. Not really. Everybody had their own lives and their own crap to deal with. Nobody, not even Jenn, needed my baggage as well.

"I know," I said, dismissing her words.

"Do you?"

I glanced away, unable to bear the weight of all that concern in her eyes. "I *will* be fine. Is that better?"

"Rain, this wasn't like an audition for some chintzy local orchestra. We both know this was your dream. I saw how hard you worked on that video audition. How you squealed when you got the letter for the in-person callback. You don't go from squealing in excitement to the bullshit of 'I'm fine.' We both know you're not fine, so please just talk to me."

Crap.

Why did she have to go and say that? I waited for a second and... There it was. That far too familiar anger bubbling up inside me. My natural response to any time someone tugged on the safety blanket of denial that I needed to feel normal.

"What do you want me to say?" I snapped, jumping to my feet and pacing around the room. "Do you want me to say you're right? That I blew the opportunity of a lifetime? That I'm so completely messed up in the head that I couldn't overcome my panic attacks long enough for one freaking song? A melody that I know better than the sound of my own voice? Are you happy now? Because no, I'm not fine. I will never be fine. People like me don't get to be fine."

Jenn cringed at the venom in my voice, and it killed me to see that small sliver of fear in her eyes.

I slumped against the wall beside the couch. "People like me don't get to have their dreams come true."

She was silent for a minute. Then, in the quietest voice, she asked, "People like you? Or people like *us*?"

"That's not what I meant," I argued.

She eyed me cautiously. "But didn't you? Neither of us has any money. We're both struggling after impossible careers. How are we any different?"

"Because you're not..." I bit back the word. I hated even thinking *that* word.

"You're not crazy, Rain," she insisted, filling in the painful blank. "Your brain just works differently. If you had continued your therapy, maybe..."

"With what money? I can barely afford the doctor visits to get my prescription refilled. I'm never going to get any better, okay? This is just how my life is."

A depressing silence settled over the room as we sat there, the only sound the ticking of the broken old fan propped up in the window. Once again, Jenn's abundance of optimism had run out, and I had never had any to begin with.

Optimism was nothing but a useless emotion for a mentally damaged orphan from Jersey.

Chapter Two

The rest of the afternoon was spent in a careful dance of avoidance, neither of us knowing what to say. It wasn't the first time we'd argued about my pessimistic outlook, and it wouldn't be the last.

By the time early evening rolled around, I could no longer take the awkward silence and decided I needed to get out of the apartment. I had work later, but after the morning's tragic audition, my turbulent brain demanded a drink. Besides, it wasn't like I needed to be totally sober for my job at the Taco Hut. Making crappy fast food for stoners wasn't exactly complicated.

I grabbed my blue hoodie with the gray pocket I added years ago and tied it around my waist. Pausing in the hallway, I debated whether I should tell Jenn that I was leaving. When a giggle filtered through the door, I decided against it. If she had her good mood back, I didn't want to ruin things again.

We would talk tomorrow like nothing ever happened, like I had never screamed at her, and everything would be back to normal.

Or back to whatever passed for normal in my life.

A blast of cool air from the AC sent a delightful shiver through my body when I stepped into Dingo's Den, the best dive bar in Passaic. The owner might be too cheap to repair the torn brown vinyl on most of the booths, and he was definitely too cheap to replace the wobbly stools tucked up at the bar, but at least he splurged on a solid air conditioner. A feature I was immensely grateful for during the hot Jersey summers. I could deal with sticky floors, body odor, and dirty bathrooms provided I endured them in sixty-eight degree temperatures.

Rum and coke in hand, I headed over to the booth with the fewest rips and no mystery stains. It was early evening on a Tuesday, so the place was fairly empty aside from the usual three or four hardcore alcoholics hunched over the bar.

I threw back a swig, savoring the delicious burn that rolled down my throat. Aside from Klonopin, liquor was the only thing that helped quiet the anxious voices in my head.

My booth shook slightly when a body slid onto the bench opposite mine, and my hand tightened on my drink in annoyance over my peace being disrupted. "Hey buddy, I'm not looking for..."

The rest of the words got lost somewhere between the table and the face of my new companion.

"Me?" the man supplied, the corner of his lip curling up into a knowing smile. A smile that actively showcased the most perfect dimple in the history of mankind. I was pretty sure my mouth hung open slightly as I took in his smooth tan skin and chin-length blond hair that draped artfully over his rich amber eyes.

My gaze slid further down, settling on the toned muscles of his arms. They were strong and robust, complete with strangely faded tribal tattoos winding around them to disappear under his gray shirt. They didn't look like steroid muscles, but I couldn't fathom the gym hours needed to build them naturally.

The man cleared his throat, and I brought my attention back to his face, hoping he hadn't noticed my blatant ogling. I was not usually the type to drool over a pretty face. "I'm sorry. I was just, uh... not expecting anyone to join me," I blurted out.

"As I am the one intruding it would seem apologies are not necessary, Miss...?"

I paused, trying to analyze his unique accent before replying. "Rain. Just Rain. No Miss."

He smiled at that, like my words were somehow amusing. "Oh, I do not believe that you are *just* anything, Rain. But if I was required to select only one, I would say..." His eyes searched mine, excitement brewing in their depths. "You, Rain, are *just* marvelous."

I shifted under the weight of his gaze, unaccustomed to anyone saying such awkwardly poignant things about me.

"Umm..." I bit my lower lip, searching for a clever response to his compliment. "Thanks, I guess."

Oh yeah... real clever.

I shook my head to wake up my sleeping brain cells and tried again. "I'm sorry, did you need something?"

He leaned forward on his elbows, the energy of a delighted puppy coming off him in waves. "I understand my presence here is confusing, but yes, I do very much need your help."

Wiping a bit of condensation off my glass, I took a second to process his words. Surely there was no legitimate reason this walking statue of a Greek god could need my help.

"Okay, I'll play," I said a moment later. I had a little time to kill after all, and he *was* gorgeous. "How about we start with your name and follow that up with how you found me and what you seem to think I can help with?"

"Your request is fair enough," he replied. "My name is Deylan. Though most refer to me as Dey. I found you by simply following you from the place you currently call home. As for what I need your help with..."

"Excuse me?" I interrupted, my brain focusing on one specific part of his statement. "Did you just say you've been following me?"

"I have," he confirmed, not appearing even the slightest bit unnerved by my outburst.

"Yeah, I'm going to stop you right there," I said, tossing back the last of my drink and gathering up my canvas bag. The guy might be hot, but I had enough drama in my life without adding a potential stalker. "This has been... bizarre.

But I need to go to work, and you need to find someone else to creep on because whoever you think I am, I'm not her."

He frowned and opened his mouth to say something, but I was out the front door before he could utter the first syllable.

Chapter Three

I only made it a few blocks before I heard steps pounding the sidewalk behind me. Maintaining my steady stride, I mentally prepared myself for the challenge of telling the world's hottest stalker to leave me alone. Again.

"What is your deal?" I huffed out as the bronze beefcake matched my brisk pace.

"My deal?" he asked, not even slightly winded from the jog. "I apologize, but this is not an expression where I come from."

"And where exactly is that? Your English is decent, but clearly not your first language."

"I am from Rivella," he replied, puffing up his already expansive chest.

"Sorry, geography isn't exactly my strong suit. Is that in the Middle East or something?"

He moved in front of me, impeding my progress down the sidewalk. "Rivella is in Vitaea," he answered, "but it is not in the east, middle or otherwise. It does, however, pose some complications with what I need to tell you."

I laughed mirthlessly. "Yeah, not really interested in continuing this conversation any further. I'm going to be late for work."

I tried to step around him, but he settled his hands on my shoulders, locking me in place. The scent of smoke and applewood wafted off him, and I crinkled my nose. The smell reminded me of camping, something I never enjoyed since it gave me flashbacks of the few weeks Jenn and I spent living out of her car.

Analyzing him a little more closely, I took in the details of his outfit. The gray top I thought was a t-shirt was actually some kind of tunic with laces at the neck. Brown leather pants clung to his powerful thighs, and a pair of soft black boots stretched just past his calves. Overall, he looked like he wandered away from a renaissance faire, and it occurred to me that I should probably be more worried this guy was legitimately unstable.

"Look, Deylan, or whatever your name is, I've had a rough day, so would you mind finding someone else to harass?" Smoothly ducking under his hold, I scurried off down the sidewalk.

"It is about your parents," he called, his words bringing me to a screeching halt.

Fuck.

Of course he had to say the one thing that might actually get me to listen to him. Granted, there was a chance he was lying, manipulating me for some endgame, but I couldn't just walk away. Not if there was a chance he knew something.

"I mean you no harm," he continued, sidling up beside me once more. "I promise you this will all become clear if you would allow me the opportunity to explain."

I scrubbed my face for a minute, cursing the hot, humid air that was likely impacting my decision-making skills. Maybe I was a huge idiot, but there was something so genuine and honest in his eyes that I actually believed it when he said he wouldn't hurt me.

I let out a long breath. "Okay," I conceded, my curiosity getting the better of me. "Let me send a quick text to my boss, and then we can go chat."

He gave me a wide grin, and if I had a better sense of self-preservation, I might have been concerned that I was about to end my day as a lampshade.

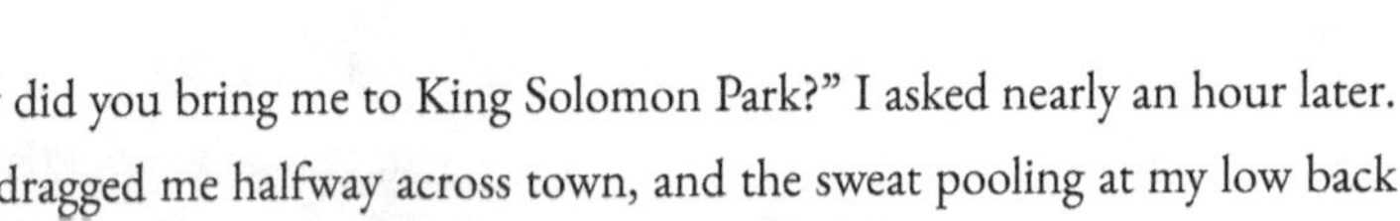

"Why did you bring me to King Solomon Park?" I asked nearly an hour later. He'd dragged me halfway across town, and the sweat pooling at my low back was reaching swamp levels. "We can't even go inside." I pointed to the chain and padlock.

Dey laughed, and the hearty, amused sound had me forgetting all about my exhaustion and sore feet. "The flimsy metal here is little more than a mild inconvenience," he replied, strolling over to the gate. Plucking a hefty stone off the ground like it weighed nothing, he smashed the lock, and the cacophonous sound echoed into the night.

I glanced around to see if anyone would come running to investigate, and when it became clear we were still alone, he tossed the now useless hunk of metal behind him. Pushing the gate open, he gave me an expectant look.

"Fine," I huffed out dramatically, dragging my ass after him. "But if you get me arrested for breaking into a cemetery, I don't care what you have to tell me, I'm seriously going to kick your ass."

He scanned up and down my thin, malnourished frame. "I welcome the challenge," he purred, amusement dancing in his eyes.

At least he didn't outright laugh in my face.

"So... what now?" I asked. "You wanted a private place to talk. Here we are. Although, I'm not sure I would have chosen a graveyard when literally anywhere else would have worked."

He held out a hand which I reluctantly accepted. It was soft and warm, lacking the callouses I would have expected from someone with his muscles.

"Literally anywhere else would not have had what I need to show you." Tugging me forward, he led me deeper into the cemetery.

I contemplated the various headstones that we passed by. What could possibly be here that I would need to see?

A thought crashed into me out of the blue, and I froze, unable to continue along the small path.

Dey cast a look at me over his shoulder, his eyes questioning my lack of movement.

"Dey..." I began slowly, trying to process the thoughts whirling through my brain as they all coalesced into one solid notion. One reason he would need to bring me to a cemetery.

"Are my parents dead?"

The thought gutted me, even though I told myself it shouldn't. It was only natural, after all. Every orphan dreamed that somewhere out there they had parents. Ones who had a good reason for giving them up. Ones who searched the world for them, obviously realizing the terrible mistake they had made. And one day those parents would show up to whisk them away to a perfect existence with food on the table, constant laughter, and the security that came with knowing you were not alone in the world.

I had always pretended that I was an exception to that rule. That I lived firmly in reality and didn't care about the people who left me at the orphanage with nothing more than a gray blanket and a name. I knew that life was cruel and unfair, and no amount of dreaming would ever change that.

Lying to myself was possibly my greatest skill.

"No, Rain," Dey replied softly. "Your parents are not here."

It was embarrassing how much relief flooded back into me as I followed close on his heels. "Okay," I said, shoring up my heart once more. "So out with it, then. Why all the secrecy? Were my parents high-ranking politicians and my birth was a scandal? Or was it like a rockstar and groupie thing? Oooh, maybe they're royalty, and I'm a secret princess or something."

Dey's steps faltered at that last one, and he glanced back at me, his mouth curving up into a knowing smile that spoke volumes.

"No... No way," I protested. "That was a joke. You're just fucking with me. Come on, are they like drug dealers or something? Because there's no reality in which I'm a princess from some foreign country."

He came to a stop in front of a flowering shrub. "No, Rain, you are not a princess from a foreign country... " His words trailed off, and he pulled the shrub back. "You are a princess from a foreign *world*."

I blinked repeatedly as if that might change what I was seeing.

"What the actual fuck?"

Dey frowned. "You keep using that word differently."

I didn't even bother to respond to his comment while I took in the sight in front of me. A shimmering mirage hung suspended between two weeping willows, its edges glowing with a faint blue light that pulsed with an electric energy.

Moving closer, I could start to make out details in the image. It depicted something like a maze, except the tall hedges were all covered in sizable flowers, similar to roses save for their brilliant, almost neon colors and obscenely large petals. Two suns hung in the clear blue sky: one up high, just reaching its apex, while the other lingered nearly halfway to the horizon. Both cast their honeyed light over the manicured shrubs, offsetting the vividly green leaves and swirling pink, blue, and purple flowers with an ethereal glimmer. Beyond the exquisite garden, huge oak trees sporting early fall colors stood proudly in a row, like steadfast soldiers holding the line.

And behind it all, a massive castle climbed high into the sky, the light gray stones of its walls sparkling in the afternoon light.

Only the front of the castle was visible, but I could see at least six impressive towers and even more turrets with crenelated parapets. The two largest rose up out of the back of the main keep, lording over all the smaller ones. Dark, almost black, spires crowned each turret, and burgundy flags atop the tallest ones listed in the breeze.

It was insane. It was unreal. It was...

"Is that a hologram? Cool."

I looked back over to Dey who now sported an even deeper frown.

"You are not reacting the way I had expected."

Now it was my brow that crinkled in confusion. "What were you expecting? Yeah, it's a sweet display, but what does this have to do with my parents?"

He just stared at me, his mouth opening and closing, his head shaking slightly.

"You are... I was not..." He ran his fingers through his hair repeatedly, the slight wave to his blond locks turning messy. "You are not reacting in a way that I have been prepared for."

A small snort escaped me. "Okay, so why don't you tell me how I was supposed to react?"

"I was told that the inhabitants of your world were rather delicate. And when you first saw the rift, you would likely respond with something akin to hysterics or possibly mania."

"Mania?" I scoffed. "I don't know what technology is like in your country, but here we don't really freak out over a few lasers. And we don't use the word mania. Gross."

I turned to inspect the hologram a bit more. "Don't think I haven't forgotten that you promised to tell me about my—holy hell!"

I was not expecting the image to have changed while my back was turned, but sure enough, the view was different. Well, the background was still the same, but a rather pissed off old guy stood in the garden, glaring out at us.

To my even further surprise, he began speaking, but the words were harsh and not in any language I recognized.

"What's he saying?" I checked behind me to see how Dey was reacting and flinched when his face was only inches from my own, his features twisted in sadness.

"I am so very sorry, Rain. This was not what I intended at all." Resting his hands firmly on my shoulders, he leaned in close. "Do not hate me for this."

Then he pushed.

Chapter Four

"Ow!" I rubbed at my sore tailbone where my ass had bounced off the stony ground.

A wrinkled hand reached in front of my face, sending fear rippling through me. "Son of a bitch!" I shouted, scrambling backward.

In a flash, I went from irritation to complete and utter panic. My heart thundered in my chest, and a thin sheen of sweat spread over my brow.

It wasn't the cantankerous old man from the mirage leaning over me that had thrown my anxiety into overdrive. No. It was what rose up behind him. The castle. The one from the hologram. Except it wasn't a hologram. It was real, and I was staring right at it.

My eyes darted around as my chest heaved, flicking from the purple rose bush beside me up to the two suns in the sky.

Two suns. How were there two suns?

I was inside the fucking hologram which... maybe wasn't a hologram at all. I whipped back to Dey in time to see him step toward me.

One step. That was all it took, and suddenly he wasn't in the real world anymore. He was here with me inside this illusion.

The older man shuffled past Dey and waved his hand through the air. The clearing I stood in moments before vanished into nothing as the blue light folded in on itself.

I shot to my feet. "What did you do to me?" It had to be drugs. He slipped me something, and now I was hallucinating.

Backing away from the two men, my eyes searched frantically for something familiar to latch onto. Something I could make sense of. But there was nothing.

The tightness in my chest grew unbearable, and my vision blurred as I cracked under the full weight of my anxiety. I had to get out of there. Had to get away from them.

I bolted, blindly sprinting toward the copse of oak trees at the edge of the garden. I needed to get somewhere safe to take my Klonopin. Then maybe I could hide out until the drugs wore off. If I could just get to those trees...

I saw my path coming to an end, so I hooked a sharp left to keep running.

I collided with something hard and warm.

Bouncing off Dey's chest, I flew backward, landing smack on my tailbone again and likely adding yet another bruise to my already injured ass.

I stared up at him, my whole body trembling. "Please don't hurt me," I begged.

The last thing I saw was Dey reaching out to touch my cheek, and then darkness swallowed me whole.

Groaning, I squeezed my eyes shut, fighting off the bright light that tried to pull me from sleep. I should get up and close the curtains, but the pillow under my head was warm and comfortable and...

My pillow twitched.

I jerked upright so fast it hurt my neck. I was not in my small but comfy bed in Jersey. I was in a rose garden. And my pillow was Dey's firmly sculpted chest.

Scrambling to my feet, I eyed him warily as he observed me from the stone bench where apparently I had been cuddling him.

Between one heartbeat and the next, everything came crashing back into me. The hologram that wasn't a hologram. The castle that still loomed over me. And my desperate attempt at an escape that had clearly failed.

"What did you do to me?" I demanded, panic knocking on the door to my mind.

In one impressively smooth motion, Dey swung his legs around and popped to his feet.

I promptly stumbled backward, making it all of three steps before the cool stone of another bench pressed against the backs of my legs.

He lifted his hands in a placating gesture that did little to actually reduce my fear. "I simply helped you to sleep for a short while," he said. "You had succumbed to hysterics, and I feared you would injure yourself further without intervention."

"You helped me to sleep? You mean you drugged me!" Panic no longer knocked but instead kicked the door down. "You slipped me some kind of hallucinogen in the bar, didn't you? Then you brought me here and drugged me again to knock me out. Shit, I don't even know where we are."

No. It couldn't be... Was he...?

"Am I being sex-trafficked?"

Before he could even respond, I shot forward, grabbed his shoulders, and kneed him in the balls as hard as I could.

He pitched forward, groaning, and I used the opportunity to flee.

I barely made it around the first corner of the maze before Dey's muscular arms circled me from behind, scooped me up, and deposited me back on the bench as if I weighed no more than the yowling alley cat that I sounded like.

Crossing my arms, I glared at him, wondering how he had possibly recovered so quickly. "You're gonna regret this," I hissed.

If my declaration phased him at all, it certainly didn't show in his expression, which now vacillated between exhaustion and mild frustration. He knelt in front of me and placed his hands on the sides of my face. I tried to jerk away, but his grip held firm.

The instant his eyes locked on mine, every trace of anger vacated my body. A soothing warmth blossomed under my skin, penetrated my muscles, and nestled into my chest.

"What did you do to me?" I whispered.

It was the same question I asked earlier, except this time I wasn't as concerned about the answer because I knew Dey wouldn't hurt me. Why did I ever think he would? There was a perfectly good explanation for everything.

He straddled the bench to face me, his hands sliding down to cup mine. "I am so very dismayed that things played out this way," he professed. "It was my intention to educate you back in the Other Realm so bringing you over would be less of a shock. Unfortunately, the rift can only remain open so long, and Lorduin was about to seal it off. I had no choice but to push you through despite how much it pained me to do so."

I turned his words over in my mind, trying to decide what to address first. "What's an Other Realm?"

His hands grasped mine a little tighter, as if he were afraid I might bolt again. "The Other Realm is the world that you know. The reality that you and humans like you exist in. We use the term Other Realm to refer to any realm other than our own. Lorduin, the male you saw earlier, is a World Walker. He opened the rift that allowed me to find you and bring you here."

"Ok," I responded, still strangely unrattled by what he was saying. I opened my mouth to ask him exactly where 'here' was when a massive hawk landed on his shoulder.

"Fucking hell!" I shrieked, throwing myself backward and promptly falling off the bench. Sitting in the dirt, I gaped wide-eyed at the creature that was not, in fact, a hawk.

Dey tilted his head to the side, and the intimidating bird mimicked his motion. "You have now used that word in many different ways," he said. "Are you entirely sure you know what it means?"

I ignored him, too engrossed with the creature that was now vigorously preening Dey's hair. It was roughly the size of a hawk with a hooked beak and reddish-brown color, but that was where the similarities ended.

It scurried on four legs from Dey's right shoulder down into his lap, where gray talons loosely gripped his thigh. Two sets of feathered wings sprouted out of its back, gently beating independently from each other as it traversed Dey's terrain. The crowning glory of the creature, though, was its chest where opalescent scales glistened in the sun, shifting between purple and deep blue depending on the angle of the light.

It dipped its head at me, then bounced around excitedly before hunkering down to rub its face on Dey's pants.

"You are welcome to pet him," Dey offered.

Scaled chest, extra wings, four legs. I hit my head harder than I thought during one of my recent falls because this was not a creature that should exist. An observation that didn't stop me from extending my hand to see if those wings were as soft as they appeared.

They were.

The creature let out a dove-like coo and arched into my touch as I caressed its back feathers. When I pulled away, it screeched sharply and flew off.

"Oof," I said with a grimace. "I don't think your bird likes me."

"He is not a bird; he is a crescia, my bonded companion. And Thorell very much likes you. Though I believe he felt that he was entitled to a few more pets."

I laughed as we both watched Thorell fly away, and then I fixed my attention back on the guy sitting across from me. "So... other realms exist."

"Yes."

"And I'm in one of them."

"Yes."

"And I'm not freaking out." I tapped the bench to confirm it was real and solid. "I feel like I should be freaking out right now. It's like my brain is fighting itself. One part believes I shouldn't be okay with any of this, or at the very least I should assume this is a dream that will end soon, but another part keeps saying relax and accept what's happening." I paused, then added, "I think that part is winning."

Gazing into his amber eyes, I felt a warm safety blanket wrap itself around my mind. "Why do I trust you?"

Dey ran his hand over my cheek, and I leaned into the gesture, enjoying how much security came from his simple caress.

"That," he said soberly, "would be my fault."

Chapter Five

I eyed Dey suspiciously. Something about his statement shifted the tide of the war within my mind, and the unfettered trust began to bow under the weight of my unease.

"And how exactly is it your fault?"

Every aspect of his body—from his face to his shoulders, right down to his massive thighs—slumped in resignation. "It is my magic that is affecting you so," he confessed. "I am, among other things, a mental caster. I can influence the emotions of others when I touch them." He lifted his chin to look at me. "You were terrified, and I meant only to ease your suffering. That is what I do. I reduce the sorrow of those burdened by feelings they cannot control. I promise you it will fade. The alteration of one's mind tends to lessen once they have been made aware of the change."

I blinked twice as the comforting feeling receded from my brain. Slowly at first, the reality settled in, eventually picking up steam as a deluge of thoughts raced through my mind, threatening to drown me. Magic wasn't real. But neither should this place be real, yet it clearly was. And if this place was real, then that meant... he had actually messed with my brain. My brain that never worked quite right and caused me untold grief, but at least I knew my fucked-up thoughts and uncontrolled emotions were my own. He just waltzed in and tinkered with everything, changing me to suit his needs.

I felt dirty. I felt violated. I felt… angry.

Without thinking, I hauled my arm back and punched him in the face with the full weight of my fury.

"Motherfucker!" I screamed, partly at Dey for invading my mind and partly at the stinging pain now coursing through my right hand. Was his face made of granite?

The asshole didn't even have the decency to pretend he was injured, to give me that small satisfaction. He opened his mouth, but I cut him off before he could utter a single word.

"No!" I shouted, pointing an accusatory finger at him. "You don't get to speak right now."

My anger burned under my skin like a living entity, forcing me to my feet. Pacing back and forth behind the bench, I clenched and unclenched my fists. I wasn't dumb enough to hit him again, but I needed something, an outlet for my wrath. Lifting my face to the sky, I screamed with everything I had left, letting my pure primal rage escape into this new world.

A flock of birds scattered from a nearby oak tree, shrieking their indignation.

"How dare you," I demanded, stalking closer to him. "Who the hell do you think you are, kidnapping me to some fucked-up dimension and violating my mind? What gives you the right to play with my emotions like I'm a goddamned toy?"

"I am sorry," he whispered. "My ability here is widely regarded as something beneficial. I honestly believed I was helping you. I did not consider how it might be viewed as a violation." His head dipped low, and a small piece of my anger faded, recognizing that he truly didn't realize the extent of what he had done.

I sat stiffly on the opposite side of the bench, in no hurry to be within touching distance again. "You owe me answers," I gritted out. "A lot of them."

"Of course, Princess."

"Ah! That, right there. Great place to start. Back in... in my world," I said, still struggling with the concept that other worlds existed, "you told me that I was a princess. Explain."

Dey hesitated for so long I feared I might have to punch him again to get some damn answers. My aching hand throbbed dully at the thought.

"I do want to tell you everything," he admitted. "But there are some things that perhaps you would be better off hearing from your father. You are likely to have many more questions only he can answer, and it is not..."

I didn't hear a word Dey said after 'father.' The word hammered through my brain on repeat. Father. I had a father. One who was alive, and here, apparently.

Wait, if I had a father, did that mean...

"Do I have a mother?" I asked, my voice barely above a whisper. I was trying, and failing, to keep hope from seeping into my heart, terrified of what he might say.

But hope, that constantly useless emotion, lasted mere seconds before I saw the sympathy cloud Dey's eyes.

It shouldn't have ached as badly as it did. I spent twenty-five years without a mom. I shouldn't be mourning the loss of something I never had.

Dey rose to his feet and extended his hand. "Come. We will go speak with your father, and he can explain everything."

"Okay," I huffed out, disregarding his offered palm as I slid off the bench. "I'm pretty sure this day can't get any weirder, so let's throw in a long lost parent. Why not?" I took a step forward, indicating for him to lead the way.

He strode off through the rose bushes, navigating the maze of twists and turns with ease while I followed a few steps behind, trying to decide if the butterflies in my stomach were nerves, fear, or possibly excitement.

"So where exactly are we going to find my father?" I asked as we made one last turn, the garden exit looming up ahead.

We passed beyond the grassy walls of the maze, and Dey simply lifted a hand toward the intimidating structure of glittering stone that I had somehow forgotten about.

I don't know why I didn't put it together sooner. If I was a princess, then my father had to be a king. With his own freaking castle.

My head still swirled from the implications of my potential princesshood while Dey led me across the drawbridge toward the portcullis.

"This river is beautiful," I remarked absently, pausing on the bridge to take in the crystal clear, slow-moving water running beneath. Leaning over, I could make out schools of pale blue and green fish swimming against the current. They were massive, twice the size of the largest koi I had ever seen. The bright sun glittered off their pearlescent scales, and the dancing light was so hypnotizing that my fingers drifted toward the water to touch one.

"That is a very bad idea," Dey interrupted, grabbing my hand inches before it broke the surface of the gentle river.

"Why?" I glanced back at the beautiful creatures right as one opened its mouth wide and snapped at me, revealing two rows of razor sharp teeth.

"Because those are stiroi," he explained. "This moat is fed by an underground stream that flows into the castle, providing us with water for drinking and bathing. The stiroi act as a filter, eating anything that comes near them. I have been told their bite is quite painful."

"Damn," I whispered as one nipped at another that had gotten too close. Dey was right, those were some seriously vicious fangs.

"Shall we continue on?" he asked, tugging me away from the water. "Perhaps with a bit more focus? At this pace, I fear I will be old and gray before I present you to the king."

Rolling my eyes, I followed after him, crossing under the portcullis to enter the courtyard. I stumbled a bit when the dazzling brilliance struck me, my eyes watering and my pupils shrinking to pinpricks. Glittering swirls of light ran through the stones beneath my feet and across the walls. The patterns intertwined among one another in bursts of greens, purples, yellows, pinks, and brilliant white, reminding me of oil drops swirling on water. In the center of the courtyard, a trio of fountains fractured the light a million times over into tiny rainbows that danced and skittered among the stone figures and splashing geysers.

I threw up a hand to block the intense display. Why was everything so damned sparkly? And where was everyone?

"Shouldn't a castle have like, I don't know, people running around? This place is dead."

"I believe your father is currently holding council with the majority of his courtiers in the throne room," Dey answered. "Also, most know to avoid the courtyard when the suns are high in the sky."

"Yeah, I can see why," I muttered, still holding my hand up to ward off the dazzling assault. I walked over to the nearest wall and examined the bricks, trying to figure out exactly why everything here was wreaking such havoc on my retinas.

"Is that...?" I leaned closer to the stone, inspecting the strange veins of glass-like mineral running through every brick in the courtyard. My mouth dropped open, and I spun to look at Dey.

He grinned.

"Welcome, Princess, to the Diamond Palace."

Chapter Six

I thought the news that other realms existed would break me. Then I thought hearing that I had a living father would break me. Nope. It was the damned diamonds that did it. I took in every single inch of that glittering courtyard and simply… laughed.

It started small at first. Just a giggle that grew to a chuckle. Then I could feel it—this writhing creature crawling up from the pit of my stomach, like a dragon that had been awoken by the presence of shiny jewels. My laughter morphed and twisted into something terrifying, but I couldn't hold it back.

Maybe I had been too quick to dismiss Dey's earlier notion that my people were prone to bouts of hysteria and mania.

I don't know how long I stayed there like that—howling like a grazed goblin. It could have been a minute or an hour. Eventually, though, I regained some tiny semblance of control and was able to look up at Dey, who appeared to be debating with himself about whether to help me or flee in terror.

Between lingering sobs and giggles, I asked, "Are you telling me that while I was in the real world making shitty fast food tacos and wondering if I was going to have enough money to keep a roof over my head, my father was living in a damn palace made of diamonds?"

He edged slightly away from me. "I... well... that is to say..."

I had to admit, flustered was a good look on him. "It's okay, Dey. Seriously. Just breathe. I'm not gonna go feral on your ass or anything."

I'm not sure my words helped as much as I intended because he took another small step backward, and his right hand shifted toward his rear as if he genuinely thought it might need protection.

I snorted. "Maybe we should just go inside." I paused. "Unless... It doesn't get worse inside, does it? Please don't tell me my father has some tacky diamond throne."

He chuckled softly. "I will not tell him you said that."

"So that's a yes," I groaned. "Well let's get it over with. I doubt it's getting less tacky as we stand here."

Dey straightened, clearly relieved to be back on task, and he gestured toward a wooden door at the back of the courtyard. "This way, Princess."

He led me down a long corridor with hallways on each side interspersed with doors featuring ornate diamond knobs. While the exterior of the castle was primarily sparkling gray stone, the interior walls were more beige in color, making the entire palace feel light and bright. The bricks that comprised the high-ceilinged walkways were infused with fewer diamonds, but there was no ignoring the occasional glittering vein that ran through the off-white stone.

The ceiling opened up above me as the corridor came to an end, and I found myself in a sweeping antechamber. Two massive ebony stone doors took up the majority of the back wall, flanked on either side by guards dressed in burgundy tunics boasting a Celtic-looking symbol on the chest. A flicker of light caught my eye, and I glanced up.

All forward momentum halted. My feet might as well have been in quicksand for how strongly I was immobilized by the beauty above me.

Swirling hues of black, purple, and dark blue decorated the ceiling perhaps thirty feet above my head with thousands of tiny diamond stars embedded throughout that midnight mural, luminous and twinkling like celestial fireflies guiding the way to the heavens. Many were arranged purposefully to form constellations, and though I didn't recognize any of them, they somehow felt familiar.

A hand grazed my shoulder, but I couldn't tear my attention from the stars. Outside, the diamonds were abrasive and intrusive, but here they were mesmerizing. They were the very definition of breathtaking. They were... magic.

I wanted nothing more than to let all my worries drift away so I could embrace the perfect serenity of this stardust sea.

"Rain?" Dey prompted, forcing me painfully back into the present.

Wrenching my gaze away from the ceiling, I gave him a rueful look. "Sorry. I, uh, got a little distracted."

"There is no need to apologize. The mural is quite magnificent. Your mother was actually the one to commission it during her brief time in the palace. Now, if you would wait here, I need to alert the king before I bring you in to see him. He will likely need time to compose himself before receiving you."

Dey left me standing awkwardly in the middle of the room while he spoke with the guards. They gave him a curt nod and pushed the heavy doors open just wide enough for him to slip through.

I spent a few more minutes examining the enchanting ceiling before the crick in my neck brought me back to reality.

Reality, however, was an otherwise empty room with two males regarding me with a mixture of awe and confusion.

"Hey," I greeted, strolling over to them. "I'm Rain. I was hoping to—"

Before I could finish my sentence, they both moved in unison, dropping to one knee and crossing an arm over their chest.

"Princepa," they intoned, bowing their heads to me deferentially.

Well, that was a far cry from the greetings I got in Jersey, which usually consisted of leers from guys and sneers from girls. I glanced down at my attire. Yeah, I was still me. Old and dirty Converse, tattered blue hoodie around my waist, torn jean shorts and a black Linkin Park tank top.

"You don't have to do that," I insisted, waving a hand near the face of the guard closest to me.

He remained kneeling, his brow furrowed, and he asked, "Nesto auxum?"

I shouldn't have been surprised by their response. Just because Dey spoke to me in English didn't mean that everyone here could. I was contemplating whether or not charades would be even remotely effective when there was a loud rap on the stone door.

The guards leapt to their feet, braced their palms against the huge slabs of stone, and began to push.

Inch by inch, the room beyond gradually opened up to me, each creak of hinges plucking my tightly wound heartstrings.

I took in a deep inhale, feeling like I was passing some point of no return, and entered the throne room.

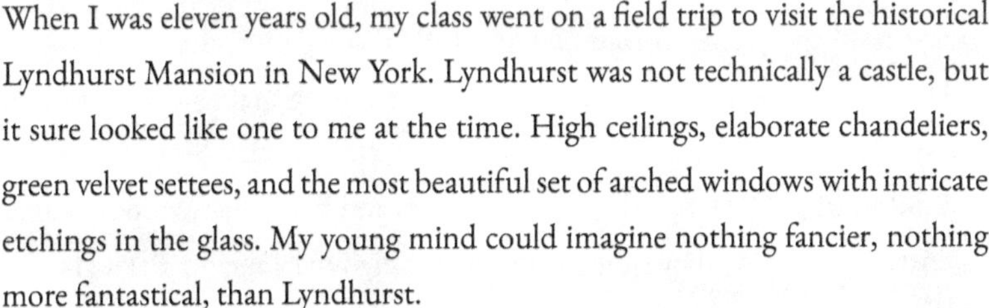

When I was eleven years old, my class went on a field trip to visit the historical Lyndhurst Mansion in New York. Lyndhurst was not technically a castle, but it sure looked like one to me at the time. High ceilings, elaborate chandeliers, green velvet settees, and the most beautiful set of arched windows with intricate etchings in the glass. My young mind could imagine nothing fancier, nothing more fantastical, than Lyndhurst.

And my father's throne room made it look like a damned bouncy castle in comparison.

Hundreds of pairs of eyes rested on me when I stepped tentatively into the expansive hall, and I tried to focus more on the room and less on the oppressive feeling of being judged.

A row of exquisite diamond chandeliers hung from the exposed wooden beams of an arched ceiling, and a gentle tinkling sound flitted down as the crystals swayed in an invisible breeze. A long stretch of burgundy velvet carpet sat atop white marble flooring, running through the middle of the room from the entryway to a raised platform at the back. Seven tall windows loomed over the curved dais, casting rays of light onto the glittering diamond throne. The effect was stunning, as if the very light of heaven fell approvingly upon the ruler of this place. From my distance, I could faintly make out broad shoulders, dark hair, and a diamond crown atop his head.

I wanted to move closer to see if his face was kind or cruel, but my body denied the request. I hadn't made it ten steps, but my feet were determined that we would go no further.

While I stood there locked in place, whispers began to filter over to me. Only a few at first, then more and more the longer I remained immobile. Spacious upper balconies lined each side of the massive hall, filled to the brim with people dressed in the finest clothing that appeared straight out of the books of Tolkien, while even more stood below the balconies in small crowds. Hundreds, maybe a thousand, all staring at me, their faces wrinkling in disdain. I had no idea what they wanted from me, but when a small snicker broke through the quiet, I decided I wasn't going to stick around and find out.

My feet that refused to move forward had no issues reversing. I took one step backward, then another, before spinning around and dashing for the door.

Shocked gasps rang out behind me, and a strong male voice bellowed, "Raynella!"

I didn't stop. I flew back to the stone doors and flung my full body weight against them, hoping they would crack just enough to let me slip through.

They didn't.

Pounding as hard as I could, I screamed to the guards on the other side, "Open the door!"

A hand landed on my shoulder, but I didn't dare glance back to see who it belonged to. If I did, I would see *them*. See them laughing and sneering and judging me.

"Rain! Rain, look at me!"

Someone was shaking my arm, but it wasn't until they forced themself in front of me that recognition hit.

"Please," I begged Dey. "Take it away."

He studied my face, and I saw that hint of uncertainty and concern like he wanted to help me but didn't understand what was happening. I'd seen that look on so many faces, so many times. The confusion that said my response to a very normal situation was anything but.

"Take what away, Rain?"

I clutched his tunic in my hands, pulling him closer to me, wanting him to feel my racing heartbeat, to understand that my lungs ached for oxygen I couldn't give them.

"All of it. Take it all away. I know I was upset before. I know I said never again, but it's too much. Please. Just take it away."

Clarity rolled over his face, and then a wave of peaceful calm swept through my body as he gingerly lowered me to the floor of the throne room. My vision narrowed, blackness creeping around the edges, and fatigue pressed in like a warm, heavy blanket.

A shadow crossed my eyes, and I took in a new masculine face staring down. As I fully succumbed to the weight of exhaustion, a single thought ran through me.

We have the same eyes.

Chapter Seven

I awoke to the sensation of hot air on my neck, a pressing warmth against my back, and the familiar scent of smoke and applewood.

A spark of panic sprouted inside me, but I quickly shut it down when I remembered the throne room. I couldn't say I appreciated waking up in bed with Dey, but I finally understood what he meant about his power being a gift.

My eyes swept over the room, taking in the stone walls and lack of anything remotely modern. The space was fairly open, yet it still had a pleasant cozy feel to it. A low fire crackled in the hearth opposite the bed with two plush chairs before it. Thick burgundy drapes with veridian stitching along the edges framed each side of the three wide windows. Celestial tapestries adorned the walls, and I recognized some of the constellations from the ceiling in the antechamber. A small table sat below the window nearest the bed featuring a diamond vase filled with a rainbow bouquet of fresh flowers.

Dey shifted slightly behind me, and the movement drew my attention to his tattooed arm lingering on my hip, a thin beige quilt the only thing between us.

His steady breathing told me that he likely still slept, but before I could decide whether I should wake him up or just attempt an escape, his arm tightened, pulling me into a deeper embrace against his chest.

Three revelations hit me simultaneously:

Dey was awake.

Dey was naked.

Dey was aroused.

I racked my brain for any information about what had happened between us, but only came up with a black wall. I remembered the throne room. I remembered the panic attack. And I remembered begging Dey to help me. After that... there was nothing. How could there be nothing?

Grabbing the edge of the quilt, I lifted it to look beneath and let out a sigh of relief when I realized I was still dressed.

Well, mostly. Someone had put me in a thin burgundy nightgown.

Dey shifted again, this time pressing his hips closer, and it was all the confirmation I needed for one of my concerns. Dey and I did *not* have sex last night, because if the hard length pressing into my ass had ever been between my legs, I would definitely be feeling sore.

I rolled onto my other side so I was facing him and noted that I had been wrong about one thing—he was not actually awake. Naked and aroused, yes, but his eyes were shuttered, and his face displayed a soft, easy relaxation that only came with sleep.

As much as I knew I shouldn't, I reached out and ran my fingers along his jaw, caressing the spot near his mouth where I knew the dimple would pop up when he smiled. There were no lines on his face. No scars or imperfections to mar his smooth sun-kissed skin. He appeared almost inhuman. Angelic, even. The more I contemplated his face, the more I felt... sad. Imperfections were what made us unique and told the stories of our lives. His dimple when he smiled was dazzling, sure, but right then, with his face completely relaxed, he was just this blank canvas waiting for someone to paint the story of his life.

I let my gaze wander a little lower, to the tattoos that adorned his arms. The swirling design that appeared darker than it had in my world started at his wrists and ran all the way up both his arms to brush the very edges of his clavicles. I resisted the strong urge to trace the pattern with my fingers. Touching his face was one thing, but running my hands over those muscles was a bad idea.

Especially since rolling over had lined up the hardest parts of him with some very soft parts of me. Parts that were beginning to pulse with heat as I allowed my eyes to drop a bit lower to take a peek at...

"Rain?"

Every muscle in my body tensed at the sound of his voice. Painfully, I dragged my eyes away from where our bodies were pressed together and forced myself to meet his eyes.

He was definitely awake now.

"Yes, Dey?" I asked, trying to sound casual.

His eyes filled with amusement and a hint of male satisfaction. "What are you doing?"

"I was, um, about to wake you up."

His knowing smile spread a little wider. "I see. And now that I am awake, was there something you... wanted?"

My mind went to a disturbingly smutty place, and another wave of heat thrummed through me when my treacherous eyes started to wander south again. I took in the hard plane of his chest, the definitive ridges of his abs, the dusting of golden hair just below his navel...

"Princess, I need you to tell me exactly what you are thinking right now."

Something about the word "princess" hit me like a cold shower. A reminder of exactly where I was and what I had been through. The rational part of my brain woke up, and I shifted back enough to put a space between me and his enticing body.

"I was thinking," I began, confident that my libido was now on the back-burner, "that it would be great if you could answer some questions for me. Specifically, where are your clothes, where are my clothes, and where the hell am I?"

Dey sighed, seemingly realizing that his chances of things progressing more physically had ended. Rolling onto his back, he stretched like a giant cat, then adjusted himself to face me.

"I can assure you, Rain, nothing inappropriate happened last night."

I narrowed my eyes on him. "We might have somewhat different definitions of the word inappropriate. I can promise you I've never woken up with a naked man and thought, 'oh, what a chaste evening we just had.' I'm going to need a few more details."

"Allow me to assuage your fears, then," he said gallantly. "You had another episode in the throne room yesterday."

"Yeah, I remember that. Can we skip ahead to the part where you're naked?"

He let out a deep exhale and ran a hand through his sleep-tousled hair. "Of course. After you fell asleep, the king had me bring you here to rest. He was very concerned for you, Princess."

I grimaced. *Great first impression, Rain.*

"We both felt it would be best after your ordeal that you got some sleep," he continued. "I remained here with you in case my abilities were needed again. You must have been very exhausted because you did not stir once throughout the night."

I fought back the urge to roll my eyes. "Yeah, it's not every day you get abducted to a different dimension. Tends to take a lot out of a girl. Now, about my clothes?" I glanced down pointedly at the nightgown.

"The servants took them to be washed. They also dressed you as I thought you might not appreciate if I were the one to do so."

He was right about that. "And your clothes?"

Dey gave me a sly grin. "It was very warm last night."

"Warm enough that you had to take off your underwear?" I wasn't the smartest person, but even I recognized a suspect story when I heard it.

"Males here do not wear additional garments under their breeches," he replied plainly.

"That's it? Your excuse is that you were hot?"

He had the decency to look a little chagrined. "My people run a bit warmer than humans. I lit the fire because I did not want you to be cold, but I became a bit overheated. I did not intend to fall asleep without my clothing on. I must have drifted off."

I found myself so hung up on his first sentence that I completely disregarded the absurdity of his explanation.

"Did you just imply that you're not human?" I asked, my mouth hanging slack-jawed. "Because I saw pretty much all of you just now, and there was no tail or pointy ears."

Dey shifted away from me, and I could swear he seemed almost insulted.

"Of course I am not human," he replied stiffly. "I am Vitaean."

That word tickled something in the back of my mind, and I recalled what he said in the cemetery—that his home, Rivella, was in Vitaea.

"Okay, but like, you're still basically a human though, yeah? Only you have a different word for it?"

"No, Princess. I am not a man. I am a Vitaean male."

"But you look..." My eyes scanned his body again, lingering in certain areas way longer than was necessary, but I told myself it was in the name of science.

"If you keep looking at me like that, Rain, it will be very difficult to refrain from educating you in the many ways Vitaeans are superior to humans."

"I'm sorry," I sputtered, his words dousing my lusty thoughts. "Did you just say you're *superior* to me?"

His brow furrowed. "Of course not. I would never say such a thing."

"Oh, okay. Good." I relaxed back into the pillow.

"I said I am superior to humans."

I shot back up and glared at him. "I'm human, you dick!"

The pity in Dey's eyes dropped straight into my stomach where it morphed into a churning, uneasy feeling.

"No, Princess. You are not."

I was still reeling from Dey's words an hour later as I stepped out of the shower. He had left to go prepare the staff for my arrival at breakfast after promising it would only be him and my father in the king's private dining hall. No crowds. No staring eyes. No whispers and giggles.

Closing the shower door behind me, I shook my head in amazement that they even had showers in this world. It only had two temperatures, but the hot setting had been perfect for rinsing away the trauma of yesterday. It was what I often did after a panic attack. Something about a near-scalding shower always seemed to reset my brain.

I mentally added the existence of indoor plumbing in a world without electricity to the list of questions I was determined to get answers to at breakfast. Starting off with the bullshit about me not being human. After dropping that little bomb, Dey had resumed his firm stance of letting my father handle the explanation, which pissed me off to no end. You can't tell someone they're not human, then trot off to get a damned bagel.

Cursing his name under my breath, I grabbed the fluffy burgundy towel hanging from a rack and dried myself, relishing the luxury of it. Every scratchy towel I had at home came from the Dollar Store, but this thing felt like velvet. Tossing it on the floor, I snagged the matching robe that was just as soft and opened the door back into my room.

I stopped in my tracks when I found two ladies in front of me, patiently waiting. They appeared only a few years older than me and might have been sisters given their similar appearance. Same height. Same long-sleeved gray dress. Same blond hair that was braided and twisted into a top knot.

As I stepped out of the bathroom, both women made a sweeping gesture, their left arm flowing up their body then back down while simultaneously dropping their weight on their right leg. It was actually quite pretty, and for a second, I thought they might start dancing.

"Ummm... Hi?" I said, somewhat confused as to why they were in my room at all.

"Salwhay," they both replied in unison as the one on the left stepped forward, took my hand, and drew me over to a cushioned seat beside the hearth.

Reluctantly, I sat in front of the newly kindled fire. "So, just confirming for my own sanity here, you guys don't speak English, huh?"

Neither responded, and I slumped back into the chair. While I sat there mulling over my communication predicament, one of the women took up a position behind me and tugged on my wet hair. I whipped my head around with a few choice curse words on the tip of my tongue until I clocked the brush in her hand.

"Oh, sorry," I muttered. The ladies must be servants, but I had no idea what that actually entailed.

Settling back into the chair, I resigned myself to my current fate. The feeling of the brush running through my thick strands in front of the warm fire was actually kind of nice. My eyelids drifted shut, and for the first time, I let myself enjoy a little pampering.

Before I could get too comfortable, though, Dey's voice pulled me from my relaxation. "I see you have met your servants," he said, laying a hand on the shoulder of the female brushing my hair. "This is Kiahna, and her sister over there is Niahna. They have been at the palace for many decades, so they will do an excellent job of taking care of you."

I stared at him. "Decades? No way. They can't be more than twenty-five."

He scratched his chin thoughtfully. "I believe they are in their late sixties, though I am not certain. It has never come up."

I scanned the women, searching for any signs they were nearing retirement age, but saw nothing. Not a single crow's foot or frown line. "So this is more magic, then? You guys have some kind of power to look young forever?"

Dey chuckled. "Something like that. Vitaeans with healing abilities live much longer lives since our power repairs the damages of aging. As long as we remain near the Source, our lifespans are quite lengthy."

I opened my mouth, but he raised a hand in a placating gesture before I could speak. "If you could hold that thought, Princess, the king is waiting in the dining hall." He frowned at my robe. "And you are not yet dressed for some reason. Did I not give you enough time to prepare?"

My cheeks warmed when I remembered how long I'd spent under the hot water since I didn't have to worry about the utility bill for once. "Sorry. I think I might have taken a bit longer in the shower than usual."

"I understand," he replied, his lips twitching up into a grin. "I imagine you were very *dirty* from earlier."

The way he said dirty had my knees wavering. Was this how things were going to be? He knew I had been ogling his package, so now he was going to bring it up every chance he got?

I glared at him, hiding my embarrassment behind anger the way I often did. "I was actually," I snapped. "From you sweating on me all night long."

His grin faded.

Stomping over to the nightstand, I snatched up my hoodie and shorts. Clothes in hand, I headed for the bathroom.

"There are many fine dresses in the wardrobe that you could wear," he called.

"I think I'll stick with my own clothing, thank you very much." Then I shut the door in his face before he could get another word out.

Chapter Eight

We approached the dining hall, and my heart kicked into a higher gear at the anticipation of meeting my father.

Lingering just outside the entryway, I found myself pleasantly underwhelmed by the space in front of me. After yesterday's throne room, I expected more opulence, more grandeur, more... Just more. This dining room, while spacious by normal standards, was actually fairly intimate. Only one unlit diamond chandelier hung from a much lower ceiling, and the brown wood flooring had an elegant maroon marbling effect throughout. A fire crackled merrily in the hearth that was set into the left wall, and a row of paintings hung above it, all portraits of males that I wagered were the past kings given their proud postures.

The long table in the center of the room—made of thick slabs of dark wood with various patterns carved into it—had chairs for about twelve people on each side, all vacant. The only occupied seat was at the head of the table, and after a tense moment, my father raised his head and looked over to us.

A smile swept over his face, and a hundred butterflies took flight in my stomach, all beating their wings at maximum speed while I rubbed my sweaty palms on my shorts.

"Raynella!" he boomed across the length of the table as he leapt to his feet. I had only seconds to take in his appearance before his long legs ate up the distance, and he enveloped me in a rib-crushing hug. His hair, so black that it appeared to absorb all the light in the room, cascaded down his back in thick waves nearly as long as my own. His beard was trimmed short and neat, and diamond-studded crown sat atop his head, though it was smaller and more subdued than the extravagant one from yesterday. A few scattered wrinkles at the corners of his mouth and eyes had me putting his age around forty-five, though he could actually be a hundred for all I knew.

He pulled back from the hug to look at me, that silly grin still plastered across his face, and I finally realized what I was seeing on his chest. What I initially thought to be an elaborately decorative shirt was actually bare skin. Swirls of black ink covered his arms, shoulders, and chest—similar to Dey's tattoos yet far more expansive and intricate.

My attention moved away from the hypnotic designs to analyze his eyes. Identical to my own, they were an abnormally light shade of sky blue that almost glowed in the light, highlighting the faint golden ring around the pupil.

An intense need to say something filled me, but no words sprang to my lips. This was my father. An actual living parent. I had played this scenario out in my head so many different times as I lay awake at night in the drafty orphanage, but all the things I thought I might say simply vanished from my brain.

How do you even act when the father that you never knew existed was also a king from a different world?

Any hope of saying something meaningful flew out the window when I instinctively blurted out, "Call me Rain."

With his arms still clutching my shoulders, he laughed, a loud, boisterous sound that filled the room. I didn't know what to make of it—I hadn't thought my name was a joke—so I just gave him a subdued smile.

He pulled me back into another brief hug, then dragged me over to the table.

"Please sit, Raynella. We have much to talk about." He gestured toward the chair to the right of his, and Dey slid into the seat to the left. "And you may call me Verren," he added.

"Thank goodness you speak English because I have so many questions," I gushed, plopping into the cushy chair. "Dey said earlier that I wasn't even human which is ridiculous because—"

"Yes, yes, dear Raynella," my father said pleasantly, cutting me off. He waved to the servants behind him, and they scurried away, hopefully to bring back breakfast. "All in due time. I have much to tell you as well, but first allow me to simply look upon my daughter. I had long thought we might never find you."

"Sorry," I replied, feeling like I had been apologizing a lot lately simply for being curious. "I haven't been able to speak to anyone besides Dey, and he hasn't really been super forthcoming."

"I suppose that might be a bit irksome," he agreed. "You see, there are very few in my court who speak your language. Only those hand selected by myself were imbued with the knowledge. It is very taxing on the caster, so it was given only to those who needed to cross the rift."

"What do you mean by 'taxing on the caster?'" I asked, feeling like I missed something important. "What's a caster?"

Brow furrowed, he turned to Dey, addressing him in their foreign language. Whatever my father said made Dey drop his chin in submission.

"Hey," I said, waving my hand at them. "It's generally considered kind of rude to talk about a person right in front of them. Especially when they don't know what you're saying."

My father shot Dey a stern look that promised he wasn't done with him, then turned back to me. "I had been informed that Dey spoke to you about our people and the magic we hold, but it seems there was much that was not discussed."

"I mean, yeah, he told me a little about his emotion power and how you guys don't age very fast. I'm guessing there's more to share?"

"I would not even know where to begin, Raynella," he replied, settling back into his chair. "Our world is so very different from yours. To answer your earlier question, there are many powerful mental casters who reside in the palace. Among them is one who has the ability to impart knowledge. He was sent through the rift first to study your language and customs. After he returned, we had him transfer the knowledge to a select few."

"Wait," I interjected, holding up a hand. "He just dumped a bunch of information into your head? That seems, well, I'm not going to say impossible because I've learned that word means nothing here, but it sounds like it would hurt at least."

"It is a unique experience," Dey supplied. "Though painful is not quite accurate. Disorienting perhaps."

The servants returned then, carrying heaping plates of food and carafes of pink liquid that they placed in front of us. I didn't recognize most of the items on my plate, but I knew a pastry when I saw one, and I tore into it with a ferocity that lacked any of the refinement the table was probably used to seeing. My hand was reaching for a piece of something I prayed was bacon, when I noticed both men watching me.

"Oh, shit," I cursed, dropping my hands to my lap. "Is there some kind of protocol for eating here?"

"No, no," my father said reassuringly. "Please, enjoy the food. We were not aware how hungry you were, or I would have had something sent to your room."

"Yeah, it's weird to me too," I replied, grabbing the bacon and shoving it in my mouth. It wasn't pork, but it was crispy, salty heaven, nonetheless. I picked up another slice, then said through a mouth full of food, "Normally, I don't get quite this ravenous from skipping dinner."

"Ah," my father mused, taking a sip of the pink liquid. "Our days here are longer than in your world by several hours. When you arrived yesterday, it was shortly before the midday meal. You slept for nearly an entire day."

"Oh," I said, chewing on the bacon thoughtfully. I guess that made sense. There was no reason this planet would rotate at the same speed as Earth.

Taking a sip of the juice, I savored the sweet yet tart taste that reminded me of strawberry lemonade, then asked, "So, can you do that brain transfer thing that lets me speak your language?"

Even though I didn't plan to stay long, I wasn't opposed to the occasional future visit to see my father. Now that the shock was starting to fade, I found myself somewhat curious about everything.

Dey's eyes brightened at my suggestion. "I think that would be a wonderful—"

"A wonderful idea, yes," my father interjected. "Though we should wait a while first. It is a very invasive process usually only attempted with the strongest of Vitaeans. I would not want to risk anything happening to you, Raynella."

I looked to Dey, but he just frowned for a moment, then shrugged and returned to his plate of food.

"Ok," I said, wondering if there was more to it than that. "I don't have a while, though. My sister's gonna freak if I'm not home soon."

"Your sister?" My father raised an eyebrow.

"Well, not my biological sister," I clarified. "We grew up together in the orphanage and took care of each other, so she's basically my sister. I sort of disappeared without saying anything." I shot a pointed look at Dey who suddenly found his breakfast extremely interesting. "I would like to come back later so we can actually get to know each other. Maybe I can bring Jenn next time? Don't worry, she'll probably handle it better than I did."

I bit into a piece of yellow fruit and let myself dream a bit about the future. If my father gave me even a few diamonds to take back to my world, it would set Jenn and me up for life. No more Taco Hut. No more canned beans for dinner. God, no more worrying about making rent.

The wary looks on Dey and my father's faces told me that my plans were about to come crashing down.

"As much as I would like to," my father began delicately, "I cannot send you back just yet."

"Excuse me?" I screeched, jumping up and knocking my chair over in the process. "What exactly do you mean by 'just yet.' When can I go home?"

"Soon," he said, approaching me with a mixture of trepidation and fortitude.

"How soon is soon?" I gritted out.

He sighed. "It takes a great deal of power for a Walker to open a rift. Their magic is not like ours. Lorduin needs time to rest before he can open another one."

"So find someone else," I demanded, fighting off the rising panic within me.

"Unfortunately, there are only two remaining Walkers, and Lorduin is the only one who resides here."

I took in a deep inhale and smoothed back my braid. "Okay," I said, more to myself than them. "This is okay. Jenn might freak out a little bit, but I'll explain everything. It'll be fine. Everything is fine."

I would have killed for a Klonopin, but I at least managed to get my breathing relatively under control. "So when can I go home? Another day or two?" I looked at my father expectantly.

"I am afraid it will take longer than a day."

I sucked in a sharp breath. "How much longer?"

He hesitated, then said, "An entire lunar cycle."

A lunar cycle? What the hell was a lunar cycle? I sorted through my memory until my brain snagged on a werewolf movie Jenn made me watch years ago.

"I can't go home for a fucking month?!"

My legs dangled over the castle parapet, a sense of complete and utter numbness settling into my bones. It was mildly concerning because I didn't think I should feel numb. Normally I would be a drooling puddle of panic in a situation like this. Yet when I glanced over the ledge at the long drop that would inevitably result in a painful death, there was simply nothing there. It was as if my body had reached its capacity for emotion, and now I was officially tapped out. It would probably be kind of nice if it wasn't for the whole trapped in a different realm thing.

Still, I admired the landscape before me, amazed at how far I could see in a world not choked with pollution. Situated on the coastline atop a vast hill, the castle nudged right up to the edge of a steep cliff. A grand bay twinkled in the morning light off in the distance, but none of the boats moored there were leaving the docks. Probably hindered by the thick fog that concealed any traces of the sea beyond the harbor.

Staring out at the ocean was one of my guilty pleasures back home. I would take the train out to Montauk, to the very tip of Long Island, so I could feel like I was surrounded on all sides by nothing but water. I never liked the beach—the heat, the people, the sand, any of it—but I loved the sea with a passion deeper than its darkest depths. It was open and endless and lacking any of the weight of the city. My mind was always quieter around large bodies of water.

Turning away from the shoreline, I surveyed the rest of the castle. Servants rushed around the main courtyard below, the females clad in plain gray dresses and males in matching long-sleeved tunics, their arms full of trays and linens. Courtiers dressed in fine sleeveless tunics and dresses that showed off the tattoos everyone seemed to have lingered around the fountains, engaging in private conversations away from the servants.

Neither sun was anywhere near its peak, so the diamonds only twinkled faintly, though in a few hours I knew they would become hazardous to the eyes.

Beyond the courtyard, the pseudo-rose garden stretched out for at least a couple acres to the right of a cobblestone path. Past that, tiny cottages with thatched roofs were sprinkled throughout the copse of oak trees.

To the left of the road, a grandiose coliseum sank deep into the ground with the entrance just outside the palace. Rows and rows of seats filled the stadium, and the pit at the bottom was littered with boulders and small blast craters.

And surrounding all of it—the palace, the garden, the arena—was a massive outer wall stretching over twenty feet high. The only break in the defensive structure was the imposing front gate where the cobblestone road led away from the castle, twisting and winding until it reached a sparkling walled city that spilled down the side of the hill like a jar of glitter tipped on its side.

There appeared to be even more buildings at the bottom of the mountain beyond the far side of the town, but I couldn't tell for sure. I would have plenty of time to explore later. I had no intention of sitting around for twenty-eight days trying not to worry about Jenn.

My heart ached as I was reminded of what she must be going through. God, she probably thought I was dead. The thought gutted me. If our roles had been reversed and she was the one who disappeared, I didn't think I could survive it.

Jenn was strong, though, and she had friends she could lean on. We paid rent two days ago, so she'd be fine until I got back, hopefully with a bag of diamonds in tow. Still, twenty-eight days of not seeing her smile, hearing her laugh...

The scuffing sound of boots behind me broke up my pity party.

"I suppose you're ready to take me to the dungeons?" I said dramatically, sliding off the wall.

Dey's eyes widened in horrified shock. "Where would you get such an idea?"

"It was a joke," I replied dismissively, any earlier annoyance I'd felt toward him fading under the weight of my predicament. "You know, since I'm being held here against my will. Like a prisoner." He let out a strangled noise when I passed by him and entered the stairwell.

"I know this is difficult for you, Rain, but you are not a prisoner. And I can assure you that we would never put you in the dungeons."

"Right. Because I'm a princess."

Dey followed me down the twisting staircase. "I actually came to bring you to the library. King Verren has asked that I explain a few things while he meets with his advisors. He will join us there shortly to answer all your questions."

"All?" I asked, raising an eyebrow suspiciously.

"Well, as many as he has time for. We are honestly not trying to withhold anything from you. I promise."

I wanted to believe him, but the way they parceled out information like I was a dog getting treats made me a tad distrustful.

Damp, musty air clung to my skin when we descended into a darker part of the castle. Halfway down a dimly lit hallway, we came to a small, unceremonious wooden door.

Despite it looking considerably less opulent than the rest of the castle, I still expected the library to be an grandiose room filled with numerous shelves of books. Instead, the space was actually similar to my father's personal dining hall—warm and cozy with a hearth off to the left. The only difference was the luscious rugs that covered most of the wood flooring.

What surprised me the most, though, was the lack of actual books. I figured a palace this size would have a library with tens of thousands, yet the few shelves on the right wall held a couple hundred at most. The rest of the room was filled with small tables, upholstered chairs, and a desk in the back buried under a mountain of scrolls.

I moved further into the room, and another ceiling mural unfurled above my head, this one composed of interconnected scenes that appeared to tell an overarching story.

"This is what King Verren wanted you to see before he spoke with you," Dey said, moving up beside me. "He thought it might make your conversation a bit easier."

"How?" I asked, studying the mural. "I don't know what it means."

"I can help with that," a voice chimed in as a door at the back of the library opened. The male looked to be about my father's age with extra gray peppered throughout his short and neat wavy brown hair. He crossed over to the desk, his brown robes making a slight swishing noise as he moved.

"You speak English." My mood perked up at having someone new who could understand me.

"Of course I do, Raynella," he replied cheerily. "Who do you think taught everyone else?"

I studied him for a second until it clicked. "Oh, so you're the scholar. The one who can impart knowledge." His robe fit what I'd envisioned in my mind, but that was about it. For some reason, I had pictured a Gandalf-looking guy with a white beard down to his waist who leaned on a twisted staff clutched in gnarled and shaky hands. This guy looked more like my high school algebra teacher.

He sketched a little bow and said, "My name is Corym, Princess, and I am at your service." He walked over to a group of three chairs and gestured for us to join him. "Now, would you like to know what the mural is depicting?"

At last, someone eager to answer questions. "Absolutely," I replied. "Dey said it was going to explain some things."

"I imagine it will, yes." Leaning back in the chair, Corym rested his head on a small pillow attached to the seatback that supported his neck while he gazed at the ceiling. "This is the origin story of Vitaea."

I took in the first image depicting islands with glittering orbs underneath. Above the planet, three humanoid beings were encased in a glowing nimbus of bright yellow light. I found myself sinking into the chair, a feeling of relaxation settling into me as Corym's melodic voice washed over me.

"In the beginning, the Gods created many worlds and bestowed upon these worlds a source of power that granted the inhabitants unique abilities. In creating Vitaea, they gifted our planet with healing so we could live long lives in a peaceful paradise. Each island was given its own Source, buried deep underground with hundreds of ley lines distributing the power throughout the land so all could bathe in the gift of the Gods.

And for a time, there was harmony in all of Vitaea.

Then the World Walkers came. Fleeing their own dying planet, three of these Walkers escaped to our island of Rivella through a rift, each bringing with them their retinue of non-magical slaves they had stolen from other worlds over the years. Their humans.

The Walkers sensed the pure strength of the Rivellan Source and knew that it could hold so much more power than this planet was born with. Each Walker ripped a hole into an uninhabited world and funneled the magic from that planet's Source directly into the Rivellan one, flooding our world with new abilities. The first to a world of elemental magic. The second to a world of mind magic. And the third to a world of creation magic.

Believing they had now created a perfect existence, the Walkers built a black stone palace over the Source and sent their humans to live among the Rivellans to tell them of all the Walkers had done for this world.

There was no peace in Rivella, however, because the creation magic began to overload the ley lines. It filled our people with power we could not control, many being driven mad or harming others with their unbridled abilities. Our populace began aging faster, unable to heal the damage from this raw new magic. Many attempted to flee to other islands, but the Walkers created a thick mist to encircle Rivella and filled the deep waters with monstrous creatures to prevent them from abandoning their utopia.

While the Rivellans began to slowly die off, the magicless humans thrived, their children unaffected. Rivellans feared that soon the humans would overpower them by sheer numbers alone. So a king from the Diamond Court traveled to this Onyx Palace to beg the Walkers to close the rifts and save his people.

Two of the Walkers were offended that their gift was being shunned and refused to address the king's demands. They believed, given enough time, Rivellans would adapt to the increase in power.

The king did not believe they would survive long enough to evolve, so he turned to the third Walker, the one who had opened the creation rift. This Walker actually sympathized with the king, believing no one should have to watch those they care for suffer. So he offered a solution: he was unable to close the rifts as they had grown permanent from remaining open for so long, but he could condense the hundreds of small ley lines into three central lines that would connect to each of the three Rivellan courts. A cascade of power would emanate directly from their palaces, the strength of the magic fading the further away one got, allowing weaker Rivellans a safe place to live.

The solution was only meant to be temporary, as he believed the Rivellans should all have their full magic again once they adapted. He told the king that one day, a powerful Rivellan would be born, one who was strong enough to hold all four types of magic within them. When that happened, they would be able to separate the ley lines and restore the power of the Source to all.

With his decision made, the Walker created a dark forest around the Onyx Palace, filled with vicious creations to protect the Source until such a time as the child was born. He told the other Walkers of his plan and begged them to leave the castle, to protect his slaves and watch over Rivella. Once alone, the remaining Walker merged the ley lines and allowed himself to slip into a death-like sleep so he could hold tightly to the condensed power for as long as needed.

It is rumored he still slumbers deep within the Onyx Palace, waiting for the chosen one to restore the ley lines and release him from his prison."

I sat quietly, taking in the final image above me of a black castle with a figure sleeping below.

"Okay..." I said, debating the best response and landing on what I egotistically considered to be the most important thing. "What exactly does all that have to do with me?"

"Actually," Corym said, rising up and walking over to his desk, "it has everything to do with you. The mural depicts what is believed to be the full story. That we are all forced to wait here until magically a person appears with all four abilities. A somewhat fruitless plan since creation magic has all but died out over the millennia."

Corym removed a key from around his neck and unlocked a drawer. He pulled out a scroll and handed it to me.

I unrolled it carefully, afraid the aged paper would fall apart in my hands. "I can't read this," I told him, holding the fragile papyrus gingerly with the tips of my fingers.

"Of course, apologies," he said. "That scroll contains the second part of the story which has been withheld from all of Rivella since the time of the first Diamond King." He paused, his eyes gleaming with excitement. "Would you like to know what it says?"

I was pretty sure I didn't.

"Yeah, okay."

Corym clasped his hands together and settled back against his desk. "The scroll details the rest of what occurred between the Walker and the Diamond King. How they decided that the fate of their magic could not be left to chance. The Walker called upon his most beloved human, a silver-haired female, and placed a dormant kernel of his Walker magic into her blood to be passed through the generations. Within the king, he placed a kernel of his stolen creation magic. He said that one day, when the two came together, the powerful child would be born. This descendant of the king and the silver-haired female would be strong enough to withstand the power flowing from the open rifts long enough to separate the ley lines and restore magic throughout Rivella once more."

Tense silence filled the library after Corym finished speaking, and he watched me for any reaction to his life-altering words.

I wanted to say it wasn't possible. I wasn't some chosen savior of a far off land. That was fairy tale garbage. I was just an orphan from Passaic, New Jersey.

But as my hand slid to the top of my head where the silver streaks that I religiously dyed would soon begin showing at my roots, I knew in my gut that I was the one who was wrong.

Chapter Ten

I always hated the word destiny. And fate. They were just flowery ways of saying you don't have any control over your life so nothing you do matters.

"No," I said, giving Corym my best defiant glare.

"Apologies, Princess, but I do not understand," he replied, his face twisting in confusion.

"Did I stutter? I said 'no.' As in, 'no, I don't give a shit about some ancient prophecy.' Or maybe 'hell no am I going to get sucked into this madness.' Take your pick, but it still comes out as 'no.'"

I knew I was being a bitch, but I didn't care anymore. I'd been at the whims of these people ever since I landed in this strange world, and I was done with it.

Shock didn't really describe Corym's expression so much as horrified. Like the thought of someone not wanting to fulfill a prophecy was unfathomable.

"But... but..." he sputtered, at a loss for words.

I handed him the scroll, then wandered back over to the chairs where I slumped down, leaning my head back to view the mural again. It really was spectacular.

"Look, I get it. You guys think I'm the one all this refers to. And maybe I am. I'm willing to accept that the king of this place is my father because he looks just like me, and I'm not surprised to hear my mom was human. But none of this means anything to me. I have a life back home and someone who needs me. I'm sorry, but I can't help you. You're going to have to wait for the next human/king offspring."

Dey knelt beside my chair and placed his hand on my shoulder. "Princess..."

"Stop," I interjected, squirming under his stark appraisal. "I'm not a princess, I'm not a savior. I'm just Rain."

He shook his head and pulled his hand back to his side. "You are wrong. This"—he gestured to the mural—"is who you *are*. You are not just some girl from the Other Realm. You never were. Surely you must have realized at some point that you did not belong there?"

I chewed on my lip, annoyed that he was wasn't entirely off base. I always thought I hadn't fit in because I was an orphan. I didn't know anything about my parents, and by extension, I didn't know anything about me. I had no siblings. No grandparents. No one to tell me how I might turn out based on my genetics. Of course I would feel lost.

"That doesn't mean anything," I croaked, failing to hide the catch in my voice. "I get it. You grew up with all this. It's very real for you, but it's just a story for me. Saying I'm the chosen one doesn't magically make me believe it."

Forcing any emotion I felt back into the vault where it belonged, I stood up, threw back my shoulders, and faced Corym, giving him a look of firm resolution. "I can't help you," I insisted, staring him down and daring him to say anything to the contrary.

"I am afraid it is not that simple," came a voice from behind me, and I whipped around to see my father standing in the doorway.

"Thank you for your help, old friend," he said, crossing the room to clap Corym on the shoulder. "I will take over from here. Raynella and I have much to discuss."

"Yes, of course," Corym said, rolling up the scroll he had been clutching for dear life. "It was a pleasure meeting you, Raynella. If you have any questions, I am most often here in the library."

"Thanks," I said, then left to follow my father, leaving Corym sitting on his desk looking a little like a lost puppy.

"Where are we going?" I asked when my father led Dey and I back up into the castle proper.

"The Sylvarium," he replied without pausing his brisk pace. "It was one of your mother's favorite places in the palace."

"I'd love to see where she spent her time," I said, feeling a tingle of excitement that I was going to learn more about my mom. "But what's a Sylvarium?"

He gave me a sideways glance and smiled. "Wait and see, my little Raynella."

I was tempted to remind him that my name was Rain, and also I wasn't little, but something kept the words from coming out of my mouth. Maybe I still really wanted him to like me despite everything.

We rounded another corner, and I saw the hall ended at a set of tall glass and metal doors. As we drew closer, it became evident that the glass panes were not actually glass.

"You have doors made of diamonds?" I didn't know if I should be disgusted at the opulence or amazed at how beautiful they were. Up close, I could see all the different carvings of trees, animals, and flowers that made up the eight panels.

"The Sylvarium is built mostly from glass," he explained patiently. "But my own mother decided many years ago that the doors needed an upgrade. She spent a lot of time here as well and felt it deserved a more elegant entry."

At the mention of his mother, it dawned on me that I might have more than just a father. I might have grandparents or even siblings.

My mind was reeling with the familial possibilities when he pushed open the diamond-accented doors, and all other thoughts were lost to the wonders within.

Frosted glass walls and ceilings inlaid with small diamond clusters shaped like flowers filtered the late morning light into the room, casting a rainbow of colors that danced across the scene before me. Numerous woven baskets hung from the ceiling, filled with exquisite flowering plants that spilled over the edges, their berry covered vines cascading toward the ground like rippling verdant curtains. Mossy cushioned benches were scattered throughout the open room, and ropes of falling ivy encircled the soft looking sofas. Narrow trees similar to skinny willows sprouted from the ground around the edges of the space. It appeared that the Sylvarium was built directly over soil, allowing everything within to grow naturally.

And all of its beauty faded into the background because I was completely mesmerized by the small creatures flying around the room. At first, I thought they were butterflies with their vibrantly colored wings, but most of them were closer in size to sparrows. As they fluttered about, soft dove-like cooing and musical chitters filled the air.

I took a few steps into the room, and two of them flitted over to me. After stretching out my arm, I held perfectly still and waited for them to land so I could get a closer look. They both perched just above my elbow, and I let out a tiny gasp when I saw they didn't have compound insect eyes, but instead had feline, oval-slitted orbs. The piqued curiosity in their expressions as they regarded me mirrored my own. One had thin, translucent crimson wings with white speckled throughout, while the other had bolder wings of deep purple with an opalescent sheen. The red one scooted further up my arm, and the miniscule claws at the end of its thin black legs gently dug into my skin as it moved. With one finger, I lightly caressed its velvety soft thorax.

I turned to my father and Dey who stood behind me waiting patiently, and the creatures flew away at the slight jostling. "What are they?" I whispered, a child-like wonder lighting up my face. There had to be a hundred or more flying around under the glass dome, some with wings of a solid color and others with spotted or sheer ones that sparkled in the rainbow light.

"They are crescia," Dey answered.

I blinked at him, "But your pet I met in the garden... Thorell, right? You said he was a crescia. These don't look anything like your hawk lizard."

He chuckled at my assessment of his companion. "That is because these ones are unbound. Once a crescia chooses their Vitaean, they go through a metamorphosis. Their final form is determined by the strength and soul of their bonded."

I had about a thousand questions I wanted to ask, but my father took my arm and guided me over to one of the sofas. "Dey can tell you more about the crescia a little later. I do have responsibilities, Raynella, and we need time to discuss things before I am pulled away to attend to the demands of my people."

A twinge of sadness caused a slight pressure in my chest as I claimed the cushion beside him and tucked one leg underneath me. Of course he would be too busy to hang out all day and chat. It's not like you could call in sick when you were the king. The logic of the situation failed to make me feel better, though.

Dey sat on a nearby sofa, seemingly content to bow out of this conversation.

"Raynella," my father said, drawing my attention back to him. "I know that you are feeling very overwhelmed right now. I should have been the one to explain the prophecy to you, but Corym is the palace scholar and far more adept at telling the story of our people." He cupped my face in his large, soft hands. "You are a Vitaean, Raynella. You were born here. I know you feel human because you spent your life surrounded by them, but you are not one. Not completely, anyway. Your mother was human, so you do have her blood in you, but your Vitaean side is much stronger."

"I don't even know what that means," I replied, still trying to wrap my brain around being a different species. "You all look human to me."

He folded his hands in his lap and gave me a sympathetic smile. "I understand your confusion. The Gods who made all the worlds created life from the same template, so we look similar, but I assure you that we are not. Dey can go over the differences another time since I must soon return to my courtly duties. I brought you here because I thought perhaps if I told you about your mother, you would be more inclined to consider fulfilling the prophecy."

It was only the desire to learn more about my mom that kept me from telling him it was a waste of breath trying to convince me.

"You must know," he continued, "that my family has guarded the secret of the prophecy for over a thousand years. When the original Diamond King returned here to the palace, he decreed that no Vitaean of the Diamond Court would be allowed to mate with a human since he was terrified of the child being born before his people were ready. He cared only for the wellbeing of his citizens and believed it was the right thing to do. His decree has remained in place ever since."

"So what changed?"

My father ran a hand through his hair, hesitating. "My people started to get sick. It began about forty years ago. A plague born of the dark forest began infecting Vitaeans. The strongest healers attempted all they could but were unable to save those afflicted." He closed his eyes for a second, visibly struggling with his words. "My wife and children all succumbed to the illness."

Oh, od.

I felt like I should hug him or something, but the thought made me too uncomfortable. Sympathy wasn't really one of my strengths, and I doubted he would appreciate any stiff gesture I could manage. "I'm so sorry," I offered soberly, the weak words the best I could summon.

"It is all right, Raynella," he said, patting my knee. "It was a very long time ago. You have to understand that most Vitaeans live much longer than humans. I myself am 137 years old and still young compared to many that reside in the palace."

I almost choked at the number. He barely appeared middle-aged.

"I realized that the only way to stop this plague is for the ley lines to be restored," he said, oblivious to my shock. "The Walker created the dark forest to protect the Onyx Palace. To protect the condensed lines. Once they are separated, that forest should be no more, and stronger healers will be able to eradicate any remaining disease. So I did the only thing I could do. I had my people search for a silver-haired human. It took over a decade, but they found her. Your mother, Leeara."

Leeara.

It was a beautiful name.

"They told me where she was staying. The moment I saw her, with that long silver hair flowing like water around her perfect face..." He trailed off, his eyes going distant at the memory.

"You fell for her?" I ventured.

A dreamy look claimed him. "I did indeed. I brought her here, and we were happy, Raynella. After a few months, she became pregnant with you. Not because I forced her, but because she wanted to have a child. I planned to tell her about the prophecy one day when you were older, but seven months after you were born she fled the castle with you for reasons we may never know." He paused before continuing, bitterness now lacing his words. "She took you to the Walker that lived in the dark forest. By the time we found her, it was already too late. My soldiers arrived just as the Walker murdered her and stole you away through a rift."

My father lifted a hand to my cheek, and his thumb wiped away a tear I didn't realize had formed.

"I have been searching for you ever since that day, Raynella. I found the last remaining Walker and convinced him to help me. Every lunar cycle when the rift could be opened, I sent one of my best soldiers to seek you out. I was beginning to give up hope, until now." He pulled me into a tight hug. "You are finally home, Raynella. Rivella is where you belong."

Ignoring the awkwardness of his touch, I let him hold me while I grieved for the mother I never knew and wondered about her possible reasons for stealing me away.

The sound of a throat clearing pulled us apart before I could ask any questions about her, though.

A short, elderly male in a red button-up frock hovered uncomfortably a few feet away, and my father waved a hand at him in acknowledgement. "I must leave you in Dey's very capable hands now, but I implore you, Raynella, please take some time before you reject your role in the prophecy. Now that you are in Vitaea, your magic will awaken, and you can be the one to save your people." He gave me one last squeeze, then stood. "Think about it. This could be your home." And with that, he left the Sylvarium, his steward close behind.

Dey joined me on the bench. "Are you well, Princess?"

I was most definitely not well. My brain was reeling, and I was pretty sure my capacity for new and insane things had surpassed its limit. There was, however, one prevailing thought that begged immediate attention.

"Dey… do I have magical powers?"

The son of a bitch just grinned.

Chapter Eleven

"Where are we going?" I asked, accompanying Dey through the castle. He still hadn't answered my question about having magical powers. He just grabbed my hand, tugged me out of the Sylvarium, and took off down a labyrinth of hallways.

When I was about to ask if maybe he had gotten lost, he halted abruptly in front of a wooden door. I followed him through, but the blinding sunlight on the other side caused me to miss the first step down. A surprised squawk flew from mouth as gravity flung me unceremoniously into Dey and knocked us both to the ground.

I nearly ate a face full of dirt, but he twisted at the last second to cushion my fall so I landed on his chest instead. He burst out laughing, and I couldn't help but join him for a second, pulled in by the sweetly innocent sound of his unfiltered joy.

When his laughter subsided, I waited for him to shift me off his body, but his arms only wrapped around me tighter. His heart beat out a brisk tempo under my ear, my own speeding up to match.

I pulled back far enough to see that the amusement in his eyes had changed into something more serious and heated. Brushing a lock of hair from his face,

I felt him grow hard underneath me. My own body melted in response to his obvious arousal, but the sane part of me recognized sex was a complication I didn't need.

Extricating myself from his arms, I rolled off his chest.

"You could have stayed where you were," he offered tenderly.

I climbed to my feet and assessed my body for new bruises. "I was crushing you. I'm not exactly petite."

"You are to me," he pointed out. "And I was not complaining." He didn't move from the spot where we landed, looking at me with something like wishful dreaming.

The light in his eyes faded when all I did was put out a hand to help him up. "Where are we?" I asked. We had entered a courtyard similar to the one at the front of the castle but much smaller with only one fountain and thankfully no diamond veins in the stone walls.

Dey led me over to the sculpture that continually tossed a fine mist into the air, and we sat on the bench beneath it.

"This is King Verren's private courtyard. The Sylvarium is lovely, but the crescia would have made conversation a challenge."

"Why?" I asked, brushing a bit of dirt off my bare legs. "I liked their soft, gentle coos."

"Yes, they are charming creatures, but I was worried they might become a distraction since they are drawn to the potential power inside you."

"Inside *me*?" I squeaked, glancing at my arms as if I might see some crackling energy leaking out.

"Yes, Princess," he said, scooting closer until our thighs touched. "I am bonded to Thorell, and the king's crescia died many years ago, so we are less appealing. You, however, are unbonded, and they can sense the rising power within you."

"Yeah, about that..." I shoved a few loose strands of hair behind my ear and shifted on the bench to face him fully, breaking the contact of his warm leg against mine. "Can we talk about this whole magic thing? Because I'm pretty sure I would know if I had powers. It's not like walking around all day with a coffee stain and wondering why people are snickering."

He chuckled. "You would not have abilities in the Other Realm," he explained, placing his hands on the bench behind him and settling back. "Your world is a place void of all magic. It was a very disconcerting feeling in truth as our power is tied to the Source. When I stepped through the portal, I could feel my magic being drained from my body as it fought to stay in this realm. Now that you are here, we have no idea how long it will take before your abilities emerge."

"What does that mean exactly?" I asked, exasperation filling my voice. "You all seem to have different powers."

"Yes, that is accurate," he agreed. "There are four types of magic. Our native healing magic is the most common, as our bodies are naturally drawn to it. Mental magic is what you felt when I soothed your emotions, and it can manifest in many different ways. Elemental magic is, of course, the ability to manipulate an element such as water or air."

I took a second to digest his words. "Okay, that sort of makes sense. And the fourth type?"

He shrugged and brushed a bit of sand off his tunic. "Truthfully? Not much is known about creation magic. Most likely because they used to execute those who exhibited the ability."

"What?" I gasped. "They murdered innocent children?"

He sat forward and took my hands in his. "Not children, Princess. Abilities do not manifest until adulthood. You must understand that in the early days, people still feared the return of overwhelming magic, and creation wielders are dangerous. Their magic allows the caster to bring forth something from nothing. There is no telling what someone could create with that ability. Thankfully, there has not been an emergence of creation magic in many years."

I pulled my hands from his grasp and folded my arms. It horrified me that people were killed for something they couldn't control, yet at the same time, I'd never been an idealist. I knew what humans were capable of, and it would be ignorant to think Vitaeans would be any better. Still, there had to have been a better option than murder.

It was all too much to process, and the pressure in my throat grew tighter. "I need to get away from these walls so I can breathe. Is it okay if I go for a walk?" I climbed to my feet and a took a few steps away from the bench.

"Of course," he said, beaming at me as he stood. "I would be happy to escort you anywhere."

"Ummm..." I shifted from foot to foot awkwardly, jamming my hands into the pockets of my shorts. "I was kind of hoping to go alone."

Dey's face fell so fast you would think I kicked him in the balls, and I knew in that moment there could never be anything between us beyond friendship. Calling him attractive was an understatement, but I was familiar with his kind. He was the type that got too attached. The type that wanted things I couldn't give him. Things I couldn't give anyone.

And despite the fact that he technically abducted me here, I didn't want to break his heart when I left.

Tumultuous thoughts bounced around in my head as my feet took me out of the castle, past the rose garden, and down to the copse of trees. When I got closer, I could see that they weren't actually oaks. The leaves were the wrong shape, and fruit that looked like pudgy, pink bananas hung from their limbs.

I was seconds away from snatching the fruit and shoving it in my mouth when another smell hit me. Taking a deep inhale, I let out a near-sexual groan as the smell of cooked meat wafted over on the breeze. I followed the intoxicating scent that took me deeper into the woods, heading in the direction of the small houses I'd seen earlier.

Boisterous male laughter reached my ears, and I tracked it to a quaint cottage that couldn't be much larger than my apartment back in Jersey. A stone pathway cut through the grass and ended at a set of stairs leading up to a spacious front porch. Blue shingles and white shutters added adorable accents to the sun-bleached wooden walls, one of which was mostly covered in untamed ivy.

Smoke wafted up from the back of the home, and I made my way toward it, determined to convince them to share their food despite the language barrier.

Two dark-skinned males roughly my age sat on the back porch steps, laughing and drinking from glasses filled with amber liquid. But my eyes barely skittered over them before landing on what I truly sought. A few feet from the house, in a section cleared of trees and grass, a hunk of meat rotated on a spit above a low fire.

Taking a few steps closer, I cleared my throat loudly, and two heads twisted around to stare at me.

Twins, I realized. They were identical in every way that I could see, with matching mops of short dreadlocks, wide upturned smiles with gleaming white teeth, and swirling tattoos along their arms that stopped short of their necks.

They both stood when I took a step forward. "Hi, um, I know you probably don't understand me, but I was hoping to have some of your food?" I pointed at the meat, then back to myself, my hands making the motion of putting something in my mouth. "Meat," I said louder, as if volume was the problem. "Can I have your meat?" I mimed chewing an invisible burger.

To my surprise, both males burst into laughter, collapsing against each other like they just heard the best joke of their life.

"What's so funny?" I demanded.

"You are, Princess," the one on the right said.

My jaw dropped. "What the hell?" I blurted out, enraged not only that they spoke English, but that they were clearly laughing at me.

"We are sorry," the one on the left said, "but we do not think it is a good idea for you to... eat our meat."

That set them both off again, and they collapsed to the porch steps in a fit of laughter. I glared at them, trying to mask my embarrassment with anger, but the bright red of my burning cheeks was probably giving me away.

I stomped over and kicked the boot of the one on the left. "Hey, care to explain who you are and how you know English? I thought I met everyone who knew my language. And don't call me princess. My name is Rain."

Their laughter died off, but the amused grins wouldn't leave their faces.

"Sorry, Princess," the right one said, ignoring my request to be called Rain. "We are two members of the team that has been searching for you over the years. Dey told us this morning that you had arrived at the palace. We meant to introduce ourselves, but..."

"We wanted to enjoy our time off more," the other twin finished unabashedly, taking a hefty swig from his glass. On the porch behind them, I saw a jug of the liquid that was nearly half empty.

"Are you drunk?" I asked incredulously, eyeing their glasses with a not small amount of envy.

The right brother grimaced. "Just a little," he confessed at the same time the left brother grinned and said, "Quite a bit."

I couldn't help but smile at the two of them, my anger over their earlier teasing ebbing. They were the first people I'd met in this world who weren't taking everything so damned seriously. The pressure of supposedly being the chosen savior of an entire realm was just too much, and I needed a break, if only for a few hours.

"So I'm your princess, yeah?"

They both nodded.

"Awesome. In that case, consider my first royal decree that I need a drink and some food. Whatever you're cooking smells insanely good."

The brothers glanced at each other, a wordless conversation passing between them. The one on the left jumped up to offer me his seat on the porch while grabbing a discarded plate, and the other refilled his glass then handed it to me. I didn't even bother to ask what it was before I downed half the liquid in two gulps. All I cared about was that it tasted delicious, like a rum and coke with honey.

I took another sip, and my eyes drifted down to the dying fire that flared back to life of its own accord as the spit started to rotate once more. I blinked a couple times. What the hell was in my drink?

"Am I hallucinating, or is there no wood in that fire?" I asked the brother beside me who was lazily spinning his hand through the air. "Also, how is it turning?" The spit was nothing more than a metal rod set onto a few pieces of wood, yet it rotated in a smooth regular rhythm.

One brother laughed while the other brought me a plate of meat and said, "We are elemental casters. I am an igniservian, so I am holding the fire in place. My brother is an aeriservian, so he funnels the breeze that allows it to rotate."

"Dang," I said, starting to understand the appeal of magic in this world. "That's badass."

I tore into the food he handed me, devouring it in minutes. Then I tossed back more of the honey-booze, enjoying the feeling of relaxation that had started to wend its way through me. "So who are you guys, anyway?"

"My name is Camden, but you may call me Cam," the one beside me said.

"And I am Ramset," the one by the railing added. "But call me Ram."

My eyes darted back and forth between them. "You go by Cam and Ram?" I tried not to laugh, but a small giggle snuck out anyway.

Crap. That couldn't be good. I only giggled when I was drunk.

"I like you guys," I said, laying my head back on the porch and staring up at the blue sky. I had a belly full of food and a pleasant buzz in my brain. Maybe I could get through these next few weeks after all.

"You are definitely not what we expected from our conversation with Dey," Cam said. Or maybe it was Ram. I already forgot which was which.

"God, I can only imagine what he said about me. Wait, when did you talk to him?"

"This morning," Cam or Ram said.

I remembered my morning encounter with Dey, and my cheeks flushed. "Do not believe a thing he said. He was the naked one, and I swear I didn't touch anything. I mean, yeah, I peeked, but who wouldn't..." My words trailed off when I caught both brothers grinning at me mischievously. "He didn't say anything, did he?"

"Only that you had arrived, but please continue. Naked, you say?" The one by the railing waggled his eyebrows at me, and I smacked him on the leg. The cottage tilted beneath me, rocking gently like calm ocean waves.

"It wasn't like that," I said, yawning. "Or it kind of was, but nothing happened. And nothing is gonna happen. Dey and me is not a good idea for a lot of reasons."

"Such as…?" the brother beside me asked.

"Oh, you know," I waved my hand around loosely in the air, fighting to keep my eyes open. "Sex complicates things, and right now my life is complicated enough. Better if I don't go down that road." My eyes drifted shut, and I didn't try to open them. I would sit up when the world stopped spinning.

"Now you sound like Sin."

"What's a Sin?" I slurred, trying and failing to fight off the strong tug of exhaustion.

I didn't hear their answer. The warm blanket of sleep had become too enticing to resist.

Chapter Twelve

I was dying. It was the only logical answer for the amount of pain coursing through my body and the fireworks exploding inside my skull.

I cracked one eye open, and then promptly shut it tight when the sunlight burned my eyes. A pathetic moan escaped as I rolled onto my side, the creaking wood underneath me sounding like gunfire to my ears.

"Rain? Rain, please look at me." Dey's voice barely penetrated the pain.

"No," I grumbled. "Too bright."

"Rain, I need your permission to heal you. I do not want you to feel as if I did anything against your will," he said, stroking the side of my face.

The only word that broke through the thunderous pounding in my head was 'heal,' and I was more than eager to approve that. "Yes, heal please," I choked out.

His hands shifted around to cup the back of my head, and then... bliss. His power flowed through me like a peaceful river, coating everything it touched. I wanted to bathe in his magic and float in that cloud of ecstasy for all time.

Too soon, I could feel it retracting, slithering out of me. I lay there for a second, trying not to cry at the loss of euphoria, until I realized that I no longer wanted to vomit, and the drummers in my brain had gone to find someone else to torture. I opened my eyes to see Dey staring down at me, the sunlight behind him casting a halo around his head.

"Was I dead?" I asked, feeling like I was staring at an angel.

Dey's smile illuminated his entire face as he placed a hand behind my neck and helped me into a sitting position. "No, Princess, you did not die. I simply healed the aches and pains that came with drinking too much Cevisa."

"Aches and pains?" I muttered. "It felt like I'd been put through a cement mixer and injected with acid. What was that stuff anyways?"

His hand rubbed my upper back in soothing circles. "Cevisa is similar to mead in your world, though much more potent since most of us have healing abilities that subdue the more negative effects from consuming copious amounts. For you, however, a few sips would have been more than enough for relaxation purposes. And that is something that you *should* have been told." He tossed a glare over his shoulder, and I noticed Cam and Ram standing behind him, both looking rather sheepish.

"Sorry, Princess," they said in unison, though the slight curve of their mouths told me they weren't really that sorry.

I scooted back on the porch to lean against the cottage wall. "How long was I out?"

"Perhaps an hour or so," Dey answered. "Ram alerted me to your situation when he was unable to wake you." He nodded to the twin on the right who raised a hand.

I analyzed them once again for any possible differences I could use as identifiers and came up blank. "I don't mean to be rude, but is there a way I can tell you apart?"

They looked at each other and laughed. "Beyond the clothes we wear? No, not really," Ram replied.

Dey gave them both a withering look. "I am fairly confident they prefer it that way. They rather enjoy tormenting people."

Ram gave me a sly grin and stepped forward. "For you, Princess? We will make an exception." He gestured over to the fire, and a spark leapt into his hand, growing until a small flame danced merrily between his thumb and first finger. He lifted it to his head, and one of his beautiful locs began sizzling.

"What are you doing?" I asked, horrified at both the visual and the smell.

"Making it easier for you to tell us apart." When the loc was mostly burnt off, he pulled his hand away and snapped his fingers, dismissing the flame. "Perfect. Now you can look for the shorter bit and know that I am Ram and he is Cam."

I gaped at him. "You didn't have to do that for me."

"It is only hair," he said, shrugging. "And the least I could do for the one who is going to save Rivella."

I whipped my head over to Dey. "I thought the whole prophecy thing was a great big secret?"

"It is. Beyond King Verren and a few of his advisors, only myself, Cam, Ram, and Sin know the truth."

Wrinkling my brow, I turned back to the twins. "One of you mentioned Sin earlier. Who's that? It'd be nice to know everyone who speaks English so people won't keep messing with me." I gave them a pointed look.

"Dreisin is the king's Cennux," Dey answered. "I imagine the closest word in your language would be commander. He is in charge of the king's guards and soldiers. Camden and Ramset are two of his generals."

"Gotcha. And when do I meet Dreisin?" I asked.

"Sin will be back tomorrow," Cam said. "I would not be in a hurry to meet him, though. He is a little... prickly. Has been for about the past forty years."

Note to self, avoid the grumpy old commander.

"Thanks for the warning," I told the twins before turning back to Dey. "So, if they're generals, what do you normally do?"

"He mostly charms the ladies," Ram chimed in.

"Please feel free to ignore him," Dey said, leading me a few steps away. "The filter between his brain and tongue rarely works."

Ram shrugged, not even looking affronted at the comment.

"You didn't answer my question, though," I pointed out. "What do you do around here?" I wandered over to the closest tree and picked a piece of the pink fruit. "Is this okay to eat?"

"Of course," he replied, showing me how to peel the thick skin back. "These are kinna fruits. We would not have anything on the castle grounds that could harm you."

I thought about the murder koi in the moat but didn't mention it.

"As for what I do here," Dey continued, "I am the king's Foster. It is tradition that a child from a strong magic line is selected to be raised by the royal family as a precaution in case the king is delayed in producing a male heir. Because Vitaeans are so long lived, kings must abdicate their throne after a time, passing the title on to their son. Or their daughter, so long as she is wedded. If the king has no male child at the end of his reign, the Foster steps in to rule temporarily. The majority of my day is spent observing and learning from your father."

I bit back my comment about garbage sexist policies since I had zero interest in who was on the throne. "So, you're like a back-up kid?" I asked instead. "Does that mean you didn't get to see your family growing up?" I felt a sudden pang of sympathy for Dey. Maybe we had more in common than I thought.

He shook his head. "No. I was brought to the palace at the age of two. My family was well compensated, and all ties were severed."

My mouth dropped open. "Are you saying your parents sold you to the king?"

Growing up, I always thought being abandoned was the worst possible thing, but at least I could tell myself maybe they had a good reason. Parents selling their child was barbaric.

"It is a great honor to be selected," Dey boasted, "and I was gifted a life much better than my parents could have provided for me. Is that not the kindest thing any parent could do for their child? Offer them the best life possible?"

"I guess," I said reluctantly. Though I wasn't sure I agreed. I thought the best thing a parent could do for their kid was to be there for them. Hold them when they got scared and nurse them back to health when they were sick. Basically, just love them.

"Do not feel bad for me. I had a wonderful childhood in the palace," Dey said, taking my hand in his and leading me back toward the castle. "Now come. I have a surprise for you."

I let him pull me away from the cottage and the twins, but not before I shouted over my shoulder, “Thanks for the drink, guys!”

“Anytime, Princess!” they called out in unison.

“And don’t call me princess!”

They chuckled, and I had a feeling it was a useless mission to get people to call me Rain.

Chapter Thirteen

I followed Dey back to the castle, and we passed through four long corridors and three flights of stairs before I recognized my surroundings.

"Are we going back to my room?"

Dey flashed a grin at me over his shoulder. "Do not worry, Rain, my intentions are purely honorable." He pushed open the door, pausing at the threshold. "In case you were wondering, my chamber is the one at the end of the hall on the right. Should you find yourself in need of... anything."

I swallowed. I was definitely not memorizing that factoid and tucking it away safely for later.

Once inside, Dey marched over to the wardrobe in the corner of the room and threw open the double doors. "For you, Princess," he announced, stepping aside to reveal the numerous dresses that threatened to explode out into a pile of colorful lace and fabric.

Each dress was a similar style to those I'd seen on the courtiers earlier, if not a bit more elaborate. I pulled out a green one with a corset top and silver ribbons crossing through at least twenty eyelets. It was sleeveless except for two fabric cuffs with organza attached that would loop around my upper arms in flowing waves. Small diamonds sewn into the sheer material glittered in the light.

I felt Jenn's absence strongly as I ran my hand over the delicate fabric. She would have absolutely loved these. They were exquisite. They were flawless. They were... not me at all.

I put the dress back and shut the doors. "Thanks, but I can't wear these."

Dey stared at the closed wardrobe for a long moment, unblinking. "What do you mean you cannot wear them?" he protested. "Are they not resplendent?"

"Oh, they're gorgeous, no doubt. But it's still a hard pass. I wouldn't feel comfortable wearing any of these dresses."

I thought Dey's eyes might actually pop out of his head. "You must! The palace seamstresses have been working on these ever since you arrived yesterday. They toiled throughout the night to ensure you would have the most beautiful gowns for your first dinner with the court this evening."

I shrugged and picked at a chipped nail. "Well, I'll make it easier for everyone. I'm not interested in some fancy-ass dinner tonight, or any night, so I don't need a dress. I'm sorry they worked so hard, but I didn't ask anyone to do that."

I took in Dey's silent look of sheer disbelief and started pacing restlessly around the room. "Did anyone here think to talk to me first? All of you are so set on me embracing life as a princess, but did it ever occur to you that I don't want to be a princess? I'm not royal or refined or any of that crap, and I don't want to be. Yeah, I hate being poor back home, but at least I'm free to live my life however I choose. You have no idea what it was like for me growing up. I spent my whole life in foster homes where I had to do exactly what I was told or risk getting sent back to the orphanage." I gulped. "Or worse. The constant fear and pressure to be perfect was torture."

My chest constricted at the reminder of my traumatic adolescent years. I couldn't go back to being judged and scrutinized all the time. I just *couldn't*. My knees trembled, but Dey lunged forward, catching me before I could fall altogether.

"It will be all right," he said, running his hands over my back in long soothing motions. "We will find something else for you to wear, and I will tell King Verren you are not able to dine with the court this evening."

"Thank you," I said, though it came out muffled since my face was firmly pressed against his chest.

Eventually, I pulled away and sat on the bed.

"I will see if I can find you some breeches and a tunic," he said, moving toward the door. "I will return shortly."

I waited until I heard the door click shut, then pulled the chair from the hearth over to the window so I could watch the people moving about the courtyard below. The suns were low enough that the diamonds were no longer a concern, and everyone down there just seemed… happy.

Was it wrong to not even consider a possible life here? Maybe. The truth was no matter what anyone said, I didn't feel like a princess or a Vitaean. I felt human. And that part of me would never belong in this world.

The first sun had fully set by the time Dey returned with a stack of sleeveless shirts and tight pants. He offered to escort me to dinner in the king's personal dining room so I could avoid the courtiers, but I declined, telling him I needed some time alone. He left, but not before I saw the disappointed look on his face.

I spent the rest of the evening at the window, lost in thought as the day bled fully into night.

Before heading to bed, I decided I should at least say goodnight to Dey and maybe apologize for my meltdown. He was just doing what my father asked, yet he kept taking the brunt of my anger.

I padded down the uncomfortably silent hallway, my bare feet cool against the stone floor. As I passed the room next to mine, a flicker of candlelight caught my attention, drawing me toward the open door. Looking for any excuse to stave off my awkward apology a bit longer, I peeked inside.

A young lady slept on a spacious bed in the middle of the room, candles spread throughout tossing a warm glow onto her porcelain face. I turned to leave before I woke her up, but my hand hesitated on the door knob. There was something about her, something off, so I took a step further into the room.

She lay flat on her back, arms against her sides, a look of youthful innocence on her sleeping face. I guessed her to be no older than sixteen. She didn't shift or make any indication that she even knew I was there. Edging closer, I feared at any moment she would wake up and start screeching at me in Rivellan to get the hell out of her room.

She didn't stir, so I moved right up to the side of the bed. Her hair was long and dark, like mine, yet her lips and face were pale. Too pale. Everyone here had at least a hint of the sun's kiss to their skin.

I leaned over and could see that she was breathing at least, though the blanket tucked into her sides barely rippled. That strange feeling kept pulling me to her, and there was something so familiar about her face. I reached my hand out hesitantly, just to touch her cheek, to confirm for myself that her skin was warm and she was alive.

As my fingers were about to make contact, her eyes flew open, and her hand shot out to grab mine. Gasping, I tried to pull back, but her grip was painfully firm, holding me in place. Her eyes, wild and unseeing, were identical to my own, and a word came unbidden to my lips—sister.

This had to be Verren's daughter. He told me his children died, but there was no denying my resemblance to the girl on the bed.

She held me in her grasp, unmoving beyond the one hand clutching my arm tightly. Her eyes connected with mine, and her lips parted.

"Selvarea."

Then her eyes closed, and her hand released mine to drift back to her side.

Before I could register what happened, the door to the bathroom opened, and a servant stepped into the room. Her eyes took in the scene, saw me leaning over the king's daughter, and then she gave me a horrified look.

I threw my hands up, backing away hurriedly. "I swear I wasn't trying to hurt her."

I couldn't tell if the servant was angry or scared, but I didn't wait to find out. I tore out of the room as fast as my legs would take me.

Spinning to the left, I took off back down the hall, but I barely made it two steps before crashing into a hard body.

Strong hands gripped my shoulders and slammed me roughly into the stone wall. Pain from the impact shot down my spine, ripping an anguished cry from my lungs.

I struggled against my attacker, but he didn't budge, his arms locking me in place. A glowering face appeared in my vision, and the scent of salt and something darker surrounded me. Pale green eyes practically glowed in the dim lighting, but any beauty was overshadowed by the anger raging in them.

The male barked at me in Rivellan, pushing me harder against the stone.

"Stop!" I cried out. "You're hurting me."

His hands held firm, and he snarled something that sounded like a question.

"I don't know what the fuck you're saying!" I shot back, pissed that this asshole assumed it was okay to push me around. I thought people in this castle were supposed to kiss my ass or something, but this guy clearly didn't get the memo. He wasn't dressed like a servant, but he also wasn't dressed like the courtiers. He wore tight black leather breeches and a long sleeve purple tunic. It was the first time I'd seen someone who wasn't blatantly displaying their tattoos.

He shoved me once more, then dropped his hands, taking a step back but maintaining the scowl on his face. Now that I wasn't being manhandled, I could actually make out his features. Appearing slightly older than me, maybe late twenties or early thirties, his face was all hard lines and dark edges. He had a strong chin, sharp cheekbones, and a slightly crooked nose that had likely been broken and not set correctly—an oddity in this world of perfect beings. The only soft thing about him was his wavy, espresso-colored hair tied loosely at the nape of his neck, the length kissing the back of his shoulder blades. He looked like an angel of death, beautiful and terrifying all at once.

His eyes were still fixed on mine, anger blazing in them, and his hands clenched at his sides like he was forcing restraint upon himself. I had no idea what I had done to enrage him so thoroughly, and that only fueled my own anger more.

Closing the gap between us, I shoved him backward. He obviously wasn't expecting a return assault because he actually stumbled, shock flashing across his face.

At least a head taller than me, his body was all tight, lean muscle, and it occurred to me in a brief moment of clarity that I rarely had to look up at a guy. At five-foot-ten, I usually met them eye to eye, and if I was wearing my chunky boots, it was basically a guarantee. This guy, though, had to be at least six-foot-four. Taller even than Dey.

His anger rekindled, and he was up in my face, yelling at me in Rivellan.

"What is your problem, asshole?" I shot back, a darkness inside me rising to meet his wrath head on. It was hard to intimidate someone you had to look up at, but I was doing my damned best. I would not roll over for this jerk.

He glared at me, our bodies so close I could feel the pressure of his chest on mine as I breathed in and out. The silent confrontation lasted longer than it should have, but we were both seemed trapped inside our own fury.

Finally, I took a small step back, needing a break from the heat coming off his body and the swirl of his intoxicating scent surrounding me. It was such a familiar smell, but I couldn't place it.

The side of his mouth curled into a smirk. Clearly he thought he won our little standoff.

"Don't you know who I am?" I demanded. I felt a little dirty saying those words, but for the first time since I was brought here, I actually wanted to claim my title. If only to force him to his knees. "Princepa," I hissed, recalling the one Rivellan word I knew.

I expected his eyes to grow wide. I expected him to drop to his knees and begin groveling. I expected he might even shed a tear while he begged my forgiveness.

What I did not expect was the loud bark of laughter that echoed through the hall as he invaded my space once more, shaking his head. No begging, no groveling, not even a head tilt in deference. Instead, he spoke softly in Rivellan, paused, then leaned in close to my ear and growled, "Fea Remia." Those two gravelly words punctuated the silence and settled into my brain.

He stalked off down the hall, leaving me with my chest heaving, pulse racing, and fire coursing through my veins.

I took in a deep breath, trying to calm myself and caught a hint of that lingering scent of his. It hit me then, what it reminded me of, and I remained in the hallway until it dissipated, wishing I could bottle it.

He smelled like the ocean during a thunderstorm.

Chapter Fourteen

A loud knock on the door pulled me from sleep the next morning. Groaning, I yanked the pillow over my head, hoping whoever it was would go away. I'd spent most of the night tossing and turning, my brain unable to power down after everything I'd experienced.

The knocking continued, and I sat up so I could shout at whoever it was to fuck off. Before the words came out, the door swung open, and the blonde sisters entered.

I buried my head under my pillow again. "Hey guys, can I get a few more hours of sleep?" I knew they couldn't understand me even if my voice wasn't half muffled, but I was hoping the tone would convey my desires.

It didn't.

They went bustling about the room, opening curtains, turning the shower on, and stoking the fire in the hearth.

I groaned louder. What was the point in being a princess if I didn't have the power to decide when I woke up?

One of the sisters tugged the blankets off me, and I surrendered. They clearly had marching orders to get my ass up, so I slid off the bed and dragged myself into the bathroom.

After luxuriating in another perfectly hot shower, I wrapped a fluffy towel around me and went in search of the new clothing that was dropped off last night.

The towel almost slipped from my grip when I stepped back into the room and saw Dey lounging on my bed, casually leaning against the headboard as if he belonged there.

"Good morning, Princess," he said, smiling brightly and looking like he just stepped off the cover of a magazine. "I am pleased to see you are finally awake."

I despised morning people.

Stalking over to the pile of clothing, I grabbed a pair of navy blue breeches and matching short-sleeved tunic. I started toward the bathroom, pausing when I noticed Dey's expression had gone from chipper to slightly wary.

"What?" I barked.

"Are you well?" he asked, his brow furrowing slightly.

"Fucking dandy," I muttered, cursing the lack of coffee in this stupid world, then trudged back into the bathroom. I never did apologize to him for my earlier behavior, but I doubted my foul, sleep-deprived mood was the best for attempting a 'sorry I'm such a bitch sometimes' conversation.

I spent over five minutes fighting with the weird lace-up bra contraption before I finally got it secured, then pulled on the pants and tunic. As ready to face the day as I was going to get, I left the bathroom, casting up a silent prayer that caffeine of some kind existed in this place.

We entered the dining room, and my father was sitting in his usual place at the head of the table, once again shirtless, though his loose pants were burgundy today.

"Good morning, Raynella," he said cordially. "You were missed at dinner last night."

"Yeah, sorry," I said, sliding into my chair. "I wasn't really up to a big fancy meal. In fact, I meant to tell you that I was kind of hoping to keep things a little low key during my time here."

He waved a hand to the servants who promptly disappeared, then turned back to me. "Raynella, you are the princess. The entire court is most excited to meet you."

"I get that," I said, avoiding his disappointed expression by tracing one of the swirly designs carved into the table. "But I'm not going to be here for long, and I'm not super comfortable with big groups of people, especially ones that are all staring at me

"You are still planning to leave, then?" he asked with a heavy sigh. "What about your kingdom, Raynella? Rivella is your home, and your people need you."

I kept my mouth shut since I had no desire to get into the same argument again. When a servant set a plate of food in front of me, I tore into it, grateful for an excuse not to talk.

The three of us ate in silence, until Dey commented, "I heard you had a bit of an incident before bed, Princess."

I thought back to the attack in the hallway, and the guy who reminded me of dark nights on a turbulent sea. "Oh yeah, I had a run in with a supreme asshole."

Dey's fork halted halfway to his mouth. "What are you talking about? Did something else happen last night?"

I glanced between him and my father, both staring intently at me. "Uh, yeah? I sort of ran into this guy in the hallway. He pushed me around a bit. Isn't that what you meant by incident?"

"No, Princess," Dey said, "I was referring to your encounter with Jeylana. One of the servants mentioned you were in her room."

"What?!" my father bellowed, and I cringed at his oddly explosive anger.

Dey was out of his chair in seconds, kneeling before his king. "Apologies, Your Highness, I thought surely you had been informed as well. I can not imagine that a servant would tell me before discussing it with you first."

Clenching his teeth, my father waved a hand sharply at Dey. "Leave us. I wish to speak with my daughter alone. Go find Cennux Dreisin. He was supposed to join us for breakfast."

Dey stood and briskly exited the dining room.

"You didn't have to treat him like that. It wasn't his fault," I pointed out.

My father's features softened, and he slipped back into the kind male I met yesterday. "You are right, Raynella. I should not have been so curt. I was... unavailable this past evening, so it displeased me to hear about your encounter with Jeylana. I had hoped to be with you when you met her."

I took a sip of the pink kinna juice and eyed my father, wondering if his Jekyll and Hyde routine was normal. "Sorry. I shouldn't have been snooping, but her door was open, and I was curious." I hesitated, trying to think of the best way to phrase the question I was itching to ask. "Is she, um... Is she your daughter also? Because I thought your kids all died."

Well that didn't come out quite as smoothly as I'd hoped.

A look of pain washed over my father's face as he lowered his fork. "Raynella," he began slowly, "when I told you that my children succumbed to the plague, I was being honest. I had hoped to spare you the unpleasant details, but the disease is not a physical one. It is a plague of madness, driving those infected to take their own life or..." He paused, and I couldn't bear the sadness in his eyes. "Or we are forced to take it for them."

"You kill them?" I asked, horror contorting my face. "Couldn't you tie them down or something?"

"We tried," he insisted, meeting my gaze so I could see the painful truth in his eyes. "We attempted to restrain them, but none of our efforts to force them into sleep worked. It was as if the madness had taken control of their entire body, forcing them to seek out death as the only escape from their torment." His head drooped. "You did not have to see their agony, Raynella. You may think it was monstrous to end the lives of my people, of my family, but it was far kinder than allowing them to suffer eternally."

"What about Jeylana?" I asked. "She doesn't seem trapped in madness. I mean, not much anyway. She did say something to me, but then she went back to sleep."

My father's head shot up, his eyes widening. "She spoke to you? What did she say?"

I bit my lip, trying to recall the Rivellan word. "Um, she said 'selvarea,' I think. What does that mean?"

His eyes flickered off to the side, and then he placed a hand over mine, sadness on his face once again. "It means 'save me.' I am so sorry you had to experience that, Raynella. Jeylana has not spoken since she was afflicted, has not even stirred until now. Her magic had not yet manifested when the madness took hold, and that was the only reason the healers were able to suspend her mind. They have been unsuccessful with any who have already formed their link with the Source."

"So why did she speak to me?"

"Perhaps because you are the only one who can save her."

There it was again—the prophecy. For some reason, it didn't hit me like it did before. I rubbed my hand over my face, fighting back the rising bile in my stomach. If it were Jenn lying in that bed, I would do whatever was necessary. I'd crawl through burning coals and crushed glass to save her.

I didn't know Jeylana, though. I didn't grow up with her, didn't spend nights holding her while she shivered from cold and hunger in a drafty orphanage.

And yet, she was undoubtedly my sister as well. I couldn't bring myself to just abandon her.

"Okay," I said, straightening with a confidence I didn't actually feel. "I'll give it a shot. That whole thing with the ley lines. I can't stay forever, but since I'm stuck here for a bit, I guess I can try at least. What do I need to do?"

I braced myself for my father's joyous reaction to my acceptance, but he merely gave me a small smile and dipped his head in a nod. Not that I expected a parade in my honor, but given his vehemence in convincing me, I thought a little more excitement was due.

"This is perfect," he said sedately, picking up his utensils as if nothing much had happened. "Cennux Dreisin should be here shortly, and we can discuss preparing you for the challenges ahead. Foremost, we will need your abilities to manifest."

"Cool," I said, digging back into my food. I might be absolutely terrified about this whole situation, but there was no denying that I was excited to experience real magic.

"Now that has been settled," he said, stabbing a piece of fruit, "tell me more about this individual who accosted you in the hallway. I cannot imagine any reason someone would want to harm you."

"I don't know who he was," I said around a mouthful of bacon. "He grabbed me when I left Jeylana's room and shoved me against the wall. He shouted at me a bunch in Rivellan, then left."

My father swallowed his bite and frowned. "That is very concerning. Everyone in the castle has been alerted to your presence and should treat you like the princess that you are. What did he look like?"

"He looked like..." I trailed off when the door opened and Dey entered the room with a male in head to toe black leather following close on his heels. I sucked in a sharp breath. There was no forgetting that face. Those hard lines and dark edges that were made even more prominent by the light of day.

"Him," I said, pointing to the newcomer, my face blanching. "It was him."

My father glanced between me and the scowling male beside Dey. "Are you certain?"

"Yes, completely," I said, without tearing myself away from the intense gaze of the one who had attacked me. "Who is he?"

Dey stepped forward and slung his arm around the other male's shoulder. "Princess, I am pleased to introduce Cennux Dreisin. Although most of us just call him Sin."

A vicious smirk rolled across Sin's face, and he gave a small bow without lowering his head, those mint-colored eyes never leaving mine for a second.

So much for the grumpy old commander.

Chapter Fifteen

My father was out of his seat and striding toward Sin before I could even blink.

"Explain yourself, Cennux Dreisin. My daughter tells me you attacked her last night?"

Sin cast a dark look my way, then straightened, facing the king head on. He responded to him in Rivellan, and I was dying to know what possible explanation he could have.

While the two of them engaged in a heated argument, I leaned back in my chair and suppressed a wicked grin that Sin was likely going to get punished because of me. Taking a sip of the sweet juice, I waited for the king to lay the smack down.

A loud bark of laughter had me whipping my head up in time to see my father pat Sin on the back, both of them now sporting relaxed smiles.

What. The. Fuck?!

I'd thought Sin might drop to his knees and beg forgiveness while my father called for someone to chop off his traitorous head because he dared to touch the princess but nope. They looked like old drinking buddies.

Dey took his place across from me, and Sin claimed the seat beside him.

"Would someone care to loop me in on what the hell is going on?" I demanded.

My father patted my hand in a condescending gesture that did nothing to quell my annoyance. "All is well, Raynella. Cennux Dreisin was explaining how last night was all merely a misunderstanding."

I glanced over to Sin, who just shrugged.

What kind of game was he playing?

"It was dark in the hallway," my father explained, "and all he saw was a stranger fleeing the room of my comatose daughter. He reacted on instinct. While I do not appreciate him laying hands on you, I cannot fault him for his trained reaction to a potential threat."

Sin took a long sip of the kinna juice and held my gaze over the rim.

Okay, I'll play your little game.

"Of course, that all makes so much sense." I gave Sin a syrupy sweet fake grin. "I can't blame him for making a mistake, now can I?"

"Excellent," my father said, settling back in his chair. "Now we can move on to more important matters. Raynella has agreed to work with us in restoring the ley lines."

Two sets of eyes flashed toward me. Dey looked pleased. Sin looked... pissed.

"I knew the princess would never abandon her people," Dey said, pride gleaming in his eyes.

Sin mumbled something under his breath, and Dey elbowed him in the ribs.

"Of course she would not," my father chimed in, ignoring whatever passed between the guys. "We must now move forward with our established plan to prepare Raynella for her journey through the dark forest."

"Plan?" I nearly choked on my juice. "I just agreed, like, five minutes ago. How do you have a plan already?"

"Raynella, we have been preparing for this for many years now. We were simply waiting for you to arrive."

Right. Because everyone was so convinced that I would jump at the chance to travel through a damn forest of monsters to restore some ancient magic while having no pertinent skills or knowledge to accomplish said task. Who wouldn't sign on for that?

Resigned, I said, "Ok, let's hear the plan."

He smiled brightly. "As I mentioned before, the most important thing is that we awaken your magic. Deylan will work with you on this front. There are a few things that have been known to accelerate the process."

I shot an inquisitive look over to Dey who winked in response.

"Generals Camden and Ramset will handle your education," my father continued. "It is imperative that you learn as much as possible about Rivella and the creatures you may encounter in the forest, as well as what it means to be a Vitaean. I believe you will find the generals to be excellent tutors."

I took another drink to hide the laugh that threatened to escape. The two drunken jokers I met yesterday were going to be my teachers? At least it wouldn't be boring.

"And Cennux Dreisin will handle you physically."

"What?!" I shouted, spewing liquid all over the table. My head shot toward Sin.

He glared but said nothing as he picked up a napkin and overemphasized wiping my spit from his face.

I whirled on my father. "Sin is going to do what to me?"

"He is going to handle your physical training," he replied as if that explained everything. He snapped his fingers, and two servants rushed over to the table. One cleaned the mess while the other poured me another glass of juice.

"My physical training? Do you mean working out and stuff, because I'm not sure I've ever seen the inside of a gym. I thought this was just about magic."

"Vitaeans cannot hold their magic once they are separated from the Source," my father said in a placating tone. "Your abilities will return as you move closer to the Onyx Palace. On the outer edges of the dark forest, however, you will find yourself to be little more than human. My soldiers will accompany you of course and protect you with their lives, but we cannot know what you will encounter. So you will be trained in combat as best we can in the short time we have. Cennux Dreisin is a very skilled warrior. You will learn much from working with him."

I didn't know what was more ludicrous. The fact that I signed up for a potentially lethal stroll through the woods or the fact that my underfed, scrawny body was somehow supposed to become a honed weapon.

"I'm sorry, but let's be realistic. This is moving past ridiculous into pure insanity. How much can I possibly learn in a few weeks?"

Sin snorted, muttering something again in Rivellan, and it pushed me over the edge.

Shoving back from my chair, I leaned over the table and snarled, "And you! How the hell can you help me with anything when you won't even speak fucking English?"

Sin shot to his feet, slammed his hands down, and shouted back in Rivellan.

"Cennux Dreisin, take your seat," my father commanded. "I understand your frustration, but you will address the princess in a manner befitting her station."

Sin gave me a nasty look, then slid back into his chair.

I turned to my father and jabbed a finger toward Sin. "What's his problem?"

"Cennux Dreisin is understandably concerned about your training interfering with his other duties," my father replied. "Duties that are ultimately less important than preparing you." He gave a pointed look at Sin, who was suddenly very focused on his plate of food.

"And will Cennux Dreisin be speaking to me in English anytime soon?"

Sin looked up at me, his scowl morphing into a smug grin. "Whatever the princess desires."

At the head of the table, my father gave a sharp nod as if that resolved everything. "Please sit, Raynella. Finish your meal." He gestured at the nearly full plate of food in front of me.

"I'm not hungry," I grumbled, hating that I sounded like a petulant child. It was also a lie since I was still ravenous, but I wasn't about to sit down and make nice with the asshole across the table.

"In that case, perhaps Cennux Dreisin is ready to begin your training. Deylan and I are needed in Civi Adasa today." At my look of confusion, he clarified, "The city beyond the gates. The King's Council will be held in six days, and we must prepare for our guests. It is unfortunate that the timing coincided with your arrival, but there is nothing to be done about it."

I was too tired to even care what the King's Council was. It sounded political and boring, and I was sure someone would tell me about it eventually. That's how I got all my knowledge here—eventually.

Noting Sin's mostly full plate of food and feeling more than a little spiteful, I said, "That sounds like a stellar idea. Right now would be perfect."

The scowl never left Sin's face, but he pushed back from the table and grunted, "Whatever the princess desires."

I was beginning to wonder if that was all he knew how to say.

Dey came around to meet me and clasped my hands in his. "I wish I could stay with you today, but Sin will take good care of you, I promise. He might seem a little rough, but he is very skilled and will train you well."

I looked down at my small hands cradled tightly within his larger ones and felt a little tug at my heart. Dey genuinely did care about me, it wasn't just sexual attraction, and a small part of me wished I felt the same. "I'll be fine. I can handle grumpy pants over there."

Sin muttered something in Rivellan, but I ignored him. "Do what you gotta do," I told Dey. "I'll see you when you get back. Maybe sometime you could actually take me into the city with you. It would be nice to get out of the castle."

He smiled. "It would be my pleasure, Princess. The city can be a very dangerous place at times, but so long as I am your escort, you will be safe."

I gave him a matching smile, then strode briskly from the dining room. "Will you be coming, Cennux Dreisin?" I called over my shoulder as I pushed through the wooden doors.

"Whatever the princess desires," he said in a low voice, and I flinched, not realizing he was right behind me.

My pace didn't falter as I passed into the hallway. Whatever I desired, huh? We'd see about that.

The moment we turned the corner and I knew we were out of earshot, I whirled around and shoved Sin into the wall before he could brace himself. "Okay, you want to tell me what the hell your fucking problem is? You absolutely knew who I was last night, so what kind of shit are you trying to pull here?"

Grinding his teeth together, he pushed off against the wall, forcing me to step back. "You're my problem, Rain," he growled, keeping his voice low. "You being here is a great big problem."

I scoffed. "Glad to see we've moved on from 'whatever the princess desires.' I knew your English was just fine." I jabbed him in the chest. "And how the hell is my being here such a problem? Everybody else seems pretty damned thrilled about it."

"Oh yeah?" he mused, moving forward leisurely like a panther stalking his prey, forcing me backward until I hit the opposite wall. He slammed a hand down near my face, but I didn't flinch this time. I wouldn't give him the satisfaction of seeing my fear.

"Well I'm not everybody else," he continued, leaning in closer until there was barely any space between us. "I want you gone. You don't belong here."

I tilted my chin up defiantly and said, with as much venom as I could summon, "I don't want me to be here either, but since I'm stuck, I thought I might do some good in the meantime. Haven't you heard? I'm the fucking savior."

He let out a low chuckle, and his breath was hot on my face. I inhaled sharply at the intensity in his gaze, immediately regretting it. The scent of him overwhelmed me, and I wanted nothing more than to close my eyes so I could picture myself alone on a pier at night, waves crashing angrily against the rocks as they fed on the might of a rising storm. If I couldn't see him, then I could imagine literally anybody else in front of me, their hard body pressed so close to mine without actually touching.

I wouldn't give in, though. I kept my eyes open, unblinking. He would not break me.

"I know exactly who you are, Rain," he hissed, and I hated the way he said my name with a sharp bite at the end. "The important question is... do you?"

The hand near my face curled into a tight fist, and I could feel it shaking, as if it cost him a tremendous effort not to strike me. "What the hell did I ever do to you?" I demanded, wondering how someone I just met could despise me so much.

A muscle in his jaw ticked, and the tension lines on his face deepened. There was a war going on inside him, and I had no idea what I had done to cause it. He closed his eyes and took in a deep breath. A painful grimace crossed his face, like my scent was the most repulsive thing imaginable.

Just as I opened my mouth to say something, he pushed himself away from the wall and stomped off down the hallway. "Let's go," he barked over his shoulder. "Your training awaits, Fea Remia."

I waited for my heart rate to ease before sprinting after him.

God, this was going to be a disaster. There was no way we could get through weeks of training. One of us would definitely kill the other one first.

I followed Sin through the castle and out into the front courtyard. Each guard we passed snapped to attention in his presence, and I wondered if they were all as terrified of him as I was.

Once outside the castle, he veered left toward the arena, and my stride faltered when we stepped through the arched entryway. I had seen from above that the space was big, but being inside was a whole different perspective. There had to be over a hundred circular rows of pale stone seats bisected by a massive set of stairs that descended into a pit the size of a football field.

"Move it!" Sin shouted from halfway down the steps, glaring up at me.

"Yeah, yeah, I'm coming," I muttered, rushing after him. Each stone step was polished from probably centuries of use, and I nearly ended up on my ass a handful of times since my Chucks weren't exactly slip resistant.

I made it to the bottom in one piece and looked around, taking in the sand covered arena with boulders larger than dumpsters scattered throughout. A handful of scorch marks along the walls had me curious as to exactly what kind of battles happened in this place.

"Over here," Sin called from off to my left.

Set a few steps lower than the level of the pit, a covered walkway ran along the entirety of the outer rim with entrances every ten yards or so and several doorways leading back into what I guessed were training rooms. Or maybe preparation rooms for whatever kind of fighting they did here. This place was giving off some serious Gladiator vibes.

I followed the sound of Sin's voice through the open hall until I came to a door on my right. Racks upon racks of swords, maces, flails, and other strange weapons I didn't recognize filled the room.

Putting my hands on my hips, I stared expectantly at Sin. "Now what?"

"Now you learn how to fight." He gestured to the arsenal around me, indicating I should pick one.

Shaking my head, I surveyed the terrifying assortment of medieval-looking weaponry. Surely he didn't mean for me to take up sword fighting on day one...

When I didn't move, he selected an impressively ornate broadsword that was mounted above a rack of more basic silver blades. He swung it around in his hands a few times, and I hated to admit how good he looked doing it. Something about a guy expertly wielding a sword was undeniably hot.

He handed me the weapon. "Here. I'll even let you use my personal sword. It's perfectly balanced. Excellent for a novice."

When my hand took hold of the hilt, my arm sank under its immense weight, and the tip of the sword slammed a few inches into the hard-packed dirt.

Well, shit. These things were heavier than they looked.

I glared at Sin who didn't even bother to hide the satisfied smirk on his face.

"What am I supposed to do with this?" I heaved the sword up, using all my strength just to lift it, yet my arms gave out within seconds. No way would I be able to swing it with any kind of accuracy. It had to be at least twenty-five pounds, too much for my scrawny arms to control, and the asshole had to know that.

"It's too heavy," I huffed out.

Stalking over to me, he snapped, "Then come find me when it isn't."

In one fluid motion, he grabbed the sword from my hand and spun it with a little flourish to effortlessly sheath it behind his back.

Without a word, he strode off, leaving me surrounded by weapons I couldn't even use and wondering why the hell I ever agreed to any of this to begin with.

Chapter Sixteen

I probably stood in the weapons room looking dumbfounded for a solid minute before I charged after Sin.

"Hey, jackass!" I yelled to his retreating back when I popped out from under the covered walkway. "Are you freaking kidding me right now? What kind of bullshit was that?"

Sin whipped around and stormed over to where I stood at the edge of the pit. "It was every kind of bullshit, Fea Remia. It's like you said earlier, a handful of weeks is not enough time to learn anything. It's fucking pointless for me to waste my time on you when I have more important things to do than babysit a child."

"Excuse you? I'm twenty-five years old. I'm not a damn child, so stop treating me like one."

He folded his arms and gave me an amused look. "Your handful of years mean nothing here. I'm seventy-seven, and do you know what I've done for most of those seventy-seven years? I've trained. It took me decades to master the art of combat, and I can assure you, three weeks will do nothing but give you enough confidence to get yourself killed."

Seventy-seven? Damn, he looked good. I kept forgetting how people didn't really age here. He wasn't wrong about my lack of combat ability, though I refused to give in and let him call the shots. I grabbed his hand before he could walk away again.

He stilled and pivoted slowly back to me, his entire body stiff.

"You might be right, but I'm pretty sure my father gave an order," I countered. "So how about you get off your high horse and show me something useful. Anything useful. Even if it's just enough to defend myself for five minutes until one of you big strong males can swoop in and save me."

That last part was dripping with a level of sarcasm he didn't seem to appreciate given the deep furrow lines carved across his forehead.

He snatched his hand away from mine, then growled at me again in Rivellan.

I ran a hand across my face in frustration. "English! Fucking English! Is that so damned hard? Hell, you speak it even better than the others around here. Which I meant to ask you about. Why are they all stiff and formal and you aren't?"

Something dangerous flashed in Sin's eyes. "You want to know why my English is better than theirs? Because I spent years looking for you in the human realm. Cam and Ram went a handful of times, and Dey had gone exactly once when he found you. Before that it was me. For over twenty years, I was the sole person looking for you. So yeah, I picked up a bit more of your colorful language than they did. They only know the proper shit Corym studied before passing it along."

He searched for me for twenty years? Was he actually just jealous that Dey found me first?

I really examined him then—his tense body, the fists clenched at his side, his teeth grinding together, his breath that came out in short bursts. He was seconds away from snapping, and I didn't think I wanted to see what would happen when he did.

"Is that why you hate me?" I asked. "Because you failed to find me where Dey succeeded?" It was the only thing that sounded reasonable, even if I thought his reaction was a bit over the top. Trying to find one human amongst billions must have been like looking for a needle in a haystack.

"Maybe," he replied, his voice low. "Maybe I do hate you for my wasted time. Maybe I hate you for being useless to me and my realm in your current condition. Maybe I hate you because you simply don't belong here. And maybe I hate you because the fate of our world shouldn't rest in the hands of a ridiculous child who doesn't even speak our language. Take your pick." Then he whipped around and stomped up the stairs.

"Will you at least tell me what Fea Remia means?" I shouted after him.

"Learn Rivellan if you want to know so bad. You're not in Kansas anymore, Dorothy," he called back without even pausing, his long legs taking the stairs two at a time to leave me in the dust.

When I finally reached the top of the arena, I spent an embarrassing amount of time trying to catch my breath before deciding to go in search of the twins. Maybe they would be more willing to help.

I found Cam and Ram back at their cottage, dressed in the burgundy sleeveless tunics of the royal guard. Theirs were a bit nicer, though, with gold stitching along the edges. I walked up to them just as Ram unsheathed a sword from his back and dropped it onto the porch. Cam followed suit with the belt of daggers around his waist.

"Hey guys," I said pleasantly, having shaken off my earlier irritation. "Is this a bad time? Looks like you're getting off shift or something."

"Not at all, Princess," Ram replied. I still felt bad about his burned off loc, but it did make my life easier knowing who I was speaking to. "We were actually preparing to train some new soldiers when Sin came by and told us to find you instead."

"Seriously?" I couldn't imagine Sin doing anything remotely helpful for me. He'd made it clear he thought I shouldn't even be here, let alone take part in studying or training.

"He came by a few moments ago," Cam chimed in. "He said something along the lines of 'she is your problem now.' Then he left to go prepare for the upcoming King's Council."

Now that sounded more like Sin. "Fucking asshat," I grumbled. "He handed me a sword that I could barely lift, then said I was basically useless to him and left."

The twins exchanged a curious look.

"You honestly could not wield a sword at all?" Cam asked.

"You don't need to take his side," I groaned. "I get it, I'm weak. But come on, that thing weighed like twenty-five pounds, and sorry, but I don't have your muscles."

They both stared at me for a second, then fell against each other laughing, their loud guffaws echoing through the trees.

I glowered at them, feeling like I was once again the butt of some unknown joke. "I don't think it's that funny."

"Apologies, Princess. We were not laughing at you," Ram insisted once he calmed down. "We were laughing because Sin gave you his personal sword, correct?" At my nod, he grinned knowingly. "His sword is made from a very special, *very heavy*, metal. He only handed it to you because he knew it would be too much for you to use. Any other sword would have weighed no more than five pounds." He plucked out a longsword from his pile of weapons and handed it to me.

I took it tentatively, and my jaw dropped when I felt how much lighter it was. "That son of a bitch!" I bellowed, my vision turning red with anger. "He did that on purpose so he wouldn't have to train me."

Gripping the weapon tightly, I worked to fight off the urge to go find Sin so I could give him a piece of my mind. Or the pointy end of a sword. How dare he stand there and call me useless when he set me up to fail?

It took a few deep breaths before I controlled my fury enough to formulate a plan. Maybe it was petty, but I couldn't ignore his insult. "Any chance you guys would be willing to help me get even?" I asked the twins.

Wariness settled over Cam, but Ram looked intrigued. "What did you have in mind?" he asked.

"I need you to steal Sin's sword and hide it in my room. If he asks you about it, you have no idea where it could be. Got it?"

Cam shot his brother a concerned look, then turned back to me. "You are not going to damage it are you? Sin has had it for a very long time."

I shook my head. "I'm not going to hurt his precious toy. I doubt I even could. I just want him to feel as helpless as I did for a little bit. So are you in? I promise I'll never mention your names."

They shared another long look, and then Ram grinned at me. "I think Sin could use some humbling. It would be our pleasure, Princess."

"Sweet," I chirped, excited to see the look on Sin's face when his special sword disappeared. "So what now? My father said you guys were going to tutor me?"

Ram reclined against the porch railing. "Something like that," he replied coyly.

"We were told to educate you about Rivella and perhaps some of the monsters you might encounter in the dark forest," Cam clarified, removing a dagger that had been tucked in his boot. "I can tell you right now that little is known about those creatures. Most who venture too far in never return. Those that do, well, their accounts are unreliable to say the least."

"So that just leaves educating you about Rivella," Ram said with a mischievous grin, and I had a feeling he wasn't referring to textbook teaching.

"Okay." My lips curved up into a smile. "I'll bite. How are you going to teach me about Rivella?"

"The only way we know how," Cam said.

"By experiencing it," Ram finished.

Cautious optimism bloomed in my chest. "Wait... Does that mean we're leaving the castle?"

"Of course. What did you think we were going to do?" Ram asked.

"Honestly, I kind of expected something like a lecture." I pictured the twins dressed in tweed jackets with bifocals propped on their noses and had to stifle a chuckle.

"Would you like a lecture?" Cam proposed, looking somewhat intrigued by the idea. "That can be arranged."

"No!" I shouted before they could change their minds. "Please no. I've been dying to go into the city."

When they didn't immediately move, I frowned. "What's wrong?"

"You have no ramentum," Ram said, gesturing at the intricate whorls of ink across his arms. "Given your age, your bare arms would suggest to anyone we passed that you were likely not Vitaean."

"And if you are not Vitaean," Cam added, "that means you are an abicario. A non-magic user. A shunned one."

"A human?" I guessed. "So only Vitaeans are allowed to get tattoos?"

"It is not like that," Cam said. "The ramentum appear on our skin when we first manifest our magic, indicating the level of our abilities. Amplissarios, like King Verren, hold three types of magic, and they have markings that cover their arms, shoulders, and chest or back."

Well that explained why my father never wore a shirt. Apparently a crown wasn't enough to confirm his power.

"Secunnarios, like Ram and myself, hold two types of magic," Cam continued. "The further the ramentum spread, the more powerful the magic." He puffed up his chest and beamed at me. "That is why Ram's do not go as high as mine."

Ram chuckled. "Of course, brother, your extra three inches there make up for your missing three inches elsewhere..." He glanced down at Cam's breeches, then winked at me.

A hint of red crawled over Cam's cheeks, and he glared at his twin. "That joke is never funny, Ramset."

"Yes it is," Ram replied, nudging my shoulder.

Trying not to laugh, I asked, "And what about people with one kind of magic?"

"Immies," he answered, snorting with derision.

"Imminarios," Cam clarified, "generally only have ramentum up to their elbow or possibly just above depending on the strength of their one ability."

"I see," I said, glancing at my bare arms. "So when people see I have none..."

"They will think you are a human," Ram finished.

"And that's a problem because...?"

"Humans are not allowed in Civi Adasa," Cam explained. "You might find some hiding in Civi Obsura, the village at the bottom of the hill, but even those humans risk being imprisoned. Or worse."

"Well that's some antiquated separatist nonsense. My father seriously allows this?"

If he cared about my mother, how could he let her people be treated so poorly?

Cam placed an arm around my shoulders. "Please do not think ill of your father, Princess. He is simply upholding the traditions of our people that were established a millennia ago. Not to mention things between humans and Vitaeans became even more strained after the plague hit. It is for the human's benefit that they are banned, trust me."

I tried to let his words assuage some of my anger, but my ire dimmed only slightly. I would definitely be having a conversation with Daddy Dearest when I saw him next. I had some serious reservations about saving a world that shunned my kind.

"All right," I conceded, determined to actually make it out to the city. "So I just need a jacket or something, then? Or a long-sleeved tunic?"

"No," Ram answered. "Secunnarios would never hide their status."

Cam pursed his lips for a moment, then turned to his brother. "I know. We could use a—"

"Shen'Valla shroud," Ram finished. "Of course. We still have the one from when our mother departed." He dashed into the cottage, his brother hot on his heels.

They returned a minute later with a piece of silky purple fabric attached to a thin ring of silver with runic symbols carved into it. They placed the circlet over my head, and the soft material cascaded around me like a poncho, ending just above my waist. Only a thin slit allowed me to see, and the whole thing felt rather suffocating. I would endure pretty much anything to get out of the palace, though.

The twins stood back, admiring their handiwork. "Perfect," Ram declared. "Now you look ready to go."

Cam nodded and pointed me toward the road. "You can take it off until we reach the city gates if you would like. I know it can be stifling."

Yanking the mess of fabric off my head, I followed them down the cobblestone road.

We'd made it only a few steps when a loud squawk above me drew my attention to the sky where two imposing birds with lustrous black and blue feathers circled above us.

"Hey guys, should I be worried about them?" I asked, pointing up. "I'm still trying to figure out which animals are friendly, and which animals want to eat my face."

"Not at all," Cam said. "Those are our crescia, Flax and Flinx. They are only squawking because they want to come into the city with us."

"Do they normally follow you everywhere?"

"When they can," Ram answered. "They have their own lives, but the drive to be near their bonded is strong." He whistled, and one of the raven-like birds flew down to his shoulder. It was even larger than Thorell, and despite Ram's muscular build, it barely fit.

If I somehow ended up with my own crescia, it better be tiny.

The creature nuzzled the side of Ram's face, then took to the sky again, and we resumed our trek with the crescia accompanying us overhead. They were quite majestic once I knew their sharp talons wouldn't be sinking into my flesh.

"It should not take too long to walk to Civi Adasa. We could take a horse, but that would be unwise unless you are a skilled rider," Ram said as we approached the outer gate. "Well, not a horse technically. We ride unguisens here, but they are close enough."

Since I'd never even seen a horse in person let alone its weird cousin, I didn't argue. My legs were more than used to getting me where I needed to go.

We passed through the gate, and the path curved as it made its way down toward a high stone wall. The salty sea air caressed my face, and a flash of annoyance passed through me since I now seemed to associate the scent of the ocean with Sin. He simply had no right to smell that good yet act so awful.

Pulling my thoughts from the ill-tempered male, I examined the bundle of metal and fabric in my hand. "What is this thing, anyway?"

"When a Vitaean offers their body to Shen'Valla," Cam answered, "the ones they leave behind generally don the shroud for a few days as a way of grieving. It is perfect because no one would ever look too closely at one who mourns."

"Very disrespectful," Ram added. "So make sure not to draw any attention to yourself, and you will be fine."

We continued on in silence, and I took the time to just enjoy the clean air. I knew Jersey had its share of pollution, but I had no idea just how bad it was until now. This was a world without cars, factories, or anything industrialized. The fresh smell alone was making it harder to think about going home.

"You seem sad, Princess," Cam observed, breaking my quiet contemplation.

I ran my fingers over the purple fabric in my hands. "Not sad, just confused, I guess. About everything. My life is back in Jersey, but this place is so beautiful..."

The twins swooped around in front of me, and I pulled up short before I crashed into them.

Ram cocked his head to the side. "Would it truly be so bad to stay here?"

I shrugged. "Maybe not, but the problem is that I can't just abandon my sister. And she's fully human, which means I can't bring her here either. So you see? Conflicted." I moved past them and continued down the road.

When we approached another curve, Cam held an arm out. "You should put the shroud on now. The entrance to Civi Adasa is just beyond the turn."

I settled the stifling fabric back over my head, and we rounded the final bend. Even with the shroud obscuring my vision, I could see the impressive walls of the city and the massive double wooden doors with guards on each side. They must have recognized the twins because they promptly pulled the gate open when we got closer.

Passing through the exit, I held up a hand to block the suns so I could fully take in the sight before me. Now that I could actually get eyes on the city up close, I realized what I had been unable to see from the parapet.

Civi Adasa was not your average city.

Civi Adasa was magnificent.

Chapter Seventeen

I stalled just beyond the entrance, letting the beauty of the glittering city wash over me. Homes with varying degrees of opulence spread out across the left side of the road, some smaller with thatched roofs while others were practically mansions. They all held one thing in common, though, an insignia carved into their white stone walls that glistened brilliantly in the sun. No doubt made of diamonds, every house had their own, like a family crest. The largest homes sat at the top of the hill, nearest the palace, while the smaller ones spilled down the left side of the mountain interspersed with sculpted trees and the occasional green space. Every yard was neatly manicured, every house was maintained in perfect condition, and every street was impossibly clean.

Businesses took up the right side of the road, and while the neighborhoods to the left were calm with only a few people moving about, the other side of the city was a bustling hive of commerce with restaurants, shops, and vendors pushing around small carts loaded with wares and trinkets. A wave of delicious smells wafted over, and my stomach quickly reminded me that I hadn't finished my breakfast.

I turned to the twins and saw them watching me, amused grins on their faces. I almost felt bad for them having to wait on me while I took it all in. They grew up in this incredible place and were used to it, but compared to the cities in my world... it was overwhelming how beautiful it all was. No homeless people sleeping in the streets or begging for change. No stray dogs peeing on the sides of buildings. No trash littering the sidewalks. It was all so... perfect.

The twins stuck close to my side as we moved deeper into the city, and I peered in each shop window that we passed. As promised, nearly everyone gave us a wide berth, a few of them whispering solemn words in Rivellan as they made room for me. I felt a twinge of guilt that I was using such a revered garment to go sightseeing, but not enough to stop my eager exploration.

There were shops selling exquisite pieces of jewelry made with gems so enormous they were almost comical. Another store displayed fine clothing that appeared to hover in the windows, shifting gently to show off each angle of the fashionable dresses. We passed by a home furnishings store, and I jerked to a halt when I saw a male crafting a chair with what could only be magic, the wood twisting and bending to his will as he moved his hands over it in smooth motions. I might have watched him all day if I hadn't sensed the twins getting restless behind me. I kept forgetting that magic was old hat to them.

Moving on, we came to another shop selling the oddest collection of items that looked like they belonged in both a hardware store and a high-end clothier. "What is all this?" I asked Ram when he came up beside me at the window.

"It is an elemental support shop," he replied snidely. "It sells devices that assist various elemental casters who are not particularly strong. That, for instance"—he pointed to a thick metal cuff—"is used by igniservians. When the small button is pushed, it generates a spark that combines with an accelerant to produce a spit of fire. Only weak casters need that kind of help."

"And you don't need anything like that?" I asked with a hint of teasing.

He put his hand to his chest and gave me a look of mock indignation. "Princess, you wound me. I am the strongest igniservian in Rivella. I can pull fire down from the suns if needed."

"Wow," I said, legitimately impressed, until I cast a sideways look at Cam who just shook his head.

Leaving the shop, I caught a whiff of something savory and followed the intoxicating scent to a food cart selling a tried and true classic—meat on a stick. I gave the twins my best pleading look. "I don't have any money, but is there any chance you would buy me one? I'm starving."

"It would be my pleasure," Cam said, stepping forward and speaking some words in Rivellan to the vendor.

The male pulled a fresh hunk of meat out of his cart and flicked his wrist. Flames rushed up to sear it for a second so it was nice and toasty when he handed it over to us.

Without thinking, I reached up to take it from him, and the shroud slid back just enough to expose my bare forearms.

The vendor's eyes locked on my skin, his pupils growing wide as he registered my lack of tattoos. "Abicario!" he shouted, backing away with a look of pure horror on his face.

I jerked my arm back, dropping the meat stick as I tugged the fabric over my body, but it was too late. Someone behind me yanked the shroud from my head, and my blank skin was exposed for all to see.

Many of the people around us moved away hastily, and I heard more shouts in Rivellan—some angry, some scared—but the only words I understood were 'Shen'Valla' and 'abicario.' Someone spat on me while another female stepped forward, waved the shroud in the air, and shouted loudly to the crowd growing larger around us.

"Princess, we need to go now," Cam hissed in my ear, pulling me away from the vendor.

Not expecting his sharp tug, I lost my balance and fell backward, twisting midair so I took the landing roughly on my hands and knees. Before Cam could help me up, someone rushed forward to kick me in the gut, and the harsh impact tore an agonized scream from me. I crumpled to the ground, my head striking the hard stone and briefly blurring my vision.

I struggled to get back on my feet, but a throng of bodies descended on us, shoving Cam and Ram behind them. Another blow slammed into my stomach, forcing the last bit of oxygen from my lungs, and a boot struck my jaw hard enough to snap my head back. Pain shot through me as I spat a mouthful of blood onto the stone. My vision started to fade, and I fought to remain conscious, drawing my arms up to fend off the worst of the attacks to my face. Curling myself into a ball, I cried out each time a particular strong kick hit my kidneys or neck.

Just as I began to pray for death, a huge blast threw the crowd off me, tossing them against a nearby building. I lifted my head weakly, and blood streaked down my face. One of my eyes was swollen shut, but through the other I could make out Cam standing in the middle of the street with his arms raised, his face twisted in fury.

Air magic, I remembered as I fell limply back to the ground, the weight of my head too heavy to remain upright.

Cam shouted at the people while Ram guarded his back with fire rising up from the palms of his hands. The flames hissed and spit as he urged them to grow larger, forming a shield that was pure inferno. The twins moved in front of me, holding the crowd at bay with the threat of their magic, yet the masses still pressed closer.

An enormous stone ripped from a nearby building, flying straight toward the brothers, but Cam whirled around before it could reach them. Lifting his arms, he caught the boulder within a wall of air just before it collided with his head.

Out of the corner of my eye, I tracked a male creeping forward, a bucket of water clutched in his hands. I opened my mouth to shout a warning but could only croak out a strangled noise. The assailant dropped the container to leave only the liquid suspended in midair, then thrust his hands forward. Thin jets of water flew at the brothers like aqueous missiles.

They crashed into Cam and Ram, knocking them off their feet. The mob wasted no time grabbing them and binding their arms at their backs, preventing them from using their powers.

Dismay spread across their faces when their eyes met mine, and I knew they couldn't save me.

The crowd fell upon me again, kicking at my already broken body, and seconds before I lost consciousness, I heard a loud roar that sounded like my father's voice.

Chapter Eighteen

"Princess? Princess, please say something." There was an edge of panic to the voice that brought me back to life, and I pried one eye open. I should be used to waking up groggy and confused, but it wasn't getting any easier.

"Dey?" I croaked out, recognizing the face swimming in and out of focus.

His features were pinched tight in worry, and I wanted to smooth his furrowed brow. He breathed out a sigh of relief, uttering something that sounded like a solemn prayer.

"Why am I on the ground?" I asked, my voice hoarse and cracking.

I heard a derisive snort, and then a familiar male voice said something in Rivellan. A glance over my shoulder confirmed that yes, Sin was standing just off to the side, glaring down at me.

"Sin, you are not being helpful," Dey gritted out.

Groaning, I pushed to sit up. "Where am I?" Soft grass spread out beneath me with several weeping willow type trees forming a circle around us.

"Princess, please lie still. You are not finished healing," Dey urged when I tried to climb to my feet.

I abandoned my attempt to stand, but only because things were still a little blurry. "Will someone please tell me what's going on?"

Everything bouncing around in my brain was disjointed and confusing. There were flashes of the twins, some birds, a glittering city, then... nothing.

"I remember going to Civi Adasa with Cam and Ram," I mumbled, "but then it's like a black wall in my mind. My memories are just gone."

Sin muttered something again in Rivellan, and Dey snapped back at him in kind. I had never heard him so angry before; it was making me nervous.

The scowl on Sin's face deepened, and he moved away from us.

"Dey," I said softly, pulling his attention back to me. "Tell me what's going on. Why can't I remember anything?"

"I was forced to use an extensive amount of magic to heal you," he explained, caressing the side of my face. "I am sorry for the side effects."

My brain supplied the memory of waking up in bed with him, and the feeling of confusion that had resulted from his help then as well. God, was that just yesterday? It felt like weeks had passed.

"Princess," Dey continued in a pained voice. "We nearly lost you. You were in town, and there was a crowd of people who thought you were an abicario mocking their religion. The citizens became infuriated and assaulted you."

I touched my head, recalling the Shen'Valla shroud that Cam and Ram used to hide my bare arms, and a terrifying thought popped into my mind.

"The twins?" I gasped out. "Are they okay? If I was attacked, then... Dey, please tell me they're okay."

"They are being punished," he said gently, and I heard Sin grunt something behind him. Apparently he hadn't gone very far.

"What? Why?" I tried getting to my feet again, but Dey held me firmly in place.

"Because they put your life in danger, Princess. When King Verren found you covered in blood, being viciously beaten..." He shook his head. "I have never seen him so enraged. If we had not been in a meeting close by and heard the commotion—"

"I would have died." Flashes came to me, triggered by his words. The shroud pulled from my head, the people shouting, the pain.

"You did die," Dey said, pulling me into his arms and holding me against his chest.

Sin barked something in Rivellan that sounded more pained than angry, but it only made Dey clutch me tighter. He held me for long enough that I started to squirm, then pulled back to look me in the eye. "Your heart stopped twice on the ride back here. I thought... I thought we were going to lose you."

I couldn't bear the anguish on his face, so I relaxed back into him and touched my forehead to his. "I'm alive. I'm okay."

We sat there quietly until Sin growled something, and Dey dropped his arms from my shoulders.

I tried once more to stand, and Dey finally stopped fighting me. Rising to my feet with only a small wobble, I took in my surroundings. The little hidden glen was quite peaceful, until a sharp caw broke through my reverie, drawing my attention up to the trees where Thorell sat on a branch beside Flax and Flinx. More bird-like creatures—some barely larger than a sparrow while others would make an eagle look small—lounged on nearby limbs, regarding us warily. One of the crescia even had fur and a swishing tail similar to an otter except with wings and wickedly-hooked talons. They weren't kidding when they said each one was unique.

Dey answered my question before I could ask it. "We are at the back of the castle," he confirmed. "This grove is a favored gathering place for many of the crescia when they are not with their Vitaean. Thorell can usually be found in that tree which is why I brought you here."

"Why did you need Thorell?"

"He is able to hold a reserve of my power within him," Dey replied, smiling up at the hawk-like creature. "All crescia are able to do so for their bonded. Should we find ourselves away from the Source, we have access to what you might consider a small emergency supply. I had to bring you back from the brink of death twice, Princess. I needed the extra magic from Thorell, or I might have drained myself before you were healed enough."

He rubbed at his arms, and I noticed his ramentum appeared faded again, even more so than when I'd met him in my world. If the tattoos acted like a battery, he wasn't lying about being drained.

I peered up at Dey's regal-looking crescia. "Thanks for the help, buddy."

He gave a squawk and bobbed his head a few times.

"Where is my father?" I asked Dey. Now that I could function again, finding him needed to be a priority so I could stop whatever punishment Cam and Ram were enduring. I only knew a few people in this world, and I wouldn't let anything bad happen to them because of me.

"King Verren returned to Civi Adasa," Dey replied. "He remained long enough to feel confident you would be all right, but once you were stabilized, he was forced to leave."

The answer wounded me like a dagger to the chest. I had only known my father a handful of days, but his apathy for my near death experience still caused my heart to clench.

Dey must have seen my pained expression because he quickly added, "He very much wanted to stay until you woke. King Verren was most distraught over what happened, but we did not know how long you would be unconscious. With the Council approaching, he has responsibilities that cannot be ignored, you see."

"He'll always be a king first and a father second, huh?" I understood, but it still hurt more than it should have. I always imagined that any parent would put their child first before anything else, but I guess family only counted for so much when that parent ruled a kingdom.

"Please do not look so sad, Princess."

"It's fine," I replied dismissively. Just because I shared some genetics with the king didn't mean he owed me anything. It only made my decision to leave in a few weeks that much easier. "He stayed long enough to make sure his savior would survive, and then he went back to work. I get it." I was shooting for indifference, but the bite to my words revealed otherwise.

Dey opened his mouth to protest, but I stopped him.

"Seriously, I'm fine. I just want to go see Cam and Ram." He winced, and nausea bloomed in the pit of my stomach. "Where are they?"

"They're in the dungeons," Sin snapped, striding up beside Dey. "You dragged them into the city, and now they're suffering for it. I hope you had fun on your little adventure, because I lost my two best generals so you could go shopping."

My blood boiled at his accusation. "Yeah? Well if you had been training me the way you were supposed to, then I wouldn't have been with them, would I? So maybe it's your fault."

He reeled back as if I slapped him, and I felt a small amount of triumph from his reaction.

Turning back to to Dey, I asked, "Can you please take me to them?"

"No, he can't," Sin cut in before Dey could speak for himself. "They're being held in the Sonaria. It's a room made from the only mineral on this planet that can block a Vitaeans access to the Source."

"Why put them someplace like that?"

"It's so they can't heal their wounds," he spat out. "King Verren had them beaten for endangering you." He dropped his voice low enough that Dey couldn't hear and added, "That's what happens here, Rain. Good males suffer because of you. Because you know nothing of this world." Then he pushed past me, knocking me to the side with his broad shoulder.

"Come, Princess," Dey said, taking me by the elbow and leading me out of the glen. "You need rest. The wounds you suffered were many, and your body will need more time to fully heal."

Dey escorted me back to my room and helped me get settled before pulling the thick drapes shut to block out the suns.

The bed dipped when he laid down next to me on his side, propping his head underneath one arm. He tugged on the hair tie that held my braid in place, and I started to object when he tucked it into his pocket—it was the only one I had. The feeling of his hands running through my hair silenced any protests, though. His attention never wavered from his task as he carefully loosened each section before fanning the strands out behind me on the pillow.

"Your hair is so beautiful, Rain," he murmured quietly.

A small slice of sunlight cut through the gap in the curtains, casting a golden glow upon his face that drew me in. He was perfection made human, not a single freckle, mole, or scar tarnished his smooth skin.

His hand slid out of my hair and dropped down to caress my neck. He lowered his face, meeting my gaze, and the space between us was so small it would be nothing to close the gap and feel his mouth on mine.

There was desire in his eyes alongside a silent challenge. He wouldn't do it, wouldn't make the first step. It would have to be me.

But I had more important things to do than complicate my life even further.

The decision must have shown on my face because he gave me a small smile and said, "Rest, Princess." He ran a hand across my cheek, then stood to leave.

"Dey?" I called after him. "I was just curious... What is the Rivellan word for 'now?'"

He frowned. "Why do you wish to know?"

I did my best to summon a blush to my cheeks. It wasn't really something I did often, but I pasted on my best coy smile that hopefully portrayed innocently sexy. "It just seems like a word that might be good to know. For the future."

Apparently it worked, because his frown smoothed into a grin. "Cotio," he said. "Roughly translated, it means 'at once.' Any Rivellan would know what you meant should you choose to use it."

"Thanks," I said, leaning back against the pillow and shutting my eyes.

"You are most welcome," he whispered, closing the door behind him.

I counted to a hundred in my head in case he lingered outside my room, then jumped out of bed. Cracking the door open ever so slowly, I peered out into the hall. After confirming it was empty, I crept toward the staircase.

I had myself some twins to rescue.

It took me less than ten minutes to find my mark. The guard who stood in front of a closed door at the bottom of the staircase appeared no older than twenty-one. Even from my hiding spot at the top of the stairs, I could tell he was perfect. His back was stiff, his hand was on the sword at his side, and his eyes never stopped scanning his surroundings—all signs of a soldier who took his guard duty far too seriously. He had to be new. All the older soldiers had a slight air of relaxation about them when they thought no one was watching, as if they trusted their instincts to kick in should the need arise. This guy? He was wound so tight that all I had to do was nudge, and he would crack under the pressure.

I pushed my shoulders back into my best regal posture and stomped down the stairs.

The guard's eyes landed on mine when I approached, and he dropped into the signature knee bend they were so fond of giving me.

"Princepa," he said solemnly, his face cast to the ground.

"Soldier," I barked, yanking him to his feet.

I hated being rude, but my tone and actions had to be spot on if this was going to work. He gave me a wide-eyed look, and I made a mental note to apologize later.

"You will take me immediately to the Sonaria," I growled in his face, doing my best imitation of Sin.

His head darted around frantically as if searching for someone to save him.

I snapped my fingers in front of him. "Do you know who I am, soldier? Princepa."

He blurted out something in Rivellan, panic rising in his eyes.

Perfect. He was right where I wanted him.

I leaned in close and snarled, "Sonaria! Cotio!"

He gave one last distressed look down the hall, then gestured for me to follow him. Once his back was turned, I sighed in relief that it had worked.

I traipsed after him, and eventually we arrived at what I thought was the lowest floor of the palace until he unlocked a concealed door to another stairwell. We must have gone down five more flights of stairs before we hit the bottom, and another long hall stretched out. The cool air underground was stale and felt... wrong somehow, like thin shards of my bones were peeling off to burrow into the surrounding muscles. The sooner I got Cam and Ram out the better.

We passed a handful of empty, non-descript jail cells until he stopped halfway down the hall in front of an intimidating metal door barred with a thick latch.

I touched it tentatively, and the uncomfortable wriggling feeling under my skin intensified. It also wouldn't budge when I tried to lift it. Stepping back, I glared at the guard and pointed to the door. "Cotio!"

He kept glancing around, and I could see a bead of sweat forming on his temple.

I didn't come this far to give up, though. I grabbed hold of his tunic and shoved him toward the door. Activating the fullest level of my bitch mode, I hissed out, *"Cotio,"* the promise of death lacing my words.

Reluctantly, the soldier lifted the latch.

Once it was up, I pushed past him and yanked on the handle of the door. It was heavy, *shit it was heavy,* but I managed to pull it open.

Pure darkness filled the cell, and I could barely see anything with only the small hint of light from the hallway.

"Cam? Ram?" I called out tentatively. A figure shifted in the gloom, catching my eye. The brothers shuffled forward, and a distressed cry escaped me.

They hadn't been beaten. They had been tortured.

Dozens of ragged gashes that oozed blood crisscrossed the entirety of their shirtless chest and arms. Bits of rock were embedded across their faces, pushed so deep into the skin that they formed small craters. One of them had a right arm that was twisted at an unnatural angle, and it hung limply at his side. The other hobbled forward on what was clearly a broken knee judging by the excessive swelling visible even in the low lighting. They were dirty and bloody and there was only a vacant expression where the joy in their eyes normally lived.

What really broke my heart, though, was their hair. Their beautiful locs had been burned off, the scorch marks on their scalps still raised and angry.

Rushing forward, I slung an arm around each of them, knowing I couldn't support them for long, and my body writhed under the onslaught of wrongness in the cell. God, how long had they been trapped in here, forced to endure that sickening sensation?

I managed to get them through the doorway and about ten steps down the hall before I collapsed under the weight of their massive bodies.

One of the brothers heaved himself off me and clambered to his feet. The swelling in his knee was receding, and the sight of his healing abilities kicking in sent a wave of relief coursing through me.

"Can you walk yet?" I asked from my position on the cold dungeon floor.

"I think so," the standing brother said, his voice thick and gravelly.

"We will be better once we get further from the Sonaria," the other brother added, climbing slowly to his feet then casting down a hand to help me up. "It is still siphoning our magic even from out here."

Moving as quickly as we could despite my weakness and their injuries, we made it up the stairs and back into the castle proper. Slowly, the gashes across their bodies sealed up, and the ugly red welts on their heads faded into smooth brown skin again.

I ran my hand over the scalp of the nearest brother. "How will I tell you apart now?" I asked, choking back a sob. Sin was a nasty jerk, but he had been right. This was my fault. I wasn't in the city five minutes before I let the disguise falter, and they paid the price.

"Do not be sad, Princess," the one I was touching said. "Wounds heal. Hair grows. We have suffered worse before and would do it again in a heartbeat if it brought you happiness."

"Besides, you can still tell us apart," the other twin offered, snapping his finger to pull a spark of flame from the nearest torch. He ran his finger across his left eyebrow, burning a tiny line through the center of it like a scar.

"Stop it, Ram," I protested, pulling his hand away from his face before he got any more crazy ideas. "You need to stop burning off your hair for me."

He only laughed and gave me a hug. Then Cam joined in, both of them cocooning me in a warm embrace that should have felt awkward yet didn't. I savored the comfort of the two brothers holding me, knowing they were safe again. It was such a strange feeling, the affection I had for these twins I met only days ago.

I never knew what it was like to actually have friends, but when a huge smile broke out across my face, I realized that just maybe I was starting to get an idea.

Chapter Nineteen

I kept watch while Cam and Ram snuck out of the castle after I ordered them to lay low until I had a chance to speak with my father. I didn't want to risk any overzealous guards trying to throw them back in the Sonaria.

Since I didn't know when exactly my father would be back from Civi Adasa, and I was too antsy to rest like Dey suggested, I decided I might as well take the time to explore the palace a bit.

Wandering aimlessly down the halls past a few open doors, I loitered briefly in front of each one to watch what was happening.

In the first one I came to, servants moved their hands in circular motions over tubs filled with clothing and soap, their magic churning the water. Off to the other side of the room, one female used her power to suspend wet clothing in the air while another made sweeping gestures that pulled every drop of liquid from the fabric down to a grate in the floor.

They were just doing laundry, but I still watched longer than was necessary, fascinated by how much effort went into something that was so simple in my world.

The next room was even more intriguing, and it took me a few minutes to figure out what was happening. Six servants stood around a wide pool in the middle of the floor with their arms swirling about them. Undulating orbs of water rippled out of the basin and bobbed across the room to snake into a series of pipes along the wall. Other servants stood near the ducts, using fire in their hands to heat the metal as the water passed through it.

So that was how I got my hot shower. Everything in the castle functioned because elemental casters made it so. I felt a pang of guilt when I saw the boredom on every single face in the room. They would be gods in my world, but here they were using their magic for mundane labor.

Continuing down the hall, I saw no more open doors and was about to give up my exploration in favor of picking fruit in the orchard when I caught a whiff of something savory. I really hoped I'd finally located the kitchen so I didn't have to go searching for smells every time I got hungry.

Following the scent to a closed door in the next hallway over, I knocked twice, then cracked it open. "Hello?"

"Come in, Raynella," a scratchy male voice answered.

I hesitated for a second, then pushed the door further open. It didn't sound like my father or Corym, and I had been told no one else in the castle spoke English.

Stepping cautiously into the small room, I noted that it was definitely not the kitchen. Instead, it resembled an office with a wooden desk against the back wall beside a bookshelf full of neatly organized scrolls. There was a hearth off to the right side with two comfy-looking high back chairs facing the crackling fire.

I crossed the room and found the source of the smell that had captivated me so strongly. A platter of food with steam wafting off it sat on a small table between the chairs. An elderly male rested comfortably in one of the cushy seats, looking up at me with curiosity. He appeared to be in his sixties or seventies with thinning gray hair and copious wrinkles. What caught my attention the most, though, were his eyes. I would recognize that shade of pale blue anywhere, and the golden sunburst around the pupil only confirmed it.

He gestured to the chair beside him, and I sat down, staring at his plate of food with thinly-veiled desire. "Please, help yourself," he said. "I can have a servant bring me another meal later."

I didn't even hesitate. I grabbed a fork and began devouring the meat and veggies.

"Thank you," I mumbled around a mouthful of food. "I didn't realize how hungry I was until I smelled this from the next hallway over."

The elderly male smiled and settled back into the chair. "You are Vitaean, Raynella. Our senses are somewhat heightened when compared to those of humans, so you will often pick up smells and sounds."

I took a few more bites. "How do you know English?" I asked, swiping my palm across my messy mouth to remove any bits of sauce. He cringed slightly at the action, and I quickly folded my hands in my lap.

"The same way the others do; Corym gave me the knowledge," he replied matter-of-factly.

"Oh," I said, my face wrinkling in confusion. "I was told I already met everyone who knew my language."

"Ah, yes, well, I took it upon myself to make the request of Corym shortly after you arrived. Naturally, I wanted to be able to speak with my kin. Let us keep this between you and me, though. Your father would be displeased if he knew I learned the language. He worries, you see, that I am too old for such things." The male gave me a conspiratorial wink, and I grinned.

I liked this guy.

"Yeah, okay," I agreed. "It's not like my father doesn't have his own secrets." My hand strayed back over to the fork, and I couldn't help myself from scraping up the last bits of food.

When I finished, he handed me a cloth, and I gently dabbed at my mouth. Setting the napkin on the table, I settled back into my chair, mirroring his relaxed pose. "So, I'm guessing you're like my grandpa, then? The eyes kind of gave it away before you even said we were related."

"You are very observant, Raynella," he replied. "Our eye color tends to be one of our strongest genetic traits. And yes, I am your grandfather. I have been looking forward to meeting you."

"Yeah, likewise," I said enthusiastically. "I mean, not that I've been looking forward to meeting you because my father didn't tell me you existed, but it's really cool to find out I have grandparents."

I hated that I was babbling, but I really wanted him to like me. Maybe there was hope that I could still have one good familial relationship. "What should I call you? Grandpa? Grandfather? Gramps?"

"You may call me Belarius," he said with a slight wince, as if the idea of me calling him Gramps was painful.

"Belarius it is," I said quickly, hoping I didn't offend him. "How come I haven't seen you before today?" I asked, changing the subject.

"I spend much of my time resting these days," he replied. "I am very close to returning my body to Shen'Valla."

"Oh." I shifted in the chair awkwardly, unsure how to respond. Shen'Valla was definitely a touchy subject around here. "So, if you're Verren's father, and he's over a hundred, does that mean you're like two hundred or…?"

"Raynella, are you trying to ask how old I am?" He gave me a knowing smile, and I blushed in embarrassment.

"Yeah, kinda. I know everyone here lives a long time, but I was just wondering exactly how long. You aren't a thousand, are you?"

Belarius let out a low chuckle. "No, Raynella. I am not quite that old."

I mentally kicked myself for the stupid question. "Sorry, that was rude. I'm just a little nervous." He let out a small yawn, and I hopped out of the chair. "I should let you rest. It was really nice meeting you. Hopefully I'll see you around. I'm going to be here for a bit and it'd be nice to talk to you some more."

He searched my face for something, smiling at whatever he saw. "I would like that very much, Raynella."

I headed for the door, but when my hand hit the knob, Belarius called, "Raynella?"

I turned back to him. "Yeah?"

"Have a nice day."

Something twisted in my stomach, there and gone before I had a chance to analyze it.

I gave him a wide smile, then left, feeling lighter than I had in a while. It was nice to have a grandfather, someone who liked me for me. I wasn't the savior with him, I was just his granddaughter.

It was all so… nice.

"RAYNELLA!"

I heard the loud roar as I neared the exit of the rose maze where I'd ultimately decided to spend the afternoon wasting hours searching for my lost purse. Well, I wasted maybe one hour searching and another hour or two trying to find my way out.

At the sound of an enraged voice, I was tempted to disappear inside again. My father was back, and from the sound of it, someone told him I had released Cam and Ram. Squaring my shoulders, I strode toward the castle with my head held high, prepared to make him see reason.

I found my father in front of the portcullis surrounded by guards and a cluster of horse-like creatures, all anxiously stomping their hooves.

When I got closer, I could see what Ram meant earlier about 'close enough' when he referred to the creatures. Unguisen were like battle horses—as beautiful as they were fierce. Despite being slightly larger, they were roughly the shape of a horse, except they had a series of bony protrusions running from their head down their back and even more along their tail, which ended in a cluster of three wickedly sharp, foot-long spikes. Short coarse hair covered their massive bodies with colors ranging from black to shades of brown, though I noted one was almost like a deep blue. Across the chest, shoulders, and underbelly, thick slabs of armor scales glittered in the late afternoon sun like dragonhide. Great ridged crests of bone sprouted from the base of their skull, wrapping around from ear to ear. They looked like the result of a wild weekend between a triceratops, a stegosaurus, and a very brave, *or very drunk*, stallion.

My father spotted me and stomped over, leaving his entourage to wrangle the creatures back to wherever the stables were located. Despite their vicious appearance, the unguisen trotted after the guards without fuss.

"Raynella," he gritted out with barely contained rage. "Is it true that you coerced a guard into releasing Camden and Ramset?"

I affected my best regal posture and met his gaze, refusing to flinch at the anger burning there. So much rage in those pale blue eyes, but also something else, something I couldn't decipher.

"Yes, I did," I said firmly. "You had no right to punish them."

"I had every right to punish them!" he exploded. "They are generals in the king's guard which means I command their every action. They had one job, to keep you safe while educating you about Rivella. Instead of following orders, they took you into Civi Adasa and nearly got you killed. How could I do anything but punish those brainless fools?"

Fear. That's what I saw hiding in his eyes. He wasn't just angry, he was also afraid. What could he possibly be scared of?

"The attack wasn't their fault," I said calmly, refusing to let my own anger rise to the surface for once. I didn't think a shouting match would help keep the twins out of the Sonaria. "I wanted to go into the city. I knew it could be dangerous, and they did tell me that I needed to make sure no one saw my bare arms. I messed up. Not them."

"None of that matters because you should never have been there in the first place. I cannot imagine what they were thinking. Is there nothing between their ears?"

"Hey," I said, feeling defensive for my new friends. "Did you give them a direct order to keep me out of the city?"

"Not a direct order, no," he admitted, folding his arms across his broad chest. "But they knew how dangerous the city would be for one who appeared to be an abicario. They risked your life, Raynella. I would come across as weak to my people if I did not punish them adequately."

"Ah! Don't you see?" I pressed, taking a step closer. "You didn't specifically tell them not to take me. They honestly thought I would be safe with them and could learn more about Rivella by getting to experience it. Maybe going into the city was a mistake, but not one that deserves torture. And I'm just as much to blame, so if you want to send them back to the Sonaria, then you have to send me too."

He flinched. "You are my daughter, Raynella. I will die before I let you be put in the Sonaria."

"Then let this go," I pleaded. "If you care about me at all, can't you just call it good? Hasn't their suffering been enough?"

I could see the war raging inside him as he stared at me, and I didn't know who would win, the king or the father. His eyes flickered to a spot just over my shoulder, then landed back on me, his internal battle ended.

To my complete surprise, it was my father who won.

"All right, Raynella. Only this once will I allow their time served to be punishment enough."

"Thank you." I breathed out a sigh of relief.

"I have one condition, though," he said firmly, and I tensed back up. "You must attend the court dinner this evening. In proper attire. For your sake, I will keep the number of attendees small, a few courtiers and advisors only."

Damn.

I chewed on my lip, debating, then felt disgusted with myself that I had even considered saying no. Cam and Ram were my friends. I could endure a single stuffy meal in an uncomfortable gown for them.

"I accept your terms. And I'll make sure we keep our lessons on the castle grounds from now on."

He waved a hand. "No need. Camden and Ramset will no longer be your tutors. I simply do not trust them with your wellbeing anymore."

A protest rose in my throat, but he cut me off. "I am firm on this, Raynella. You may be able to overlook the danger they put you in, but I was the one who had to witness the aftermath of your assault. I will not take that risk again."

"Fine," I grumbled. He didn't say I couldn't be friends with them, they just couldn't be my tutors. Semantics, really. "Corym can help me, then. He seems like an excellent teacher. He's literally all about knowledge."

"Corym is not available," he said brusquely, his eyes briefly focusing on a spot behind me once more. "He received word yesterday that his sister has gone to the Shen'Valla Temple. He is saying his goodbyes and will return in a few days."

"So who is going to answer all the questions I have about this place?"

He smoothed his long hair back and straightened his mantle, the kingly persona locked in place once more. "I have decided you do not need a formal education. Deylan or Dreisin can answer any pertinent questions that arise, but I believe it is best if you take things slow. Your curiosity has nearly gotten you killed once already."

My jaw dropped. Was he serious? I made one mistake by going into the city, and now I had to fight for every scrap of information about this world?

"I am needed in a meeting, Raynella, so I will see you at dinner shortly. You should go prepare." He leaned forward, kissed the top of my head, then strolled off to rejoin his guards, completely unphased by the stunned expression on my face.

Chapter Twenty

Back in my room, I yanked open my wardrobe and grabbed the first green dress I saw. It was pretty enough and likely to be just as awkward as the rest.

Pushing the other gowns aside, I was pleasantly shocked to see a familiar sword tucked behind all the clothing. The twins had been tortured and broken, yet they still took the time to steal Sin's precious weapon for me. I was starting to understand why they were such high ranking generals despite their laissez-faire attitude. If they could pull that off, then they were equal parts gutsy and stealthy.

Chuckling to myself, I headed to the bathroom to hop in the shower. Even though someone had wiped most of the blood off me after the attack, it was like I could still feel it coating my skin.

I exited the bathroom almost an hour later to find Niahna and Kiahna hovering by the fire, and I wondered if they just hung around all day waiting to be of assistance.

The sisters began their usual routine of pampering me, and I relaxed back into the chair, enjoying the soft touch of Kiahna's fingers in my hair as she brushed and sculpted my long locks into something more befitting a princess.

I was standing in front of the mirror wondering who the hell was looking back at me when a knock sounded at my door.

Pulling it open, I found a scowling Dey on the other side. I was about to make a crack about him taking lessons from Sin, but the moment his eyes settled on me, his anger vanished, and he took in a sharp inhale. I waited for him to say something, but all he did was stare, his eyes crawling up and down my body in long, lingering glances.

I couldn't blame him too much since I knew my appearance was a drastic change, and damn did I look good—the dress fit me perfectly, clinging to my breasts and smooth stomach without making me appear too emaciated. The sisters had braided my hair and twisted it into a coronet atop my head. Thirty or more diamond flowers were clipped in at carefully selected intervals, and the whole effect was actually quite breathtaking.

I endured about a minute of Dey's hungry perusal of my body before I started to feel a little uncomfortable. "Um, did you need something?"

His eyes slowly rose to mine. He gave his head a little shake, then focused on me. "Yes, apologies, but you look... absolutely stunning."

I let out a half-hearted laugh. "Yeah, well, who knew a Jersey girl could clean up so well?"

He reached out and ran a hand down my cheek. "I did," he whispered. "I have always seen the beauty you work so hard to hide."

Blushing, I opened the door wider and gestured him inside. I plopped on the bed with all the grace of an elephant, not caring much if I wrinkled the gown, and faced him. "So, what brings you up here? I figured I would see you at dinner."

He paused just inside my door, his smile fading. "I came to inform you that I heard what you did earlier with the twins. I must say that I am disappointed. I thought we were beyond subterfuge with one another."

The look on his face speared me with guilt. "I'm really sorry, Dey. I didn't want to hurt you or anything, but I couldn't risk you stopping me. So far you've always sided with my father, and I couldn't just leave them there. Honestly, I'm surprised you could. I thought they were like family to you."

"They are," he replied, taking another step into the room. "However, there are things about this world that you do not understand."

"So tell me," I pleaded. "Explain to me how you justify the torturing of two people who were only trying to make me happy. Two people that you claim are like brothers. Did you see what happened to them?"

His eyes dropped to the floor. "No, I did not witness it," he admitted. "Though I have seen punishments in the past. Princess, you must understand that this world is not like yours. To control a population of magic wielders, King Verren must rule with a firm hand. If he shows any weakness, the people might rise up against him."

"Maybe they should," I suggested bitterly, turning away from him. A sharp gasp had me spinning back around. The horrified look on his face was almost comical in its severity.

"You... you cannot sincerely believe that," he said, his voice barely above a whisper.

"Come on, Dey, is equality really that strange of a concept? This same thing happened in my world, and yeah, we're still working on it, but things are getting better. Rivella could be better too if you all stopped judging people based on their magic."

He gave me a pitying look. "Princess, what could the people of the Other Realm possibly know about creating a better world? Humans are little more than savages."

His words slapped me in the face.

"I'm half-human," I snapped, leaping to my feet, anger exploding like fireworks inside me. I knew he felt Vitaeans were superior to humans, but I never fully grasped the extent of his bigotry.

"I know," he said, his calm tone fueling my rage further. "The fact that you will rise up to save us in spite of your heritage makes me truly in awe of you."

"*In spite of*?" I spat out. "Maybe it's *because of*. You ever think of that? Maybe if I was just some pompous Vitaean, I wouldn't care enough to even try to save you jerks!"

I pushed past him and stalked down the hall.

"Wait!" Dey called after me. "You need an escort to dinner. It would be unseemly for the princess to enter alone. Please, come with me and allow us to discuss this further."

Like hell I was eating dinner with him.

I neared the end of the hall just as a door opened to my left, and a wave of cool salty air swept over me. Seconds later, Sin stepped out, looking devilishly handsome with his dark chocolate hair tied back, and his standard black tunic replaced by a deep purple one embroidered with silver around the edges.

Heavy footsteps pounded behind me, so I made a split decision and chose the lesser of two evils. Grabbing Sin's arm, I dragged him toward the staircase.

"You're escorting me to dinner," I said, allowing just enough pleading into my voice to not sound like I was full on begging. "Just this once, please don't fight me."

I honestly expected him to resist, but something in my voice must have halted whatever he was about to say. He glanced behind me at Dey, then took my arm and wrapped it under his. We walked down the staircase toward the dining room in complete silence, which was pretty much the best I could have hoped for from him.

A guard stopped us at the entrance to the smaller dining hall and asked Sin a question in Rivellan. Surprise momentarily sparked on the guard's face at Sin's answer, but he turned to the dining room and loudly announced, "Princepa Raynella au Cennux Dreisin."

The nearly full table of courtiers all stood when we entered, and I could feel every single pair of eyes on me as Sin guided me through the room.

Breathe.

Just keep breathing.

A hundred thoughts raced through my head, none of them pleasant. Were they judging my dress? My hair? They were probably all staring at my bare arms. I half expected someone to spit on me.

I waited for Sin to say something snarky, because there was no way he couldn't feel my body tensing and my breath coming out in short bursts, but he just pulled out the chair to the right of my father's mini throne, then pushed it back in once I was settled. He briefly hesitated before taking the empty seat beside me. My breathing only leveled out once the other courtiers sat and the low hum of chatter resumed.

The spots opposite Sin and I were already occupied with two stiff-looking males I had seen hovering around my father previously—likely his advisors—which meant the next empty seat for Dey to claim was… I suppressed a grin when I saw it was over halfway down the table.

Minutes later, he arrived and scanned the room until he found me. Dey looked crestfallen until his eyes shifted to Sin sitting beside me. He lifted an eyebrow, but Sin just shrugged and glanced away, focusing his attention on the drink in his hand.

Dey's shoulders dropped as he took the remaining empty chair. Shortly after, the guards loudly announced that the king had arrived, and my father strode confidently through the room to the head of the table. He stopped without sitting and surveyed the people gathered with a brilliant smile on his face. A smile that wavered when he took notice of Sin beside me, though it promptly slid back into place as if nothing was amiss.

He started speaking in Rivellan, and it sounded like some sort of grand speech.

I squirmed when I heard my name a few times and also caught the word 'princepa' more than once.

"What's he saying?" I asked Sin. I leaned in closer to keep my voice low and immediately regretted my action when his scent threatened to pull me under like a dark tide.

"He's saying the Gods have cursed him with a useless daughter, but not to worry because he's working very hard to fix the situation."

"He is not, you ass," I snapped, smacking his shoulder. Apparently I had been a little too loud because my father faltered in his speech. I gave him my most beatific smile, and he continued.

"Seriously, what is he saying?" I asked again, keeping my voice controlled and my hands to myself.

Sin sighed. "Blah blah blah, searching for you forever, blah blah blah, greatest gift, blah blah blah, future of the kingdom. It's all quite ridiculous if you ask me."

"Why do you say that?" I didn't entirely disagree with him, but I wouldn't call my father's speech ridiculous.

He brought his face close to mine, his eyes flashing with something like accusation. "Because we both know you aren't staying here, Fea Remia. The sooner you leave, the better for everyone."

My teeth clenched at his harsh comment. I'd allowed myself to think maybe, just maybe, he could be someone worth getting to know, but first impressions never lie, and he was nothing more than a heartless asshole.

Keeping my eyes fixed on his and my voice as low as possible, I said, "Yeah, well fuck you too, Sin. Why are you the only one in this damned place who is so set on me leaving as soon as possible? Don't you want me to fix the lines? Save your world?"

He snorted derisively. "Everything comes at a cost, Fea Remia. Maybe I'm not willing to pay the price required just so everyone here can have more magic."

I blinked at him. No one had said anything about a cost to me. Though it did make sense that if the dark forest was truly dangerous, then people might get injured or die helping to get me through. Maybe he was concerned for his soldiers and wanted to protect them. The idea of Sin actually caring about other people felt absurd, but if it was true—if he hated me for the knowledge that I was dragging his fighters off to potential death—maybe I was a little hasty in my decision to pursue the mission.

Then I recalled what Cam and Ram told me about the imminarios and their segregation. This was about more than stopping the plague. It was also about restoring the magic to everyone, not just the privileged.

"No price is too high to pay for equality among the people," I hissed.

His eyes narrowed. "Spoken like a true idealist. Tell me, Fea Remia, when did you start to care about others? I thought you always looked out for number one?"

My retort died on my lips because he wasn't wrong. Back in Jersey, I literally only cared about Jenn. Even the guys I dated ranked lower than a decent grilled cheese sandwich in terms of my affection.

Before I could tell him where to stick his assessment of me, a heavy silence settled over the room. Tearing my eyes away from Sin, I saw not only the king but the entire table observing us closely.

"Raynella," my father said with barely contained annoyance. "Would you care to stand and greet your court?"

Crap. How long had everyone been watching our argument?

I reluctantly rose to my feet. The number of people staring at me threatened to kick off another panic attack, but I forced it down. I told my father I would do this, and so I would. Wiping my sweaty hands on the soft material of my dress, I summoned a wan smile.

The faces regarding me ranged in expression from adulation (that was a young female with short red curls that reminded me of Jenn) all the way down the spectrum to outright hostility (that was the two advisors across the table from me). Most landed on haughty indifference, and that was fine with me.

I gave a little wave, then hurriedly sat back down.

My father must have been satisfied with that because he gave one more booming proclamation, and then everyone relaxed into their chairs once more. Servants spilled into the room with plates of food, and my awkwardness was soon forgotten as people indulged in conversation with those around them.

I focused on stuffing my face, praying I could get out of this situation quickly and painlessly.

Without dropping his kingly smile, my father leaned over toward me. "Raynella, why is Deylan not sitting beside you? He was supposed to escort you to dinner this evening."

I gave him a wide-eyed, innocent look. "Was he? How strange. When I left my room, I only came across Sin here, and since you were so keen on me working with him, I figured he would make an excellent dinner companion. Was I wrong to make such an assumption? If so, I deeply apologize."

Anybody who spent more than ten minutes with me could hear the mockery dripping from my words, but my father hadn't quite picked up on my nuances yet.

"Of course. Cennux Dreisin is an excellent choice. It was just a bit surprising as Deylan is usually seated at my side. He is my Foster, after all."

I dropped my eyes to my lap, doing my best to look remorseful. "Of course, Father. I didn't mean to cause a disruption. I am so new to all of this. Perhaps I shouldn't come to these dinners any more. I don't want to embarrass you with my ignorant ways."

At this point I might be laying it on too thick, but it was a shot I had to take.

"No, no, Raynella. It is quite all right. In fact, I think it would be best if you dined with the court from now on. It will help prepare you for the King's Council banquet."

"Come again?" My head whipped up, and my beautifully constructed act dropped away entirely.

He took a bite of his meal that he chewed far too thoroughly before finally swallowing and turning to me. "You are my daughter, Raynella. Your presence at the Council banquet is mandatory. My search for you has been well known throughout the land, and attendees from all three courts will be excited to meet you."

My mouth opened and closed as I gaped at him like a dying fish.

"You will have a wonderful time," he continued, spearing a chunk of squishy yellow vegetable. "The King's Council happens only once every hundred years, and we are lucky to be hosting it. There had been talks of moving it to the Gold Court after that... debacle we had with the Silver Court some years back."

Beside me, Sin choked on his food, but my father paid him no mind.

"We simply must have you there, Raynella," he continued as if his Cennux wasn't dying on the other side of me. "You will not be required at the morning meeting, of course, but your absence would be noted if you did not attend the Elemental Games or the banquet. And of course, there is the ball afterward." He paused. "That does remind me, we will need to get a tailor here immediately to fit you for your gown. Your tiara is being fashioned as we speak by some of the finest terriservians in the whole of Rivella, and your dress will need to be just as extravagant."

Silence settled over our end of the table while I took a second to envision all the different events he'd mentioned. "You know," I said casually, suppressing the soul deep urge to run as fast and as far as my legs could take me, "I always thought hell would be hotter. More demons and pitchforks, you know? I guess this works too."

I heard a coughing sound, and turned to see Sin choking again, this time on the water he had been drinking. I gave him a wicked smile. "Manners, Sin. You're at a royal function after all. You should try to be more refined."

If looks could kill, I really would be in hell, but his irritation was far from my greatest concern. The only thing keeping me from dissolving into a puddle of hyperventilating goo was the firm knowledge that I would be doing none of the things my father had listed off.

I showed up to his dinner. I met his terms. Cam and Ram were safe. He had nothing left to force my hand with, so unless he wanted to drag me kicking and screaming, there was no fucking way I was attending some Cinderella-esque fairy tale ball.

No. Fucking. Way.

Chapter Twenty-One

Okay, so there was one way to get me to cooperate, I discovered the next morning at breakfast.

"You've got to be kidding," I said, my mouth hanging wide open.

My father took a bite of his pastry and chewed sedately before responding. "No, Raynella, I believe I was quite clear. It is absolutely necessary for you to be present at the Council events. I had hoped you would do it simply because I asked it of you, or better yet out of some semblance of pride for the Diamond Court, but alas, this is where we find ourselves."

"But... but..." I sputtered, words utterly failing me. He was my father. Granted we barely knew each other, and I had no basis for father-daughter relationships, but this just seemed... evil. "You saw what happened when I first arrived. I can't do crowds of people staring at me. I just can't."

"Deylan can assist if you find the emotions overwhelming."

I glanced over at Dey who wouldn't meet my eyes. He knew exactly how I felt about that but would never stand up to the king. So much for the damsel in distress mentality. The one time I would actually embrace that patriarchal nonsense, and he just sits on the sidelines.

I didn't even bother looking to Sin for help.

"It is ultimately your choice, Raynella, but my decision stands firm. If you are so determined to return to the Other Realm once the magic is repaired, then there is little I can do to stop you, no matter how saddened I am. However, if you want to leave with enough of my diamonds to improve your station in your world... then you must agree to uphold your royal duties." As he took in my shocked expression, he added, "I am sorry if this seems harsh or cruel, but I am the king here, and appearances are everything within the royal courts. I would appear weak if I could not make my own daughter attend the necessary functions. I am sorry this upsets you, Raynella, but you have left me with no other options."

Flashes of staring eyes, whispering mouths, and judging scowls raced through my mind. Dey probably could help, but I just wasn't comfortable letting him hack my brain for a social function. What if he calmed me too much and I did or said things that I never would otherwise? I doubted his power had the same precision as a klonopin tablet.

Then I thought back to my tiny apartment in Jersey. The disappointed look on Jenn's face any time I told her I would be short on rent that month. Could I really return to her empty-handed after being gone for weeks? Would she even believe my story if I had no proof? Our bond was near unbreakable, but even this pushed the limits of sisterhood. It might destroy us, and I couldn't risk that all this was for nothing.

"Fine," I snapped, feeling once more like even the illusion of choice had been ripped away from me. "I'll do it. I'll let you parade me around in front of your subjects. But when it's all done? You will give me all the diamonds I can carry, and then I never want to see any of you ever again. You won't try to find me. You won't keep tabs on me. Once I leave, Raynella is dead. Do you understand me?"

It was petty to meet his ultimatum with my own, but I needed to see if the thought of losing me might change his mind. If I was ever going to come back here, ever try to have a real relationship with my father, then I had to know if there was a chance that he would ever put me before his precious crown.

To his credit, I could see the decision was at least difficult. He opened his mouth and closed it multiple times. His eyes locked on my own, then flickered off to the side. He grit his teeth and clenched his fists.

In the end, this was one battle I lost.

"I accept your terms," he said with a bone deep sigh, his tight features sinking into resignation. "The King's Council is in five days, and you will make every effort to manifest at least one of your powers before then. After the Council, you will focus on obtaining the rest and restoring the magic to Rivella. Then, and only then, will I allow you to return home with whatever compensation you desire."

My heart sank that he actually agreed to my idle threat. Once again, I had let that bitch hope taunt me with something I would never have.

"And if I fail? If I can't fix the ley lines or whatever?"

He glanced away. "You will not fail," he said softly. "We will do whatever is necessary to ensure your success."

I glared at him for a long moment until the sound of something breaking shattered the tense silence.

Across the table, Sin's hand dripped red, and shards of glass littered the table. He snatched a towel and wiped off the blood, the small gashes in his skin closing up within seconds.

Shoving back from the table, he said something to my father in Rivellan, then left. I frowned at his retreating form. What exactly did he have to be upset about?

"I take it I can be excused as well?" I asked bitterly.

My father waved a hand at me. "Yes, you may go. Deylan, you will be needed in my office when Apha Solis reaches its peak, so please work with Raynella on manifestation techniques in the meantime."

Dey nodded and pushed back from the table, gesturing for me to follow him.

I guess I would be the ever obedient little princess and go do whatever the intelligent males in charge told me to do. I tried not to throw up in my mouth. I might be the savior, but in reality, I was just a puppet, and they were all pulling my strings.

Come on, Rain, let's go dance for the nice people.

Dey held open the ornate diamond door, and a huge smile spread across my face as I entered the Sylvarium—it was just as wondrous as the first time I'd seen it. The crescia all flitted about, chittering softly, and two of them promptly landed in my hair. I laughed as they nuzzled my scalp.

Making my way further into the dazzling space, I appreciated how the glow from the early morning sun cascaded through the glass walls, giving everything within an ethereal glimmer.

I settled onto one of the benches in the center of the room and closed my eyes, enjoying the smell of flowers and the rhythmic beating of tiny wings all around me.

"Look," I said, refusing to open my eyes just yet. "I'm not stupid. I know you grew up in this world and were raised to believe humans are somehow less than. But being taught something as a child doesn't make it okay to continue the belief as an adult. Not when you should be able to think for yourself."

"Princess," he began, but I stopped him.

"Tell me the truth, Dey," I said, finally opening my eyes. "For once, ignore what you were taught, and think for yourself. If this all was just a huge mistake and I ended up being nothing more than completely human... would you still care about me?"

He didn't have to say a word because the answer was written all over his face.

"That's what I thought. So how about we just stick to the task at hand, and in a few weeks, you'll never have to see me again."

"I do not want you to leave, though," he protested. "I am sorry, Rain, I..."

"It doesn't matter," I said hastily, not wanting to hear anymore. "I wanted a lot of things in life that I'm never going to get, so right now I just want to focus on this."

I took a deep breath and forced myself to ignore that sore spot in my heart. Dey was never going to be the guy for me, and all of this made it so much easier to resist the attraction. He might not be as bad as the people in Civi Adasa that violently attacked me, but I was fairly certain he wouldn't have stopped it either if I was any other human.

"So, why did you bring me here? Not that I'm complaining, it's beautiful, but what does this have to do with awakening my magic?"

He looked like he wanted to say something more, but my body language must have told him it was a lost cause.

"There are a few different ways to awaken a Vitaean's power," he started. "Manifestation typically occurs between eighteen and twenty years of age, and—"

"Has anyone ever not manifested?" I interrupted.

"No, Princess," Dey said, seeming a bit shocked at the idea. "Our ability to access magic is a defining characteristic of who we are. Nothing short of forcing a Vitaean to live their entire life cut off from the Source could prevent manifestation."

"Like me?" I asked dryly.

"Yes, like you. That must have been torture." He tried to lay a comforting hand on my thigh, but I brushed it off.

"No, Dey, it really wasn't. You can't miss something you never even knew about." I huffed out an annoyed sigh. "Can we please get back on topic. What do I need to do to jumpstart this whole magic thing?"

"Yes, right, apologies," he stammered. "Since many families of lesser status rely on magic for their income, elemental casters are very desirable for a number of occupations, and it behooves them to gain access as soon as possible. It also gives the families more time to plan should their offspring's magic prove to be less... in demand."

"Yeah, heaven forbid your kid turned out to be just a lowly healer," I said sarcastically, hating the clinical way Dey spoke about people's lives.

"You are correct. Healers are less desirable given that most in Civi Adasa have their own healing power," Dey replied, clearly missing the sarcasm. "Yet it can still be a useful skill to those living in Civi Obsura."

I hadn't seen any of the town outside the high wall, but it was becoming apparent they basically considered it the slums. The place where they hid those with lesser magic so they wouldn't taint their perfect society. He had the gall to think this world was better than mine when, in reality, they were both fucked up.

"There are three circumstances that have been shown to be helpful in the past," Dey continued, oblivious of my frustration. "There is no guarantee any of these will work, but there has been enough recorded success to warrant an attempt. The first is extreme emotional and physical distress. Young Rivellans who suffer a truly traumatic event often manifest their power as a result."

"Almost dying yesterday was pretty fucking traumatic and nothing happened," I replied.

Of course my broken brain chose that moment to flash back to a different horrific experience—that night years ago when I'd been just a naïve teenager. I quickly stuffed that memory back into the recesses of my mind, though, refusing to go there just yet. "What are the other two?" I asked. Anything would be better than going back to that night.

"The second one I do not think you would be interested in entertaining. At least, not anymore."

There was a slight blush to his cheeks, and my lips popped open into a small 'o' as I realized what he was referring to. "You're talking about..."

"Yes, Rain. Intercourse has actually been proven the most effective of the three. So if you were planning to forgive me at any point in the near future..."

"I'm not," I interjected, cutting off his train of thought. Had he told me that bit of info twenty-four hours ago, I probably would have already been naked and riding him at a gallop if it meant I might get home faster. Now, when I searched for that small flare of heat low in my abdomen I'd felt every time I thought of Dey naked... there was nothing there. No heat, no desire. Just sadness that he wasn't the person I thought he was.

I cleared my throat, banishing the flash of melancholy. "So what is the third one?"

"As you know, most Vitaeans bond with a crescia after they manifest. While there are some unbonded crescia in the wild, residents of Civi Adasa are usually invited here to see if any of these will bond with them after they manifest. Waiting for a wild crescia could mean waiting years, if ever."

"And the people in Civi Obsura, do they get invited here?" I don't know why I asked. I already knew the answer.

He at least looked a little ashamed as he replied. "No, Princess. Only the best families of Civi Adasa have that privilege."

"Color me shocked." I sighed. "So if I need to manifest my power first, then why am I here? This seems like an after thing, not a before thing."

"I was getting to that point. On occasion, spending time with the crescia can be beneficial. They sense your potential and are drawn to it as I mentioned before. It has also been theorized they give off a pheromone that the magic inside you reacts to, rising to the surface to seek out your bonded."

I glanced around, noticing that nearly every crescia in the room had moved closer to us at some point. Most lingered in the branches just above where we sat.

"Okay, so basically I just hang out here? Wait to see if anything happens?"

"Yes, that is about the extent of it," he said, standing up. "I am due in King Verren's study shortly. I will let Sin know you are in here so he may fetch you when he is ready for your training."

Dey headed for the exit but paused before leaving. "I do hope we can be friends again, Princess," he said solemnly. "It would mean a great deal to me."

I lifted my head to respond, but the door had already closed behind him.

Could we be friends? He wasn't evil, I knew that much. He wasn't even as much of a jerk as Sin was. Yet every time I looked at him, I heard those same words over and over again—'humans are little more than savages.' I honestly didn't know if I could be his friend.

"He feels very sad."

"Holy shit!" I yelped, jumping up and scattering a cloud of crescia. I searched the room for the source of the voice even though it had felt like an echo inside my brain.

"I apologize. This is the only way I can speak to you. Please do not be upset."

The voice rolled through my head again, and I managed to contain my scream. It sounded innocent—not childlike, but soft and feminine—though it was still the most unsettling experience I had in the palace so far.

"If you don't want me to be upset, then why won't you show yourself?" I demanded, brushing aside the hanging vines to my right.

The leaves behind me rustled, and I whipped around to see a young woman with ginger curls tentatively emerge. It took me a second to register where I had seen her before. She was the only one at dinner who had been openly smiling at me.

"I remember you," I said when she cautiously approached.

Slight of frame and barely over five feet tall, she moved almost as if she were afraid that *she* would startle *me*. Her lavender short-sleeved dress showed off the tattoos swirling up the entire length of her arms, but they were different than the others I had seen, more delicate, with swirls that were more thin and spread out.

"My ramentum are different because both of my powers are mental based. I can both push my thoughts in as well as pull another's thoughts out. I am still a secunnario, though only just." She kept her expression completely neutral as she spoke inside my head.

"Okay, first, can you please stop doing that? The mind speaking thing is creepy. Second, how are you speaking English?"

Her eyes darted over my face, studying me. *"You have questions, but they are jumbled inside your head. You must focus if you want answers, Princess."*

She took a seat on the bench I had previously vacated, and I wondered if she even could talk out loud.

"I am somewhat able to speak aloud, but it would be difficult. And it would be in Rivellan. To be honest, I prefer this method of communication. Right now, I am connecting my mind to yours while projecting my thoughts and intentions. Your brain is interpreting those thoughts in English. Perhaps it would be helpful to think of it like I am sharing a very detailed image with you, along with the emotions that accompany it."

I nodded, settling onto the bench beside her. "So, when I speak English like this, you don't understand me?"

She traced her finger in the dust on the bench, drawing a stick figure. *"I hear the words,"* she replied, *"but they have no meaning. Your thoughts, however, I can pull from inside your head. At least when you are thinking clearly. Your mind is... very busy."*

She kept her eyes focused on her doodles, and I wondered if it was for my own comfort since her vacant staring had unsettled me. "Okay you're kind of freaking me out here. Does this mean you can just read my mind anytime?" If she could, I doubted she would like what she found. My brain was not a happy place.

She added a second figure to her drawing. *"Only when you are projecting. If you do not want me to hear you, you need only wish it so."*

"But you said earlier that Dey was sad. How did you pick that up?"

"He was projecting; he just didn't realize it. When a Vitaean is experiencing strong emotions, I can pick up on them with little effort. The message is not detailed or clear, but I can sense what they are feeling. Deylan was experiencing a great deal of sadness as he left you."

I didn't want to know that he was suffering because of me when it wouldn't change anything. He still hated humans.

"So what's your name? I can't just keep thinking of you as the red-headed female."

She smiled. *"My name is Josira. You may call me Jo, if you wish."*

"Well, it's nice to meet you, Jo. It's been all testosterone since I arrived, and not a single one of them has any concept of proper footwear." I gestured to my Chucks that looked wildly out of place against the black breeches and oversized pale yellow tunic. "They tried to give me boots with a two-inch heel. Like I'm going to walk around all day in uncomfortable shoes. Hard pass."

I glanced down at Jo's feet. Peeking out from under her dress were a pair of slim, feminine boots much like the ones Dey had offered me.

She giggled at the embarrassment on my face. *"You become used to them over time. Perhaps we can go shopping and find you better ones?"*

I scuffed my shoe in the dirt. "Yeah, I don't think that's a good idea. I kind of almost died last time I went into town."

She frowned. *"Yes, we all heard about that. Perhaps another time, then. After you have been introduced at the King's Council."*

I really didn't need any reminders about that. I was still uneasy about mingling with the people who tried to kill me yesterday. Knowing I was the king's daughter didn't change the hatred that lived in these people's hearts.

"You should give them a chance," Jo said. *"People only know what they are taught. It takes someone new with new ideas to help them grow and evolve. You could be that person."*

I sighed. "Honestly, I'm not going to be here long enough to try to change the Rivellans. I told my father I'd separate the ley lines, and then I'm going home. I'm not the kind of person who changes the world, Jo. I'm just trying to survive as best I can."

She scrutinized me for an uncomfortable amount of time before the cool breeze of her words flowed into my mind. *"It does not matter what I think you are capable of. You must choose on your own to be more than what life has offered you. I can feel what is in your heart, Raynella. You want to be more."*

"Call me Rain," I said, not wanting to even address the rest of what she said. People around here really needed to stop thinking so highly of me.

Beside me, Jo stiffened. *"You have company coming."*

Sure enough, Sin barreled through the door seconds later. He scanned the room, and once his eyes came to rest on me, he made a beeline in my direction.

"There you are," he barked out. "Dey said you'd be in here. I gotta say—" He faltered when Jo brushed aside a cluster of hanging ivy, making her presence known.

I rolled my eyes at his abrasive entrance. "Hello, Sin. Nice to see you too. I hope you had a lovely morning. I'm sure you've met Jo."

"Yes," he gritted out. "I have."

He didn't elaborate, but I heard Jo's voice inside my head. *"I must go, Rain. Sin needs you. Will I see you at dinner this evening?"*

"Yeah, I'll be there," I said as she stood to leave. "And thanks for the offer to go shopping. I hope we get the chance to do that someday."

She gave me a wink and exited through the diamond doors.

I glanced back to the bench, to her drawing. I scanned the two crude yet obviously female stick figures holding hands—one with long hair and one with short curls—and smiled.

Turning back to Sin, I said, "Okay, let's go train. Any chance you're planning to help me this time? Not just laugh at how weak I am?"

He smirked. "What can I say? The truth hurts. You are weak, and nothing I do will change that." He spun on his heels and headed out of the Sylvarium, leaving me behind.

I quickly untangled the two crescia that had been lounging in my hair, ignoring their sad keening chirps as I placed them on the bench and tried to reign in my anger at Sin's barb. Though I wasn't sure why it even mattered to me if he thought I was useless. Sin and I were never going to be friends, so why bother trying?

That logic still didn't stop me from chasing after him, though, determined to set the record straight.

Chapter Twenty-Two

"Hey!" I shouted when I caught up with Sin.

He ignored me and hooked a left down a dimly lit hallway, not pausing until he reached the door at the end.

"What?" he snapped, finally acknowledging me.

"Do you have to be so rude?" I panted, out of breath from chasing after him. "It's not like I signed up for any of this."

He folded his arms over his broad chest, the movement pulling his black tunic even tighter. "You agreed to fulfill the prophecy, didn't you? Kind of sounds like signing up if you ask me, Fea Remia."

"Stop calling me that," I demanded, pushing my wild hair out of my face in frustration. "My name is Rain. Not Raynella. Not princess. Not princepa. And definitely not whatever the hell 'Fea Remia' is. Why is it so fucking hard for people here to get that? And for the record, you guys brought me here against my will and basically forced my hand with all this prophecy crap. So back. The fuck. Off." I jabbed his chest hard on the last words to ensure I got my point across. His boorish behavior was getting really old, really fast.

His scathing glare bounced right off me as I waited for him to decide on whatever snarky comeback he'd go with this time. He must have been tired, though, because he just yanked the door open and disappeared down a wide staircase that led into a suffocating, inky darkness.

I only hesitated a moment before plunging in after him.

Once we hit the bottom of the stairs, flickering wall sconces every few yards illuminated the space, and I could make out an old tunnel with a mild downward slope.

"Where are we?" I asked.

"This leads to the arena," he replied without stopping. "You slipped on several steps yesterday, so I figured you'd prefer this route. If you're scared of a few cobwebs, we can always turn around."

I didn't know which surprised me more. That he noticed my struggles, or that he even cared enough to go a different way.

"No," I said quickly. "This is better." I watched his retreating back for a second, then raced after him. "Thanks," I said, matching his stride as best I could. "I appreciate it."

Sin scoffed. "Don't go thinking any pretty thoughts about me, Fea Remia. I'm still the same asshole."

I groaned internally. It felt like every time he did something nice, he had to immediately act like a jerk to counteract it. I just wished he would pick a personality and stick with it.

I nearly crashed into Sin's back when I entered the weapons room and found him standing just inside, unmoving. He snarled something in Rivellan, then rushed over to a rack of weapons at the back wall. The assortment of plain swords hung in their usual place, but it was the empty wall mount above them that Sin was staring at.

"Examenti!" he cursed, whipping his head around to scan the room frantically.

I took a step back. "Um, what's wrong?" I asked innocently.

"My sword is missing," he growled, kicking a rack of maces and sending them scattering across the floor.

I jumped back before one of the pointy weapons hit my foot.

"Sorry," he bit out, running a hand angrily through his hair. "I just need to find it. It was supposed to be cleaned yesterday, and I assumed the soldier would leave it here after."

Panic contorted his face in an all too familiar expression, and an arrow of guilt struck me hard. I had thought it would be funny stealing his sword. I'd watch as he got all red-faced and grumbly, maybe stomp around a bit. But this? He seemed genuinely worried, and I didn't like it as much as I thought I would.

"It's probably still being cleaned," I suggested.

"No, if that were the case, then it would be here." He pointed at a cabinet in the corner of the room. "That's where we keep all the supplies. I should have made sure it was returned last night, but I was..."

His voice cut off, and I filled in the blank. Distracted. He was distracted because of me.

"Maybe they left it in your room? I'm sure it'll turn up. Plus we don't need swords anyway. I was thinking we could focus on self-defense today."

"No," he muttered, brushing past me as he headed for the exit. "I need to find it now. Training can wait."

I saw my opportunity to actually learn anything slipping away, and before I could stop myself, I blurted out, "Sin, wait. I might know where it is."

Every muscle in his body went rigid, and slower than I had ever seen him move, he turned around.

"What did you say?" he asked, his face scarily neutral.

I gulped. I had wanted this, to punish him for thinking he could push me around. I couldn't show weakness.

"Nothing," I said coyly, pretending to examine a shelf of wicked-looking daggers.

"Rain..." he warned, and I could see him out of the corner of my eye moving closer, like a tiger stalking its prey.

I couldn't help the sharp laugh that escaped. "Now you use my name? I didn't know all it took was your toy going missing to knock some sense into you."

He didn't stop his forward progression. "Where is my sword," he demanded in a low tone that promised violence, pain, and other dark things I shouldn't be thinking about.

I wiped every trace of emotion from my face and tossed my messy hair behind my shoulder. "How would I know? I can barely lift it, remember?"

Apparently that was the wrong thing to say.

He surged forward, pressing me back into the shelf of knives with his hands braced against the wood structure on either side of my face.

And now I was now trapped in a cage with the tiger.

His eyes scanned mine, and he smiled. "You're scared of me, Fea Remia," he accused, his voice low and gravelly. "And you should be. Now tell me where my sword is before I prove to you just how much of a monster I can be."

I gulped as his turbulent ocean scent washed over me. Sin was dangerous, and right now, I was the object of his rage. I should just tell him where it was and pray he decided not to take it out on me.

I couldn't bring myself to say the words, though. I didn't want him to let me out of the cage. I wanted to keep the tiger angry. I wanted to keep him pacing and snarling. I wanted to see what he might do, how far he would go, because I honestly believed he wouldn't hurt me. Not really.

But then again, maybe that was what every victim thought just before they died—that the wild beast could surely be tamed.

"And what happens if I don't tell you?" I asked, keeping my voice level, not willing to show him any of the fear I felt racing through my body. Fear and... something else.

I allowed myself to breathe him in deeply, and his eyes flared as I did so. Arousal stronger than I ever expected to feel for this male filled me, the heated pulse in my lower abdomen catching me so off guard that my knees wobbled. It might be twisted, but right then, I didn't want Sin to fight off his urge to hurt me.

Maybe there was something wrong with me. Scratch that, of course there was something wrong with me, but it didn't stop the surge of desire I felt. I wanted to fall prey to his violence and passion, because I knew if he let go, it would be all consuming. I wanted to feel that kind of intensity, if only once before he decided to hate me again.

Without thinking, I closed the gap between us and pressed my lips against his.

My entire body lit up at the contact, the slight roughness from his stubble more delicious than I imagined.

Sin tensed, and for a second, I thought he would push me away, curse my name, and storm off.

He didn't do any of those things.

Before I even knew what was happening, his hands were off the shelf and wrapped around my waist, drawing me to his chest. A slight groan slipped out of him, and he finally unleashed every bit of that passion I had hoped for, deepening the kiss to the point I could barely remember my own name.

I melted in his arms as one of his hands snaked upward into my hair, clutching my loose strands tightly, while the other moved low to grab my ass and mold our bodies even closer together. If I had any reservations about his desire, they disappeared the moment his hard length pressed into my stomach.

I met his fervor with my own, prodding my tongue at the seam of his lips. He opened to me, and I moaned softly into his mouth, desperate to taste him fully.

Daggers fell to the ground around us when his intensity pushed me harder into the shelf, and I cried out when one of the remaining knives lodged itself in my shoulder blade.

The pain of the physical wound was nothing compared to the agony of Sin releasing me and turning away. My body mourned the loss of his heat and that exquisite pressure.

I stood there panting, breathlessly waiting for him to say something. Preferably he would say nothing, and instead take me back into his arms. It was stupid to kiss him, but that didn't mean I wanted to stop. I had a taste of his violence, and I wanted more.

"Are you hurt?" he asked, refusing to even look back at me.

I reached behind my shoulder and saw the blood on my hand when I pulled it away. It wasn't much, but enough to warrant a bandage.

"I'm fine. Just a flesh wound," I joked. If he got the reference it didn't show.

"You should have Dey heal you," he mumbled.

"I don't want Dey to heal me."

I wanted him to look at me. I wanted to know what he was thinking.

"He's very skilled, and it won't scar if he does it," Sin continued, still ignoring me.

"I said that I don't want Dey," I reiterated.

"I doubt you know what you want these days, Fea Remia." Any softness in his voice was gone. He turned to look at me then, and there was no emotion, no passion in his eyes. Just the cold hard reality that he didn't want anything to do with me.

"Maybe I'm not the one who doesn't know what they want, Sin," I replied, proud of the unwavering strength in my voice.

He took a step toward me and growled something in Rivellan. But right as I was hoping he would grab me and we could pick up where we left off, his face closed off again.

"Get someone to heal that wound and bring my sword back here within the hour or there won't be any training today," he said, his voice tight.

"Fine," I snapped, heading toward the door.

"And Rain?" he called out behind me.

"What?" I asked, whipping back around and smacking myself in the face with my unruly hair, losing any sense of the upper hand in the situation.

Sin stared at me for a moment, his stone cold eyes a contrast to my fiery ones. "Don't ever do that again."

I ground my teeth together at his statement. I had gotten my wish to feel Sin's intensity, but it clearly came at a price.

If he wanted to pretend he didn't feel anything, I could do the same. "Not a problem," I tossed out as I stormed off to find a healer for my shoulder.

The wound to my pride, however, would not be so easy to fix.

Chapter Twenty-Three

It wasn't until I emerged from the tunnel back inside the castle that I realized I couldn't go looking for Dey to heal me. He was with my father, and the last thing I wanted to do was tell them how I ended up with the wound. I doubted either would believe me if I said I bumped into a shelf of daggers.

So I went in search of the only two people I could trust. Thankfully, I ran into Cam right outside the castle.

"Princess!" he shouted, rushing over. Before I could stop him, he threw his arms around me for a quick hug. "Wait, what is this?" He pulled his hand back to look at the blood coating it, and his eyes widened.

"Yeah, about that... I was coming to find you or Ram. I was hoping you could help."

"Of course. Come, sit," he said, leading me over to a bench. "Ram is somewhat better at healing than I am, but he is on the king's guard duty today. Let me see if I can help, though." He shifted around to look at my back, then cleared his throat. "Apologies, Princess. I need access to the wound, and your... well, your tunic is in the way."

I glanced over my shoulder, and I could have sworn I saw a blush on Cam's dark skin. "Can't you work around it?" I pleaded. "Dey was able to heal me with my clothes on when I almost died."

"Dey is a much stronger healer, Princess. I would be happy to fetch him for you." Cam took a step toward the castle, but I grabbed his hand.

"Wait. It's fine. I don't want to see Dey right now." I chewed on my options. "Can you just cut the tunic a little?"

"I can try." He unsheathed a dagger from his belt, and I felt a gentle tug as he sliced through the fabric.

I clenched my teeth when several stuck fibers pulled free of the wound, but a soothing warmth seeped into my shoulder blade, and the pain receded almost instantaneously. I slumped forward, exhausted from holding my body tight for so long. "Thanks, Cam. You're a lifesaver."

He held out a hand for me. "The blood still needs to be cleaned off, and I have a short break before I must report back to guard duty. If you want to come down to the cottage, I can assist you."

I took his hand and stood slowly, twisting my back around a bit to test how everything felt. No pain. No stiffness. It was like it never happened.

Perfect. Now if I can just get cleaned up before anyone sees me, I might get out of this whole nightmare with a shred of dignity intact.

"Sounds great," I told him. "Thanks."

We made our way into the orchard, and Cam managed to stay quiet for all of thirty seconds. "I do not mean to pry, but are you going to tell me what happened?"

I sighed. "Sin happened."

Cam stopped abruptly. "Sin harmed you?"

I briefly contemplated the safest explanation. "Not exactly. It was mostly my fault."

"I see. Because you stabbed yourself in the back?" he asked suspiciously.

"Yeah, something like that. Can we just drop it? I need to get cleaned up, grab Sin's sword, and get back to the arena within an hour. So I sort of need to hurry."

With a short nod of acceptance, Cam held the door open for me, and I stepped into his cottage. Rather than the two bedroom home I had expected, the interior was all one spacious open area with four sturdy pillars in the center and two single beds flanked by small wardrobes off to the right. There was a brick hearth on the back wall with a bulky cooking pot in front of it and smaller pots stacked messily to one side. A table sat off to the left of the room with a few cabinets behind it along with two metal chests.

It would have been one of the cutest cabins I'd ever seen if it weren't for the assortment of dirty clothes, boots, weapons, and books that covered every surface in the room. Definitely a bachelor pad.

Cam walked over to the cabinet by the table and pulled out a pitcher of water, a small basin, and a handful of towels.

"Over here," he said, gesturing for me to take a seat at the table. "We do not have hot running water, so this might be a little cold." He paused. "You will need to remove your tunic."

I cursed myself for assuming he would have a shower. I trusted Cam, and yet...

"I can offer you a blanket to cover yourself," he added at my hesitation. "My only intentions are to clean your wound, Princess."

"It's not that. It's... Just promise you won't say anything."

Cam frowned. "Say anything about what?"

"My back. Just don't say anything at all. To anyone."

He placed a hand across his chest solemnly. "I would never betray your confidence, Princess."

Resigning myself to the inevitable, I took a seat in the chair facing away from him and pulled off my tunic.

There was no mistaking his choking noise for anything other than dismay. I should be used to it by now, but the reminder still hurt every time.

Thankfully, he kept quiet as he poured water into the tub and wet the cloth. He ran it over my skin, and I suppressed a shiver at the cool touch.

The silence started to eat at me as I waited awkwardly while he cleaned up my back "So, don't take this the wrong way, but it's a little weird talking to you without Ram around. I feel like you guys should have teased me at least four or five times by now."

Cam let out a sardonic laugh. "My brother certainly likes to find the fun in life. It can be very infectious at times. When I am alone, though, I am a bit more reserved, I suppose."

I thought back to the few times I'd spent with them. He wasn't wrong. Ram was definitely more outgoing, but Cam was an idiot if he thought he wasn't also amazing. "Well, I think you're both great," I said, wishing I could erase the hint of sadness I'd heard in his voice. Jenn had always been the fun one between the two of us, and I knew the kind of low-level resentment that could build from that.

He tossed the bloody rag on the table when he was done, and I cringed at how much red was on it. I knew the dagger was sharp, but it hadn't felt that painful at the time. I guess I'd been more lost in the feeling of Sin's body pressed against mine than I realized.

"Are you all right, Princess?" Cam asked.

"Yeah, I'm fine," I said, popping out of the chair. "Just didn't realize the cut was that deep."

"It was likely a fenite dagger, then. It is the same metal that Sin's sword is made of." He hesitated, then added quietly, "It is the same metal they used for the Sonaria."

I shuddered, thinking back to the awful feeling that had slithered under my skin when I'd been near the dungeons. If fenite slowed healing, no wonder the small jab bled so much.

"I should probably get going," I said, breaking the uncomfortable silence. "I need to drag that sword back to the arena before Sin freaks out again. Any chance you have a shirt I could borrow? Preferably a non-bloody one?"

Cam chuckled. "Yes. I think I can find something for you."

He pulled a tan tunic from the wardrobe on the right and handed it to me. It was practically a dress with how big it was, but at least I wouldn't be making a scene wandering through the castle in my bra.

"Thanks," I said, heading to the front door with Cam close behind me.

"I will escort you back to the castle, Princess. I am due to relieve Ram soon."

We left the small cottage behind and made our way back to the front entrance. When we hit the glittering courtyard, Cam gestured to the left. "I need to go this way. Take care of yourself, Princess. Do not let Sin push you around. As they say in your world, he is all bark and no bite."

Images of the kiss flashed through my mind, the rough way he pushed me against the rack of daggers.

"He definitely has bite," I muttered under my breath as I left Cam and headed off to collect Sin's sword.

"Here's your damn weapon," I huffed, tossing the heavy sword at Sin's feet.

He looked up from where he lounged on a bench in the arena, the picture of calm and collected with his legs crossed and his arms folded behind his head.

"Why do you even have a fenite sword?" I demanded.

"It was a gift."

"And?" I pressed, refusing to give up. There was no way he actually fought with that thing just because it was a gift.

"And it is very useful in battle," he replied. "I have become somewhat desensitized to the painful effects of fenite over the years."

It was honestly more than I expected him to share, and I seized the chance to keep him talking.

"Have you fought in a lot of wars?" I asked, regretting the question the moment I started imagining Sin shirtless on a battlefield, his chest gleaming with sweat as he cut down his enemies.

"Just the one," he said simply, getting to his feet. "And no, I'm not going to talk about it."

"Fine. Can we talk about what happened earlier, then?" I asked, attempting to provoke some kind of response. I hated this new cold Sin. I hadn't even realized how much I had enjoyed bickering with him.

"No," he replied firmly.

"No?"

"No."

"And I don't get a say?"

"No," he reiterated, turning back toward the hallway that surrounded the arena.

"So that's it?" I shouted to his retreating back, equal parts annoyed and disappointed. "We pretend like nothing happened except now you keep to one word sentences? Look, it was a stupid mistake, and you were just reacting in the moment. You've made it very clear you don't *feel* anything for me, and I'm fine with that. So can we just go back to normal?"

Sin paused at a door, and I hurried up behind him. Glancing over his shoulder, I saw a room full of metal bars and round balls of increasing size that filled the racks throughout the room.

A weight-lifting gym, then. Lovely.

"You'll start in here to build up your muscles," he said, still refusing to face me. "Start by lifting the smallest ones. When you're done, run ten laps around the arena for stamina. Get some food afterward, then come find me in the barracks at the back of the castle."

He turned to leave, but I caught his arm, refusing to let him walk away. "Sin, you said you were actually going to train me today."

"I can't train you when you're this weak," he stated, all of the earlier passion missing from his hard face. "Anything I teach you would likely just get you killed in the forest if you attempted it. You're better off trying to improve your overall strength and endurance for now."

He yanked his arm out of my grip and headed toward the stairs. He hesitated at the base of the first step, then reached into his pocket and tossed me a thin black cord. "To keep your hair out of your eyes."

He was gone before I could even say thank you.

I clutched the small bit of leather in my hand and leaned back against the wall. I hadn't thought he noticed or even cared that I was struggling with my unbound hair. Was this just Cennux Dreisin following best practices for training, or something else?

Frustrated, I twisted my hair into a messy braid, then dragged the smallest weight I could find over to a bench. Maybe I was trying to see something in Sin that just wasn't there. I'd been sleepwalking through life for so long, of course I'd be drawn to someone who was intensely alive. Didn't mean he felt the same.

Still, I'd do what he asked on the off chance it might fix things between us. At the end of the day, I needed him if I wanted to learn anything useful.

I struggled my way through a couple bicep curls, but even the lowest weight was almost more than my pitiful arms could handle. Sighing, I dropping the hunk of metal to the floor with a thud.

Maybe Sin was right. Maybe this was all just a huge waste of time.

I lifted weights for as long as I could, then started on my laps. I made it less than one loop before I was huffing and puffing, but it was a start at least.

Dragging my ass back to the castle, I decided to skip lunch in lieu of an obscenely long shower. I felt a little bad about all the magic being used, but I couldn't resist lingering under the hot spray, enjoying how the heat poured over my skin. Back home, I always had to rush my showers in order to keep the water bill low.

Clean once more, I collapsed onto the bed, not even caring that my wet hair was soaking my pillow. I just needed a short rest, and then I'd go see what pointless plans Sin had for the afternoon.

I must have dozed off, because the next thing I registered was soft hands caressing my back, and fingers running through my long hair. The ministrations felt heavenly, and I snuggled deeper into the blankets, content to enjoy the delightful dream.

My eyes popped open as reality crashed into me. Kiahna and Niahna pulled their hands away when I shot up in bed.

"Shit!" I swore, rushing to the window. Sure enough, both suns were on their descent. I slept the entire afternoon away, and Sin was going to kill me.

I sank back onto the bed, and Kiahna began brushing my hair again as Niahna selected a purple sleeveless dress with blue paneling from the oversized wardrobe.

I was debating abandoning the sisters so I could go find Sin to apologize when Dey rapped his knuckles on my door and stepped inside. He spoke to the females in Rivellan, and whatever he told them had Kiahna setting the hairbrush down before briskly exiting the room alongside Niahna.

"Princess, I wanted to talk to you," he said, lowering himself onto my bed a fair distance away from me. "I know what happened today. I do not need all the details, but I do have one question."

"Uh, ok," I replied, completely clueless as to why he was so solemn.

He straightened his tunic, steadying himself, then asked, "Do you love him?"

The gears in my brain came to a grinding halt for almost an entire minute as I processed his question. "What? No!" I sputtered. How did he even hear about me and Sin?

"It is okay if you do," Dey said wearily, folding his hands in his lap. "I know that I have not proven myself worthy of you."

I jumped up, staring at him in disbelief. "Dey, I have no clue where you got this idea that I'm in love with him, but it was one kiss. And it was a huge mistake."

Pain swam in Dey's amber eyes. "You do not need to spare me. I know it was much more than a kiss. I only hope that you and Cam are happy together."

"Wait, what?" I took a step back. "Did you say Cam? You think I slept with Cam?"

Dey's face crinkled in confusion. "Of course. Who else would I be talking about?"

"I thought you meant Sin!"

"Sin?!" Dey leapt to his feet, eyes blazing. "You slept with Sin?"

"No!" I threw up my hands in exasperation. "I didn't sleep with anyone."

"Then why did a servant tell me they saw Cam sneak you into his cottage, and you were wearing his tunic when you left?"

"Oh, for fuck's sake," I swore. "Everyone in this damn castle needs to mind their own fucking business." I took a deep breath, trying to reign in my frustration. "I got injured earlier in the weapons room. Sin said he wasn't a very good healer, so I found Cam. We only went to his cottage to clean off the blood, and I borrowed his tunic for the walk back to my room. That's all."

"You did not have sex with Cam?" Dey asked, cautious optimism on his face.

"No! I adore Cam, but it's not like that."

Dey collapsed onto the bed, his entire body sagging with relief.

I perched on the edge of my dresser, crossing my arms. "It wouldn't matter if I had, though. You don't have any claim over me."

"I know that, Princess," he replied softly. "But I can still hope that will change someday."

I grabbed the discarded brush and began raking it through my tangles. "I don't know if that will happen, Dey. It's hard enough for me to even consider being friends with you right now given your opinion on humans."

He leaned forward eagerly. "So teach me. Explain to me why you believe humans are worth defending so vigorously."

I continued to fight with the rat's nest on my head and thought about what Jo said earlier. That I should give them a chance. I didn't know about the whole of Rivella, but I guess I could give Dey a shot. "Okay. We can start over." A smile blossomed across his face, and I quickly clarified, "As friends."

Dey grinned and pushed to his feet. "In that case, I will leave you to prepare for dinner. Perhaps this evening I might escort you?"

"Sure," I agreed. "Why not?"

He stepped toward the door but halted abruptly and turned back around. "Princess..." he began, his eyes narrowing. "What exactly happened with Sin that had you assuming I was referring to him earlier?"

Crap. I really wished he had forgotten about that.

Focusing intently on a particularly nasty tangle in my hair, I said, "Ummm... Sin and I sort of... kissed. In the weapons room."

The stony silence was a palpable weight in the air, and then my door swung open violently, slamming into the opposite wall. I looked up in time to see Dey disappear.

"Shit," I cursed, leaping to my feet to run after him.

Dey must have the speed of a cheetah, though, because he was already at Sin's room before I was halfway down the hall.

"Dreisin!" he shouted, pounding heavily on the door. He rattled the knob, and when it didn't open, I thought he might yank the door right off the hinges.

I had never seen this side of him. This was bad. This was very, very bad.

The door flew open just as I arrived behind Dey. Sin stood there, freshly showered and pulling on his long black tunic. He barked something in Rivellan at Dey, and to my horror, Dey responded by punching him squarely in the face.

Sin went down hard, and Dey barreled into the room before I could stop him.

"Dey!" I screeched. "What the hell are you doing?" I lunged forward, but he kicked the door shut behind him, and I heard the loud thunk of a lock slamming into place.

Oh, God. They were going to kill each other, and I couldn't do a thing to stop it.

I pressed an ear to the door, straining to hear Sin and Dey as they shouted at each other in Rivellan. After a second, the words cut off, and I could only make out the sound of fists contacting flesh. I winced when a loud crash thundered inside the room.

Banging on the door frantically, I screamed, "Dey! Sin! Stop this!" A pained cry rang out from the room, and I was pretty sure it was Dey that time.

I kicked at the door, but it barely moved under my feeble attempt. A feeling of guilt and worthlessness swept over me, and my knees shook under the weight of it. I braced a hand on the wall, but the overwhelming anxiety left me gasping for air and dropped me hard onto the stone floor. The impact barely registered, though, as I struggled to take in even a single breath. Panic crushed my lungs in a vice grip I was helpless to break through. I tried to cry out again, to beg them to stop, but the words wouldn't come.

I never should have told Dey about the kiss. Hell, I never should have kissed Sin to begin with. They were hurting each other, maybe killing each other, and it was all my fault.

My fault. My fault. My fault.

I slumped against the door as the words ricocheted through my brain, growing louder and louder until they were screaming inside my skull.

"Please," I croaked out weakly. My entire body strained as my lungs spasmed with sharp inhales, unable to pull the oxygen any farther than my lips. "I'm begging you," I wheezed. "Please stop fighting."

The noises inside the room ceased as a familiar cloud of black started to roll over my vision. Someone yanked the door open, and I fell backward, my head slamming into the floor.

I barely recognized the two males hovering above me. A nasty gash over Sin's now swollen left eye dripped blood down the side of his face, and his jaw looked awkwardly out of place. Shredded strips of Dey's tunic were all that remained, and a dagger-sized chunk of wood stuck out of his chest.

Both males dropped to the floor at my side, but Sin grabbed me first, hauling my slack body into his lap. Dey reached for my arms to pull me over to him, and Sin curbed the action with a harsh word in Rivellan.

"What is wrong, Princess?" Dey asked, yanking the wooden shard from his chest.

"She's having a damn panic attack," Sin stated as if it was painfully obvious. "She doesn't have her medication."

I briefly wondered how he even knew about my pills, but then Dey's hands cupped my face, and my entire field of vision was filled with him.

"Let me help you," he pleaded. "Just like last time. I can fix you."

"She's not broken," Sin argued. "She just needs to work through it."

"No, she needs me to help her."

"Keep your grubby powers out of her brain!" Sin shouted, his outrage echoing loudly through the hall. "She doesn't need you messing with her head."

"And she does need you?" The thinly-veiled threat underneath his words hung in the air as I struggled to regain control of my breathing.

Sin's response was in their language, and whatever he said caused Dey to press pause on his anger. Eventually, he bit out a single Rivellan word.

The floor dropped away as I was lifted up and cradled against Sin's chest. Instinctively, I wrapped my arms around his neck. He still smelled like the ocean, but underneath it was the coppery tang of fresh blood. Tilting my face to look at him, I watched as the gash over his eye sealed itself up, the swelling visibly dissipating.

Guilt was plastered across his face as he whispered, "Breathe, Fea Remia. Just focus on your breathing. In and out. You can do it."

I closed my eyes, trying to do as he said, but I couldn't force the air down.

My body jostled in his arms slightly as we ascended a flight of stairs. More than one by the feel of it.

A gentle breeze hit my face, and my eyes shot open. We were outside, on top of one of the turrets, and the sky was on fire with clouds blazing orange, red, and purple. I took in a sharp inhale at the striking sunset, and to my surprise, the oxygen filled my lungs.

Sin carefully set me on my feet but maintained his hold around my arms, keeping me steady as my legs continued to shake.

He rotated me slowly, and the ocean came into view. The mist glowed with the flaming light of the setting suns in a glorious display of exploding color. A breeze ruffled through my hair, and I couldn't tell if I was scenting Sin or the actual ocean. I didn't care either way. The smell of fresh salty air surrounded me, and the tightness in my chest began to ebb, my heartbeat slowing to a reasonable pace.

I noticed Sin staring at me cautiously, as if afraid I might shatter in his arms. I took another deep breath, relishing the cool air as it coated my lungs, and hazarded a smile at him.

He smiled back, the first genuine expression of joy I had seen on his face, and I did shatter then. Every ounce of anger and frustration I felt toward him burst into countless glittering shards, and I knew I would do anything he asked—run a million miles or lift a thousand pounds of weight—if it meant he would keep looking at me like that.

A cough sounded over his shoulder, and the smile dropped away as storm clouds rolled over his face once again.

I untangled myself from his arms, my legs steady enough to stand on their own, and glanced over to see Dey glaring at Sin from against the wall of the turret, his arms crossed, muscles still tight with anger.

Sin gave me one last lingering look, then left down the stairs, muttering something in Rivellan to Dey as he passed.

Approaching cautiously, I placed my hand over Dey's chest where a rip in his blood-stained tunic was the only remaining evidence of the injury.

"You're healed," I said quietly, not ready to meet his eyes yet.

"Yes," he replied, his arms relaxing to his sides. "I am a fast healer. That was not our first fight, nor will it be the last."

"But it was the first fight you had over me." I forced myself to meet the pained expression on his face. "I don't belong to either of you, Dey. I'm not staying here longer than a few more weeks. You shouldn't be hurting each other because of me."

"I know, Princess," he said, caressing my shoulders. "I know that you are not mine. Sin told me he kissed you in the heat of the moment, and it was a huge mistake, but the thought of his lips on yours..." Dey swallowed roughly. "Sin is not who you think he is. And he had no right to touch you."

My mouth opened to correct him. To tell him that I kissed Sin, not the other way around. Before I could get anything out, Dey put two fingers to my lips.

"You do not need to apologize," he said, misreading my thoughts. "I should not have reacted in such a way. I am displeased you saw me like that. I do still hope I can be better for you."

We stayed like that for a few seconds, and then he pulled back and straightened. "Stay up here as long as you like. The setting suns are quite magnificent. I will have the servants bring dinner to your chambers. King Verren will understand."

He placed a chaste kiss on my forehead, then headed back down the stairs.

I don't know how long I stayed there, staring out over the calm blue waters of the ocean. I imagined hopping on one of the small boats and disappearing into the mist, leaving all of my troubles behind me.

It would be pointless to escape, though.

Not even the suffocating fog that hovered just beyond the bay would be enough to save me from myself.

Chapter Twenty-Four

I was surprised to see neither Sin nor Dey at breakfast the next morning, but at the same time, I was grateful for the brief reprieve. I had no idea what I was going to say to Sin after last night. Every thought I had about him was jumbled up with mixed signals and confusion. One minute he was a colossal asshole, and the next he was saving me. One minute he's kissing me with a blazing passion, and the next he's telling Dey that it was a huge mistake. Though, I might be partially to blame for that one. I did tell Sin I thought it was a mistake first, if only out of self-preservation.

I still didn't know if it actually was a mistake. All the same reasons I never went there with Dey applied to Sin as well, and yet... my resistance for Sin was so much weaker. Now every time I saw him, I'd be thinking of how his body had felt wrapped around mine, how his lips had burned against my own. I wanted to feel that again, to feel more even, and that was a problem I didn't know how to solve.

"Are you well this morning, Raynella?" my father asked, taking his seat at the table. I hadn't seen him since we made the deal yesterday, and I would be content with avoiding him as much as possible. He made it clear all he wanted from me was to fulfill the prophecy, and I could do without the fake fatherly concern in the meantime. Or maybe the concern wasn't fake—I was important to his kingdom after all—it just wasn't fatherly.

"I'm fine," I said curtly, focusing on the plate of food being set in front of me.

"Raynella, you do know that you can talk to me if you are distressed," he said, dismissing the servants with a wave. "I am aware of everything that happened yesterday. There is little in this castle that I am not informed about."

I almost choked on the pastry I bit into. The rumors about Cam and I were bad enough, but knowing he likely heard about the kiss as well? That was a topic I had even less desire to discuss with my so-called father.

"If you know everything, then you know I'm fine," I said before taking a sip of kinna juice to clear my throat.

"Yes, well, you do seem to be in good health this morning. I suppose the events of yesterday can be left in the past where they belong."

I had no idea exactly which events he was referring to—the kiss, the rumors, the fight, or the panic attack—but I was more than happy to let all the subjects drop. "Where are Dey and Sin?" I asked casually.

He steepled his hands under his chin. "Ah, yes. My Cennux and my Foster. They do seem to be at the forefront of your thoughts these days."

His tone indicated he had a strong opinion about that, but I couldn't quite determine what that opinion was.

"Deylan is in the city overseeing preparations today, and I have decided to heed Cennux Dreisin's advice in regard to your time with him. He was correct. Training you for combat is an exercise in futility given our short amount of time and your current lack of physical prowess. So you will not be training with him any longer. I trust my soldiers to get you through the forest safely without you needing to engage."

I dropped my fork. Was he kidding? First my lessons with the twins and now this? He was the one who said I needed all this training and education to begin with.

"Then what am I supposed to do all day?"

"That is entirely up to you, Raynella. Though I would advise you to keep your distance from Cennux Dreisin. The Elemental Games are in four days, and while I have little doubt that he will be one of the champions, I have asked him to spend the next few days honing his skills. He does not need any... distractions."

The pointed look he gave me confirmed that not only did he know about the kiss, but also the ensuing brawl.

I shoved my plate away, no longer hungry. "Great, so I'm stuck here in the palace with no TV because it doesn't exist in this world, no books because they're all in a language I don't understand, and now I can't even work out with Sin?"

I snorted. Not being able to go to the gym was something I never thought I would be upset about.

"I am sorry my kingdom has proven to be such a disappointment to you, Raynella," he said with a heavy sigh. There wasn't even a hint of sarcasm to his words, and it sounded like he was genuinely sad about the fact.

"Yeah, I know. God shits in my breakfast once again. I've learned to deal with worse situations than this." I stood from the table and strode briskly toward the door. "I'll be communing with the crescia if anybody cares."

I spent the rest of the morning hanging out in the Sylvarium, letting the same two crescia nest in my hair again. I named the red one Jenni because of her red coloring and the smaller one Opal for her shimmering, iridescent wings. I didn't actually know if they had genders, but since Jo wasn't around, they would have to suffice for girl talk. Which was considerably easier to engage in when you didn't have to worry about your companions judging you.

After a few hours of braiding the hanging vines, drawing stick figures in the dirt, and idly chatting with the crescia, I concluded nothing was going to happen in terms of my magic. And since I'd run out of steam for our one-sided conversation, I decided to call it a day.

Leaving the Sylvarium, I went in search of my father's office, thinking it might be fun to learn how to ride one of those unguisen. I had nothing better to do with my time, so maybe he could spare someone to teach me.

I realized fairly quickly that finding my father was not going to be an easy task.

Most of the doors on the first level were closed, and knocking yielded no responses. After a half hour or so, I moved to the second floor and caught a soldier coming out of a room three doors down. I made a beeline for it since there was a solid chance he had just been with my father.

The door was still slightly ajar, so I peered inside, but my optimism dwindled when I saw the room was empty. I was about to leave when a broad table in the corner caught my eye. Stepping inside, I smothered the little voice in the back of my mind that whispered snooping might get me in trouble. If they didn't want me poking around, they should have given me more answers.

What I thought was a table was actually a highly-detailed topographical map, and judging from the presence of the mini Diamond Palace in the bottom right corner, it was a map of Rivella. I poured over the rendering, excited to finally learn about the landscape of this world. There was another castle to the western side of the continent made from bits of gold, and a third made of silver was nestled among a range of craggy mountains to the northeast.

Three palaces. Diamond, Gold, and Silver.

My eyes drifted over the rest of the map, taking in the expansive sand dunes of the northwest and the bay flowing out of the east. An assortment of roads connected the three castles around the perimeter of the island, but the dark forest and jagged mountain range prevented direct access from the Diamond Palace to the Silver Palace.

I was surprised to see there was no marker for the Onyx Palace. There was only a black hole in the middle of the forest that comprised a sizable chunk of the map's center. Maybe they just didn't know what it looked like.

When my stomach grumbled, I pulled away from the table and turned to leave, but something shiny caught my eye from the desk in the center of the room.

Is that...?

I stepped closer to investigate, and sure enough, it was exactly what I thought it was—a cell phone. More importantly, it was *my* cell phone. I would recognize that silver case covered in music notes anywhere.

What was it even doing in my father's office? And if my phone was here, did that mean...?

I went around to the other side of the desk, ripping open drawers and rifling through them. Tucked in the very back of the bottom drawer, hidden in a way that could only be intentional, was my purse.

My heart bottomed out. My father had it this entire time and never said a word.

I sank into the oversized chair and stared at the faded brown messenger bag I'd carried around for years, refusing to get rid of it despite the multitude of small rips and tears. When I moved out of my last awful foster home at eighteen and finally got a job, the bag was the first thing I bought. The first thing that was truly mine and couldn't be taken away by greedy fake parents.

Practically my entire life was in that bag—keys, wallet, sunglasses, makeup, extra hair ties, phone charger, book I was reading, small canister of pepper spray—along with other assorted items like period supplies that I was suddenly very grateful to have since I had been dreading having that conversation in a few weeks. But the shining beacon of hope was the small orange bottle of Klonopin. I counted ten remaining pills, and I was tempted to pop one in my mouth just to calm my racing heart, but I knew I should save them for emergencies.

Dumping everything into my bag, I hurried back toward my room to hide my purse. I prayed my father didn't notice it was missing right away. Although, it's not like he could question me about it because then he would have to admit he had kept it from me.

As I stuffed my bag into a dark corner under my bed, it occurred to me how little I really knew about my father. He seemed so happy to see me at first that I allowed myself to believe he was a good person. That he might turn out to be the kind of parent most kids dreamed about. Instead, he forced me into doing uncomfortable things, tortured Cam and Ram, restricted where I could go, and dictated who I could spend time with. Not to mention the most recent discovery.

I had chalked it all up to him putting his devotion to his people before anything else, but… what if it was more than that? What if I actually had no idea what kind of guy he was?

Either way, I was going to find out. Starting by talking to the other male here that I couldn't get a very good read on.

Cennux Dreisin.

Chapter Twenty-Five

Loud shouts filtered down the dim hallway leading to the arena, but nothing could have prepared me for what I actually saw taking place once I exited the tunnel.

It hadn't occurred to me that I never once asked about Sin's magic. I just assumed it was the element of fire based on his personality, because there was no way someone with his temper could be anything but fire.

I couldn't have been more wrong.

Sin was a water caster. A really, *really,* good water caster.

I stood off to the side, watching with rapt attention as he took on the five soldiers surrounding him.

Moving as one, they all lifted their arms and thrust their hands forward. Wobbling orbs of water levitated from casks scattered around the arena and shifted into foot-long spears that hurled themselves at Sin.

He didn't so much as flinch. He snapped his hands out in front of him, and all five javelins halted inches from his face. The soldiers shouted at each other as they pivoted back to the tubs for more ammo, but Sin was quicker. He swirled his hands in a series of sharp movements, and each soldier's watery missile returned to them faster than I could track. The projectiles slammed into their chests, and the pure force of the impact lifted each male from his feet and hurled them into the walls of the arena.

The soldiers struggled to get up, but Sin showed no hesitation as his hands dipped low toward the ground then flew upward. Every ounce of liquid soaking the soldier's clothing squeezed out from their uniforms and danced over to Sin. He began swirling his hands around, and the cloud of water spun just as quickly, twisting into a liquid tornado suspended in front of him. He swooped his hands out in an arc, and the cyclone shot around the arena, growing even larger as it drained the water out of each barrel on the field.

The vortex descended upon the fallen soldiers, sucking them into its vicious embrace.

I watched helplessly as they flailed and thrashed within the cone of water. Then Sin flung his arms above his head, and the tornado followed suit, rising into the air and swiftly surpassing the height of the arena itself.

Horror spread across my face as he ripped his hands apart, and the cyclone burst like a balloon. Water droplets and soldiers rained down to the arena floor, hundreds of feet below.

"No!" I shouted, rushing from the tunnel. Sin's head jerked toward me, shock spreading across his face. The soldier's terrified screams filled through the air, and I closed my eyes, refusing to witness their gruesome end.

When several moments passed and I hadn't heard the sickening crunch of bodies, I risked opening my eyes.

All five males hung suspended in a now docile cloud of water less than five feet from the ground. An amused look swept over Sin's face as he flicked his hand toward the aqueous safety net, and the soldiers crashed the rest of the way onto the hard dirt.

Groaning, they all struggled to their feet and took up defensive stances to continue the fight. Sin yelled something over his shoulder, and the five males relaxed their postures and shambled out of the arena.

"What the hell is wrong with you?!" I roared, stomping over to Sin and jabbing him hard in the chest, though I was pretty sure I hurt my finger more than I hurt him.

He smirked. "Many things, Fea Remia. You'll have to be more specific."

"Wipe that damn look off your face," I snapped. "You know exactly what I'm talking about. You were about to murder those guys."

He casually dried his hands on the sleeves of his black tunic before replying. "You really need to make up your mind here, Rain. Today you don't like me being amused, and yesterday you didn't like me being reserved. I'm not sure I have another setting."

"You're forgetting about asshole mode."

"No, that's always engaged," he assured me, the damn smirk back on his face.

"It wasn't last night," I said before I could stop the words from escaping.

Shit. How had I gotten so off track here? I was supposed to ask about my father, not bring up awkward topics.

The smirk faded as Sin's facade of cool detachment slid back over his face.

"What do you want, Rain?" he asked, folding his arms over his chest.

"Well first, I'd like to know what the fuck all that was," I replied, gesturing wildly into the air where the water tornado had been.

"Training," he said simply.

"Training? People can die when they train with you? Because if so, then maybe I'm glad you asked my father to cancel our sessions."

He blinked at me once. "For the record, I asked Verren no such thing. And if you must know, those males were never in any danger. They were prepared for things to get rough, but I would never actually harm my own soldiers."

I gawked at his unfettered arrogance. "What if you missed?" I sputtered. "What if you didn't catch them in time? They would have died."

Sin took a slow step toward me. "I don't miss."

I snorted. "That's cocky."

"No, it's accurate."

I glared at him. "The two aren't mutually exclusive."

Sin grinned at my words. Not the heart-stopping smile he gave me last night. No, this grin was positively devilish. "I'm glad we agree, then," he said smoothly before slipping his mask of indifference back on. "Now, do you plan to tell me what you're doing here, or did you honestly just come to give me a lecture about my own abilities?"

"No, I came to talk to you about my father."

"And what would you like to know about the illustrious Verren?" he asked, turning to cross the arena toward the weapons room.

"I need to know if... Is he..." I tried to figure out how best to formulate my question.

"Spit it out, Rain."

"Is he evil?" I finally managed to ask. "Like, is he a genuinely bad person?"

Sin stalled halfway across the arena. "Evil is a relative term," he answered. "And I don't think I'm the best one to ask about that."

I don't know why I had thought he would make this easy.

"Fine. How about this? Is he keeping secrets from me?"

Sin resumed his trek across the arena. "Everybody keeps secrets, Fea Remia. Even you, I'm sure."

"You are being incredibly unhelpful," I growled, following close on his heels.

"Then perhaps you should ask better questions."

I grabbed his arm, forcing him to turn back to me. I wanted to see his face when I asked *this* question. "Tell me... did you know he found my purse and was hiding it from me?"

His eyes locked on mine. "No," he calmly replied.

"Liar!" I hissed venomously, his denial fueling my anger. "Last night during my panic attack, I heard you tell Dey that I didn't have my medication. There is no way you could have known about that unless my father told you what was in my purse."

Sin pivoted sharply and started to walk away. "That's not how I knew about it."

"Yeah, right," I shouted at his back. "You're clearly lying, Sin. You and everybody else in this damned castle. Is that another Vitaean trait? Are you all just a bunch of deceitful jerks?"

Sin stopped in front of the steps down to the hallway, still refusing to face me. "I'm not lying, Rain," he said, his voice even tighter.

"Oh, really? Then how you could have possibly known about my meds if it wasn't from my father?" I waited, but he remained a stone statue. "Tell me!"

"Because I've seen you take it before!" he yelled, whirling around and closing the distance between us in a flash. "Back in your world. I saw you struggling to breathe, struggling to even stand. You opened that orange bottle, took whatever was inside, and then you were fine. It was the same thing I saw happening last night. And if I had known Verren had your pills, I would never have kept them from you. I may be a monster, but I'm not *that* kind of monster."

I just stood there, our chests one good inhale from touching, as I soaked up the intensity in his eyes that had been absent since our kiss. I searched his face for the truth and saw not one hint of deception.

"But you never located me in my world," I whispered, my voice soft with confusion. "Dey found me first."

Sin squeezed his eyes shut and took a step away from me. When he opened them again, they were as cold as ice.

"There are so many things you don't know."

"Then tell me," I begged, hoping to see a hint of the old Sin.

"I can't," he said, turning his back on me again.

"Can't or won't?"

"Take your pick."

"So what can you tell me?" I asked, exhausted. I waited, watching his shoulders rise and fall as he neither spoke nor walked away. "Please, Sin. Tell me something. Something useful."

His voice was quiet when he responded, almost as if he was speaking to himself. "You need to pay attention to the man behind the curtain."

His long legs carried him from the arena before the words even registered. When they did, I was only more confused.

Another Wizard of Oz quote. I'd dismissed his earlier reference as a common saying in my world, but now...

The film played every Wednesday night at the old rundown theater in Jersey, and I knew nearly every line by heart. I think I loved it because it was about an orphan who got to visit a magical world and escape the depressing life forced upon her. The one thing about the Wizard of Oz I could never understand, though, was why she wanted to leave so badly. She could have been a queen in that world. A world full of beauty and magic. Why would she want to go back to being poor in Kansas?

I understood it now. Ever since arriving in Rivella, I wanted nothing more than to go home myself. I didn't want to be a princess. I just wanted to hug Jenn, have a drink at Dingo's, and play my violin.

What I didn't understand was how Sin knew it.

Regardless, it sounded like he was telling me that if I wanted my life back, I needed to figure out what was going on behind the scenes.

So that's exactly what I was going to do.

Chapter Twenty-Six

I returned to the castle intent on uncovering whatever was going on. I couldn't figure out why I had been so lax in speaking with my father until now. I kept telling myself it was because I respected his busy schedule, he was the king after all, but that was a flimsy excuse at best.

So why hadn't I been demanding more answers? Answers about what happened to my mom. Answers about how I ended up in the human world, or what was waiting for me when I entered the dark forest?

He assigned the twins to 'educate me,' and yet somehow I'd barely learned anything. He scheduled me for training sessions, but I'd made no actual progress. I'd been here for days, and I honestly knew little more than when I first arrived. There was more going on in this castle than I was being told, and I was determined to figure out exactly what it was.

I checked my father's study first in case he had returned, but it was still empty. Then I went out to Cam and Ram's cottage hoping one of them might know where the king was, but the small home was dark.

Dragging myself back to the palace, I tried not to feel too defeated. The only other person I knew in this place was Josira, and I had no idea where she spent her days.

I hooked a right out of the seizure-inducing courtyard and decided my only method at this point for finding my father was to go room by room. He had to be somewhere.

To my dismay, hours passed with no luck. The few courtiers I encountered had ignored me when I kept saying "King Verren," either not understanding or simply choosing to be unhelpful.

I had decided to admit defeat and was passing by the grand hall on my way back to my room when I caught my father's voice drifting into the corridor. My father's *angry* voice.

I ducked into the shadow of the doorframe and peeked around slowly to see what was happening. I wasn't about to confront him if he was in the middle of berating one of his guards.

My father stood in the back corner of the massive hall, arguing with someone hidden behind a wide pillar. I held my breath as he roared at the person in front of him, a throbbing vein prominent on his forehead. I didn't know who incited his anger, but judging by the threatening sound of his voice, it was serious.

After a few minutes of admonishments, he turned and stalked off through the grand hall, exiting out the back. I debated chasing after him, but curiosity got the better of me, and I stayed in my hiding spot, wanting to see who my father was so upset with.

My breath caught in my throat when I saw Dey step out of the shadows. As he hurried past me, I made a snap decision and decided I wouldn't give up this opportunity.

"Dey," I called, revealing myself.

His head swiveled around, and for a brief moment, he looked nervous.

"Sorry, I didn't mean to eavesdrop. I was waiting to talk with my father, but it didn't seem like a good time. Is everything okay?"

Dey briskly straightened his tunic. "Everything is fine, Princess. King Verren and I were just having a slight disagreement."

I scoffed. "You call that a slight disagreement? I thought he was about to murder you." Dey flinched. It was small, barely noticeable, but I caught it. "What was he so mad about?"

Dey gave a weak chuckle and rushed toward the door. "Just court business. Nothing to concern yourself about."

I grabbed his arm. "Dey, stop. Please tell me what's going on? Why are you afraid of him?" I held his gaze, letting him see my desperation for answers. "Please," I begged when he hesitated. If he was truly my friend, surely he wouldn't lie to me.

To my disappointment, he gently removed my arm from his and said, "Everything is fine, Princess. King Verren has a lot on his shoulders with the upcoming Council. Everything will be better afterward. Trust me." He gave my shoulders a reassuring squeeze and strode from the grand hall.

I let him go. There was no point in trying to get answers he was never going to give.

Leaning against the wall, I wondered what Dey possibly could have done to upset my father so badly that he wouldn't tell me about it. I supposed I could be reading too much into things. Maybe he made an embarrassing mistake and didn't want to admit it to me. Maybe there was no big secret and my father was honestly just stressed about the Council.

I did know one thing for certain. If I was ever going to figure out what was going on around here, then I really needed to learn Rivellan.

I just had no clue how to do that.

When I returned to my room, I found Niahna and Kiahna waiting to help me prepare for dinner. I let the sisters go about their routine as they braided my hair and secured it at the nape of my neck. I only wrinkled my face a little when they helped me into the purple corset dress with a flared waist and loosely attached gossamer sleeves. It was a little snug through the chest, but the slight compression made it look like I actually had decent breasts for once.

I stood in front of the full length mirror, evaluating the overall look. I'd only been here a few days, but the access to multiple nutritious meals meant I was starting to lose some of my hard edges. My collar bones weren't as sharp, and my ribs were becoming less noticeable.

I chuffed out a small laugh. I felt completely ridiculous, and the dress was beyond impractical, but still... I did look good. It was like catching a glimpse of who I might have been if I had grown up in Rivella.

I turned away from the mirror, dismissing that train of thought. I hadn't grown up here, and there was no point in wondering 'what if.' I stopped playing that game around age six when I realized all it did was allow disappointment to sink its claws into my heart. You couldn't change the past. You could only hope for a better future.

It was years later before I realized that hope was just as much a waste of time.

A knock pulled me from my depressing thoughts, and I hurried to the door.

Dey stood on the other side, his normal plain tunic swapped for one of brilliant azure with a silver brocade. I suppressed a frown as I realized I had been hoping to find Sin there.

"Princess? Would you care to join me for dinner?" he asked sweetly, as if our earlier conversation had never happened.

With a face chiseled to perfection, golden hair, and a toned body, he was the epitome of Prince Charming. And yet, all I could think about was how much disappointment I felt that it wasn't Sin standing in my doorway. His mahogany tresses pulled back to showcase his rough face, his knowing smirk, his crooked nose that spoke of a violent past, and his ghostly green eyes.

Dey was perfect. And Sin was perfectly imperfect.

But Dey was here, and Sin was not, so I took his hand and let him escort me to dinner.

"You look beautiful tonight," he said softly as we made our way down the stairs.

"Thanks," I replied, still feeling a bit awkward in the dress. At least it was long enough to hide my Chucks so I could walk comfortably. I wondered what all these courtiers would think if they knew what footwear hid beneath the fancy gown.

I stifled a grin at the thought as we entered the dining room, and I suffered through being announced once more.

Dey tried to direct me to the end of the table where I was supposed to sit by the king, but my eyes snagged on Jo seated near the middle, every chair around her empty. I felt a sympathetic twinge of pain because I'd been that lonely girl at the lunch table nobody wanted to sit with more times than I could count.

I slipped my arm from Dey's and took a seat across from Jo before he could stop me. "Hi," I said brightly.

Jo's face lit up when she saw me. *"Rain!"* Her voice inside my head rang with excitement. *"It is so good to see you again. I missed you last night."*

"Princess," Dey said in a low, controlled voice, his hand on my arm. "Our seats are by King Verren."

I gave him my best firm stare. "No, my seat is here tonight. By my friend. You can sit wherever you want." Jerking my arm away, I directed my attention back to Jo.

Dey must have stood behind me shifting his weight uncomfortably for at least a minute, and I realized I had effectively left him with a difficult decision—join me here in my little rebellion or retreat to the king's side. I had little doubt as to where Dey's loyalty lay, but it still hurt a little when he abandoned me and took his seat at the end of the table.

"Sorry, what were we talking about?" I asked Jo, acknowledging that I had missed what she said while I was waiting for Dey to decide.

"I asked you how your day was. Have you gotten to see more of the castle?"

I snorted. "Yeah, I've seen pretty much the whole thing at this point. It's not like I can go into town or anything."

"You should be able to soon enough. The Council is in four days, and then all of Civi Adasa will recognize you. Everything will be better afterward. Trust me."

I didn't need a reminder about my upcoming torture, but I was looking forward to being able to leave the castle grounds. My days were pretty bleak and boring now that my father had basically taken all my friends away from me. Everybody except Jo.

"Hey, will you come visit me tomorrow morning in the Sylvarium? I've been hanging out with the crescia, but their conversation skills are a bit limited, you know?"

Laughter filled my head, and it was such a surreal yet pleasant experience.

"That would be wonderful. I do wish to get to know you more, Rain."

"Awesome," I said, starting to feel a little better about my situation. Jo would be the perfect person to answer some questions about my father. Not only was she his advisor, but she was basically a mind reader. If anybody knew what he was hiding, it was her.

I started to ask about how she usually spent her days around the palace, when the guard announced a newcomer to dinner—Cennux Dreisin. He strolled into the room confidently, looking every ounce the way I had envisioned him earlier with his hair tied back and the hard lines of his face on full display. All that was missing was the smirk. When his eyes swept over the table and he noted where I was sitting, it finally made its appearance, tugging his lip up slightly into that amused little grin.

I didn't know if I should feel thrilled or annoyed as he made his way over and casually slid into the seat beside me.

"Hello, Fea Remia," he whispered, keeping his voice low. "I hope your afternoon was... productive."

"Not exactly," I said, frustration seeping into my voice. "I don't know how I'm going to learn anything about, well, anything when I don't speak Rivellan."

"I didn't take you to be the kind who gave up so easily."

"Yeah, well, you don't really know me that well do you?" I grabbed a napkin and plopped it in my lap, annoyed that he was making it seem like I even had options available.

Sin gave me a wolfish grin. "Oh, I think I know you very well, Fea Remia."

The words ignited a fire low in my abdomen, but the announcement of the king's arrival saved me from lingering in the awkward silence.

My father walked briskly through the dining hall to the head of the long table. He glanced from Dey to the empty seat beside him, and Dey rose hastily to whisper something into his ear. He scanned the dinner guests until he found me.

I gave him my best innocent smile.

Just an ignorant human here. Can't blame me for not knowing about royal dining protocols.

His lips pursed tightly for a second, and then he dipped his head in acquiescence. As he took his seat, servants emerged to present our meals.

"So, what do you normally do all day, Jo?" I asked, not looking over at Sin or his tempting mouth.

"With the Council so close, I am mostly assisting with security interrogations. With the other kings and their entourages arriving soon, it is imperative there are no traitors within our ranks."

I paused with my fork halfway to my mouth. "Wait, so my father has you reading the minds of everyone in the castle?"

"No, I cannot quite read minds. I can only hear thoughts if they are directed toward me. It is very difficult, though, for someone to hide their intentions when they answer my questions. I am able to detect if there is any deception or malice hiding underneath the words they choose. Thankfully, none have shown to be anything more than loyal to the crown."

"Oh, well that's good." It sounded a bit invasive, but precautions were probably necessary. I didn't know anything about the other courts, so maybe there was a danger to the rulers all being together in one place. My father had said they only met like once every hundred years.

"You seem tense," Sin purred right beside my ear, and if I hadn't been before, I certainly was now. How could he do that? Affect me so profoundly with just that hint of gravel to his sonorous voice. It was like every time he spoke, I could think of nothing but sex or violence. Usually both.

"I'm fine," I said, with a forced casualty. "No need to worry about me. Feel free to go back to being, how did you put it? Reserved?"

I was acting petty, but I didn't care. Our earlier conversation had left me with nothing but a million more questions, and I knew he had no intention of answering a single one. Evasions and half-truths were all I ever got from him.

"What if I want to be amused right now? I do have two settings, remember?"

I risked meeting his eyes long enough to shoot him a glare. "You know, it's getting a little annoying how I never know which Sin I'm going to be talking to."

He sank back into his seat and glowered, all levity gone from his expression. "Then maybe it would be best if you didn't speak to either one."

"You two have an interesting friendship."

I jerked at the sound of Jo's voice in my head, having completely forgotten she was even there.

I gave her an embarrassed smile. "Sorry. I didn't mean to exclude you. And I don't know if I would call us friends." I caught Sin's flinch out of the corner of my eye but ignored it.

"Do not be sorry. I can talk aloud, but honestly, I have spent so long mind speaking it feels uncomfortable to use my voice. I am accustomed to being more of a passive presence during others' conversations."

I frowned. "Just because you're used to it doesn't make it okay. You deserve to be included."

Jo beamed at me, like no one had ever validated her existence before, and it nearly broke my heart. *"You are very kind, Rain."*

"I'm glad you think so since it doesn't seem to be the popular opinion."

"I never said you weren't kind," Sin interjected, and I whipped my head to stare at him.

"You heard her?" I gasped.

"Of course I heard her. She was talking to both of us."

"I can speak inside more than one head at a time," Jo explained. *"I choose who can and cannot hear me."*

"Wow," I remarked. "That's actually really cool."

She blushed. *"I am glad you think so, but Dreisin is right, Rain. You do seem rather on edge this evening. Is everything okay?"*

I hesitated, then said, "Yeah, it's no big deal. Just been thinking about a lot of things lately. We can talk more tomorrow."

She must have read my intention that I didn't want to speak in front of other people because she only said, *"I look forward to it. In the meantime you should try to relax a bit."*

"Maybe visit the Laneum," Sin chimed in between bites of food.

I opened my mouth to ask what a Laneum was, but Jo answered first.

"You have not been to the pools yet? They are my favorite part of the castle. Igniservians are stationed there around the clock to keep the waters hot. They are on the lower level just past the library."

Well that piqued my interest. This Laneum place sounded like heaven in the form of hot springs.

"They tend to be empty in the evening," Sin said. He gave me a heated look and added, "They're the second best thing I can think of for relieving tension."

I almost choked on my dinner, and my cheeks burned so hot they had to be a mirror of Jo's flaming tresses.

"Is that so?" I forced out, though it didn't sound nearly as nonchalant as I'd hoped for.

Across the table, Jo attempted to hide a grin by daintily dabbing her mouth with a napkin.

"I'll keep that in mind." I focused on my meal and tried not to imagine Sin joining me in the heated pools. The thought of him shirtless had me surreptitiously clenching my legs together. He was all lean hard muscle that filled out his tunic in a way that screamed the body hiding beneath would be, well, sinful.

If I ever got my hands on his scorching hot body, it would probably burn me alive.

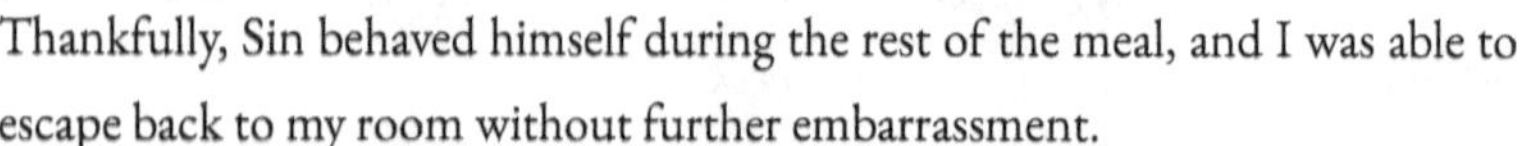

Thankfully, Sin behaved himself during the rest of the meal, and I was able to escape back to my room without further embarrassment.

I was contemplating how best to spend the remainder of my evening when Kiahna showed up at my door carrying a pile of clothing. She set the stack on the end of the bed and gave me a small curtsy before leaving.

I was pawing through the garments, grateful to have some new clean tunics and breeches, when my eyes snagged on the last two articles of clothing. They resembled a bra and underwear but were far more delicate in design and material. The fabric felt like silk yet had the elastic snap of spandex. Both pieces began as a deep rich purple that gradually darkened to a midnight black.

I picked up the top, similar to a bralette, and wondered if Kiahna had just brought me sexy underwear. I couldn't imagine why she would do that unless... Maybe this was their version of a bathing suit.

Okay, Jo, I thought, bemused. *I can take a hint.*

I pulled on the two pieces, hesitating when my hand brushed over the ridges along my low back. Sin *had* said the Laneum was typically deserted at night, and if it wasn't empty I could always come back. It was worth the effort to try at least.

Clad in the new silky-soft garments with my robe wrapped tightly around me, I made my way to the lower levels, past the library, until I heard the faint sounds of burbling water.

I rounded the corner, and a cavern spread out before me where the castle had been built into the side of the cliff. I took in the massive chamber with high ceilings made of rough stone and the five spacious pools of water that were more a part of the land around them than they were of the palace. A servant slouched against one wall, bouncing his finger through the air like the conductor of an invisible choir. Following his gaze out toward the water, I spotted a flaming construct of a rabbit-like creature hopping across each pool. Everywhere it landed, the water around it hissed and bubbled.

I cleared my throat, and the igniservian jerked up at the sound. His eyes widened briefly in recognition, and he scrambled to his feet to give me a hurried bow.

"Yeah, please don't do that," I said, turning away so the young-looking male would get the hint and leave me alone.

It took another minute, but I eventually heard him stand and shuffle off to the farthest pool to continue his duties. Apparently that would have to do for privacy.

Carefully, I lowered myself into the steaming water, letting out a huge sigh as the warmth slid over my skin. The pool was deep enough that I could sit with my legs outstretched on the bottom, and the water just covered the top of my bathing suit. I leaned my head back against the lip of the pool and closed my eyes, letting the heat soak into my sore muscles.

I was lazily drawing circles on the surface of the pool when the sound of a male voice drifted through the cavern. My eyes popped open when I recognized it—Corym.

I was out of the pool in a flash, yanking on my robe and securing it tightly. Dashing out of the room, I ignored the shouts of the igniservian.

I skidded to a stop in front of the open door to the library just in time to see Corym disappear through the door at the back of the darkened room.

I hurried toward that door, slipping more than once with my wet feet. "Corym!" I shouted, ecstatic to see the friendly librarian again.

His head whipped up, a startled expression on his face. "Raynella," he said, recovering quickly. "I am surprised to see you here so late at night." He eyed my attire and the water dripping to the floor of his small office. "I assume you came from the Laneum?"

"Yeah, Sin told me it was best to go at night when no one else was there."

Corym smiled. "Yes, that is very true. I do most of my reading down here in the evening. During the day, the voices and splashing water can echo quite loudly. Funny that you mention Dreisin; you actually just missed him."

Relief that I narrowly avoided an awkward encounter must have shown on my face, because Corym asked, "And how are your interactions with the king's Cennux going?"

I waved a hand dismissively. "Oh, you know, one second he's the biggest ass I've ever met, and the next he's actually a decent person. It's infuriating trying to figure him out."

"He can be that way at times," Corym replied sadly. "I do apologize. He was not always so difficult." Corym shifted over on the couch and patted the spot beside him.

"So people keep telling me," I said, sinking back against the plush sofa. "I don't suppose you know why that is?"

A pained look crossed Corym's face. "I do, but it is not my story to tell. I will say that Sin has lost people that he loved dearly, and it has made him... hard." He paused, then said, "You could help with that, you know."

I laughed. "Help make him be less of a jerk? I doubt that. I feel like I make him worse."

"On the contrary. I know Dreisin quite well, and when he speaks about you, there is a light in him that has been dark for far too long. You have awoken something inside him we all thought lost forever."

I smothered the rising curiosity about what Sin had been saying about me. There would be nothing to gain from pulling on that thread. "Pretty sure the only thing I've awoken is his anger," I replied.

Corym shook his head and gave me a sad smile. "I think you are wrong, Raynella."

I studied him carefully, mulling over his excessive interest in Sin, and a puzzle piece clicked into place. "You're his father."

It was so obvious now that I had met them both, I don't know how I didn't put it together sooner. They had the same wavy dark brown hair, the same facial structure, even their eyes had the same shape, though Sin's were pale green and Corym's were a deeper, mossy hue. He was basically an older, slightly softer version of Sin.

Corym sagged a little, and I knew I was right. "Yes," he confessed, "but Sin does not know."

"What? How? You guys look so much alike." I had only spent a handful of minutes with this guy, and I made the connection.

"Sin was told his father died when he was an infant, so he does not see it. I spend as much time as I can with him under the guise of wanting to be helpful, and we have become... friends, for lack of a better word. He does not believe it to be any more than that."

"And you're okay letting him think you're dead?" Did Corym not know how much a child craved their parents?

"His mother made the decision, and I supported it. I loved my family, Raynella. I loved them so deeply, but there was nothing I could do. Sin's mother and I grew up in Civi Obsura. We fell in love at a young age, but when we manifested, she was an imminario, and I was a secunnario."

"So what?" I asked. "Why would you care?"

"I did not care, and neither did she. Though rare, it is not unheard of for a secunnario to live in Civi Obsura. Most would immediately seek out work and a better life in Civi Adasa, but I could not bear to leave Sawnya. For many years, we were happy, but shortly after Sin was born, King Verren caught wind of my abilities. He decided I would serve in his court." Corym stalled, the weight of his sadness evident in his entire being. "My wife, however, was not welcome."

My jaw dropped. "So you left them? You abandoned your wife and child for a damn job?"

"It is not so simple, Raynella," he protested, wringing his hands anxiously. "My presence was not a request, but a command, and it nearly destroyed me to leave them. The last time I saw Sin's mother, she told me my child would grow up thinking I was dead. Better for him to believe that than to think I willingly left him."

"But you did leave him." I could see the pain he had suffered, but that didn't make it okay. Nothing made abandoning your child okay. "Why didn't you both leave? Go to another court? Better yet, tell my dad to fuck off." I stood up, pacing around the room. How could my father break up families so casually? He wanted me to restore the lines and give the magic back to the people, something that seemed incredibly altruistic, yet he had torn Sin's parents apart for his own gain.

"One does not refuse a king," Corym replied solemnly. "Were we to flee to another court, it would have put my family in danger of retaliation. To protect Sawnya and Sin, I had to leave them."

I sank back onto the couch, the weight of his story heavy on my shoulders. "And Sin has no idea?"

"His mother died of the plague some years ago, and as far I know, he was only ever told the lie. When he came to work for King Verren, I was ecstatic to be able to see him again yet too afraid to tell him the truth. How could he ever forgive me for what I had done? I do all that I can to help him when he needs it, but he thinks I am merely kind." Corym turned to me then, fear blanching his face. "Please tell me that you will keep this secret, Raynella."

"I will," I promised. I respected Corym despite everything, so I could honor his wishes, even though I itched to tell Sin the truth. Everybody deserved to have family in their life.

"Thank you," he replied, the tension in his shoulders easing.

Another long pause stretched out, the secret hanging between us like a tangible presence.

"So, would this be a bad time to ask for a favor?" I said, brushing back my wet hair that was slowly dripping onto his sofa.

He chuckled. "There is never a bad time for the princess." Straightening, his scholarly air settled about him as if he had just put on an old familiar coat. "How can I assist you?"

"Right, so I've been waiting for you to get back because I am in desperate need of your skills." I felt a little gross saying that after everything he just told me. Everything he gave up so his precious skills would be here at the palace for someone like me. "I need you to do that language transfer thingy. I'm sure you've heard that I agreed to fulfill the prophecy, but I can't stay here without learning Rivellan."

Corym blinked at me, and then his brow furrowed in confusion. "Get back from where? I have been in the library every day. I honestly expected you to seek me out much sooner for this very reason."

I shook my head. "No, my father said you were gone. Your sister was sick or something."

"Oh, I am afraid he was mistaken. I have not left the palace for many years now."

"He lied to me?"

Why wouldn't my father want me talking to Corym?

"I am certain it was an honest mistake. King Verren has many advisors, and much is happening with the Council. He likely confused me with another."

"Maybe..." I conceded. Though I'd bet a week's pay at the Taco Hut my father knew exactly what he was doing. He hadn't wanted me to learn Rivellan. Had said as much at breakfast the first day I met him. Was that why he lied? To prevent me from doing this very thing?

"Is it dangerous?" I asked. "The transfer?"

Corym stroked his neat beard for a moment. "I do not believe so, though I have only transferred something as complex as language to a few others. I have given immense sums of information to many individuals before, but never to one who has not manifested."

Maybe my father was right and there was a risk. Although, that was nothing compared to the alternative—continuing to feel like everyone was hiding things from me.

"Ok," I said, my voice resolute. "Go big or go home right?"

Maybe that phrase wasn't the best in this situation.

I cleared my throat. "I'm ready is what I'm saying. If you're willing to do the transfer."

Corym smiled. "Of course I will not."

I frowned. "Wait, what?"

He paused, then cleared his throat. "I said of course I will... not." His mouth opened and closed as he struggled to form words, but the message was pretty clear.

"Why?" I demanded.

Corym rubbed at his forehead. "I am sorry, Princess, I must be tired. What I am trying to say is that I will... not help you."

"Yeah, you made that part pretty clear. I'm asking why the hell not?"

His face scrunched up, and he shook his head. "I am not saying the correct thing."

I gave him a wary look. "So you will do the transfer?"

"No. Wait... Yes. I mean no." Corym's face contorted in distress, and he started scratching at his temples.

"Hey, are you ok?" I pressed. "What's going on?" I really hoped he wasn't having an aneurysm or something.

He looked up at me, his eyes wide in panic. "I want to help you, Raynella. I need to help you. My life's work is to share knowledge."

"Ok... so then let's do it."

"I want to but... something will not allow it." He wouldn't stop scratching at his temples, and I was afraid he would start bleeding soon.

I chewed on my lip a second, evaluating his distressed expression. "Corym," I began slowly, "is there a kind of magic where someone could stop you from doing something?" The idea terrified me, and I hoped I was wrong. I thought Dey's emotion manipulation was bad, but at least I still made my own choices with his power.

"Compulsion," Corym replied quietly, his hands dropping to his lap. "Compulsion could do it, but that possibility defies reason. It was decreed over a thousand years ago that Rivellans with such a dangerous ability could not be allowed to live."

I should have been disgusted, but after hearing how they executed creation casters, I was starting to see a pattern forming.

His eyes glossed over, and he appeared lost in whatever thought process he was currently analyzing.

"Corym?" I nudged his arm. "Are you in there?"

It took a second, but his eyes focused on me. "Yes, Raynella, I am here. My deepest apologies. It seems that I have developed something of a nasty headache. Could we possibly do the transfer tomorrow?"

"Um, sure," I replied. There was definitely something wrong with him, and it was probably a good idea to wait until he worked through whatever was happening. "Is there someone you can talk to? Maybe someone who can help with whatever's happening?"

"Yes, perhaps," he replied, pinching the bridge of his nose. "I will go see a healer in the morning. Come find me tomorrow afternoon. I will make sure that I am able to do the transfer."

I pushed off the sofa. "Ok, um, I'll see you tomorrow, then."

I made my way back to my room, my mind racing with everything that had just happened. The idea that someone could mess with my mind so thoroughly was terrifying, and as I got into bed and pulled the covers up to my chest, a dreadful thought occurred to me.

My father had never actually told me what kind of powers *he* had.

Chapter Twenty-Seven

My steps were heavy and slow as I entered the dining hall the following morning, and part of me wanted to bail on the whole confrontation. What kept my feet moving forward was the need to know my father didn't have anything to do with Corym's breakdown. Regardless of whatever secrets he was hiding, I had to make sure he wouldn't violate someone's mind like that.

God, what if he had used compulsion on me? How would I even know? I thought back to everything that had happened since I arrived. Was anything I had done strange or out of character?

My heart started racing, and I delved into the pocket of my tunic for a Klonopin. If there was ever a time to use one, it was now.

Every second I waited for my father felt like an hour, but right as my medication began to smooth out my breathing, heavy steps announced his arrival.

"Good morning, Raynella," he said in his pleasantly booming voice. "I am glad you are here. I need to speak with you and have precious little time this morning."

He looked the same as he did most every day—loose pants, burgundy mantle around his shoulders, long raven hair flowing loosely down his back, and a crown of diamonds nestled atop his head.

"Wait," I said firmly before he could sit. "I need to ask you something first."

His brow crinkled in confusion. "Anything, Raynella."

I stifled the bitter laugh threatening to escape at that blatantly inaccurate response and steadied my voice. "I need you to tell me what abilities you have."

He blinked at me as if it was the last thing he'd expected me to ask. "Why do you wish to know?"

"Just tell me!" I demanded, the calming effects of Klonopin bowing to my frayed nerves.

"All right. I am an amplissario, so I have three abilities," he began cautiously, as if afraid I might snap again. "Like many Vitaeans, I have my healing power, though it is not as strong as most. Beyond that, I am an aquiservian, and my mental gift is telekinesis."

His words were everything I wanted to hear, and if he was telling the truth, then he couldn't have messed with Corym's mind. But I wouldn't just take his word for it. Not anymore.

"Prove it," I demanded.

"Raynella, what is this all about?"

"Prove. It," I said again, my jaw aching with tension.

His eyes flickered off to the side, and then he sighed heavily and gestured toward the table with his right hand. The water I'd been drinking swirled up and out of the cup, shaped itself into a perfect flower, then dropped smoothly back into the glass.

"And the other?" I prodded.

He faced the wall of windows and squinted his eyes slightly. I turned to watch, and all the tension I'd been holding melted away as the curtains opened and closed.

He was telling the truth.

"Thank you," I said weakly, slumping back in my chair.

He took his seat, regarding me with concerned eyes. "Will you tell me now why that was so important to you?"

I sipped my water to buy some time to think. I couldn't exactly tell him I went to go have Corym do the mind transfer after he specifically told me to wait.

"I realized last night that I didn't know anything about you. We've barely spent any time together because you're always off doing king stuff, and I was starting to feel like maybe you were keeping something from me. It was stupid, I know, but I've never had a father before."

I forced myself to meet his eyes, and the amount of sympathy and pain in them had me reconsidering every negative thought I'd ever had. Sure, he bullied me into doing what he wanted for the supposed good of his court, but that didn't mean he had some deeper nefarious plan. This was not my world, and maybe my father's actions would be considered justified here. For all I knew, refusing to show up to his dinners might be the same as someone in my world refusing to accept a medal of honor from a world leader—insulting and unheard of.

My stomach twisted as a wave of nausea and embarrassment swept over me. What if I had been so scared about finally having a family that I was subconsciously doing everything I could to sabotage it?

"Raynella," he said softly. "I am so sorry I gave you cause to doubt me. I know I handled the situation with Camden and Ramset poorly, but I just found you. I had to witness each of my children succumb to the plague, and that day in the city, I was so afraid I had lost you as well. This King's Council has occupied so much of my time that should have been spent getting to know you better, and for that I am truly sorry. It will all be over in a few days. Everything will be better afterward. Trust me."

I pulled my braid around and chewed on the end for a second. Everything he said was what I wanted to hear except...

"What about my purse?" I asked.

He blinked. "Your purse?"

"Yeah, I found my purse in your office. I was looking for you and saw my phone on your desk. I just don't know why you've kept it from me."

"Raynella," he said calmly, "half of this court has access to my study. If someone placed your purse on my desk, I was not informed of it. That is the truth."

Something inside me broke then. Maybe having some kind of relationship with my father wasn't totally a lost cause.

"I'm sorry," I said meekly. "I should have talked to you."

His hand reached out to pat mine. "It will be all right. I can only imagine how strange this world is for you. How much our way of life differs from your own. I could never take offense at your concerns. I do hope you know you can speak with me in the future."

"I do now," I said, swallowing hard.

A servant brought in a tray of food for me, and I noted the lack of a second plate.

"You're not eating breakfast?"

"I am afraid not," he replied, smoothing down his mantle. "I would enjoy nothing more than to dine with you, but with the Council a mere three days away, I simply cannot. I only came to let you know that a dressmaker will be arriving a bit later this morning to design your gown for the banquet. Dey will retrieve you from the Sylvarium at the appropriate time."

For a short blissful while, I had actually forgotten about the upcoming ball.

Feeling like we had connected a bit, I decided to throw a hail Mary. "Are you sure all this is a good idea? I'm still leaving in a few weeks. How will you explain my disappearance again?"

My father gave me a small smile, kissed me on the forehead, and turned to leave the room. "A few weeks is a long time, Raynella," he tossed over his shoulder. "You may yet change your mind."

"Not likely," I muttered under my breath and sat down to eat breakfast.

Alone.

The Sylvarium was empty when I arrived, save for the usual flock of baby crescia. I was pleased to see Jenni and Opal make a beeline in my direction.

"I'm starting to think you guys like me," I joked. I definitely had my fair share of others fluttering nearby, but Jenni and Opal had definitely staked their claim.

"So which one of you is it going to be, then?" I asked, trying to decide if I even had a preference. Opal was smaller, quieter, and a bit more timid, while Jenni was considerably more vocal, playful, and always the first to land in my hair.

I ran my fingers lightly over both of their delicate wings. "Just so you guys know, I like you both, but I also won't be around long. You might want to hold off for someone better."

"Now who could be better than the princess?"

I whirled around as the sweetly amused voice of Jo slipped through my mind. I watched as she moved lazily through the Sylvarium, picking the occasional berry and sniffing the flowers.

"Can you teach me how to do that?" I asked as she got closer.

"How to do what?"

"Talk inside your mind. Like, can I project my thoughts or whatever into your head without speaking out loud?"

Jo popped a berry into her mouth. *"There is nothing to teach, Rain. Whenever someone wishes to speak with me, their mind essentially opens up, making it easy for me to pull out the intentions."*

My eyes followed her around the room, and I decided to give it a shot. Without opening my mouth, I thought, *"So... can you hear me?"*

She smiled. *"I can."*

My face almost hurt I was grinning so big. *"Do I have to be looking at you?"*

"No," she replied, ducking behind a massive hanging plant with vines so thick they formed a solid curtain down to the ground. *"You need only be thinking of me. Try again now that I am hidden."*

I closed my eyes, wanting to see if I could do it with no visuals at all. *"Is it insulting if I ask how old you are? I've learned that appearance means very little in terms of age."*

It was like I could feel her shrug inside my head when she replied. *"It is not a commonly asked question, but I do not mind. Given the varying lifespans of our people, it is typically viewed as irrelevant by most. Similar to asking one's favorite color. Just a random factoid about them. And for the record, I am twenty-three. I have no healing magic, so I will age much like a human."*

I settled onto the floor of the Sylvarium and leaned back against the bench, keeping my eyes closed. *"Huh. I don't think I realized that only the ones with healing magic got to live longer."*

Something like a sigh rolled through my mind before she responded. *"It is one of many injustices that may be corrected once the ley lines are restored. Let us not speak of such things, though. Why did you wish to know my age?"*

I bit my lip and fought back the twinge of guilt that I basically wanted to ask Jo a million questions. It didn't seem like a particularly balanced friendship when I barely knew anything about her.

"I can sense you are conflicted about something, Rain."

"I'm sorry. It's just... I have a lot of questions, but I don't want you to think that I only wanted to hang out so I could grill you for information."

The soft scuff of boots alerted me to Jo's presence before I felt her settle down beside me.

"I would never think that, Rain. If I can help you understand our world even a little better, then I will do so gladly."

"Why?" I asked, so unused to people openly volunteering information.

"Selfish reasons, mostly. I do not want you to leave. If there is a chance I can help this feel like home to you, then I must take it."

Her words hit me like a punch to the gut. How many people would I be leaving behind when I returned to my world? And were they all really less important than Jenn? It was an impossible question, and yet I still knew the answer. My home would always be wherever my sister was.

"I am sorry if my answer caused you pain."

"No," I said quickly, opening my eyes to look at her. *"I'm just not used to having anybody besides my sister actually want me to stick around. That's all."*

She gave me a sad smile. *"Do people in your world not see how amazing you are?"*

I glanced away as a highlight reel of abuse flashed through my head. The beatings from foster parents who would inevitably send me back. The teasing from my classmates every time I skipped lunch because I had nothing to eat and no money to buy anything. The bullying from the rich girls with private music tutors always saying that I was a waste of a perfectly good violin.

"No, not exactly," I thought weakly, though I didn't know if it even made it from my mind to hers. If it did, she mercifully didn't press the issue.

"What questions can I answer for you, Rain?"

I looked over at her and relaxed a little when I saw no pity on her face. *"Truthfully, I asked about your age in hopes you were around when my mother was here, but she would have died before you were born."*

"Yes, I am afraid that is correct. You would have better luck finding someone who knew her down in Civi Obsura. While humans are technically not allowed to live within any of the kingdom's cities, I know there are many pockets of them that reside there. It is where King Verren found her, after all."

"Thanks. I doubt he'll let me take a sightseeing trip anytime soon, but maybe I can sneak off after the Council is done."

Jo gave me a strange appraising look, but it shifted into a neutral expression as Dey entered the Sylvarium.

"Princess," he said, striding across the room toward us. "What are you doing on the floor?"

Standing up, I dusted off my leggings. "What's wrong with the floor?"

You would think I had asked what's wrong with eating dirt based off the look he gave me in response.

I shook my head. "Never mind. I take it the dressmaker is here?"

"Yes, they are waiting in your chambers. Shall we head up there?"

"Might as well get this over with." I turned to Jo. *"Same time tomorrow?"*

"It would be my pleasure."

I gave her one last smile and turned to follow Dey from the Sylvarium.

His eyes flicked up to my hair. "Are you aware that you have two crescia on your head?"

"Oh, right." I reached up to nudge them, surprised they hadn't flown away on their own like every other time I left the room. Jenni let out a string of sharp chitters, and I got the feeling she wanted to stay. "Can they come with me?"

Dey raised an eyebrow. "I am afraid not. One of them may have chosen you as their future bonded, but they must stay here where it is safe for now."

"Sorry, ladies," I said, giving my head a little shake. "You heard him. I'll see you tomorrow."

Jenni gave one last irritated chitter, and then she and Opal flew away.

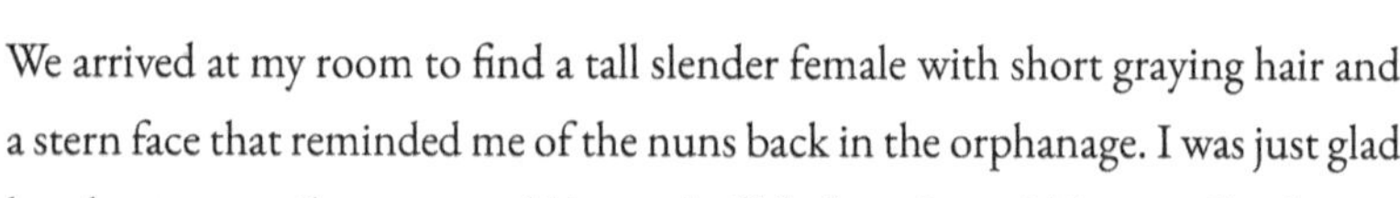

We arrived at my room to find a tall slender female with short graying hair and a stern face that reminded me of the nuns back in the orphanage. I was just glad her dress was a vibrant emerald instead of black, or I would have suffered some serious flashbacks.

She addressed Dey as we walked inside, and whatever she said was definitely not a pleasant greeting. He spoke to her briefly; then she huffed and began sorting through her box of supplies.

"She is merely annoyed that we are late is all," Dey explained, as he plopped onto my bed and leaned back against the headboard. I started to tell him to get the hell off my bed, but the seamstress locked her rough hands on mine and yanked me into the center of the room.

She studied my body from every angle, and I squirmed under her assessment. I never had a female make me feel like a piece of meat before, but I always thought I'd feel a bit more flattered if it ever happened. Judging by her scowl, she definitely didn't like what she was seeing. And here I thought I was starting to look better.

Turning back to her open satchel, she flicked her hand, and a black wooden box floated up.

Aeriservian, I realized, still not used to seeing magic used so casually.

She gave a few more flicks of her wrist, and I tried not to flinch when the case popped open to release four thin strips of fabric that wrapped themselves around my breasts, stomach, hips, and right bicep. She gave another flick, and red pins shot toward my body, weaving themselves into the fabric to mark my sizes.

She said something in Rivellan, and I craned my neck to look at Dey.

“She said to relax,” Dey translated.

“You try relaxing with sharp metal bits flying at your body,” I shot back.

Resigning myself to my fate, I held painfully still to avoid getting stabbed.

“Is she almost done?” I asked after what felt like an hour but was likely only fifteen minutes. The seamstress had stopped focusing on me a while ago and just stood there, drawing on a piece of parchment with a thin charcoal stick.

“She is mocking up a sketch for you to approve. If you are pleased with it, then yes, you will be finished,” he replied.

Finally, the seamstress revealed her vision, and I choked back a gasp.

I always hated dresses. As far as clothing options went, they were uncomfortable and made me feel fragile, like dressing too feminine somehow changed me into a delicate flower who needed a strong man to save her.

I didn’t hate this dress, though. If the final product was anything like the sketch, then it would probably be the first dress I ever put on voluntarily.

“Did she say what color it will be?” I asked, tracing a finger down the drawing as I waited for her response.

“She said that for the lost princess of the Diamond Court, nothing would be acceptable save for undyed crescia silk,” Dey replied, and I caught a hint of reverence in his voice.

“Crescia silk?” I had spent a fair amount of time in the Sylvarium, but never once saw any trace of a web.

“Crescia draw themselves into sort of a cocoon once they have bonded,” he explained. “They spend a short period of time inside, then reemerge in their new form. They only produce the silk for the transformation so, as you can imagine, it is very rare.” He paused. “And beautiful.”

“But it has long sleeves,” I mused, continuing to take in every detail on the page. “Why would they use more silk than necessary if it’s so special?”

Dey cleared his throat, and I tore my eyes away from the drawing to look at him.

“King Verren thought that perhaps it would be better if… if perhaps we…” He looked so uncomfortable it was almost adorable.

"What, Dey? It's a simple question."

He blushed, his words barely discernible as they rushed out. "He felt perhaps we should not openly display your lack of manifested power."

"Yeah, okay. I get that," I agreed, turning back to the drawing.

"You are not upset by this, Princess?"

I shrugged. "No, why would I be? I think it's a waste of the super rare silk, but I remember what happened in Civi Adasa."

"I am pleased that you are not offended," he said, sounding profoundly relieved.

I turned his words over in my head. Should I be offended? I guess it was a little strange. I highly doubted anyone would dare attack me here in the castle, so why hide my arms?

Unless... he was ashamed of me. Of the fact that I hadn't manifested any powers.

"Are you well, Princess?" Dey asked, pausing by the door after escorting the seamstress out.

I waved a hand. "I'm fine. Go do whatever you gotta do. I'll see you at dinner tonight."

"Perhaps you will sit with me this time?"

He gave me a lopsided grin, and I plastered on a fake smile in return. "Sure, why not? Just make sure Josira has a place near me, ok?"

"Of course. I will see you tonight."

Left alone with my tumultuous thoughts, I stared up at the stone ceiling of my suddenly cold and empty room.

Ashamed. My father was ashamed of me. The thoughts rolled over me, a suffocating darkness threatening to swallow me whole and drag me down into the black abyss of suffering I had spent so many nights in as a child.

Stop, I commanded myself before the spiral could dig its claws in. I wasn't going to do this again. I wasn't a kid anymore, and I was too old to wallow in my lack of parental approval. If my father was so ashamed that I didn't have any powers yet, then I guess it was time to go get some damn powers. I was tired of being the only one here without them.

I thought back to the three ways Dey said I could activate my abilities. Crescia? That hadn't helped so far. Sex? While I'm sure Dey would gladly volunteer, that was so far from being an option now. Which left only pain. I needed someone to hurt me, emotionally and physically. And it needed to hurt *a lot*.

The memory of when I was sixteen scratched at the door of my mind, and I knew nothing short of reliving that night would be enough to break me.

I bit my lip. Was I really going to have someone torture me just because my father was ashamed of me?

No, I thought. This wasn't for him. I'd been hiding from that night long enough, shoving it down and refusing to go back there. I would need to deal with it sooner or later, and if meant I could finally hold my own in this world, then I guess I was going with sooner.

And I knew just who to ask.

Chapter Twenty-Eight

I don't know what I expected to see when I entered the arena, but I did know what I absolutely wasn't expecting to see—Sin backed up against a wall with a female wrapping her long legs around his waist. They were so entangled that I wouldn't have even known it was him save for his familiar leather black tunic.

It was instantaneous, the jealousy that boiled up inside me.

"Are you fucking kidding me?" I screeched before my rational brain could catch up and warn me that this was a very bad idea. That I had no claim over Sin and even less of a say in what, or who, he did in his spare time. "Was this why our kiss was a mistake? You know, you could have mentioned you were with someone. You didn't have to play me like a damned violin!"

Sin shifted around to look at me over the female's shoulder, his face tense and strained, then it disappeared behind a long curtain of silky chestnut tresses.

My vision turned red.

He acknowledged my presence and didn't even have the decency to push her away? I had never felt like a violent person before. Sure, anger was a close and personal friend, but violence? That was new.

I stormed across the arena to do something—not that I had any bright ideas in the moment—but before I reached them, the female flew back and hit the ground hard at my feet.

I stumbled backward, tripped, and landed on my ass. Scrambling to get up, I paused only when a calloused hand appeared in front of my face. Raising my arm to block the intense sun, I saw Sin leaning over me.

"No thanks," I grumbled, slapping his arm away so I could stand up on my own.

Beside me, the female popped her to feet with the grace and execution of a warrior gymnast.

I took her in briefly, registering the short-sleeved burgundy tunic and leggings paired with tall black boots that reached nearly to her knees. A bodice made of chainmail was snug against her ample chest, but it was her face that I lingered on. She was beautiful in the kind of way that I would never be. Tall and athletic with soft features, wide blue eyes, and olive skin that practically gleamed in the sunlight.

She was like the female equivalent of Dey, and I wanted nothing more than to mess up her pretty face.

If I paused for even a second to analyze that thought, I might have realized that the jealousy coursing through me was something to be a bit concerned about, but once again, my mouth was faster than my brain.

I whirled on Sin. "What the hell is going on? And who the hell is she?" I thumbed a finger at the hottie who just stood there watching me, as if I was a curious new insect and she was debating whether or not I was worth squashing.

I added her to my brand new 'maim and murder later' list, then turned my fury back to Sin. It took all I had not to slap the smirk right off his damn face. God, he looked like a cat that ate a canary and enjoyed every last bite.

He stepped up to the female—whose gentle features had settled into a rather intimidating glare after I dismissed her—and said, "Rain, meet Peywyn."

"Nice to meet you," I replied, sarcasm dripping from every syllable. "Sorry I interrupted your little tryst," I said to Sin. "By all means, don't let me stop you from making out with someone who isn't a mistake." My words were sharper than a knife, yet the smirk never even wavered. Couldn't he at least have the decency to look a little embarrassed that I had caught him?

I spun on my heels to stalk out of the arena before I did something stupid, like hurt my hand on his rock hard chin, but Sin grabbed my arm, halting my dramatic exit. "Peywyn is one of my soldiers. We were training, Fea Remia. No need to get jealous."

"Jealous?" I scoffed, completely dismissing the first part of the sentence. "I don't get jealous. And especially not over you."

"That's not what I saw," he said smoothly. "Tell me, do you nearly claw out the eyes of every female Dey speaks to, or is this level of rage special just for me?"

My flaming crimson cheeks had nothing to do with the two suns beating down. "You son of a bitch," I growled, my tone low and laced with the threat of violence.

"You're lucky I know that's just an expression, otherwise I might be insulted," Sin replied coolly. "My mother was quite lovely."

His words dumped a bucket of ice water over me. Every ounce of anger drained away as I recalled what Corym said about Sin's mom. How she raised him alone but died of that horrific plague... And I just called her a bitch. It didn't matter if it was a figure of speech, I still couldn't believe I'd said it. Once again, my uncontrolled anger had me spouting things I didn't really mean.

Sin's smirk dropped then, giving way to confused wariness as he watched shame overtake me. He released my arm and took a step back, evaluating this strange new creature in front of him.

"I'm sorry," I mumbled awkwardly. I turned to the female who regarded me with crossed arms and a rigid demeanor. "Sorry," I said quickly to her as well, his earlier words about her being a soldier finally penetrating the haze of my rage.

I rushed to leave the arena before I could embarrass myself further and made it just inside the tunnel before a rough hand clamped on my bicep, whirling me around. The action yanked me off balance, and I found myself careening into Sin's chest.

With lightning fast reflexes, he trapped me against him. "Would you please stop for one second and actually listen to me? Peywyn is my partner in the

Elemental Games. We were training in close combat fighting. She had a band of water at my throat choking me, or I would have explained when I first saw you."

Behind him, Peywyn threw up her hands in exasperation and stomped out of the arena. It was the response of someone annoyed that their training had been interrupted, not someone upset that their boyfriend was now holding another woman. Which had to mean he was telling the truth.

Once again, I had made a complete and utter ass of myself.

"Oh."

"'Oh?' That's all I get?" His glare faded as the corner of his lip twitched up. "Fea Remia, you wanted to murder Peywyn. I believe I deserve more than 'oh.'"

"Well 'oh' is all you get," I said, now struggling to break his tight embrace. I needed to get back to my room and die of mortification in peace.

He relaxed his hold on me enough to slide his hands down to my forearms, the firm grip an indication that he wasn't letting go just yet.

"You never answered my question," he said.

"What question?"

"I asked if you get jealous whenever Dey speaks to another female."

Answering that was the last thing I wanted to do. His ego was big enough. I opened my mouth to give some flippant response, but he stopped me.

"The truth, Rain. I can tell when you're lying."

I didn't know how the hell he could possibly do that, but the confidence in his eyes gave me pause. I glared at him and tugged my arms, trying to break free.

His grip only tightened. "Tell me the truth and I'll let you go."

I didn't see any way out of it, so I grit my teeth and said, "I haven't seen him speak to many other females, but no, I don't get jealous. For some reason, you manage to bring out my violent side." When he grinned, I added, "That's not a compliment."

He leaned forward and whispered in my ear, "To me it is."

I could feel nearly every muscle in my body clench with desire at the heat in his words. The gentle scrape of his stubble against my cheek and his warm breath on the shell of my ear had the memory of our kiss flooding my brain.

He pulled back slightly, and my body protested the loss of his warmth. I swallowed roughly and tried to find my north star. Sin was like a damned hurricane. Every time I was close to him, I always seemed to lose my bearings.

"Will you let go of me now?" I asked tightly, doing my best to hide how he had affected me.

He gave me a sly grin. "Nah."

I gaped at him and pulled against his grip. "But I answered your damn question. You said you'd let me go."

"I lied," he said, his smirk widening. "Asshole, remember?"

He was lucky he had both my hands trapped, or I would have smacked the grin off his face. Or I might have thrown my arms around him and let another 'mistake' happen. My mind and body were frequently at odds when it came to him.

He let me struggle briefly before the pressure of his hold loosened, and he stepped back. "You can go if you really want to, but I'd rather you just tell me what brought you here in the first place."

I rubbed my arms absently, enjoying the slight soreness I felt there, the reminder of how tightly he had held me and how much he didn't want to let go. I shouldn't like it as much as I did.

"I need your help to manifest my powers," I confessed. "I've been here almost a week, and nothing has happened yet. I can't wait any longer."

Sin's curious expression sank into a frown. "What's the rush?"

I didn't want to tell him that my father was ashamed of me, so I settled for something safer. Lifting my chin, I said, "The sooner I get my powers, the sooner I can travel to the Onyx Palace. I don't want to be here any longer than I have to."

A muscle feathered in Sin's jaw. "And how exactly do you think I can help with this?"

I held his gaze. "Dey told me there were three things that can possibly speed up the process. He's had me spending time with the crescia because he felt it was the only viable option, but it's not helping."

A positively wolfish grin spread across his face, highlighting the lines of his crooked nose and perfect lips. He took a step closer to me, and I could feel the warmth wafting off of him despite the chill from the shadowy tunnel. My traitorous body leaned into him slightly.

Chocolate had nothing on the smoothness of his voice as he replied, "You know where my bedroom is, Fea Remia. You're welcome any time."

A steady pulsing heat blazed to life between my legs, my toes curled inside my chucks, and I struggled to breathe. The throbbing between my thighs begged for his touch as a thousand images flashed through my brain.

Images of me on top of him, sinking down until every inch of his hard length was seated deep inside me.

Images of Sin naked on top of me, pumping into me with a punishing rhythm as I cried out my release.

My heart beat faster and faster as I was drowned in the visuals of us together.

Against a wall, the rough stone scraping against my back.

On the floor of his bedroom, me on my hands and knees.

In the pools, my ass propped up on the edge with his head buried between my legs.

It was that last one that broke me. Just enough that a small gasp slipped out. There was no hiding my reaction to his words. I wanted him, unequivocally, and now he knew it.

I took a step back, needing space from his presence that muddled my brain so profoundly. I could never think when he was that close to me. My back hit the stone wall of the tunnel, and the cool brick was a balm on my overheated skin.

That gentle kiss of chill was enough shock for me to close my eyes and focus. I came to the arena for a reason, and it wasn't to jump Sin's bones and ride him at a furious pace until he exploded like warm champagne. Sure, Dey said sex was an option for manifesting my powers, but if it didn't work, then I was left with the awkward aftermath of dealing with Sin for weeks to come.

I took three deep breaths to calm my racing heart before I felt confident my libido had been tamed.

Then I opened my eyes, and my confidence shattered as my thoughts once again tumbled into an abyss of need and desire. He had a hand on either side of the stone wall, caging me in, and his face was so close it would only take the slightest shift forward to press my lips against his. To spark the firework that would inevitably burn us both.

His body was deeply rigid and perfectly still as he held himself inches away from me, daring me to make that first move. His stormy ocean scent surrounded me, and I wanted nothing more than to fall into the dark sea that was Sin. To finish what we had started in the weapons room.

It was that thought that saved me. Our kiss in the weapons room. The one he had called a mistake.

I didn't have much, but I had my dignity, and I'd rather be tortured than fuck someone who thought being with me was ultimately a bad idea.

I slid down and ducked underneath his arms, the action quite possibly the hardest thing I'd ever done.

He leaned one shoulder against the wall I had just vacated and crossed his arms, giving me an amused look.

He was so much the picture of cool and collected that I couldn't stand it. The pulsing desire low in my body shot up into my chest and bloomed into white hot anger.

"What the hell is wrong with you? You called our kiss a mistake, and now you're happy to jump into bed? Which is it, Sin? Do you want me or not? Because I'm getting a little tired of trying to figure you out."

As soon as the words were out of my mouth, I wanted to take them back. Nothing good would come from him answering that question. I didn't know what it would mean between us if he said yes, but at the same time, I didn't think I would survive if he said no.

"On second thought, don't answer that. I don't care. I didn't come here to seduce you. I said I needed your help with my powers, but I didn't have sex in mind."

Sin's brow wrinkled in confusion, and I could see him trying to recall the third possibility. I knew the moment he figured it out because his posture turned stiff and closed off. "No," he said coldly, then took off striding across the arena.

I jogged after him. "What do you mean 'no?' I told you that I need my powers to manifest. And if I really have four of them to get through, then I need to get started."

His brisk stride barely slowed.

"Would you just wait?" I yelled, closing the distance between us. "I feel like I'm always chasing you across this damn arena. For once can you just help me without being so fucking difficult?"

Before I knew what was happening, Sin had my arms pinned tight against my sides, his strong hands shackling my wrists and forcing them down. A small cry escaped at the pressure of his grip. I didn't realize he had been gentle before, but this was rough and uncontrolled Sin.

"Is this what you want?" he demanded, shaking me like a rag doll. Another gasp of pain slipped out as he wrenched my hands behind me and my chest bowed against his. "You want me to hurt you? Is that really what you want, Rain?"

"Yes," I said firmly, meeting the intensity of his gaze head on. It was all I needed to say because I placed no asterisks on my statement. I wanted my power. I *needed* to feel powerful.

There was so much rage in Sin's eyes. He let go of my hands, and I fell to the ground.

"I won't do it," he said, something dark simmering under the surface of his words. "I won't hurt you just so you can make them happy. You're doing this, all of this, for them." He spat the word, and I knew the disgust he felt wasn't for me but for the people who drove me to this point. "They don't deserve you."

"This isn't for them," I argued. "It's for me. I just need to stop feeling weak. Please, Sin. I need to stop feeling so... lost."

His entire demeanor collapsed then, crumpling under the weight of my request. His head dropped, and for a minute he stood there, not saying a word but also not walking away.

A moment later, he knelt beside me. "Oh, Fea Remia," he murmured, "why me?"

"I'm not sure," I answered honestly. "When I made my decision, you were the first person I thought of. I can't explain it, but I feel like what I need... It has to be you."

He studied my face. "What exactly are you asking for, Rain?"

"Dey said it has to be a mix of physical and emotional pain, so I need you to help me relive the worst night of my life." Turning away from him, I dragged my tunic up, exposing the wide patch of ruined skin on my lower back. "I want you to cut these scars open."

Just thinking of that night already had me quivering. When Sin sliced into my flesh... it would destroy me. I just hoped I could rebuild myself afterward.

He made no sound at the sight of my scars, and I waited for him to say something. Every second felt like agony as I sat there, hunched over and feeling more bare than if I had actually been naked.

When I could no longer take the silence, I turned back to him, prepared to see pity or shock. Maybe even disgust. I'd seen it all. Hell, more than a few guys had refused to be with me after they saw the scars.

All I saw on Sin's face, though, was pure concentrated rage. Every hard line of his face was locked in tension, and I saw the muscle in his jaw tick twice before he opened his mouth.

"When?"

I blinked at him, confused. Who, why, and how were the popular choices when someone saw the damage, but 'when' was rarely brought up. And yet, it seemed so important to him.

Whatever the reason, I felt like I could tell him the truth, the raw, dirty truth that most people who saw my scars didn't actually want to know.

The words came out sluggish as I forced myself back to that night. "I was sixteen. I'd been sent to live with a new foster family—the Thorntons. At first, I thought they were wonderful, and they even had a son my age. Jimmy was so cute, and for weeks, he made me think that he was kind and funny and..."

My throat tried to close up on me at the memory. I'd never been able to talk about it before. Not to Jenn, not to any therapists. I could feel something straining inside me, something hot and angry trying to break free from where it lay buried deep beneath layers of pain and suffering.

Dropping my eyes to the dirt at my feet, I forced the rest out. "He was my first. I thought he liked me. Maybe even loved me, whatever that means. But after we... I was laying there with my back to him, imagining how much better my life could be with a loving home and a boyfriend who saw me as more than an orphan. I was so happy. For the first time in my pathetic life, I was actually optimistic and hopeful and... naïve.

"He was halfway through the first cut before I even felt the knife in my skin. I was too small and too weak compared to him, so I couldn't do anything more than struggle, and that just made it hurt worse. He held me down and took his time. He wanted it to be perfect. I was sobbing so loudly that his dad came in and told me to keep quiet. He knew exactly what his son was doing and didn't care.

"When Jimmy finished, he went back to his room, and I spent the rest of the night curled into a ball, my blood soaking the mattress beneath me. The next morning, they slapped a bandage on it and said they would kill me if I ever told anyone. I was sent to a new foster home a week later. Their twisted son got what he wanted, and they had no further use for me."

I traced the thick ridges covering the entirety of my lower back that no amount of time would ever diminish. JRT, he had carved. Jimmy Ryan Thornton.

I pushed myself to meet Sin's gaze, to see what he thought of me now that he knew the truth. His face was twisted in agony, and I honestly might have preferred pity.

"He claimed you," he whispered, his entire body shaking, his fists clenching and unclenching at his side. "I didn't know."

I laughed bitterly. "Of course you didn't know. Nobody here does. Well, Cam saw my back once, but I told him to keep quiet and didn't give any details. I don't exactly enjoy reliving it."

He shook his head, mumbling to himself. "He needs to pay. I should have made him pay."

I gaped at him. "What are you talking about? I was sixteen, and we hadn't even met yet. I don't need your overprotective, alpha male bullshit, and I really don't need it retroactively." I climbed to my feet and pulled my tunic on. "I've hidden from what happened that night my whole life. If reliving it helps me become stronger, then... then at least something good can come out of it. So help me become strong."

He didn't get up, just remained sitting in the dirt, refusing to look at me. "I can't," he said softly.

"Please tell me you're joking," I replied, disbelief flooding my face. "I know it's disgusting, but you would be doing me a favor. You could help me awaken my power. Please, Sin."

I never begged anyone for anything, but I would crawl on hands and knees if it meant I might wake up in the morning able to wield magic.

He looked at me then, something inexplicable hiding in the depths of his eyes. "Your back is not disgusting, Rain. You could never be disgusting to me. But I won't make it worse."

He paused, then added something in Rivellan, his words soft and tender.

I was too angry to even care what it meant. I just told him my darkest secret, ripped my trauma wide open in front of him, and he was refusing?

"Why the hell not?" I yelled.

Something about my scream must have broken through to him, because he jumped to his feet and pulled me roughly into his arms, my head braced tightly against his chest. "I won't be another monster in your story, Fea Remia. I will not, could not, *ever* hurt you like that."

The words were compassionate, and I felt so safe in his arms. Any other time, any other day, I would have snuggled deeper into him, relishing that comfort and security.

Right then, it was the exact opposite of what I needed.

Ripping free of his hold, I pushed him hard and backed away quickly. "Then what good are you?" I spat, infusing my voice with all the disdain and disappointment I felt.

I didn't look back as I tore out of the arena, my hopes of gaining my powers crushed beneath his feet.

Chapter Twenty-Nine

I spent the next hour or so in the glen behind the castle, watching the adult crescia fly around. The babies were cute, but the older ones were fascinating and considerably more active—dancing, preening, cuddling, and swooping about.

I briefly wondered which one was bonded to Sin. I would have thought with as much time as he spent in the arena, his crescia would have been nearby at least once, but I hadn't seen any around him. And none of the ones in the glen drove me insane with a hot/cold attitude, so his must live elsewhere.

Laying at the base of the largest tree to stare up into the branches, I let my mind wander over the possibilities of what my crescia might look like. If they changed to suit the bonded, then I felt bad for whichever one chose me. What type of fundamentally damaged monstrosity would I end up with to match all my own issues? It almost wasn't fair.

To them.

Maybe I wouldn't even get a crescia. God, how messed up would it be if everything was one great big cosmic mistake? I still didn't have any powers to confirm I actually was the supposed savior.

I thought back to my argument with Sin. How I begged him to hurt me so I could feel an inkling of magic in my veins. I spent almost ten years with the memory of that night buried so deeply in the recesses of my mind that I forgot about the scars most days. And I ripped it all wide open for the potential of magic. The potential of power. The potential to finally feel like I was someone who mattered.

A wave of disgust rolled over me. It would almost be fitting if I endured weeks of misery only to discover I was nothing more than the waste of space I'd always been. I doubted even magic could fix my broken brain.

Feeling a spiral about to start, I dug my meds out of my tunic pocket. I knew where this was headed, and it would be better to cut it off before things got much worse.

I waited another fifteen minutes or so until the soothing calm of Klonopin washed over my brain, quieting the churning maelstrom of painful thoughts.

Both suns were fairly high in the sky, so I assumed it was safe to say the morning had officially become the afternoon. Which meant it was time to go see Corym. If Sin wouldn't help me with my power, hopefully his father could at least help me with the language.

Pushing open the door to the library, I was pleased to see Corym standing on a ladder, shelving a book with no traces of last night's distress on his face.

He shot a glance over his shoulder and gave me a huge grin. "Raynella, you are right on time." He shoved the massive tome into place and climbed down.

"How come there are so few books," I asked while I waited for him to clean up his desk. "I would have thought a royal library would be bigger."

"Ah, yes, one would think that and rightfully so. However, King Verren does not allow literature from other courts to be kept here. So we are limited to only those produced within the Diamond Court, and writing has never been much of a socially supported pursuit."

I sifted through his words, trying to determine the meaning behind his stilted speech. "Are you saying writing isn't cool here?"

"Yes, I suppose that would be the accepted vernacular," Corym said, chuckling softly. "The Diamond Kings of centuries past have always encouraged their citizens to prioritize building up the strength of our court more than anything else. For their own protection, of course."

I frowned. "Protection from what?"

"From the other courts," he stated plainly, as if confused as to why I would even ask. "There have been few wars throughout Rivella's history, but they have all been extremely destructive. The amount of damage powerful elemental casters can do is something quite terrifying to behold." His eyes shuttered for a moment. "You did not come here for a history lesson, though." He gestured toward his back office. "Shall we see what we can do about your language problem?"

I grinned, excitement bubbling up in me as I followed him into the small room. He seemed happy and healthy. Maybe the transfer would actually work this time.

Corym sat on the sofa and indicated the spot beside him.

"So, you're better today?" I asked, scanning his face for any hidden signs of distress. "No headaches?"

He gave my leg a gentle pat. "You do not need to worry about me, Raynella. Not only have I spent my life providing knowledge to others, but I have also spent many years anxiously awaiting your arrival so that I might play a small part in your journey to save Rivella. I want nothing more than to help you."

I almost asked how he could have so much kindness in him when Sin had so little, but I didn't want to rip open old wounds.

"Okay, then," I said, clapping my hands together and rubbing them briskly. "Let's do this. Anything I need to know first? Dey said the experience was disorienting."

Corym scratched his chin for a second. "I suppose that would be an accurate description. Though it does vary person to person. Do remember that I have never done this on one such as yourself before."

I didn't know if he was talking about the fact that I was half-human, or the fact that I had no magic yet. Either way, it didn't matter, I wasn't turning back now.

"That's fine," I said quickly. "I'll take the risk."

Corym let out a slow breath as he scrutinized my face. If he was looking for any sign of hesitation, he wouldn't find it.

"Take my hands, Raynella, and close your eyes."

I did as he said and waited for the crushing influx of the Rivellan language to flood my brain.

And waited.

And waited.

I cracked an eye open. Corym still sat across from me, but now his face was pinched in concentration, beads of sweat forming on his brow.

"Is there still something wrong?" I asked wearily, afraid he might be back in the same situation as yesterday.

He let go of my hands and shook his head. "There is something foreign swimming inside your mind. I have never seen anything quite like it. I want to give you the language, Princess, but I am still fighting my own hesitancy. I do not think I can work around this new obstacle as well."

"You're still fighting to help me? I thought you were better?"

"I am much better, but there is a reservation lingering inside me that I do not fully understand. Nor do I understand what this hinderance is that floats at the forefront of your mind."

I tried analyzing my own brain, but I had no clue what to even look for. It definitely wasn't something I did. I wanted this more than anything. Frustrated, I slumped back against the couch. The movement caused my Klonopin bottle to shake, and a sick feeling hit me.

"Corym, is there a chance that a medication from my world could affect your abilities?"

He rubbed his forehead thoughtfully. "What type of medication?"

I swallowed. The last thing I needed was for Corym to think I was crazy or defective in some way. "It sort of… calms my mind. I guess that's the best way to describe it."

Corym stood and paced around the room, his anxious steps threatening to wear a hole in the rug. "It is possible," he said. "There is simply no way to know how human drugs might impact your Vitaean half. It could interfere with my abilities."

I groaned. "So you're saying we have to wait until it's out of my system?" I wanted to punch the sofa. Once again, I was so close to making progress only to be shut down. Story of my life.

Corym tapped a finger absently against his chin, lost in thought. The perfect picture of a scholar trying to solve a problem.

I saw a flicker of light in his eyes and sat up. "Is there another way around it?"

"Perhaps, perhaps," he said, still not quite fully present. I waited patiently, giving him the time needed to sort through whatever he was considering.

Finally, he grabbed my hands. "Raynella, I think I have a solution, if you are amenable."

"Anything," I blurted out, and it was sad how much I actually meant it.

"This substance resides at the forefront of your active mind, yes, but your subconscious may be unaffected. I could attempt to deposit the information there, and once the medication is gone, you would be able to access it. I cannot say when that will be or how quickly the language will take root, but it is worth a try. Provided you are willing."

"Oh, I'm very willing," I said, shifting my body so I was facing him full on, the eager student ready to learn.

"Splendid. This is my first time using the subconscious, so please be patient with me."

I laughed and gave him a sly wink. "It's my first time, too, Corym." He smiled politely, and I realized the joke had gone over his head. Seriously, how was he related to Sin?

I closed my eyes and braced myself for whatever was about to happen. Luckily, it was less than a minute before I felt a tingling in my head, like wind chimes blowing in the breeze—a gentle sensation that tickled and danced through my mind. I relaxed into the couch. I could handle this.

Then everything changed. A gasp escaped my lips as the gentle tingling grew into zaps of lightning arcing through my brain, each one a dagger of crackling electric pain. I was spinning, tumbling, falling into a black abyss of torment, clawing frantically at nothing. I was lost to the darkness and the purest suffering I had ever known.

Someone was screaming, such a horrific sound, and only when it began to fade did I realize it had been me.

Corym released my hands, and I fell back against the couch, my head lolling to the side. The misery faded but not the memory. I didn't think that would ever go away.

"Did it work?" I croaked out, my voice scratchy and dry.

The older scholar's face was a mess of exhaustion and worry. I wanted to reach out and smooth the prominent wrinkles of his forehead, but I could barely move my body.

"Yes. I believe it worked." His face contorted from worry to shame. "I am so immensely sorry, Raynella. If I had known..."

"Known what? You said anything could happen. Was it the most intense agony of my life? No doubt. But it was over fairly quick, and I survived. I'll take the win." I started to sit up, but Corym placed a hand against my shoulder.

"Do not try to move yet. You should rest."

"I'm fine, Corym, seriously. I can handle a few seconds of pain."

He shook his head and kept his hand on my shoulder, gently pressing me onto the couch. "Princess, you have been screaming for over an hour."

I stayed in Corym's office a few more minutes, scarcely comprehending how what felt like seconds had actually been much longer. Mostly I was just grateful that it hadn't been the other way around.

When I was able to get to my feet without help, Corym let me leave, but not before reiterating at least three times that the language would gradually settle into my brain, and he could not predict how soon or how fast it would happen.

I gave him a hug before heading out, and strangely, it felt less awkward than the one I had given my father. Corym might not be my actual parent, but he had the empathy and kindness I still craved from Verren.

Back in my room, I collapsed on my bed, content to pass out for the rest of the afternoon. To my dismay, the sisters appeared in my room to prepare me for dinner less than five minutes after my back hit the blankets.

I never asked what the sisters' magic was, but their real talent had to be transforming me every night from a gutter rat into something frighteningly close to a princess. They had gone all out tonight with an elaborate updo held together by six-inch-long diamond encrusted pins that stuck out of my hair in an explosion of sparkles. Combined with a lemon-colored gown that faded down through shades of orange into a deep crimson, I looked like a walking sunburst in the best way possible.

Dey's timing was once again impeccable, arriving just as they secured my bodice, and he escorted me to dinner, happily chatting about the upcoming ball. The entire time he remained oblivious to my slow steps and quiet murmurs of agreement.

True to his word, Dey had made sure Jo was seated across from us, and I was pleased to see the jubilant expression on her face.

"I have never sat so close to King Verren before," she cooed happily inside my head. *"Normally only his senior advisors are allowed here. I am usually lucky if I don't have to sit with empty seats all around me."*

It was still a gut punch every time I remembered how the people here treated Jo simply because her method of communication made them uncomfortable.

"I will tell my father you should be allowed to sit here from now on. This archaic seating arrangement is just a stupid power move that serves no real purpose that I can see."

My father arrived then, and I was surprised to see his step falter when he observed Jo seated across from me. Apparently Dey hadn't given him a heads up. Interesting, considering he always seemed like a total scaredy cat when it came to anything involving his king. My father quickly recovered and took his seat at the head of the table.

Our meals followed shortly after, and I tried to ignore the disappointment I felt when I realized Sin wasn't coming to dinner. I hadn't wanted to cause any permanent damage to our friendship with my request. Not that we actually were friends. I honestly had no clue what we were, but something had definitely changed when I walked out of that arena.

"How did your meeting with the seamstress go, Raynella?" my father asked, and I shifted to face him, letting Dey strike up a conversation with the courtier on his other side.

"It actually went okay," I said once I swallowed the bite in my mouth. I was still working on my princess manners, but I wasn't a total lost cause.

"Wonderful," he replied, the smile on his face reminding me of how he had been when I first arrived—genuinely happy.

"Tomorrow," Dey said, and I turned to face him.

"What's that?" I asked, his back still directed away.

He shifted to look at me. "I am sorry, Princess. I was speaking to Ferdin here. He doesn't know English, so I must converse in Rivellan." He gave me an apologetic look, then returned to his conversation.

I frowned. He'd definitely said 'tomorrow', and it hadn't been in Rivellan. I rubbed at my temples, trying to massage away the headache that had taken root.

"Are you all right, Raynella?" my father asked.

"Yeah, just a headache. I'm fine. Probably need to drink more water." I grabbed the glass in front of me and chugged half in a single go.

Further down the table, the word 'absolutely' caught my attention, and it was followed up with a boisterous guffaw. I glanced over, but the only person laughing was a portly fellow who definitely shouldn't be speaking English.

What the hell is going on?

The pressure at my temples was steadily increasing, and I continued rubbing at them, hoping to alleviate even a hint of the pain.

"Rain, are you sure that you are all right?" Jo asked inside my head, her voice thick with worry.

"Yeah, yeah, I'm fine," I muttered and attempted to give her a reassuring look. I must have failed because the concern on her face held firm.

"Simply atrocious," a high-pitched female voice said, the sound grating and unfamiliar. I whipped my head back around and pinned the voice on a snooty-looking courtier a few seats away that was draped in far too many jewels for a casual dinner.

"How...?" The word just slipped out, and both Jo and my father gave me a curious look.

"How what, Raynella?" he pressed.

Before I could answer, a sharp bolt of pain exploded inside my skull, and I let out a pitiful whimper, clutching my head. A red hot knife attempted to pry my eyes from their sockets, and I pushed back from the table. "I'm sorry," I managed to grit out through tightly clenched teeth. "This migraine is only getting worse. I think I need to go lie down."

"Of course," he said hesitantly, as if he could tell it was more than a mere headache. "I will send a servant up with the rest of your meal shortly."

"No, that's okay," I said, backing away from the table. "I had plenty. I don't need anything else. I'll... I'll see you at breakfast tomorrow. I think I need some rest."

Sprinting to my room, I only just closed my door when the searing pain detonated with such intensity I could no longer hold back my screams. The agony was not the sharp lightning from earlier. It was acid. Venom. It was a cancerous poison that devoured every cell in my brain, only to spit them back out so it could do it all again.

I managed to crawl onto my bed moments before the torturous sensation fully consumed me, and a wave of darkness pulled me under.

Chapter Thirty

I wandered aimlessly through the rose maze. Everything around me was awash in a dreamy haze, and my eyes swam in and out of focus. I felt lost, yet a strong wave of déjà vu swept over me.

I rounded a corner and stopped when I saw... myself.

Pausing, I watched the scene unfold before me. The open rift that stole my life away glowed with that striking blue light, and a past version of me stood on the other side, peering through at the Walker. The familiar events occurred only a few days ago, yet I felt like I was looking at a stranger.

It was like I was a ghost in my own mind.

The Walker glared at the other Rain still standing in Jersey, then opened his mouth to speak. Only this time I understood him.

"I take it you're the girl everybody has made such a fuss about? Well come on, I don't have all day."

Before I could even take a step toward the rift to warn my past self to run, there was a harsh tug inside me, and the world shifted, dumping me into another memory.

This time Past Rain stood outside the throne room, pacing in front of two guards. I watched silently as the scene once again played out just as I remembered it.

"Princess," the guards intoned, bowing their heads.

"You don't have to do that," Past Rain said.

The guard furrowed his brow. *"Do you need help?"*

I wanted to scream yes, I did need help, but once again, I was tossed through a kaleidoscope of images.

Scene after scene, memory after memory, played out in front of me, and I was helpless to stop them or even slow them down.

I watched my past self meet the sisters.

"Greetings," they said in unison.

I watched my father speak to Dey at the breakfast table the first day I met him.

"I thought you prepared her?" my father asked.

"Apologies, my king," Dey replied. *"She has not been adjusting well. I mentioned our magic, but I was afraid I might damage her psyche if I tried to tell her too much. She is quite fragile."*

"Yes, I can see that. This may be a bigger challenge than anticipated," my father confirmed.

I watched as I approached Jeylana, and she grabbed my arm.

"Save yourself," she uttered, before her eyes closed once more.

I tried to lock onto that memory. My father told me that she had said, 'save us,' but that wasn't what she said at all. What could I possibly need saving from? Or who?

I was helpless to stop the pull that dumped me outside Jeylana's room just as my past self slammed the door shut, panting.

My head whipped toward the stairs. He would be coming soon.

This was when I first met Sin.

Sure enough, he rounded a corner, and Past Rain plowed straight into him.

He gripped her shoulders and slammed her into the stone wall. My past self cried out as she struggled to push him away. The expression on Sin's face went from anger to confusion back to anger.

"You can't be here," he barked at Past Rain.

"Stop!" she cried out. "You're hurting me."

"Do you know what I have done to keep you away from this place? What I have sacrificed?" he shouted.

"I don't know what the fuck you're saying!"

I watched, hypnotized, as Sin pushed her away and stepped back, clenching his fists. Past Rain closed the gap and shoved him, sending him stumbling backward. I laughed at the shock on his face. It wouldn't be the last time I would catch him off guard.

He quickly recovered and was back in Past Rain's face. *"You're in danger here, and I won't sit back and watch you die!"*

"What is your freaking problem, asshole?" Past Rain glowered at him.

As they stood trapped in a silent standoff, I recalled the warm sensation of his body so close to mine. I had known then, felt it then. I thought it was hatred, but now I knew the truth; I just despised how much I was drawn to him. To the darkness haunting his eyes that so closely matched my own.

Sin smirked as my past self took a step back. He'd probably thought I was conceding to him. As if I would ever.

"Don't you know who I am?" Past Rain snapped. "Princepa."

Sin laughed. *"Is that what you think you are?"* he asked. *"You are so much more than that..."* He leaned in closer and growled, *"My lost queen."*

Then he stalked off down the hall, leaving me and my past self standing there, alone, trying desperately to slow our racing hearts.

Chapter Thirty-One

I jolted upright in bed, sweaty and panting heavily. Clutching the blankets to my chest, I sat in the nearly pitch black room, listening to the soft crackling of the dying hearth as I recalled my dream.

It had worked. The language transfer worked. I could speak Rivellan. I opened my mouth to say something, anything, but when my brain went searching for the words, it came up empty.

"What the hell?"

I willed myself to say 'this place is crazy' in Rivellan, but nothing came out because... I didn't know the words. I recalled every translation from my dream but not how to actually speak it. It was like I had been watching a movie dubbed in my mind without paying any attention to the language.

Groaning, I fell back against my pillow. *My subconscious*, Corym had said. He put the information in my subconscious, and now that I was awake, I couldn't access it. Couldn't match a single Rivellan word to an English one.

Except one phrase—Fea Remia. My lost queen.

That translation had stuck. Maybe because he said it so many times, or maybe because it was the last thing in my dream, I had no idea. It didn't matter, though, because it didn't make any sense. Princess, sure, my father was the king after all, but while I might not agree with some of the decisions he made as a ruler, I had no intention of kicking him off the throne.

I replayed the words from my first meeting with Sin, but knowing the translation didn't help me understand our bizarre conversation. What had he sacrificed? And what did he mean that he wouldn't watch me die? If he was so worried, then why not tell me what was going on?

I ran my hands through my hair and felt something hit my arm. I reached up and touched my head. The diamond pins. I yanked them out, yelping slightly when one stabbed my finger with it's sharp tip.

Once I got them all, I tossed the whole pile in the general direction of my nightstand and shook out my long hair. Pulling the uncomfortable dress off, I decided to just sleep in my underwear.

Staring out into the dark of my room, I waited to see if the past would come calling once more.

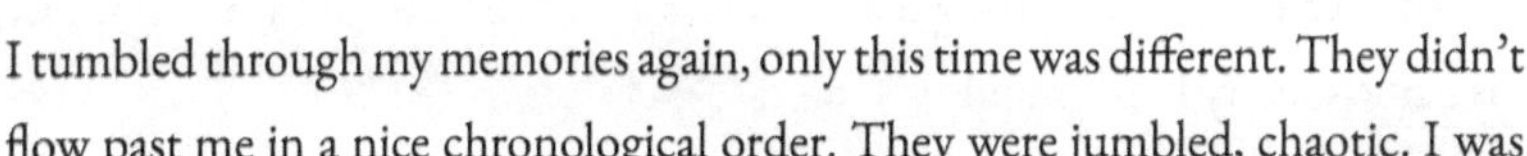

I tumbled through my memories again, only this time was different. They didn't flow past me in a nice chronological order. They were jumbled, chaotic. I was flung from scene to scene, catching only snippets.

I listened to Dey tell the seamstress that I liked the dress before she left. Then the scene rewound to the beginning, and I heard Dey apologizing for our tardiness. "*Truly we meant no offense to one so talented as yourself,*" he said.

Then I was thrown like a ragdoll to the ground in another memory. Lifting my head, I saw the young guard that had showed me to the dungeons.

"I will surely be beaten if I take you down there."

I didn't have a second to feel bad for what I had done before I was falling into another moment in time.

I tried to close my eyes when I saw the glittering city appear around me, but there was no hiding inside my head.

"Sacrilegious!"

"How dare an abicario use the Shen'Valla shroud to sneak in here!"

"She will pay in blood for her blasphemy."

I was helpless to do anything but listen to the insults and watch the mob nearly beat me to death.

For once, I welcomed the forceful tug that hurled me through a tunnel of memories and deposited me in the dining hall where I saw Dey clasping my hands.

"I wish I could stay with you today, but Sin will take good care of you, I promise. He might seem a little rough, but he is very skilled and will train you well."

"I'll be fine. I can handle grumpy pants over there."

"I might not be so grumpy if he would keep his damn hands off of you," Sin muttered.

The scene reversed around me then, everyone moving backward like a tape rewinding.

Action resumed as I heard Sin telling my father he thought he was restraining an intruder, but quickly realized I was far too inept to be an assassin.

At least now I knew what made my father laugh. Thanks, Sin.

I could feel the pull alerting me that I was about to be tossed again, but I let his name solidify in my mind.

Sin. Focus on Sin. I wanted to see more of him. Hear all the things he kept from me.

It worked too well. Suddenly my brain was flooded with memories of him, all jumbled up and bouncing around like my mind couldn't pick just one. Fractured glimpses of time, each one passing by before I could latch on.

Sin walking away from me at our first training session. *"I won't let you kill yourself. Not for him."*

Sin talking to Dey on the roof after their fight. *"You said that you could take care of her."*

Sin yelling at Dey outside his room. *"Neither of us is good enough for her!"*

Faster the memories flew by me, little more than hiccups, then gone once more.

"And it'll happen again because you can't always protect her."

"Because you are too reckless for your own good."

"She doesn't need your hands groping her right now."

Then it all came to a screeching halt, and Sin was kneeling by me in the arena. I immediately registered the moment; it was when I bared my soul after begging him to hurt me. My heart stopped as I recognized the emotion I hadn't been able to identify at the time. The painful tenderness I saw hiding in the depths of his green eyes that had been so foreign I simply dismissed it as unimportant. Maybe I hadn't realized what it was because I had never seen it before. Never felt it before.

"Your back is not disgusting, Rain. You could never be disgusting to me. But I won't make it worse." He paused, then added softly, *"I love you too much."*

I couldn't move. Couldn't breathe. Couldn't stop what was happening in front of me. The memory began looping, replaying his words over and over again. I had wanted to latch onto something, and I finally managed it.

"I love you too much."

Except it couldn't be this. Anything but this.

"I love you too much."

I had to get out. Had to stop it.

"I love you too much."

I needed to break the loop. Needed to wake up.

"I love you too much."

My brain was on fire, burning with the intensity of the memory.

"I love you too much."

I just. Needed it. To stop.

"I love you too much."

"No you don't!" I screamed as I was hurled violently out of the memory and flung backward through time. No matter how hard I tried to make it stop, I couldn't silence the words.

Tumbling through my own mind, a tornado of memories swept me up and forced me to relive every interaction I ever had with Sin right up until he slammed me against the wall the first night we met.

The force of the impact ripped me from the dream state, and I shot upright in bed, still screaming that he couldn't love me. Not like that. I didn't deserve it.

Because I was far too broken to ever be able to love him back.

Chapter Thirty-Two

Judging by the faint sliver of light peeking in through my curtains, it was still quite early. The sisters wouldn't be in to wake me for some time, but there was no way I could possibly go back to bed. I couldn't risk falling into my memories again. Into *that* memory.

I threw on the first clothes I saw and stormed out of my room. I would wait in the library until Corym showed up and demand that he fix whatever went wrong with the language transfer. I needed to be able to understand people, speak to them, not be sucked into memories every time I closed my eyes.

Pushing open the entrance to the library, I caught a hint of light spilling out from under the door to Corym's back office. I didn't even stop to wonder why he would be awake so early. I just marched over to the door and yanked it open.

"Corym, I need to talk to—" The words caught in my throat as I scrambled to understand what I was looking at. Flashes of my past filled my vision.

The sharp edge of a knife.

Smooth skin being sliced up.

A pool of blood.

My feet were in motion before I even knew what was happening.

I ripped Corym off the sofa and flung him against the wall. "Stop! You're killing him!"

He clearly didn't share his son's self-defense skills, because he hit the wall hard and slid to the floor, his body going still.

I rushed to the sofa and knelt by Sin who lay prone, his eyes wide in fear. I forced myself not to look at his back. At the mess of blood and flesh I'd seen when I opened the door. Fuck, could he even survive that?

"Sin, what did he do to you?" I brushed a lock of sweaty hair out of his face. "Tell me how to help you." A terrified voice in the back of my head whispered that I was too late. Too late to prevent Sin from suffering a fate even more awful than my own.

"Rain," he said with a slight tremor. "I need you to listen to me very carefully."

"Yes, of course, whatever you need me to do." I tried so hard not to look, but I couldn't stop my eyes from flickering past his shoulder to the gore beyond. I was right. It was so much worse than what I had endured.

Sin's hand clamped onto my chin, drawing me back to him.

"Focus, Rain," he said firmly, and I nodded, giving him my complete attention. "I need you to make sure Corym is okay. It sounded like he hit his head, and I need you to see if you can wake him up."

Had he lost his damn mind? He wanted me to go help the person who butchered him?

"I am all right," Corym said, and I whipped my head over to see him climbing to his feet. "Just a minor contusion."

I jumped up and got in his face, my inner Jersey girl emerging in full force. "Oh, it's going to be a hell of a lot more than that if you don't have a damned good explanation for why you were carving Sin up like a fucking side of beef."

"Rain," Sin croaked from the sofa. "While your willingness to do violence on my behalf is extremely attractive, it's not actually needed right now. He was helping me."

"And I am nearly finished," Corym interjected, "so with your permission, I would like to get back to work."

I stood there, horrified, trying to make sense of it all while Corym retrieved the knife and began cutting into Sin's back once more. He removed a thin flap of skin and tossed it into a bucket at his side.

My hand slapped to my mouth to hold back the rising gorge as the strip landed with a sickening plop atop of a mound of bloody flesh bits.

As long as I lived I would never get the image of exposed muscle tissues out of my head.

I dropped back to my knees beside Sin. "What happened?" I choked out.

"Oh, Rain," he said softly. "I never wanted you to see this."

"See what?" I pleaded. "What is he doing to you?"

He dropped his face to the couch, offering no response.

"Whatever is going on, please just tell me, Sin." I couldn't help him if he wouldn't talk to me, and I needed to help him.

Sin remained silent, and Corym announced that he was finished a few minutes later. The scholar uncorked a glass jar full of silver flecks and sprinkled them liberally over the bloody mess that was Sin's upper back and shoulders.

"The fenite is in place, Dreisin," Corym announced as he levered himself to his feet. "I will leave you to decide how you would like to handle Raynella." He gave me a small bow. "Princess. I wish I could say that it was lovely to see you again, but we both know that would be false given the circumstances." He paused, then added, "Do please allow him some time to recover before you make any rash decisions."

Corym left, and I turned back to Sin, relieved to see that his face was no longer drawn tight with pain. "Please," I begged him. "Tell me how to fix this."

He sighed and pulled his arm out from under his body to curl it beneath his head so he could rest atop it. If I ignored the small tension lines around his eyes, I could pretend things were casual, relaxed even. Just Sin lounging on the sofa, looking devilishly handsome as always. Except he wasn't relaxed, and this wasn't casual.

I scooted closer to the couch so I could lay my head near his. Face to face, we both took a second to breathe the other one in. His stormy ocean scent was tinged with the coppery tang of blood that permeated the air, yet his eyes shuttered in bliss as he inhaled deeply.

"How can you do that?" I asked, our faces so close that I could nearly touch my nose to his.

"Do what?"

"Smell all that blood and look happy about it."

He gave me a small, genuine smile, not a smirk, and it reminded me of the rooftop. When he smiled at me for the first time.

"Because I don't smell blood, Fea Remia. I only smell you. And you smell like sweet apples and sunshine."

I winced at his endearment for me. "I'm not a queen, Sin. I'm barely a princess."

His brow furrowed. "I take it you asked someone for the translation?"

"No," I replied, not ready to deal with everything that came along with admitting to him that I sort of knew Rivellan now.

"Then how did you learn?"

"You first," I said firmly. Reaching out, I trailed a hand down his neck and over his shoulder, stopping just shy of the pool of blood that covered his upper back. "Tell me why Corym was flaying off strips of skin. I don't think I can ever go to sleep again without seeing the image of you sliced up like a half-butchered pig."

Regret flooded his pale green eyes. "I'm so sorry you had to see that. Nobody is supposed to know about this, least of all you." He took a deep inhale and closed his eyes on the exhale. "I'm an amplissario, Rain. Corym was... He was cutting the ramentum out of my skin so no one would find out the truth."

I pulled away from him, a mixture of shock and horror twisting my features as the bile in my stomach rose once more. "Why? I thought power was a sign of status here. The more the better. Why would you ever hide who you really are?"

"Because the king would kill me if he knew," Sin replied. "He does not allow amplissarios to exist outside his own royal line since we are a threat to his power. You can't tell anyone, Rain. My life is in your hands."

The bile climbed higher in my throat, burning my lungs, and it took all my willpower not to throw up.

"Say something," he pleaded.

I shook my head at him, trying to figure out some way this atrocity could possibly be justified, but there was nothing. Nothing to explain this away. Nothing that would ever make this okay.

Sin had to mutilate his body just for the right to exist, and I wanted to vomit because I had asked him to do the same thing to me.

All because I wanted to feel special.

Chapter Thirty-Three

The air was suffocating with so many unspoken words and unanswered questions. What could I even say? I wanted to apologize for my father, and I really wanted to apologize for stupidly asking him to cut my scars open, but anything I said would be too hollow, too insignificant when compared to the damage done.

I turned away from Sin, unable to avoid looking at his back and seeing all the blood my father was responsible for.

Since I couldn't take the silence either, I asked the first question that came to mind.

"How often?"

"About once a lunar cycle," he replied slowly, as if afraid the words would upset me.

He was right.

"Oh, God," I gasped out, dropping my head to my hands. Once a month. Once a month he had to carve up his back to keep his secret. And if he was seventy-seven that meant... I didn't want to know the answer. Didn't want to do the math. Whatever the number, it was too many. Too many times he had been forced to endure this.

"The fenite flakes Corym adds to the wound help. They cause some pretty awful scars, but it takes longer for the ramentum to fully reappear that way. They always come back, though. They're part of me, part of my magic, and this is the only way to keep them hidden. I cannot risk that I might get injured in training and a healer would need to remove my shirt."

I let out a bitter laugh. "This is what you meant the other day, isn't it? When you said you had grown somewhat desensitized to the fenite."

Sin exhaled, and his breath tickled the back of my ear.

I wanted so badly to turn around. To take him in my arms and hold him until this world wasn't so awful anymore.

But the world would always be awful. His world. My world. It was all the same. Everyone suffered in the end.

Shoring up my nerves, I shifted to face him, bracing myself for the sight of his back but knowing he deserved a comforting presence. I wouldn't abandon him, no matter how difficult it was.

I gave him a sad smile. "I guess I can't complain about my scars anymore, can I?"

He ran a hand down the side of my face and rested his thumb on my bottom lip. "Don't worry, Fea Remia," he replied, smirking. "I have complete faith you'll find something else to complain about."

I laughed as I sank against the couch, allowing my head to fall beside his on the soft fabric. The heaviness in the room lifted, and my body relaxed slightly. If Sin could make jokes, he would be okay.

Nothing outside of this room would ever be okay again, but at least for now, we could hide from the world.

"I'm proud of you, you know," he said, taking my chin with two fingers and gently tilting my head toward his.

"Why?" I asked, feeling wholly unworthy of the light shining in his eyes.

"Because you didn't panic," he whispered, leaning forward to brush his lips against mine, gentle, inquisitive, like he was giving me the chance to pull away. "You got a little angry, sure." Another feather light kiss. "And I have to admit watching you rough up Corym was a little hot." A deeper kiss. "But you didn't break down. You didn't have a panic attack." Even deeper. "I'm so proud of you."

I couldn't take it anymore. Curling my hand around the back of his neck, I let myself sink into his kiss. And when he parted his lips, my tongue slipped in to meet his.

He kissed me like it was our first time. I kissed him like I was drowning and he was my only source of air.

"Wait," I said breathlessly, forcing myself to pull away. "Not like this. You're lying on the couch unable to move, and I have your blood on my hands."

"Seems to be a common theme with us," he replied, laughing. "One of these days, I'll kiss you and neither of us will end up bleeding."

One of these days.

His words had a sobering effect, and I tried to mask the uncertainty I felt.

'One of these days' implied a future.

'One of these days' implied there was something real happening between us.

'One of these days' reminded me that he said he loved me. Even if he knew I didn't understand it at the time.

Picking at the blood drying on my fingers, I couldn't help but feel like it was a sign.

I cleared my throat. "So, um, what happens now?" When he gave me a wicked grin, I clarified, "With your back, I mean. Can I help somehow?"

Sin twisted his body a few times. "The fenite slows my healing ability, but I think it's mostly scarred over. I would appreciate it if you could go find Corym so he can clean me up. I don't want to drip all over his antique Parellan rug. This thing was crafted before Rivella was sealed off from the rest of Vitaea, so I can't exactly buy him a new one."

I cast him a withering glare. "If that's all you need, then I think I can handle washing your back, Sin."

He propped himself up on his elbows and matched my scowl with his own. "Go get Corym, Rain. I don't want you to see how bad it looks under all that blood."

"How bad it looks?" I folded my arms and let out a mirthless laugh. "So what, I show you my back, but I can't see yours? I doubt it's that much worse."

"Gods dammit, Rain," he growled. "This is not a competition to see which one of us is more fucked up."

"Good, cause I'd win," I snarked bitterly.

A strangled sound escaped Sin, and he collapsed face first onto the sofa. "Shen'Valla take me now," he muttered. "Are you always this difficult?"

"Are you?" I shot back. When he offered no response, I started searching the room. It didn't take long to find the small bucket of water and stack of hand towels Corym had tucked behind the sofa. I knelt by Sin's back and said, "You can grumble all you want, but you told me my scars didn't make me disgusting. Well guess what? Neither do yours."

He mumbled something under his breath that sounded vaguely like consent, so I dipped a towel in the water and started to mop up the pool of blood.

My hands trembled slightly as I made the first pass over his back. There was so much blood that it saturated the towel, and I had to wring it out in the bucket, turning the water from crystal clear to a sickening shade of pink that only got darker as I continued.

Sin shifted on the sofa, twisting his head to look back at me. "I don't suppose you'll talk to me now? It would help keep my mind off what you're doing back there."

"Maybe," I said, meeting his gaze. "What did you want to talk about? Personally, I want to discuss why you quote my favorite movie all the time. Or better yet, let's discuss how you knew about my anxiety medication. Either of those sound good?"

I returned my attention to the task at hand, finally clearing enough blood away to see what was underneath. The ropey muscle was no longer visible, and the last edges of the deep cuts were slowly knitting back together before my eyes. I ran my fingers lightly over his back and down the mess of peaks and valleys. His skin was a topographical map of suffering. I would never say a word about my scars again. At least I could forget about mine most of the time. But Sin? He had to reopen his every month. They would never fade, the edges would never soften. It would always be a fresh new hell from which he couldn't escape.

I looked down and saw him watching me closely. Wiping away any trace of pity, I gave him a weak smile. "So? What did you decide for the topic of conversation?"

"You," he whispered. "You said no one translated Fea Remia for you. Care to elaborate?"

I had really hoped he would forget about that. Me and my damn mouth.

"Sin, I don't think this is the best conversation to have when I'm wiping blood off your back." Or ever, if I could possibly avoid it.

He craned his neck to look further over his shoulder. "Looks like you're about done to me. Seems like a great time."

I narrowed my eyes at him as I wiped the last of the blood from his back and tossed the towel back in the water tub. "How come you get to keep so many secrets, but I can't have just one?"

"Because I want to know everything about you," he said, shifting onto his side and tucking his arm under his cheek. If I thought passionate and intense Sin was hot, then casual and relaxed Sin was a whole other form of torture. It was so rare to see him as anything other than angry or distant, but now, with him stretched out, lounging on the sofa... I could almost picture us as a real couple, back in my apartment in Jersey about to watch a movie on a Friday night.

The thought tugged at my heart, and I had to look away from him. He didn't belong in my world any more than I belonged in this realm of magic and fantastical creatures. If for even a second I started imagining him in my real life, then...

I couldn't go there. It wasn't an option. No matter how much it might kill me, I still had to leave him at the end.

"How about an exchange?" he asked when I had been silent for too long. "Ask me one question, any question. If, and that's a strong if, I am able to answer it, I will."

He sat up on the sofa to make room for me, but I kept to my end. Touching him right now was a bad idea.

"Okay..." I had spent enough time with Sin. I could play this game of half-truths and evasion. I racked my brain, sifting through all the things I wanted to know about him. There were so many, and yet I had to pick only one.

To spare myself a mental breakdown from over-analyzing my options, I went with the first one that solidified. "Why the Wizard of Oz?" I blurted out. "I mean, how do you know it well enough to be quoting it all the time? I doubt you spent your trips to my realm watching old movies instead of searching for me."

Sin leaned back against the couch and closed his eyes. "That is dangerous knowledge to have, Rain. You still have the chance to walk away from this. From me." He opened his eyes, and something like fear lurked in their depths. "If I tell you... everything will change."

I met his inquisitive gaze with my own resilience. "Everything has already changed, Sin."

And I wasn't even talking about his secret. I was talking about him, us. As much as I knew that I should run and save myself from the inevitable heartache, that ship sailed the second I first kissed him and realized nobody else ever had or would make me feel the way he did. Leaving was going to hurt whether he told me or not, so I might as well make it burn.

"I suppose you're right," he admitted. "You want to know how I know the Wizard of Oz so well?" The question came out cautious, as if he was giving me one last chance to back out.

I nodded my head, and the explanation fell from his lips in a shower of pretty words that destroyed everything I had ever known about him.

"I know it so well because you know it so well," he started slowly. "You went to that old rundown movie theater at least a few times a year to watch it, and many times I was lucky enough to be there with you, sitting a few rows back. It let me feel connected to you, to share something you loved so much. The truth is, Rain, I found you when you were fifteen. It was winter and snow dusted the streets, but you didn't even have a decent coat on. I watched you leave the foster home you were staying in and walk over an hour to that theater. You couldn't stop shaking, but you never once ducked into a store or restaurant to warm up.

You had a destination, and you were determined to get there. I couldn't help but admire you from the first time I laid eyes on you.

"I had to know where you were going that was so important you would suffer to get there, so I followed you. I barely caught any of the film that first time because I spent the entire movie watching you, marveling at all the emotions you displayed—fascination, sadness, a longing to be anywhere else. I knew then that I couldn't bring you here. You would have fallen for this place, Rain. You would have been like Dorothy, captivated by the land of Oz, only you wouldn't get the happy ending. So I told myself I would watch over you and wait until you were older, let you live a little first.

"I lied to Verren every time I returned, insisting I still hadn't found you yet. For ten years, I kept you safe from this place, witnessing your evolution from the awkward teenager I first met into this incredibly fierce, beautiful woman. It was the night you moved into that awful apartment with your sister, when I saw pure joy on your face for the first time, that I stopped lying to myself about ever being able to bring you here. You weren't an innocent creature anymore, yet I knew I would still die to keep you from being harmed. Every night after that it got harder and harder to walk away from you." He swallowed roughly. "I don't know if I can keep walking away from you."

My heart thundered in my chest, beating too fast, too hard, keeping my entire body on edge. After everything he just told me, I should have had a million questions. And yet there was only one that mattered.

"Why did you need to walk away?"

Pain contorted Sin's face as if my question physically hurt him.

"Because I'm not a good male, Rain. I've done things that no amount of time can ever erase. You have endured so much already, and I can't bring myself to cause you more suffering. I will never be worthy of you... but I might not be strong enough to resist you either."

His words melted into my skin, embedding themselves deep within my heart. He saw all the broken pieces of me and felt like he was the unworthy one. It was too much. I was teetering on the precipice of a bottomless chasm. One wrong move, one wrong word, and I would be gone.

But as I stared into his icy green eyes, I realized that I didn't have to fall.

I could jump.

So I did.

The kiss was not a gentle meeting of the lips. The kiss was flame and fire, and I would happily let it burn me alive.

Sin hesitated only briefly before his hands snaked around my back, clutching my body tightly against him as he pulled me into his lap. My fingers wound through his hair, feeling like they belonged there tangled up in the soft darkness that was Sin.

I pushed him back into the couch, pulled my tunic over my head, and grinded my hips deeper into him. The heat spread from our lips, and I could feel it burning through me, begging for a release that only he could give. I craved the feel of his body against mine more than I craved sunlight or air. I wanted to remove every layer that separated us until there was only my skin and his.

I felt like I might burst into flame if he wasn't inside me within the next few seconds.

"Sin," I gasped, pulling away from his mouth and rolling my hips again. "I want..." I couldn't finish the sentence. I knew exactly what I wanted, but the words fought me. They struggled to stay inside my brain. This was a bad idea for a thousand different reasons, and I should definitely stop before it went too far. Or maybe it had already gone too far because I couldn't bring myself to crawl off him.

"What do you want, Fea Remia?" he whispered, leaning forward to sprinkle kisses down my throat.

I arched into him, baring my neck and chest, and his lips continued their journey south. I cried out when his teeth nipped at the soft skin above my collarbone, his bite like lightning that shot straight down my body to ignite my core.

"I need you to tell me what you want, Rain," he whispered as he licked the mark he left on my neck. "I need to know that all of you wants this." His hands slid from my back up along the sides of my ribcage, sending tingles dancing across my skin. They settled just below my bra, and his fingers tightened around the edges of the ribbon that held it in place. He didn't pull, though. He kissed his way back up to the outer edge of my ear and breathed out, "Are you with me, Fea Remia?"

Sin's intoxicating scent overwhelmed me, drowning each and every reason we shouldn't be together. He was a thundering ocean that would drag me under and never let go, lost forever to his dark storm.

"I'm with you, Dreisin. Every single part of me wants this. Wants you."

His eyes went molten, and he yanked on the ribbons. The bra fell apart, scraps of fabric dropping to my sides to expose my heavy breasts to him.

"Decoria," he murmured as he ran his tongue lightly over one peaked nipple.

I didn't care what the word meant so long as he kept his mouth on me. Writhing underneath him, the desperation inside me boiled up too fast, too hot.

"I need to feel you, Sin," I begged, and I barely recognized my own voice so thickly laced with need and desire. Gripping his bare shoulders, I rubbed my aching core along his cock that strained against his breeches.

"I want this to last, Fea Remia," he insisted, his left hand cupping my breast tightly as he flicked my nipple with the tip of his tongue. "Do you have any idea how long I've dreamt about this? How many nights I've touched myself, imagining that it was you?" He shifted over to my other breast, and I moaned unabashedly as his teeth grazed the sensitive skin there. "I didn't think I would ever get to have you. And now that I do..." He rose up to press his lips roughly against my own. A kiss that was punishing yet promising at the same time. "...I fully intend to take my time."

His words added fuel to an already blazing need, the throbbing between my legs beating in time to my racing pulse. "I... I can't wait, Sin. I need you." I fumbled at the strings on his breeches that kept me from what my body hungered for most.

A soft groan escaped Sin's lips. He gripped me tightly, rolled us, and pressed me into the sofa, settling himself between my thighs.

He gazed down at me greedily, and I swallowed, ready for him to unleash the passion I'd gotten only the smallest taste of that day in the weapons room.

It was almost painful when he pulled back to survey the small room. I needed his focus on me. I needed him to quench the flames that licked at my skin.

"You deserve better than this," he said softly, his breath hot against my neck. "Close your eyes."

I obeyed, if only out of fear that he might stop touching me if I didn't.

He tensed for a moment, and then his body relaxed back into mine. "Now open them."

I gasped. The small, dark room forgotten at the bottom of a castle was gone. Instead of a cracked ceiling, an endless blue sky stretched above Sin. The loud crash of waves echoed through my ears, and I twisted my head to look at the ocean that spread for miles beyond the edge of the vast cliff we lay on. Birds chirped pleasantly, and a round stone tower rose up in the distance.

"The Cliffs of Moher," I breathed out. Everything looked exactly like the image that had been my laptop screensaver for years.

"Look at me, Rain," Sin commanded, his voice rough, textured, and I was helpless to do anything but. "I told you I was an amplissario. Healing. Water." He exhaled. "And illusion."

There was so much hesitancy in his words, as if he feared I might be upset by his ability. But how could anyone hate a power that produced such enchanting beauty?

"It's incredible. You're incredible." I pulled my gaze from him to stare at the realistic wonder around us.

"I can't take you away from here, Fea Remia," he said, drawing me back to him with a kiss to my neck. "Illusions are all I have to offer you." A kiss to my breast. "You deserve so much more than me." Then to my stomach. "But I'm selfish." A slide of his tongue across the skin below my navel. "And I'm going to claim you anyway."

The entire world tilted when Sin yanked my panties and leggings down with one swift movement. There was only a second of chill against my overheated skin before he dipped his head and flicked his tongue against the tight bundle of nerves that was the source of all my wanting.

"Sin!" I cried out, my hips bucking against his face as the searing warmth between my legs threatened to consume me. My body writhed under the sensual assault of his tongue that only increased in speed the louder I moaned.

My eyes squeezed shut, and I was lost to the sensation, his carefully constructed illusion taking a backseat to the pleasure.

He slipped a finger inside me, and the flames under my skin flared hotter. I rolled my hips in a circular motion, riding his hand as he added a second finger, stretching me even wider.

My body was a blazing inferno, and if I didn't release the fire soon it would incinerate me from the inside out.

"I'm burning up, Sin," I panted as his tongue and fingers worked together to push me to the brink of furious ecstasy.

His fingers slipped out of me, and I whimpered at their sudden absence. I was so close to the edge. Too close. I wanted to walk straight into his fire and let it take me.

"Look at me, Rain," his rough voice growled, and my eyes shot open.

He grinned wickedly. "Burn for me, baby."

Then he ran his tongue straight up through the center of me.

"Sin!" Fire exploded inside me with the intensity of a volcanic eruption, flames dancing over every inch of skin as I gave in to the heat and let it consume me.

It was hot.

Too hot.

I was burning too bright, and I couldn't stop it.

"Rain!" Sin cried out, the fear in his voice strong enough to cut through the haze of the orgasm still rippling through me.

I forced my eyes open. I was definitely burning.

Only the fire wasn't inside me anymore.

Chapter Thirty-Four

I should have been scared as I took in the small room around me—Sin's illusion destroyed as he fought to put the fire out with a blanket—yet there was no fear to be found. The flames coated my entire body like a second skin, and the acrid smoke stung my nose, but my mind lingered in the orgasmic haze.

I think Sin shouted my name, but I couldn't fully register what was happening. I could only lay on the couch, unmoving save for the slight twitch of my hips as my body continued to savor every last drop of pleasure despite the raging inferno.

The fire consumed everything around me, and yet... it didn't burn *me*. The opposite, in fact. The flames caressed me, soothed me.

As my heart rate finally settled back to normal, I lifted my hand to my face and watched the fire fade away, as if crawling back into my skin to slumber until summoned again. My eyes scanned the length of my arm, studying the new black swirls with accents of red that spread from my wrist to my elbow. I had never seen a Rivellan with color in their ramentum before, and I briefly wondered if I should be concerned about that.

I swung my legs around and pushed up to sitting, surveying the damage surrounding me. The sofa was covered in black scorch marks, some of them still letting off wisps of smoke as the last embers died. The fire must have spread to the rug because it, too, was deeply singed. That would be tough to explain to Corym.

The only damage I cared about, though, was the damage that I had done to Sin. His chest and arms were covered in deep burns—charred, cracked, and oozing blood. The ruined blanket hung limply at his side as he gaped at me with an emotion I couldn't decipher.

I reached down to pull up my leggings and found nothing but charred bits of fabric flaking off my lower legs. Searching the room, I found my tunic bunched up off to the side, mostly intact save for a few burn holes and gray smudges.

I tucked my knees under me on the destroyed sofa and tried not to focus on the ashes that continued to float up into the air. "I'm sorry," I said soberly, refusing to look at Sin. It was the most underwhelming apology, given that I had roasted him and destroyed half the room, but it was all I could manage. I was barely able to sift through my own thoughts enough to figure out exactly what I was feeling.

Regret? Worry? Yeah, I had both of those. But there was also a giddy thrill coursing through me, and I hated suppressing that excitement. In the aftermath of what happened, though, it didn't seem right to embrace it.

I wanted magic. I wanted my abilities to manifest. I wanted to feel powerful. I just didn't expect anyone else to get hurt in the process.

I could still feel the fire underneath my skin, a soft thrum of warmth that felt... right. Like it had always been there, eager for the moment I might set it free. The sensation reminded me of that split second before an argument started, when my anger would burn deep in my chest and demand to be released. Except now, it was content to laze inside me. Not fading. Not flaring. Just waiting.

Sin's silent stare was agonizing. Yelling I could handle—Sin and I were great at fighting. If I had to look in his eyes and see disappointment or regret, though... that would be a far worse fate.

After a few more heavy exhales, Sin made his way to the burnt sofa.

"Thanks for not dumping the bucket of bloody water on me," I mumbled, needing to break the painful silence somehow.

"It was a challenge not to reach for the only water in the room, but I didn't want to traumatize you." There was a hint of amusement in his voice, and I didn't know how he could find anything funny about what just happened. "Rain, I need your attention right now. This is important."

My pulse pounded in my ears, and his knuckle slid under my chin to gently, but firmly, tilt my face up. As my eyes lifted to meet his, I prepared myself to see the worst.

What I saw when I met his gaze had me sucking in a sharp breath. There was no shame or pity on his face. Just... pride?

"You are extraordinary, Fea Remia."

My heart bottomed out, and I collapsed in on myself. It was the last thing I expected after nearly burning him alive and damaging priceless antique furniture. He should hate me. Fear me. I would have understood either of those emotions. But this love in his eyes? He spent the morning having his back sliced up, and the first thing I did was subject him to more torture.

"I'm so sorry," I repeated, waiting for him to unleash the anger I deserved.

"Don't do that, Rain. Don't apologize," he replied firmly. "Do you have any idea what you've done?"

"Yeah," I said bitterly. "I manifested my first power and almost killed you in the process."

"Is that why you look like I just broke your favorite violin? Because you think you're a danger to me?" He leaned forward and tucked a strand of hair behind my ear. It was such a small, innocuous action, and yet the tenderness of it nearly destroyed me. "Rain, you are breaking my heart right now. What you did..." He glanced around the room, but only awe remained in his expression. "When an elemental caster first manifests their power, do you know what happens?"

I shook my head, realizing once again how naïve I had been. Not once did I ask what the manifestation process entailed. For some idiotic reason, I'd assumed I would be walking down the street and then voila! Magic.

"It's different for every caster to some degree," he began slowly, taking my hands in his, "but most of the time, you feel a tingling inside you, and that sensation is typically tied to whatever the ability is. As you feel the magic start to bubble up, you have this urge to seek out your element. When I first manifested, I could feel the call of a nearby river, and the magic coursed like rushing waters through my veins, demanding I go to it. Once you've found it, something snaps inside you, and the element jumps to your hand, ready to be wielded. It takes training to master it, but anytime you see your element, you can call it to you and manipulate it as an extension of your being. You, on the other hand..."

He pulled me into him so my back was to his chest, and he wrapped his arms around me. If I could have stopped feeling bad for a minute, I might have enjoyed the gentle touch of him nestling his chin on top of my head.

"The sconce behind you didn't so much as flicker," he finished. "Do you understand what I'm saying?" His arms tightened just enough for me to wonder if he was afraid for me.

Or afraid *of* me.

"I don't know what any of this means," I admitted.

"It means, Rain, that you didn't pull the fire to you like every igniservian has done throughout history."

I took in a sharp inhale.

"It means, Fea Remia, that you *created* the fire."

Sin left shortly after to go find Peywyn, indicating she would have some clothes I could borrow and wouldn't ask any questions. I fought to suppress the spark of jealousy at how close they were, but the wretched emotion burned inside me all the same, and for a second, I thought flames might erupt from my skin again.

When no fire appeared, my body sank into the sofa, and my mind sank into the dark place I spent far too much time in. I should have asked Sin not to leave me alone. Should have told him abandoning me with nothing but my thoughts—especially after dropping a bomb like that—would not end well.

I didn't even know how to process the fact that I created fire. All of this magic was such a foreign concept to me that I honestly couldn't see a difference between creation and manipulation. A week ago, I would have laughed and said it was all absurd. It was like someone told me unicorns existed, then I stumbled upon one that could also fly. Okay, sure, why not? If we're hopping on a crazy train, might as well ride to the end of the line.

Banging my head against the sofa frame, I tried to think of anything other than Sin. Per usual, I failed miserably, and my brain kept circling back around to what a tragic idea it was for us to be together. Not to mention, I still didn't know how I felt about him watching over me for ten years. On one hand, it was kind of sweet, his need to protect me from whatever dangers he thought Rivella posed. On the other hand… it kind of left me with stalker vibes.

And the fact he showed up when I was only fifteen? Little weird. I knew it wasn't like that for him at first—he'd been pretty clear it was more 'protect the innocent' until well after I was an adult—but still… If he thought I was in so much danger, why not talk to me?

And why was he still not talking to me?

"Do you know what I have done to keep you away from this place? What I have sacrificed?"

If there was truly a threat to my life in Rivella, then why not warn me?

It was the first thing I brought up the moment Sin returned.

"You're keeping things from me," I blurted out when he walked through the door carrying a pair of leather fighting pants and a long-sleeved beige tunic.

My question must have caught him off guard because he stilled just past the threshold. "Yes, I am," he confirmed, his tone lacking any emotional reaction to my accusation. He handed me the clothing, then turned his back so I could change.

I snorted at his modesty given where his mouth had been less than twenty minutes ago.

I tapped him on the shoulder once I was dressed. "Talk to me, Sin. If you were so afraid for me to come here, why not warn me back then? And why are you still not telling me what's going on?" When he refused to look at me, I grabbed my hand and twined my fingers through his. "I can't do this anymore. If you really care about me, you'll tell me the truth."

He pulled his hand from mine and walked backward to lean against the closed door, but the space between us felt so much greater than the few steps he took. “It’s not that simple, Rain.”

“So make it simple, Sin.”

He ran a hand through his dark hair, and I hated how much I wanted it to be my fingers running through those soft waves.

“I can tell you that I never approached you in your world simply because I had no idea what to even say. How would you have responded if I showed up one day claiming you were the lost princess of another world when I had no proof to back it up? I didn’t have my magic in the Other Realm, Rain. And I couldn’t show you the rift because the Walker would have seen you and told Verren. Even if by some miracle you did believe me, what then? You spend every waking moment afraid that any stranger you saw might be someone who had come to kidnap you?” He shook his head. “There was no good option, Rain. The only way I saw to keep you safe was by lying.”

“And now?” I asked, taking a step closer but leaving a gap between us. A gap that needed to be filled with answers. “Why keep me in the dark now?”

“I want to tell you everything, Rain. I do.”

“Then open your mouth and start talking,” I begged.

“I... I want to,” he gritted out, his fists clenching and unclenching.

It took all my willpower not to grab his arms and shake the answers out of him. “So do!” I shouted, a hot sensation crawling under my skin.

“I can’t!” he screamed in anguish, sinking to the floor and throwing his head back against the door. “I want to tell you so many things, Rain. I want to tell you so bad it hurts, but I can’t make myself say the words. It’s killing me to hide things from you, but I just... I just can’t.”

This was not the Sin I knew—the confident, seductive, occasional asshole. This male in front of me that I found myself caring about more than I should, more than I had any right to, looked so defeated. So confused.

My anger dimmed under the weight of a deeper emotion I wasn’t ready to think about, and I knelt to press my forehead against his. Twisting my fingers around the long strands of his hair, I searched for something to say. I wasn’t good at this. The ability to comfort a person who was hurting was not part of my repertoire. I wanted to help in some way, though. I wanted to take away his pain.

I pulled back, caught his eyes, and pressed a soft kiss to his lips. "It's okay," I murmured.

"No, it's not," he replied. "Nothing about you being here is okay."

"I know," I said, shifting to lean back against the door beside him, his thigh a warm presence next to my own. "I think I understand why you can't tell me what's going on. I asked Corym to transfer the Rivellan language to my mind, and it almost broke him. He kept saying he wanted to, but he couldn't." I paused, angling my head so I could look into his beautiful, sad eyes. "He looked exactly like you do right now."

Something snapped inside Sin, and he crumpled in on himself, his body succumbing to the pressure he had been fighting for so long. I took his face in my hands, kissed him with enough force that it was hard to pull away, then lowered his head to my lap.

We stayed like that for a long time—not saying a word, just me running my hands through his hair, forgiveness and understanding filling the silence. I didn't have any pretty, comforting words I could give him, so my presence would have to be enough.

Chapter Thirty-Five

I still had a million things I wanted to ask Sin, but it all seemed rather pointless if he was locked in the same mental prison Corym had been in. So instead of demanding answers to questions that would likely only cause more distress, I let him direct the next steps.

"What do we do now?" I asked as we left the small office and passed through the library. Sin had said he would stay and explain to Corym what happened, though I hoped it would be a somewhat modified version of the truth.

"You need to go to breakfast," he said, stopping at the door to the hallway. "Verren might get suspicious if you don't show up. I think for now it's best if he believes nothing has changed."

"Just about us, right? You can't possibly mean you want me to keep my magic a secret?"

To my complete and utter frustration, his firm expression confirmed the ridiculous idea.

"Sin, I was literally prepared for you to slice and dice me yesterday, that's how badly I've wanted this. Now you want me to hide it? No. Sorry, but no."

He leaned against the door frame, studying me with narrowed eyes. "Why is it so important that everyone knows?" he asked with a familiar apathetic tinge to his voice.

I leaned against the opposite side, mirroring his posture. If he wanted to slip back into these roles, fine.

"I already told you," I said, my voice a mimic of his casual disinterest. "I want everyone here to stop making fun of me behind my back. I'm not stupid. I see the looks I get at dinner. I don't enjoy feeling like a lesser citizen. I got enough of that in my world."

"Try again, Fea Remia," he replied smoothly, that infuriatingly hypnotic smirk making a reappearance to my own twisted delight. "That excuse doesn't work on me. I saw you back in your world, remember? You never once tried to be someone you weren't just to fit in."

I scoffed. "Please. You saw me for a handful of days. It doesn't make you an expert on all things Rain Solis."

He blinked a couple times, his cool mask slipping for a second.

"What?" I asked.

"You never use your last name. I forgot I even knew it, that's all."

I wrinkled my brow. "It was just a random word that sounded cool. When Jenn and I turned eighteen, we decided on new last names. Neither of us was a fan of the state chosen 'Smith.' They weren't too creative, I guess. Jenn helped me pick mine out, but it never mattered much to me. A last name is a family name, and I never had a family." I paused, then asked, "What's yours? I actually don't think I know anyone's last name here."

"We don't have surnames in Rivella," he replied. "Only a first name and sometimes a title or designation. I'm Cennux Dreisin. Dey is Deylan, the King's Foster. It doesn't matter what family you come from here. Only what you can do."

I considered that. "I suppose that's a nice change of pace from the rampant nepotism of my world."

"Indeed." He was quiet for a moment, then added softly, "It means sun."

"What?" I asked, nudging his boot with one slightly burnt sneaker.

He straightened and cleared his throat. "Solis. Your last name. It means sun in Rivellan. I think it's just kind of fitting."

"Because of my fire magic?"

He moved into my space and wrapped his hand around the back of my neck. I let out a tiny shudder at the contact. He had always been the hotter one, but now his skin was almost cool against my new constant warmth.

He bent down and pressed his forehead to mine. "Because you shine so brightly it cuts through my darkness."

I should have laughed. If anyone back in Jersey ever said that to me, I would be rolling on the ground. But when Sin said it... my heart thumped a little faster.

Then he kissed me, deep, passionate, and over far too soon. He pulled away before I could even get my hands on him, yet that simple kiss had me breathless.

"Whatever your reasons, Rain. Can you please trust me on this? It's a bad idea to tell anyone right now."

With my legs still wobbly from the way he pressed himself against me, I found myself absently nodding. "Okay."

"Good girl," he said, smirking, and if I wasn't trying so hard to keep my knees from buckling, I might have smacked him.

I managed to pull myself upright and started off down the hall. I made it maybe three steps before I heard his voice.

"One hundred and fourteen," he called.

I looked over my shoulder and cocked an eyebrow.

"You said I only spent a handful of days with you. It was actually a hundred and fourteen. I know you better than you think, Rain L. Solis." And with that, he gave me a wink and disappeared back into the library.

I stared at the space he vacated, trying to figure out why my stomach felt like it was full of fluttering baby crescia.

Damn.

Of all the possible dangers in this world, I was pretty sure he was the blade that could cut the deepest.

I went up to my room, showered, and quickly threw Peywyn's clothing back on before the sisters showed up. I had no doubts that if they saw my ramentum, they'd run straight to my father.

After breakfast, Dey left me at the door of the Sylvarium with a kiss on the hand and a reminder that visitors would start arriving at the castle tomorrow for the King's Council, so I should enjoy the relative peace and quiet while I could.

By the time I entered the serene indoor garden, I thought my head might implode under the weight of all the secrets I had to keep.

Opal flitted over and landed in my hair once again. Laughing at her standard greeting of nuzzles and chitters, I wondered why she seemed a bit more aggressive than usual. When she kept up the level of enthusiasm, it occurred to me that Jenni hadn't joined her. Strange, since she was normally the first one to claim a spot atop my head.

"Jenni?" I called, walking around to the different hanging vines. I couldn't spot her scarlet coloring anywhere among the sea of crescia.

"Jenni!" I called, raising my voice enough that it echoed through the room and frightened a few of the little ones. Opal started chirping anxiously, and I gave her a couple of quick, soothing caresses.

"It's okay, Opal. I'm just worried about Jenni. I don't suppose you know where she is?"

Okay, maybe talking to her was a little silly, but it was better than the alternative—accepting Jenni was gone.

Before I could return to my usual bench, Opal gave another loud chitter and flew from my hair. She tore across the Sylvarium and landed on the wide rim of a planter overflowing with enormous lily-like flowers.

"What's going on, Opal?" I asked, my voice wobbling under rising apprehension.

As I approached, the small crescia bobbed up and down a few more times, then hopped into the planter, nudging aside one of the large flower petals and disappearing underneath it.

Carefully, I shifted the leaves to the side and sucked in a sharp inhale at the small, shiny white bundle that lay nestled in the dirt. Leaning in a bit closer, I tracked the tiny movements—the way it shifted and writhed ever so slightly, the pearlescent threads that covered it expanding and growing. I pushed a few more flowers back so I could take in the whole thing and caught the slightest glimpse of a red wing before it, too, was encapsulated by the shimmery white strands.

It hit me then, something Dey had said.

"Crescia draw themselves into sort of a cocoon once they have bonded."

Bonded.

This had to mean Jenni was my crescia. A squeak of excitement leapt out.

I had a bonded crescia.

I had magic.

My world hadn't shifted this much since I landed in Rivella a week ago.

Opal sidled up to the cocoon and lay beside it, apparently happy to assume guard duty. I slumped back against the planter and let the flower petals slide back into place to protect them.

The massive grin on my face had my cheeks aching as my mind raced with the knowledge of the past few hours. It hadn't fully hit me before with Sin, but in the peace of the Sylvarium, it dawned on me that I was, in fact, not entirely human.

Holy shit.

It didn't change anything, this confirmation, but I felt like it should. I felt like my entire world had flipped upside down, and I only now learned how to walk on the ceiling. This place could be my home. I could stay here. I could stay with Sin, Jenni, and everyone else.

Then the roller coaster of excitement came crashing to an end when Jenn's face popped into my mind. The reality was I still needed to go home because gaining magic didn't change who I was, and I was not someone who abandoned her sister.

"You seem distressed."

My head shot up at the sound of Jo's voice, and I searched the Sylvarium for her.

Pushing a few vines aside, she walked over and sat down across from me, a small cloud of dust settling onto her light blue leggings as she took a cross-legged position.

"I did not see you here at first and nearly left, but your mind is so tumultuous I could sense you from across the room. What is wrong, Rain?"

I opened my mouth to tell her about Jenni being in the planter behind me, then hesitated. Sin had been very clear that I shouldn't tell anyone about my new ability. But Jo was... She was Jo. She wouldn't tell anyone if I asked her not to.

"You can keep a secret, right?" I projected into her mind.

She perked up a little at that. *"Of course, Rain. What has you so troubled?"*

"I'm just a little sad because I was thinking about my decision to go home when this is all over."

"Have you changed your mind about staying?" she asked with uncontrolled enthusiasm.

The hope in her eyes was a knife in my heart. *"I'm sorry,"* I said, looking away. *"I can't leave my sister. It's not an option. But..."* I couldn't find the words to tell her what I was feeling, but thankfully, she saved me.

"You feel bad about leaving now. Is that it?" When I nodded, she asked, *"What has you questioning your decision?"*

I gulped. It was now or never. I either trusted Jo or I didn't.

Pulling back my sleeve, I showed her the intricate ramentum that now covered my arm.

The squeal inside my head was deafening, and I wiggled a finger in my ear absently despite knowing the damage had been purely mental.

Jo grabbed my arm and pulled me closer to her, gasping as she ran her fingers over my vibrant new tattoos.

"Red," she said softly. *"You have red in them."*

"Yeah, I was curious... Is that normal? I haven't seen any colored ramentum before, but it's only a few accents, so maybe I missed it on others?"

I kicked myself for not asking Sin earlier, but we'd had larger issues to discuss at the time.

"It is beautiful, but no. I have never seen anyone with color before." Her round eyes swam with adoration. *"I knew you were special, Rain."*

I shifted uncomfortably at her praise. Sin had also said my ability was unique, but the problem was that different didn't always mean special. Sometimes it just meant you were a weirdo, and that was the more likely scenario when it came to me.

"What power did you get first? Did it happen last night? Oh dear, I hope you were not by yourself when it hit. Manifesting is such a beautiful process. It would be a shame to go through it alone."

My cheeks blushed at the reminder of what Sin and I had been doing when my power hit. *"Um, not exactly. Sin was there."*

Her brow furrowed. *"You were with Cennux Dreisin? Interesting."*

Something about the way she said 'interesting' made me think she had another word she would have rather used.

"Yeah, he just sort of happened to be around by coincidence." It wasn't technically a lie, so maybe she wouldn't sense any deceit. I still felt the need to hold back the new development between Sin and I. If she didn't like that he was there at the time, then she really wouldn't like knowing what triggered it.

"So what is your new power?" Jo asked. *"Most Rivellans get healing first, but not always."*

"I—"

I started to tell her about my fire magic but stopped. I kept snagging on the way she had said 'interesting.' It was a single word. So innocuous and completely understandable. And yet...

"It's a secret," I said quickly. When she frowned, I added, *"I thought it would be fun to reveal it at the upcoming ball. You know, for a little excitement or something."*

Lying to Jo was beyond awkward, and I was certain she could tell that I wasn't being entirely truthful. It was a secret—that part was true—I just didn't give a shit about the ball.

If she sensed my dishonesty, she hid it well. A crescia landed on her arm, drawing her attention, and I seized the distraction.

I sat up eagerly and placed a hand on her shoulder. *"That reminds me,"* I said, grimacing when my motion sent the timid creature back to its branch. *"I think I bonded to a crescia, but I don't know what to do now."*

I leaned over the planter and pulled the flowers back to show Jo the cocoon. Opal released an annoyed trill at the movement, then nestled back into her spot.

"Oh, how exciting! Yes, that must be the crescia that has chosen you. It should wake shortly, and you will be able to see what form they have taken. Make sure you save the silk after they emerge. It is very valuable."

"So I've heard," I said, thinking about my dress. The cocoon was so small, I couldn't see that amount of silk making more than a pocket square. I could only imagine how many crescia were needed to make my gown.

I dropped my arm to let the leaves fall back into place, but Jo thrust out a hand to stop me.

"You cannot leave your crescia here!" There was so much horror in her voice you would think I just threatened to go on a murder spree. *"You should keep it with you until it wakes. They draw upon your magic to help their transformation, so you must not leave them alone for too long."*

"Got it, sorry. All new to me." I gingerly picked up the cocoon and cradled it in my hands. Opal promptly flew out of the planter and took her spot against Jenni once more, the two of them filling my palm.

"They must be related," Jo mused. *"She will likely act out when you take your crescia away, but do not let her distress upset you. It is the way these things go."*

Opal let out a sharp string of chitters as if she knew what Jo said and had a strong opinion to the contrary.

"You know so much about them. Do you spend a lot of time with your crescia?" I had seen quite a few in the glen out back. Maybe I'd remember hers.

"I do not have one," she replied, and the intense sadness that filled my head felt almost like my own.

"I'm so sorry. Did they pass away recently?"

Jo stood and turned her back on me. She looked about ready to walk away when I heard her say, *"I never had a crescia. Never bonded to one."*

Oh. I opened and closed my mouth a few times, doing my best imitation of a fish while I tried to figure out an appropriate response.

"I should go," Jo said. *"There is still much to do before the Council."*

"Ok," I replied, hoping she wasn't leaving because of me.

"Take care of your crescia, Rain. You do not want anything bad to happen to it." And with that slightly ominous warning, she disappeared out the door.

I contemplated the little bundle in my hands that was roughly the size of a peach, if not slightly more elongated. I needed a nap. Manifesting a new ability then lying to the person who was arguably my best friend here took a lot out of a girl.

"Okay, Opal. I'm going to my room for a bit, and I know you're not supposed to come with me, but I don't have any energy left to fight you." I set them on the edge of the planter, then pulled the tie off the end of my braid, releasing my thick waves. "If you want to stay with Jenni for a bit longer, I'm going to need to sneak you out. So either you rest on my neck and let me bury you under my hair, or you remain here. Your choice." I lifted my mass of black hair and gave her a pointed look.

It was ridiculous to think she would even understand me, but to my surprise, she wordlessly flitted up to land on my neck. I released my hair to hide her against my nape, then carefully picked up Jenni. Cupping her inside my closed hands, I left the Sylvarium and headed to my room to get some sleep. If I was lucky, I would have a new friend by the time I woke up.

"Take your time, Jenni," I whispered as I set her down on my nightstand. When I lifted my curtain of hair, Opal flew out to resume her self-appointed guard duties.

"I'll be here whenever you're ready."

Chapter Thirty-Six

It hadn't occurred to me at any point between waking up and finding Sin bleeding in Corym's office that I might have missed a memory during last night's tumble through my past encounters. Learning Sin loved me was pretty all-encompassing of my thoughts, so it was only understandable I'd forgotten about a few undiscovered instances of people speaking in Rivellan.

It was this realization that both intrigued and frightened me as I drifted off and promptly found myself hidden in the shadows of the door to the grand hall.

I waited patiently, knowing exactly what I was about to see, yet still nervous all the same. It was the argument between my father and Dey. The one he assured me was nothing, though I knew it had to be something.

"You had one job, Deylan. One!" my father roared. *"I have treated you like my own son. Raised you in the palace and given you all the finest things in life. And this is how you repay me? She was raised among humans, and they are barely better than animals. You are a Vitaean. How hard could it be to seduce her?"* His voice dropped an octave as he bit out, *"Fix this, Deylan. You have no idea what will happen if you fail, so do whatever it takes to make her fall in love with you. We are counting on you."*

He gave Dey one last ominous look, then stalked out of the grand hall. I didn't watch him go, I just waited for the person I knew was about to emerge.

I hadn't registered it the first time I saw him. The extent of shame and embarrassment on Dey's face all because he failed to seduce me.

She was raised among humans.

Barely better than animals.

The words hurt more than a fenite dagger in my back.

I wasn't disoriented this time when I woke up. I knew exactly where I was and what I had just witnessed.

I barely made it to the bathroom before I vomited my breakfast into the diamond-accented toilet.

You had one job.

Barely better than animals.

I couldn't stop hearing the words inside my head. Any glimmer of hope that had been left inside me, any miniscule piece of my heart that still held onto the possibility that my father had a good reason for everything he had done... Gone. Incinerated by the flames coiling underneath my skin. A fire built inside me, and it wanted to rage until anybody who had ever hurt me regretted the day I was born.

If I had any sense of self left, I might have been worried about the dark thoughts coursing through my head. The voice inside me that screamed I was powerful now, and they couldn't treat me like that.

Barely better than animals.

I held up my hand, visualized what I wanted, and smiled when thin wisps of fire emerged from the tips of my fingers, curling slightly as the writhing flames coalesced into inch-long talons. I pressed my hand to the floor, and the claws burned into the stone easily as if it were no more dense than clay, leaving a red hot glowing handprint.

My father wanted to manipulate me? Fine. I could play his game.

I rotated my hand, admiring the power I was now capable of. Maybe it was my hatred driving it, maybe it was just a reaction to my father's words.

It didn't matter how it happened. He could call me whatever he wanted.

This animal had claws.

I'm not sure what I might have done if I had been alone in my room. The fire inside me demanded retribution and pain. I wanted to rake my new fiery talons over my father's face and watch him scream until his magic healed him, all so I could do it again and again until he knew what it felt like to be helpless.

Except I wasn't alone.

It was so soft, the tiny mewling noise that caught my attention.

The flames disappeared back under my skin as I spun on the cold floor of the bathroom to look behind me.

"Jenni?" The word slipped out on a stunned exhale.

A tiny red creature sat in the middle of the doorway, its head cocked to the side, analyzing me.

Jenni.

My crescia.

I held out my trembling hand, and she tentatively moved toward me, her legs unsteady as a newborn fawn. Four tiny new tails swished behind her, the miniscule scales only giving off the faintest twinkling sound as they brushed together. She was bigger than her unbonded form, but still so small that she could climb into my hand and sit comfortably as I lifted her up. She couldn't weigh more than a pound or two, but her size didn't detract from her magnificence.

"My crescia is a baby dragon?" My words were hushed and awe-struck, made only more reverent by the slight echo off the stone that surrounded me.

Jenni wasn't a baby dragon, of course. Dragons didn't usually have four tails. Dragons didn't have gauzy bat wings that looked like sky dimming into night—a deep shade of crimson that faded into purple then finally black with star-like speckles on the edges. And dragons definitely did not have adorable little feline faces, complete with whiskers that tickled as she nuzzled my palm.

She was fascinating.

She was perfect.

And when she opened her mouth and coughed out the tiniest little spark of fire before curling up in my palm and falling asleep, I knew that she was mine.

I spent the rest of the afternoon playing with Jenni and Opal. I was terrified someone would come in and find her, so I pushed my dresser in front of the door. It seemed rather unfair that every room in the castle had a lock except mine, though I couldn't really be that surprised. I was well aware my father was manipulating every move I made, so of course he wouldn't allow me the privilege of privacy. It would be pretty hard for Dey to sneak in and show up naked in my bed if the door was locked.

Dey.

I rubbed at my chest. There was still a bit of an ache from that one. I didn't even know what was real anymore. Had he been pretending the entire time? For all I knew, he might secretly loathe the amount of time he'd been required to spend with me.

Hours passed, and still, the truth ate at me. I had suspected my father's deceit from almost the very beginning, and I had no idea as to why I kept making excuses for him. All he did was mold and shape my actions to whatever end he wanted. I wasn't his daughter. I was his pawn.

I had trusted Dey, though, even considered him a friend despite him calling my people savages. I guess savages was a step above animals, albeit a small one.

But the worst part of it all, the part that had me refusing to leave my room, was knowing if Dey could fool me, then anyone could. Cam. Ram. Corym. I gulped. Even Jo.

Dey had some fucked-up, racist ideology, but I never once doubted that he cared about me. So if he was lying the whole time… then who else was lying?

I should never have made friends to begin with. It was always a bad idea for me. I knew I wasn't planning on staying in Rivella, and yet I had stupidly let so many of them into my heart.

I tried to summon my flames back to my hand, needing to express my frustration in some way that might make me feel better, but despite trying multiple times, the fire remained trapped underneath my skin. Apparently I didn't have the control I thought I did.

I punched the side of my bed instead, sending Opal and Jenni into a tizzy as they squawked and took flight.

"Sorry," I called out to them, watching as they landed on top of the wardrobe and peered down at me.

Great. Now I'm scaring my crescia. Stellar move, Rain.

I held out my arm for Jenni to return, but she only twisted her head to the side defiantly. I couldn't help but laugh at how much personality lived in her tiny body. I knew what Dey meant when he said Thorell wasn't a pet. Jenni was smart. Too smart sometimes, it seemed.

I made a sad face. "Pretty please?"

Another tiny fire burp popped out before she flew over to land on my arm. She nipped at my skin in admonishment as I ran my hands over her beautiful red scales, but her teeth were so small she couldn't even break the skin.

"I'm sorry," I said. "I didn't mean to scare you." Her cat-like eyes slitted even deeper, and then she walked up to my shoulder, curled herself into a ball, and promptly fell asleep.

Sensing the danger was over, Opal flew down and snuggled into the center of my braid that I had coiled like a nest atop my head. She was never far from Jenni, and I was starting to worry what I would do about that. I couldn't keep Opal too. She had a Vitaean out there somewhere just waiting for her bond. It would be selfish not to take her back to the Sylvarium. Then again, I wasn't exactly an altruistic person by any stretch, so I could hold off a little longer.

I glanced at Jenni sleeping on my shoulder. She was so precious with her fuzzy little snout and minuscule puffs of smoke that rippled out of her nose when she exhaled. "You might be the hardest one to leave," I whispered.

She cracked a single eye open at the sound of my voice.

"Rain not leaving."

The words echoed through my brain, similar to when Jo spoke to me, yet the voice was so innocent, so child-like. A soft, melodic sound that danced inside my head.

I gawked at her. "Did you just talk?" There was a solid chance at this point I was going crazy and had imagined it.

"Yes." Another fire burp escaped, and she squawked as if it caught her off guard.

"Why didn't anyone tell me I could speak with my crescia? That seemed like an important thing someone should have mentioned."

"Rain special."

Now it was my turn to cock my head in confusion. "Are you saying no one else can speak to their crescia?"

She dipped her head slightly in an action that appeared far too reminiscent of human behavior.

I rubbed at my eyes, still not entirely convinced I wasn't losing my damn mind. "This is insane. Nobody can speak to pets where I come from."

Jenni's eyes narrowed sharply. Then she hopped down to my knee and gave a roar that would have been terrifying if she wasn't five inches tall. The mini fireball that accompanied it barely left a noticeable scorch mark on Peywyn's pants.

"Sorry! Poor word choice," I apologized, brushing the bit of ash from my leg. "I know you are more than just a pet. Trust me, I know."

She huffed out a little puff of smoke, and I had to take a second to process the implications of this tiny creature being annoyed with me. The fact that she was intelligent enough to know when to take offense was approaching unfathomable.

I ran a single finger across the red scales on top of her head, down her back, and over the spot where her spine split into four thin tails. "Forgive me?" I asked softly.

She gave a little wiggle and one of the tails reached over and wrapped around my pinky. The swell of joy in my heart at that tiny motion bordered on painful, and I imagined it was similar to what people felt when a newborn baby held onto their finger.

"Can you tell me why I'm special?" I asked slowly, enunciating my words for her.

"Crescia know Rain. Inside. Rain is home."

I sighed and leaned back against the bed. I didn't think I was going to get any kind of straight answer out of her. Maybe her eloquence would improve as she got older.

Resting my hand on my leg so she could curl up again without releasing my pinky, I debated whether I should tell anyone about her ability to speak with me. In my world, if a human was able to talk to animals, they would likely end up in a government lab getting their brain sliced open. But how would Rivellans respond? Sin had seemed in awe of my unique fire ability, so maybe he'd feel the same about this. Although, he also had love coloring his response.

Love.

I still didn't know what to do about that. I needed to tell him I knew, but that would lead to a conversation I was terrified to have. Sin had known me for ten years, but I had only known him for a week. There was an undeniable connection between us, and when I was in his arms everything just felt... right.

But love? What did I even know about love.

A soft knock saved me from ruminating on those depressing thoughts. The door creaked open an inch, banging into the dresser.

"Just a second," I called as I jumped to my feet, cupped Jenni in my hand, and rushed over to the tall wardrobe. Yanking it open, I set her on the bottom, then plucked Opal from my hair as well.

"You have to be quiet," I said in a desperate yet hushed tone. Jenni gave a single dip of her head, and I shut them in.

I pushed my dresser away from the door and cracked it open slightly.

Dey eyed me curiously through the gap. "Is everything okay, Princess? Why is your door blocked?"

I clenched my fists at my side, summoning every ounce of willpower I had to not punch him in the face. Instead, I feigned a hint of embarrassment and said, "Sorry. I wanted to take a nap without being bothered. I don't have a lock on my door, so..."

Dey nodded in understanding. "Yes, apologies for that, but this was the only available room befitting a princess."

"Perhaps a lock could be installed?" I asked, my face a picture of innocence.

"Yes, perhaps," Dey replied flippantly. "The sisters are here to get you ready for dinner. Would you let them in?"

Shit. I had forgotten about dinner.

"Actually," I said, fanning a hand in front of my face, "it was kind of warm in my room this afternoon, so I'm feeling a little sweaty. I'd like to take another shower first. Can you ask them to come back in a bit?" I gave him my best doe-eyed princess look and prayed he didn't know me well enough to recognize the deception.

He smiled. "Of course. Enjoy your shower." He turned to speak with the sisters, and I shut the door before they could even respond.

Dashing over to the wardrobe, I pulled it open and knelt down to where Jenni and Opal were curled up together in the back corner.

"You guys were great, but I need to find a spot to hide you for the rest of the evening." Jenni unfurled her body and gave a tiny squawk. "I know, I don't like it either, but no one can know about our bond yet." I searched around frantically, then scooped them both up, crossed the room, and set them on the long marble counter that comprised the back wall of the oversized bathroom. "You can stay here, but if anyone comes in, I need you to hide in the pockets of my robe. Can you do that?" I tugged on the luxurious fabric to show them the spacious gaps.

"Jenni Opal secret. We hide."

I gave them both a quick stroke and hurried over to the wardrobe to rummage through the assortment of dresses.

Shit. They were all short-sleeved.

A panic attack began percolating inside me, but it faded when I found my salvation tucked in the very back. A silken, long-sleeved half jacket of a bright crimson hue.

I snagged the first gown that might match the color, then rushed into the bathroom. Pulling the dress on, I secured the jacket's jeweled clasp across my chest. I glimpsed myself in the mirror and fought the urge to cringe. The shades of red were just different enough to look tacky together, and the diamond encrusted bolero did not match the wispy lacey vibe of the gown at all.

I was past the point of caring, though. Maybe they'd chalk it up to horrible human fashion sense.

After all, we were barely better than animals.

Chapter Thirty-Seven

The second the sisters deemed me ready, I hurried out the door in an effort to avoid Dey. He must have anticipated my preparation taking longer because he was nowhere in sight, and I breathed a sigh of relief as I made my way toward the stairs.

My pace slowed when I approached Sin's room, though, and I briefly considered knocking to see if he would escort me to dinner. Despite the continued lies, I still wanted to nestle my head against his shoulder and breathe in his comforting scent. Hell, if I was being completely honest, what I really wanted was for him to pull me inside and ravage me until I forgot every fucked-up thing I learned today.

Heat pulsed between my thighs, and I found myself moving closer to his door as if drawn to him.

One single tap of my knuckles against the wood. That's all it would take, and we could fall into his bed, remaining there until I explored every inch of his body so thoroughly that I knew it better than my own.

Intense desire coursed through me, yet I couldn't lift my arm to knock. That intensity was also a warning. Sin was fast becoming an addiction I couldn't resist. A single taste, a single caress, and I would crumble like a sand castle at high tide.

Walking past his room was one of the hardest things I'd ever done, and I felt like I deserved a reward for showing such restraint.

Thankfully, dinner was fairly uneventful. Neither Jo nor Sin were present, which I found to be a bit odd but ultimately for the best. Even the smallest distraction might have led to me inadvertently revealing something about my new ability.

For most of the meal, I had to sit through my father making a painstakingly long speech about the upcoming Elemental Games and the banquet we would be hosting for the competitors the following night. If Dey's whispered translation was even partially accurate, it sounded like the whole thing would be a political quagmire.

When I felt like I had stayed long enough, I gave Dey and my father a polite good night and hurried to my room.

As I swung open my door and stepped into the darkened chambers, two assailants burst from the shadows. It was only by a sheer miracle that I managed to choke down the high-pitched shriek of alarm. They launched a dual pronged assault, with Opal going high to crash into my hair while Jenni went low, slipping under my dress to nip at my ankles.

"Okay, okay, ouch! All right," I managed to get out between laughs. "I'm sorry I left you alone, but I brought you some food."

That must have been the magic word because they flew up to hover in front of my face, waiting expectantly.

I had no idea what crescia ate, so I snuck a couple handfuls of nuts, seeds, and berries off my plate at dinner, filling the small pockets of the half jacket that had gotten more than a few snide looks. I dumped the pile of food onto my nightstand and waited to see what they would do.

Opal hung back while Jenni made a circle around the bounty. After careful examination, she plucked a small berry off the pile and carried it over to her friend. Opal didn't hesitate; she mashed her face into the berry, her tiny mandible reducing the fruit to a pile of mush in seconds. Beside her, Jenni promptly began chewing happily on the kinna seeds.

I left them to their meal while I shed my dress and collapsed onto the bed. With the effort of maintaining appearances all night behind me, my brain wanted to think of nothing save for Sin and his absence at dinner. Was he avoiding me? Had he changed his mind and decided he actually wanted nothing to do with me?

I squeezed my eyes shut and tried to focus on the physical sensations around me before my mind was lost to another anxiety spiral. The softness of the mattress underneath me. The slight pressure around my ribs from the lace up bra. The warmth radiating from the fireplace. I cycled through each sensation, blocking out the cascade of vicious thoughts that wanted to tear me apart. Despite my best efforts to ground myself, I started to reach for a Klonopin.

Then I recalled Sin's words to Dey.

"She's not broken."

"She just needs to work through it."

The memory swept through me on a calming wave, and I forced myself to lie still and wait for the anxiety to pass, focusing on Sin's face in my mind.

When I finally felt like I could breathe normally, I sat up in bed. Both crescia had stopped eating and were staring at me.

"Sorry," I said, leaning over to pet Jenni. "I'm afraid you bonded to damaged goods."

"Perfect Rain."

The gentle words floated through my head, and I laughed. "No, Jenni. Not perfect. Not perfect by far."

"Rain sad."

"Not sad, really," I said as she flew over and landed on my thigh. "Confused, I guess. I'm not sure what to do about Sin."

"Rain and Sin happy."

"I don't know Jenni," I replied, running a pinky over her glittering scales. "I don't know if Rain and Sin can be happy."

"Rain and Sin happy," she reiterated, then nipped at my skin to accentuate her point before flying back to her meal.

I closed my eyes and pictured Sin in my head. I didn't have to wonder what he looked like underneath his tunic anymore. I had my hands all over his smooth chest and toned abdominals only hours ago. But I never got his breeches off. Never got to feel his hard length in my hands. And judging by what I felt as I had ground my hips against him, I would not be disappointed when I unwrapped his package.

I ran my hands over my own chest and stomach, wishing it was him touching me instead. My heart sped up a bit as my fingers slid lower, dipping just under the waistband of my panties. The pleasure from my own hand would be nothing compared to how Sin had made me feel. How I clenched around his muscular digits as he thrust them deeper and deeper.

The images overwhelmed me, and I succumbed to them.

Sin running his tongue down the center of me.

My own hand slid further into my panties.

Sin flicking his tongue over my clit.

I swirled my fingers over that same spot.

Sin licking and sucking as my hips bucked against his face.

I cried out as the memory and the reality mixed together. The pulsing heat was too intense, except I wasn't burning. I was aching. For Sin.

I couldn't take it anymore. I had to know if he felt the same.

"I'm sorry, but I have to go," I said to Jenni and Opal as I slipped my robe on. "Can you stay hidden if someone comes in?"

Jenni dipped her head. *"Rain and Sin happy."*

I smiled at her words. "I hope so." Then I was out the door and rushing down the hallway.

The darkened castle was eerily silent, and anticipation pricked at my skin as I hovered outside Sin's room. This wasn't smart. Or rational. And it would only make leaving a million times harder.

But I needed him.

I just hoped he needed me even half as much.

I raised my hand to knock, but the door swung open before I could make contact.

Sin stared at me for a second, then ran a hand through his wet hair. The dark ocean smell coming from him was stronger than usual, and my eyes drifted shut as his scent washed over me. When they opened, his expression had turned molten with desire.

I swallowed roughly. His eyes were making promises that I would kill to see fulfilled.

"I was just coming to see you," he said, his low, gravelly voice sending a wave of heat through me. "Do you want to come in?" He held the door open, and I slipped inside.

I hadn't seen much of his room before when he and Dey got into their fight, only snatching a quick glimpse while I was struggling with my panic attack. It was smaller and more cozy than mine, with thick rugs covering the floor and tapestries adorning the walls. One in particular reminded me of the night sky mural my mother had commissioned for the antechamber. A wrinkled, threadbare quilt lay crumpled on top of an old steamer chest at the foot of his bed, and a glass of water sat on his nightstand beside a lantern that cast a soft, flickering glow over the room.

There was a small weapons rack in the corner, displaying a dozen daggers and small swords, and a tall bookcase dominated the entire wall beside it. Each shelf packed to the brim with extra novels shoved in sideways to fill the gaps, while even more were tossed haphazardly on top.

My eyes swept over to the entrance into his bathroom, and I noted the pile of wet towels on the floor. A neat freak Sin was not, and I kind of loved that about him. There was something so intimate about a person letting you see their mess. Letting you see the real them without any societal expectations or trappings. He didn't need to put on a show for me, and I loved his adorable, cluttered room.

I sat on the edge of his bed, struggling to slow my racing heart. Now was quite possibly the worst time to have a panic attack.

He eased the door shut and leaned back against it, watching me curiously like I was a wild animal that might bolt if he made any sudden movements.

"What's tumbling through that head of yours, Rain?" he asked softly. "What has you staring at me like that?"

"Like what?" I croaked out.

"Like you're afraid of me."

Tucking my sweaty hands under my legs, I dropped my eyes to the floor and nudged a stray sock with my toe. "Because I am," I admitted softly.

He was quiet for a long moment. When he finally replied, his voice was thick with an emotion I couldn't place. "Why?"

The answer lodged itself in my throat. God, I was being such a coward, once again refusing to allow myself any semblance of happiness because I always told myself I didn't deserve it.

Maybe I didn't deserve Sin, but I was tired of running away from the things I wanted, and I wanted him with every fiber of my being. Beyond that... any other emotions I might be feeling could be dealt with later.

I stood slowly and crossed the small room on wobbly legs to stand before him.

"Rain?" There was so much hesitation in his voice.

I closed the gap between us and placed my hands against the door on either side of his head. I much preferred being on the other side of this position, but I needed him to know I was in control.

"We can talk later," I said, leaning in to whisper in his ear. "All you need to know right now is that I want you, Sin." I pulled back enough to see his reaction.

A whirlwind of emotions ran across his face. Disbelief. Longing. Arousal. And finally that familiar smirk that was so definitively Sin.

"Whatever the princess desires."

Then his mouth was on mine, devouring me with the hunger of a starved animal. Wrapping his arms around me, he flipped us and slammed me back against his bedroom door. His tongue warred with mine, and I didn't care who won so long as I got to taste every inch of him.

His knee pushed my legs apart, causing my robe to slide open, and his muscular thigh pressed against my center.

A moan slipped out. His or mine, I wasn't sure. It didn't matter. All I cared about was getting more friction in that perfect spot.

He pulled his lips from mine, and a look of pure male satisfaction dominated his face. "Gods, Rain, your panties are already soaked."

"I know," I breathed out, unashamed of how strongly he affected me. I slid my hand down his taut chest and cupped him through his breeches. "I was thinking about you before I came here."

He covered my hand with his own, making me squeeze him harder. "Is that so?" he mused, kissing and nipping the spot just below my ear. "And what were you doing while thinking about me?" His hand slid off mine to travel up my waist, stopping only when it reached my breasts.

I arched into him and whispered, "I was touching myself."

The groan that escaped him was equal parts pain and pleasure. He captured my mouth again as he tore the robe from around my shoulders. His arms snaked around my back and pulled me into him tighter, sliding one of my legs up around his waist. The action brought my aching core closer to the thick bulge under his breeches, but I was still a few inches shy of where I wanted to be.

"Do you have any idea what you do to me?" he growled. His hand gripped my ass, and he pulled me up so both of my legs were wrapped around his midsection.

I rubbed my drenched panties against him, relishing the exquisite contact that came with this new position. Yanking his tunic up and over his broad shoulders, I lowered my head to run kisses down the corded muscles of his neck. "Tell me," I urged, needing to hear that he felt the same way I did.

"I was useless today," he replied, fisting my hair just hard enough to skate that line between agony and ecstasy. "I couldn't train. I couldn't speak with my soldiers. I couldn't do anything but think of you. I spent half the day painfully aroused, reliving the memory of you coming undone beneath me and imagining how it would feel if it were my cock instead of my fingers that brought you such pleasure."

I nipped the outer shell of his ear. "Who taught you such a dirty word?"

He laughed, a low sensual sound that only added fuel to the fire between my legs. "You have no idea what I know, Fea Remia."

He leaned forward and swirled his tongue around the taut peak that poked through the thin fabric of my bra. I pressed into him, and he sucked it into his mouth.

"Show me," I moaned. "I want all of it. All of you."

The tension on my scalp relaxed as his hand moved away from my hair, instead travelling south to dip inside my panties. He abandoned my breast so his lips could find mine, his tongue slipping into my mouth just as he stroked his fingers languidly through my wet heat, causing every muscle in my body to tighten in anticipation.

I cried out, rolling my hips faster, urging him to do more, to take more. But right as I approached the edge, he released his grip on my ass and set me down on unsteady legs.

A pathetic whimper slipped out, but before I could complain, he dropped to his knees. Looking down at him, I nearly came just from the sight of such a powerful fighter kneeling before me.

He returned my heated gaze, gave me a sinful grin, then ripped my panties off with his bare hands.

In seconds, I was back on the edge, my body begging for the satisfaction only he could give me. "Sin," I breathed out. "I won't last much longer."

With maddening slowness, he trailed kisses from my knee to my inner thigh, closer to where I burned for him. "Relax, Fea Remia. We have all night. And I do mean, all night. There are so very many naughty things I want to do to you, and I won't be denied this time."

He swirled his tongue over my sensitive clit, and my knees started to buckle. Suddenly, without a hint of warning, he swept me up into his arms and tossed me onto the bed.

I bounced twice from the impact, then stretched out on his bed, the heat under my skin roaring to life. At nearly six feet tall, I'd never been with someone who made me feel small or dainty in the physical sense, and I craved more of it.

For the first time in my life, I begged to be dominated in a way that made me feel wanted instead of weak. Sin didn't treat me like a broken doll. He treated me like someone who could take everything he had to give and more.

"You look so perfect spread open on my bed," he purred as he unlaced his breeches and released a cock that had to be impressive even by Vitaean standards. He stroked himself roughly, watching me, his eyes taking in every inch of my body.

"Please, Sin," I moaned, running my hands over my stomach and chest, desperate for him to replace them with his own.

My soft plea was all it took to break him. He yanked off his breeches and was on top of me before I could even get my bra off.

"That's my job," he breathed into my ear before gripping the strings and releasing my breasts from their confines.

I arched up into him, gasping when he slid a hand between us and brushed his thumb over my clit.

The fire building inside me flared even brighter, and I cried out from the intensity. "Sin," I whimpered as my skin started to prickle. "My fire... I can't control it."

"So don't," he offered as he notched himself at my entrance. "Lose control. I've got you." With that confident declaration, he thrust inside me in one go, sheathing himself to the hilt.

His thick cock stretched me to the point just shy of painful, and I could think of nothing save for that deliciously full sensation.

I clenched my eyes shut and allowed my fire to rush to the surface, trusting Sin not to let me hurt him.

His pace was fast and hard, yet I could still feel him holding back. I opened my eyes and met his gaze, saw the restraint he was working so hard to hold onto as he pounded into me.

"Don't," I begged. "Don't hold back. If I let go, you let go. Deal?"

"I'm not human. I don't want to hurt you, Rain," he panted, slowing enough to look me in the eyes.

"You can't hurt me, Sin. Just like you said I can't hurt you." I thrust my hips up, desperate for him to resume the furious pace. "Do it, Sin. Let go. Fuck me like a Vitaean."

He surrendered then, and I felt him plunge so deeply inside of me that I was eternally ruined for any human man.

Gripping my low back, he pulled me up against him so every bit of my skin connected with every bit of his, angling his cock even higher until he hit the spot that had me moaning uncontrollably with pleasure.

I should have been worried someone might hear us, but I was lost to the indulgence that was Sin. Flinging my head back, I cried out as my flames and orgasm erupted simultaneously, my entire body exploding with heat and euphoria.

"Sin!" My body bucked against his, drowning in the release that flooded me, and I barely registered the cool chill that swept over my hot skin.

He continued to thrust faster and deeper, dragging every ounce of pleasure from me possible. When I thought I could take no more, his entire body tensed up, and he finished inside me with a thundering roar.

We crashed to the bed in a sweaty mess of entwined limbs.

After a moment, he rolled off me, still panting heavily, and I scanned the room. No scorch marks anywhere. No smoldering ashes. Nothing burnt.

I flipped on my side to face him, letting my hands roam across his undamaged chest.

"What happened?" I managed to get out despite my own heavy breathing and thundering heartbeat. "Why didn't I burn you?"

He gave me a lazy smile. "Why Fea Remia, if I didn't know better, I'd think you wanted to cause a little pain."

I smacked his arm lightly. "Ass. You know what I meant. I saw the flames. How are you ok?"

"I told you I wouldn't let you hurt me," he said softly, running a hand down the side of my face. He gestured behind me, and I twisted to see what he was referring to.

On his nightstand, the glass of water was bone dry.

I ran a finger along my slick arm. "You..." I couldn't even finish the sentence as I gaped open mouthed at him.

"I'm one of the most powerful aquiservians in Rivella, Rain. Coating your body with a thin layer of water to smother your flames took little effort. Which is good because I needed the other ninety-nine percent of my attention to fully experience you shattering into a million pieces when I came inside you."

"Fuck!" I shouted, bolting upright in bed, his last sentence destroying my bliss. "We didn't use a condom, and I haven't taken my birth control in almost a week!"

His arm slid around my waist. "Oh, you don't need to worry about that."

He tried to pull me down against him, but I shoved his hands away. "Oh, I very much need to worry about that!"

He chuckled and tucked his arms behind his head. "I take it you still haven't gotten a lesson about the differences between humans and Vitaeans then, huh?"

I glared at him. "No, I haven't. Would you care to share with the class?"

"Well, there are a lot of differences, actually. We tend to run warmer, and most of our senses are better—hearing, smell, and so on. Though not to any biologically impossible extreme. We're still carbon based life forms, same as you."

"Oh my God!" I shouted, punching his shoulder considerably harder this time. "Can we save the lecture for a time when I'm not freaking out?"

"You did ask me to share with the class," he said, smirking.

"Sin..." I warned, my voice heavy with the promise of vengeance.

"Fine, fine," he said, tossing up his hands in a placating gesture. "Vitaeans are naturally sterile, Rain. There is no way I could impregnate you even if we fucked all night long." He grinned. "And I do intend to make that happen as soon as you stop looking at me with murder in your eyes."

I shook my head. "How is that even possible? You wouldn't survive as a species if you were sterile."

"No, we wouldn't," he agreed. "There is, however, an herb that relaxes a certain muscle inside the male body. Without it, there are no... swimmers, I guess you could say. Which means I can come inside you as often as I want. And, Rain? I very much want."

Despite the heated promise in his eyes, my tension eased at his words, and I fell back against the pillows. "So, in my world, females have to poison our bodies with side-effect riddled hormones, but here, the guys only have to take an herb if they *want* a kid?"

I hated to admit it but damn. Dey might have been a tiny bit right. Vitaeans were superior to humans. At least in this one thing.

I snuggled up against Sin, and he ran his fingers through the loose waves of my hair. "There are a lot of things about Vitaea that are different from your world. Our evolution never lent itself to a biological drive to reproduce. Possibly because our source of magic is limited in how many may draw upon it."

He ran a hand down my skin that no longer felt overheated, and I shifted so my head was laying on his chest. I wanted to ask him questions—about Vitaea, about magic—but I had put off this conversation long enough.

"Sin," I said quietly. "I need to tell you something." His hands stilled in my hair, but he remained silent, allowing me to continue. "I asked Corym to do the language transfer. He couldn't, not fully, because he was fighting against a mental block, but he was able to store the knowledge in my subconscious. I can't speak it or understand it, but... I can catch snippets if I'm not paying attention." I took a deep breath. "I've also been reliving past conversations in my dreams. When I do... I understand everything that was said in them."

Sin's body stiffened under me, and I wondered which conversation he was recalling that had him so nervous. I waited for him to speak, but he didn't.

I shifted so I could look at him. "Say something."

"How much do you remember?" he asked, his face dangerously neutral.

"Everything," I whispered. "I remember you saying that you love me. And I remember how you said that you sacrificed so much to keep me away from here." I paused when his eyes shuttered, but I had to ask. "What did you sacrifice for me, Sin?"

His eyes slowly opened, and their lovely green hue was dampened by sorrow. "I can't," he confessed. "I can't tell you, Rain."

I nodded, unsurprised by his response after our earlier discussion. "I understand that, but... do you want to tell me?"

Apparently that was the wrong thing to ask because Sin pulled away from me and sat up, swinging his legs over the side so his back was to me.

"No." The word was so quiet, so faint, and yet it thundered through my ears.

He said he wanted to tell me things, but apparently that didn't extend to whatever he had given up to protect me. And I had to decide if I could live with that.

I debated for a few seconds, but the answer came easy—I could. For now at least. I just wasn't sure if I could forever.

I sat up and wrapped my arms around his ribcage, pressing my face to his scarred back. "Okay. I can let it go."

He reached down to where my hands were clasped around his bare waist and pulled them up so he could kiss each one of my knuckles.

I drew him back to the bed, my chest pressed to his back, letting him feel my skin against his. Neither of us had mentioned the L-word, and maybe that was for the best. I didn't know what I felt for Sin, but I did know it couldn't be love.

We lay there in the heavy silence of the flickering light for a long while, languishing in this brief moment outside of time. No prophecies. No rifts between worlds. No manipulative kings. And definitely no secrets that might tear us apart.

We were just Rain and Sin. Two lost souls who had finally found a home.

Chapter Thirty-Eight

Sin and I spent the rest of the night alternating between talking and continuing to explore how well I could restrain my fire when things got heated. I never quite got the control down perfectly, but damn did I enjoy the practice.

I told him about Jenni and Opal, and he told me a little about his crescia, Cardis. When I asked to meet him, Sin just said Cardis was gone, and I thought it best not to push.

He told me about how him and Dey grew into their powers together once Sin arrived at the palace, and how they used to be brothers in the way that Jenn and I were sisters. When I told him about the conversation between Dey and my father, he grew quiet for a long while, but if Sin had any insight as to why Dey was supposed to seduce me, he didn't share it.

At some point, we fell asleep in each other's arms, and it was only the thin dagger of morning light slicing through the gap in the curtains that woke me. I had one of Sin's legs nestled between my own, and his arm was securely wrapped around my middle. I might have stayed in his bed all day, but mother nature called, and I had to answer.

When I came out of his bathroom, he was sitting up with the sheets loosely draped around his waist and sporting some of the sexiest bedhead I'd ever seen.

"Good morning," I said, trying to hide how awkward I felt. So much had happened last night, but I still feared he might not feel the same in the harsh light of day.

"Good morning, Fea Remia." His eyes raked over my naked body, and he gave me a wickedly seductive grin.

"Stop doing that," I said, gripping the door frame for support.

"Stop what?" he asked, his hand slipping beneath the sheets.

"That! You're using your sexy voice, but I need to go back to my room. I left Jenni and Opal alone all night, and I have to make sure they're okay. Breakfast at some point would be nice too. So no seductive smirks or trying to lure me back into your arms." I paused, then added, "At least not right now." I gave him a knowing smile with the promise of many more nights together.

He slid out from under the sheets and tossed me my robe before pulling on his breeches. "Here," he offered, handing me one of his long-sleeved black tunics. "It's an older one of mine, so hopefully no one will recognize it. And maybe after breakfast you can meet me at Corym's office."

"Why?" I had planned to visit the scholar so he could fix my language issue, but I didn't know why Sin needed to be there.

He tucked a stray lock of hair behind my ear and kissed me. "I want to take you into Civi Obsura. I know a way out of the castle that leads directly there, and it's near his office."

"Okay," I said, kissing him back, vacillating between excitement and nervousness about going into a city again. "I'll meet you down there shortly." He tried to pull me into a deeper kiss, but I knew where that would lead, so I smacked his bare chest. "Later," I scolded as I cracked the door open. When I saw the hall was clear, I made a beeline to my room before I lost all willpower and jumped back in his bed.

After confirming Jenni and Opal were safe, though a little irritated that I was gone all night, I showered and dressed in Sin's tunic. I took a quick sniff of his shirt and nearly collapsed when his scent hit me. Either he lied about it being old, or my sense of smell really was heightened, because all I discerned was pure, undiluted Sin.

I pulled on a pair of soft purple leggings and my Chucks, then spent a few minutes with Jenni and Opal, letting them play in my hair and chew on my shoe strings. I kept an ear out and shuffled them under the bed when I heard footsteps approaching.

Without knocking, the sisters breezed into my room, and Kiahna started in on my braid while Niahna made the bed. As they worked, I let my mind wander back to my time with Sin. I'd never had a night like that before, and I couldn't shake the tiny fear that I might not have one again.

It wasn't just about the sex either, as mind-blowing as that had been—the pleasant soreness between my thighs could attest to that. More than the physical intimacy, was the connection I felt when I was with him. Like I could tell him anything and not worry about his judgment. He had spent a long time tracing my ramentum, and even though he confirmed it was unheard of to have a color mixed in, he also said that it didn't mean it was a bad thing or that I was a freak.

"Never be afraid of how special you are," he'd told me.

Sometimes I really wished I could see myself the way he did.

When the sisters were finished, I shooed them out of the room so I could say goodbye to Jenni and Opal.

"I'm sorry, but you can't come with me," I said, staring into the mirror so I could see both of them nestled on top of my head. I didn't know if it was possible, but Jenni appeared a little bigger this morning, and it was getting a bit rough on my neck to have both of them up there.

"Jenni protect Rain."

"I know you want to protect me, but right now I can't let anyone know about you. So will you please stay here?"

I attempted to pull her from my hair, but she clung tightly, and all I managed to do was ruin my braid.

I crossed my arms and glared at them in the mirror. “You have five seconds to get out of my hair or I’m taking Opal back to the Sylvarium. Your choice.” It was an empty threat of course, but they didn’t need to know that.

I thought Jenni would call my bluff when I felt her claws gripping and releasing my hair like she couldn’t decide. Eventually, she let out a tiny wisp of flame and flew back over to the nightstand where a few nuts and seeds still remained. She gave me a derisive chuff and started eating. Opal, ever the faithful sidekick, took her cue from Jenni and did the same.

I shook my head. “Why do I feel like a parent with two petulant toddlers?”

When I found Dey waiting outside the dining hall, I nearly did an about face, but he noticed me before I could make an escape.

His nose twitched as I neared, and my step faltered.

Shit. Could he smell Sin on me?

Dey dipped his head slightly and gave me a wary smile. “Good morning, Princess. That is an interesting tunic choice. Where did you get it?”

Okay, he could definitely smell Sin.

“I found it in the weapons room a couple days ago. It was folded and smelled clean to me, so I took it back to my room. It gets chilly in the Sylvarium sometimes. I must not have the same elevated body temperature because of my human side.” I gave him my best ashamed look, and it worked like a charm.

Dey stepped into my space, and I fought the urge to cringe as he ran a hand over my shoulder. “You should not be embarrassed about your human half, Rain. It only proves how strong you are to overcome it.”

Damn he was predictable.

With Sin’s smell forgotten or deemed unimportant, Dey took my arm and led me into the dining hall where my father was already eating breakfast.

“Good morning, Raynella,” he greeted. “I trust you slept well?”

I tried not to blush at the reminder of exactly how well I had slept. “Yes, thank you.” As I took my seat, his nose twitched as well.

He asked Dey a question in Rivellan, but Dey just responded dismissively. I could imagine what he was saying, but I needed to be ignorant to sell it.

"What's up?" I asked, taking a bite of fruit and palming a couple berries at the same time to give the crescia later.

"Nothing important," my father said. "I did want to remind you that the dinner this evening will be somewhat elevated, though not quite as elaborate as tomorrow's banquet. Please make sure your servants dress you accordingly. The seamstress will return this afternoon for a fitting of your finished gown, and you will need to meet her in your chambers."

"I will come find you in the Sylvarium later," Dey added. "That way I can assist with the translation."

"Sounds great," I said, hoping it came out more authentic than it sounded to me. I snagged a handful of nuts and pushed back from my chair. "I'm actually not that hungry, and I want to make sure I get plenty of time with the crescia, so if you don't mind, I'm going to head out."

My father looked like he wanted to argue, but I breezed out the door before he got the chance.

I left in the direction of the Sylvarium in case they were watching, then hooked a right toward the stairs to the lower level. My heart skipped a beat when I saw Sin waiting outside the library, leaning against the wall. He was a harsh kind of beautiful, and I imagined most people gave him a wide berth. I wondered if it ever bothered him, this persona he portrayed. Maybe he preferred it like that. Preferred the solitude. Either way, I knew what was in his heart, and he could play scowly and growly all he wanted with everyone else because I knew the truth.

His slow grin melted my insides as he stalked toward me like a panther sizing up his prey.

He stopped just shy of me and slid his gaze up my body, causing something inside me to clench at the desire in his slow perusal.

"I wish I could dress you in my clothes every day," he said, his deep voice rough with approval.

I closed the gap and slid my arms around his neck. "Yeah? Well I think people might catch on if you did that." I gave him a placating kiss on the nose. "Is Corym here? I need to see if he can fix the language issue before we leave."

"Yeah, I think I heard him in there."

He pushed the door open and gently nudged me to enter first. I braced myself for the remnants of the destruction I left behind but was surprised to find no evidence of what occurred. The rug and couch were gone, replaced by new ones, and all scorch marks had been scrubbed from the ceiling and walls. There wasn't even a lingering hint of smoke.

"Princess," Corym called, crossing over to me, an unexpectedly wide smile on his face. Apparently my royalty status trumped the destruction of his antique rug. "It is wonderful to see you again under better circumstances. I feared this one might have scared you away." He gave a pointed look to Sin, who just shrugged and leaned against the doorframe.

Corym drew me over to the sofa and pulled me down beside him. "What can I do for you?"

"Right, so the language transfer thing? It worked, but it seems to be stuck in my subconscious. I can only remember conversations when I'm sleeping. Any way you can fix that? The medication should be long out of my system, but things aren't improving."

Corym's eyes lit up. "I would be delighted to try. It is so fascinating how your brain works. I never placed knowledge in the back of the mind before. I have spent quite a bit of time considering the practical applications of such a possibility."

That was Corym, ever the scholar. I gave him a small laugh. "Well, I'm happy to be your guinea pig. Let's see if you can push it to the front."

"Yes, let us," he said, shifting to take my hands. "Close your eyes. I do hope this will be quite a bit faster and less painful."

"Painful?" Sin asked in a low growl, the single word threatening violence against any who might harm me.

I gave him a determined look. "It's okay, Sin. I want this. Whatever it takes."

His eyes narrowed, but he reluctantly resumed his position against the doorframe, grumbling under his breath in Rivellan.

"Please continue," I said to Corym and closed my eyes.

While I waited for something to happen, my mind drifted off toward thoughts of Sin. There had been a moment after my third, maybe fourth, orgasm of the evening when I had been so completely and utterly sated that the idea of me even moving was laughable. I'd been so wrapped up in him that I forgot about my scars on full display.

Until he pressed gentle kisses along my back. "You should never be ashamed of this, Rain," he'd said. "Scars are not evidence of weakness. They are evidence that you have endured more than most, and yet you remain standing. They are proof that you cannot, will not, be broken. Wear them as a badge of honor."

It was another reason that I didn't deserve him, and yet I clung to it. This idea that I was not broken, but instead had been forged into something stronger. It was a beautiful lie, but so long as he believed it, maybe I could too someday.

"Princess?" Corym's gentle voice pulled me out of the memory.

I blinked a few times at the two male faces staring intently at me. "Is that it?" I asked warily, hoping I didn't lose hours of my life again.

"You tell us. Can you speak Rivellan?" Sin asked.

I frowned at him. "How can I tell? Do I just think of a word?"

Sin and Corym both laughed, and it only made me frown harder. "What's so funny?"

"Dreisin was speaking to you in Rivellan, Princess."

I looked to Sin who nodded in confirmation. "I thought you were speaking English... That's what I heard in my head."

Corym gave me one of his patented professor smiles—a mix of encouragement and patience. "That is because your brain converts it automatically for you. Listening will be the easiest, of course, as the translation will happen with little to no effort. Speaking Rivellan, however, may take you a second to adapt to. You will need to focus and make a conscious effort. Your brain will supply the words as they come up. Give it a try."

I glanced between them. "Okay, sure. What should I say?"

Sin smirked. "You should say I am the greatest aquiservian who ever lived."

I paused, trying to focus on the swirl of Rivellan words bouncing around in my head.

"Sin abea amplie ia." My words came out rough and stilted like a child learning to read, but Corym laughed, so the translation must have worked.

"I don't have a big ego," Sin muttered, stomping back over to the door.

Corym settled into the sofa, exhaustion deepening the lines of his face. "You should practice speaking in Rivellan as much as possible so your mind grows accustomed to forming the words. Hearing others speak it will be beneficial as well since your brain should start alerting you to the change in language. Right now, the translation is automatic, so you may not even realize someone is speaking to you in Rivellan at first. It will take a moment, but soon you will be able to recognize and speak it with ease."

I leaned forward and gave him a peck on the cheek, grinning at his startled expression. "Thank you so much. You don't know what this means to me."

He blushed. "It was my pleasure, Princess."

I hopped off the couch and bounded over to Sin, excited to try out my new language skills in Civi Obsura. "You ready to go?"

"More than," he said, turning to leave the library.

"Princess?" Corym called. "May I have a brief word alone?"

"Sure. What's up?"

He waited until Sin left, then said, "I must make a confession. When I was moving the language from your subconscious to your conscious, I found myself able to see what you were thinking about."

My cheeks burned so hot my hand unconsciously lifted to check for flames. "Oh," I said awkwardly.

Corym stood but maintained his distance. "I do not want to make you uncomfortable, I merely wanted to inform you that I was aware of your relationship with my son. Also..." His eyes dropped to the ground. "I wanted to ask you a favor."

"Anything." I owed Corym big time, so I would do pretty much whatever he wanted.

There was so much vulnerability in his wide eyes and hunched posture as he whispered, "Do not hurt him, Princess. Sin has suffered much in his life, and I know he has his secrets, but… he is a good male. Please, do not break his heart."

I swallowed roughly. Corym had asked for the one thing that I couldn't promise. "I would never want to hurt him," I replied, but I couldn't bring myself to give him any more than that.

Corym nodded in understanding. "That will have to do, then. Thank you, Princess. For bringing joy back into his life."

I didn't bother to correct him. To tell him that Sin was the one who brought me back to life. Every day since I arrived here, I thought of nothing but going home to Jenn. Now, I mostly thought of Sin. Of the times when we were together, and how perfect it felt to be in his arms. Mostly I thought about how he never once made me feel broken or damaged.

He was the light in my life, not the other way around.

I smiled at Corym and closed the door to his office. Finding Sin waiting out in the hall, I couldn't stop myself from rushing over to him. Our kiss was slow and gentle at first, but quickly became deep and demanding. It was torture to pull away from him, but anyone could turn the corner and find us.

"What did Corym want?" Sin asked, running his thumb over my swollen lip.

I hesitated, then said, "He told me not to break your heart."

Sin eyes shuttered at the solemn words. When he opened them, a fire not unlike my own burned bright. "And what did you say? Are you going to crush me, Fea Remia?"

"Not on purpose," I answered truthfully, forcing myself to meet his gaze.

He gave a shallow nod as if confirming he was aware of this very dangerous game we were planning. "In that case, let's enjoy the time we have." He tugged on my hand, and I followed him toward the entrance to the Laneum.

"Wait here," he whispered as he edged around the corner. "Off to the left is a huge boulder. Behind it is a gap in the stone. It's narrow, but we can squeeze through. We just need to wait until the attendant's back is turned."

I nodded, and we waited in silence for so long I was starting to wonder if we should abandon the plan. I was about to say as much when Sin tugged on my arm. "Now."

We dashed into the cavern, and I tried to keep as quiet as possible as he dragged me off to the left and around the massive stone. Thick and twisted veins of obsidian ran through the muted gray rocks of the roughhewn wall, and I did a double take when Sin disappeared through one. I approached it cautiously and realized that the gap in the wall was cleverly disguised as merely another vein of black stone.

Turning sideways, I slipped through the narrow space, my breasts scraping against the wall. For the first time in my life, I was actually grateful they were relatively small. I eased my way through roughly ten feet or so of tight stone corridor before I popped out on the other side, and Sin grabbed me when I pitched forward into the open space.

"Well that was fun," I muttered into the ominous darkness that now swallowed me.

"It's okay," Sin said. "I've been through these tunnels many times and can likely find the way in the dark." He pressed himself tightly against me and added, his voice a sultry whisper in the shadows, "If you'd like to make it easier for yourself, though, and create a little light, I wouldn't say no." He nipped my ear as punctuation.

"I can't," I said, my voice taking on a husky tone as he pressed kisses against my neck. My inability to see him only heightened the sensation of his lips against my skin. "I've tried. It just sort of comes out when I'm angry or..."

"Aroused?" Sin purred. His ability to soak my panties with a single word should be considered magic all its own. He guided me backward until I hit a wall of rock, and his hand began a leisurely journey south. "I don't want to make you mad."

"Me neither," I gasped out as his fingers reached the top of my leggings.

"Which only leaves one option..." His hand slipped under the waistband of my leggings, and his other hand clamped over my mouth to keep me from crying out. "Hush, Fea Remia. We're not far enough away. Someone could hear you."

He ran a single finger through my wet center, and I arched into his touch. "I need you to be a good girl and keep quiet." His finger dipped inside me. "Can you do that? Can you be a good girl for me?"

I nodded. I would have promised him anything at that point.

"Then prove it," Sin growled softly into my ear as he plunged another finger inside me and used his thumb to rub circles around my clit.

I nearly bit my tongue off to keep from crying out. My flames started to burn inside me as the orgasm built, and I shoved at Sin to get him to back away.

"I'm not going anywhere," he said, pumping his fingers faster and faster, curling them up inside me to hit my favorite angle. "I trust you. Control your fire. I know you can."

It was the most perfect kind of torture, and I wanted to give in to the pleasure, allowing myself to burn in the heaven that was Sin. His words locked themselves into my brain, though.

"I trust you."

At the last second, just as the orgasm spilled through me, I pulled at the fire under my skin, drawing it up my legs, across my torso, and out along my arms.

I threw my hands above my head right as they erupted in flames.

I breathed out a sigh of relief and let my head fall back against the stone wall. It worked. I controlled the power.

Well, mostly. Miniscule wisps of smoke curled up from where I singed a few holes in my tunic, but at least they were small and barely noticeable.

I opened my eyes to see Sin leaning back against the opposite wall, his hand rubbing over the prominent bulge straining against his breeches. "Gods, Rain, I love watching you come," he murmured, and my cheeks reddened. Despite everything we had done together, he still made me blush.

"Well, I'd like to return the favor, but..." I held up my hands which were fully engulfed in flame.

He smiled and gave one last stroke over his cock before moving closer to whisper into my ear, "It's okay, Rain. I love the idea of you owing me one."

A small shudder ran through me at the sensual promise in his words. "I can't wait for you to collect," I said, turning my head to look at him, our faces so close my lips nearly grazed his.

He shifted slightly to press a kiss to my mouth, then began the journey deeper into the tunnels. "Coming, Fea Remia?"

I squeezed my thighs together, forcing my body to ignore the pulsing ache that had already bloomed again between my legs, and jogged after him down the dim tunnels, my flames the only light in the darkness.

We walked in silence for a while so I could focus on keeping my fire lit, but after about ten minutes, I found it easier to maintain without effort.

"Can all igniservians wield their magic without burning?" I asked, waving my hands around in front of me so I could watch the reds, oranges, and yellows dance in the dark.

"No," he replied, dodging to the side when my fire got a little too close to his face. "All elemental casters are able to do is manipulate. Igniservians can still burn. Aquiservians can drown. Aeriservians can suffocate."

"And terriservians?"

Sin's footsteps stuttered, and his back stiffened, but he continued along.

"They can be buried alive."

The deep chill in his tone told me not to pry, regardless of how badly I wanted to. Corym said Sin's mother died of the plague, so who had he lost in such a tragic way?

I allowed the crunch of gravel beneath our feet to echo through the uncomfortable silence, waiting to see if he would say anything more. When he didn't, I decided to practice my Rivellan to break the tension. Remembering what Corym had mentioned, I focused on phrases I recognized to bring the foreign language to the front of my brain.

"How did you discover this tunnel?" I asked when I felt confident enough to make an attempt.

"The information is passed from one Cennux to the other," Sin replied in what I was pretty sure was Rivellan. "It is a closely guarded secret that only a handful of people know about at any given time. Not even the kings are told, lest they accidentally let it slip."

"Why the secrecy?" I asked, maintaining my grip on the Rivellan tongue.

"Safety precautions," he responded in kind. "Were the castle to fall, we would need a way to get the royal family out. The more people who know about these tunnels, the easier it is for them to become compromised."

I nodded. "So only you and who else knows about them?"

"Peywyn is the only other."

My flames flared a bit brighter at the mention of her name, and Sin eyed me curiously. "She is just my second, Rain. No need for jealousy."

I huffed out a breath and reigned in my fire. "It's not like that. I trust you, Sin. It's just..." I didn't know how to finish my sentence. How to explain that it wasn't the kind of envy he imagined. "I'm jealous that she knows you so well. That she gets to spend time with you out in the open. It also doesn't help that she's gorgeous."

Sin laughed. "You wouldn't say that if you saw her during her awkward phase."

"See," I pointed out. "It's that right there. She has your past, Sin. Even if you aren't, you know, *together*, she still has a piece of you I never will. I don't blame her, but I also can't help the little spark of envy."

Careful to avoid my flames, Sin's hand drifted up to my face and cupped my cheek. "She might have my past, but you have my future. If you want it."

It should have been exactly what I needed to hear, but I couldn't help the hint of nausea simmering in my stomach. I wanted his future. I just didn't think I was going to get it.

Sin dropped his hand and continued down the tunnel. "And for what it's worth," he called over his shoulder, "I was never with Peywyn at any point. She never felt that way about me. You might have a shot with her, though." He gave me a wink, and I nearly stumbled.

Oh.

Composing myself, I jogged forward, blushing and trying not to think about the warrior goddess naked, her legs wrapped around me the way I had seen them wrapped around Sin.

"Should I be the jealous one now?" Sin asked when I caught up to him. He gave a meaningful glance to the flames in my hand that had sparked brighter again.

"Maybe," I said, only half joking.

"It's a good thing I found you first, then," he replied. "If she fucks the way she fights, I wouldn't stand a chance."

More images spilled through my mind, and I cleared my throat, needing to change the subject before I did something stupid, like suggest a threesome. "So where are we going exactly? Is Civi Obsura pretty big? Can we get some food at some point? I didn't eat much breakfast."

Sin chuckled at my obvious attempt to discuss anything but his sexy second in command. "Civi Obsura is larger in population but condensed into a smaller area than Civi Adasa. And of course we can get you something to eat. There are a few street vendors toward the center of town. One in particular makes the most delicious roast lanfa you'll ever eat."

I decided it was likely better if I didn't ask what a lanfa was.

"And our destination? Or is this mostly sightseeing?"

He shrugged. "I thought it would be a good idea to find you a long-sleeved dress for dinner tonight. You can tell Verren you borrowed it from Peywyn. She'll back you up." Sin paused before adding, "I also thought you might want to see where your mother lived."

I stopped abruptly as Sin's words squeezed my heart.

My mother. Sin had met her. Why did I never ask him before? He was nearly eighty, of course he had been around when she was at the palace.

"You knew my mother?" I asked, my voice shaky.

"I did. She was... She was wonderful. And kind, unlike so many that live in the castle. When she found out I grew up in Civi Obsura, we would talk about it for hours on end. I missed my home, and she didn't. We were still able to share some fond memories, though."

"I want to know everything," I breathed out.

"I wasn't sure if you did," he said as we resumed our trek. "You never asked about her, and I didn't know if it would be worse for you. Her story isn't pleasant, Rain. She was a human who spent her whole life in hiding."

"I don't care," I replied firmly. "I want to know everything."

Sin spent the rest of our journey down the mountain telling me everything he knew about Leeara and how similar we were. He told me how they would sit on the parapet almost every evening because she loved looking out at the ocean at night. How she hated all the rude courtiers and all the pretensions of palace life. How she always spoke her mind and was the strongest person he'd ever met.

By the time light began to filter into the tunnel, my face was tear streaked, and my heart was close to bursting. I would give anything to be able to talk to her, even for a minute. I would ask her how she did it, how she survived in the castle surrounded by wolves. And I would thank her for taking me away from all of it. I hated my life growing up, but I hated even more the idea of who I might have become if I'd grown up in the palace with the rest of the snobs.

Talk of my mother ended as we approached a small opening in the tunnel, and I snuffed my flames.

"Let me go first so I can hold the tree limbs back," Sin said, slipping through the tiny gap in the stone.

The bright sun stung my eyes when I emerged from the tunnel, and Sin let the branches swing behind me, hiding the passageway once again.

"What's that smell?" I asked, a whiff of something foul stinging my nose.

"Sewage," Sin said, gesturing to my right where a metal pipe dumped dirty water into a massive quarry.

I took a couple steps closer, trying not to breathe too much, and peered over the edge. Rancid brown water filled the pit, and what little breakfast I had tried to claw its way out to join it.

"Makes it easier to keep the tunnel a secret," Sin commented. "Nobody wants to spend too much time here."

"No kidding," I agreed, trying not to choke on the stench.

I followed him away from the putrid smell until we came to a grove of desiccated and twisted trees.

Sin stopped me and started rolling up his sleeves. "We're almost there, so you'll want to expose your arms. Nobody will know who you are here, and it would be a good idea for them to think you are an imminario."

"I thought humans lived in Civi Obsura," I said, folding back my loose sleeves.

"They do," he replied. "But they stay in hiding and only go out in disguise. The imminarios are nowhere near as vicious as the secunnarios in Civi Adasa, but there are many who do not take kindly to humans here."

"Why? You'd think they would sympathize with being treated like lesser citizens."

"They used to," Sin said, leading me through the trees. "There was a reluctant alliance between them years ago, but that all changed after the plague hit."

I put a hand on his shoulder and stopped him. "Why?"

Sin frowned at me. "Your father never told you?"

"Told me what?" I asked, growing nervous. I was tired of finding out new and tragic things people kept hidden from me.

"The plague," he replied slowly. "They brought it into the city. Humans are the carriers."

Chapter Thirty-Nine

While Civi Adasa was charming, elegant, magnificent, and beautiful, Civi Obsura was dirty, smelly, crowded, and depressing.

Honestly, it felt like home.

"This is like the Rivellan version of Jersey," I said with a laugh as we meandered down the road.

The streets were packed with unguisen pulling wagons loaded with food and other goods, while vendors hawked their wares at anybody who passed by. The city's buildings looked like they might crumble to pieces with a strong wind, and puddles of muddy water filled the numerous potholes strewn about the road. The stones that made up the sidewalks had more cracked pieces than solid ones.

All that aside, though, it was the people that made the biggest difference between this city and the one up the hill. There was very little joy on the faces of Civi Obsura's citizens. Their eyes were downcast and their shoulders rounded forward. Children tucked tight into their parents' sides tended to be crying rather than laughing, and more than one fight broke out during the first five minutes we were there.

And the smell. It wasn't quite as bad as the sewage dump, but it was definitely not the vanilla and rose petals I had scented in Civi Adasa.

The longer we walked, the more I realized maybe Jersey wasn't so bad.

When we passed by the food vendors, Sin bought me a hunk of the roasted lanfa he swore would change my life.

He wasn't far off. The tender meat nearly melted in my mouth, and the salty, spicy flavor had me drooling.

"What do they season this with, cocaine?" I asked as a moan escaped me.

Sin laughed and led me down a side street while I devoured the tasty snack. We moved away from the center of the city into a more residential area, and I noticed at least in this part of town, things weren't quite so depressing. Children actually played in the streets while mothers chatted nearby in the shade.

"What's that?" I ask, pointing to a symbol on a crumbling brick wall.

"That's the sign of the Lissentia," Sin said in a quiet, maybe even respectful, tone. "I suppose you would call them anarchists. They are, or were, a group of Rivellan imminarios that opposed the royal family being situated over the Source while the people here on the outskirts struggled with scraps of magic."

"That's considered anarchy?" I asked, licking the remnants of the lanfa off my fingers. "It seems like the people here far outnumber those in the castle. Why don't they overthrow the royal family?"

"There have been attempts," Sin said as he directed me to continue walking. "Though the attacks really only began in earnest after the plague tore through each court's outer cities. The imminarios always suffered the most. The Silver Court had the first uprising, maybe thirty years ago. They just wanted their king to open his castle grounds to the masses for a few hours each day. They believed that more of the imminarios would be able to develop as secunnarios or even amplissarios if they were nearer to the Source." Sin stopped walking. "The king had their heads removed, Rain."

His statement drew me to an abrupt stop. "Wait," I said, once I was able to move past the Silver King's brutality. "Are you saying that proximity to the Source can affect how many abilities a person can get?"

Sin let out a sigh that carried the weight of someone witnessing injustice but was helpless to prevent it. "Yes, Rain. If a Vitaean doesn't have access to the Source, then how would they be able to manifest their magic? Those forced to live on the outer edges so far from the well of power will never know how much magic they might have been able to wield. A lion will never know how fast he can run if he is never released from his cage."

I placed a hand along a wall to steady myself. "So those that are born out here will never have a way to improve their situation? It's a never ending cycle of suppression."

"For the most part," he agreed. "Occasionally a powerful secunnario will emerge, but it is very rare."

"Like you," I said, and Sin nodded.

"If I wasn't accepted into Verren's guard and spent so much time around the Source, then I never would have developed my third power."

My fingers twined through his, and we continued walking, but I couldn't stop thinking about the people around me. All throughout my life, we had been taught about injustice, and yet no amount of schooling prepared me for seeing it in person. I inspected the city around me, the slums, and really saw it for the first time.

A young girl spilled the glass of water she was carrying, and her mom struggled to catch the stream of liquid before it hit the ground. A little boy on the ground was crying, and his father struggled to heal the scraped knee, barely able to get it to scab over. Behind me, a street vendor struggled to keep the fire going under the meat he was cooking.

Struggle, struggle, struggle. It was all I saw. Every one of them struggled to do things that would be so simple if they only lived a few miles closer to the castle.

I spent my whole life below the poverty line, barely able to make ends meet, but I always believed that if I worked hard enough, trained with my violin long enough, maybe things could change.

These people couldn't even have the dream. Only the cold, hard reality that their lives would never be more than what they were now.

"How do they live like this?" I asked, my voice laced with despair.

"They don't, Fea Remia. They only survive. It's all they can do. The people here will only ever go as far as the ramentum on their arms allows, and for most, this is the end of the line." He gestured to the ramshackle homes falling apart around us.

"Nobody should ever be okay with this," I declared as we crossed down another alleyway. My mind was running rampant with thoughts I was afraid to voice, but the more I saw of the city around me, the more I had to know. Gripping Sin's hand, I forced the question out. "Do you think restoring the lines will change things for them? If it returns their full access to magic?"

Sin flinched slightly, and I nearly missed it. I recalled how hard he tried to convince me to abandon the prophecy. To leave the ley lines as they were because he said the risk wasn't worth it.

"Maybe," he admitted. "Maybe it will change everything. And maybe it will change nothing. People in power tend to want to stay in power."

I bit my lip. "Do you think if I agreed to stay here as princess—and I'm not saying I am—but if I was... do you think I would be able to change anything?"

His hold on my hand tightened, and he lifted it to press a kiss to my knuckles. "I don't know. I won't hide the fact that I do want you to stay now. When you first arrived, I could think of nothing beyond pissing you off enough to get you to leave. To go back to your world where you would be safe. I would have spent my very long existence alone, comforted by the knowledge that this place could never harm you. But now that I've touched you..." He paused for a beat. "Now that I've tasted you, I can't fathom the thought of letting you go. It doesn't matter who you are—a princess, a queen, a human from Jersey—I will never be worthy of you. There is so much in my past that I can never atone for, but I would do everything in my power to earn your trust, and your love, if you stayed here." He swallowed. "If you stayed with me."

There it was. The topic we had been tiptoeing around since yesterday, neither of us willing to bring it up for fear of what might be said.

I leaned forward and sank into the warmth of his lips. He wrapped his arms around my waist and pulled me tight against him, deepening the kiss. We devoured each other, forgetting for a moment that we probably shouldn't draw attention to ourselves. I couldn't help it, though. I let his dark ocean scent wash over me for as long as possible.

Resting my cheek against his shoulder, I whispered, "You could come back to Jersey with me."

Sin's hands at my low back gripped me tighter, as if he was afraid to let me go. "I can't, Rain. I'm a Vitaean. We need access to the Source. It killed me a little every time I visited your world. I felt like I was missing an intrinsic part of me, like a piece of my soul was just gone. I can't live like that."

I wondered if I would feel something similar when I went home. Would I miss my magic? Would I miss it enough to abandon Jenn forever? I couldn't imagine anything feeling bad enough to do that.

"So you have to stay, and I have to go."

He squeezed his eyes shut. "That's what it sounds like."

I ran a hand over the deep furrow in his brow. "What does that mean for you and me?"

He opened his eyes, and my knees practically buckled at the heartache I saw in them. "It means I lose part of my soul either way."

A tear slid down my cheek. Then another. I wiped them away, cursing my inability to hold them back when I was usually so good at that. "Why is my stupid heart making me feel like this?"

"Hearts will never be practical until they can be made unbreakable."

His words hurt like knives stabbed deep into my soul, and the tears only poured out faster at how casually he quoted my favorite line from The Wizard of Oz. The motto I based my entire life on because it never failed me. And the first time I decided to ignore it, the first time I let someone into my heart, was when I was reminded why it was such a bad idea.

"Don't cry, Fea Remia," Sin said, lifting my chin with a single finger and brushing away my tears. "There's still the possibility that we both die in the dark forest before you even have the chance to leave me."

Barking out a sharp laugh, I jabbed him in the chest. "Oh my God, Sin, did you really just say that?"

He smirked. "I got you to stop crying though, didn't I?"

I sniffed, but there were no more salty droplets streaming down my cheeks. He always knew how to save me from myself.

Refusing to fall back into the despair of losing him, I decided it was time for me to do what I did best. Avoidance and dismissal.

"So, I don't see any shops around which I guess means you're taking me to my mom's place?"

"It's right around the corner," he said, but when I turned in that direction, he put a hand on my shoulder. His face darkened, any semblance of the earlier levity gone. "All joking aside, I know you're still planning to fulfill the prophecy before you leave. But you also need to know that I won't let you restore the ley lines if it means you might be harmed in the process. I would let them suffer, all of them, if it keeps you alive. I won't apologize for that."

I gulped, hearing the truth in his voice.

And it made me wonder what he knew that I didn't.

The house where my mom grew up shocked me more than I thought possible given everything else I'd seen. Mostly because it wasn't really a house. It was a brothel.

Half-naked ladies lounged on a sagging front porch while a few others escorted random males in or out of the run-down, two-story home. They reminded me of beautiful harem girls from the Arabian nights with their swishy, transparent outfits.

I turned to Sin. "My mother was a sex worker?"

He laughed and tugged me toward the house. "No, Rain. Your mother just lived here. She was taken in by the Madame who runs this place and kept hidden. Come on. If Yanda is around, she can tell you more about your mother than I can."

Letting Sin drag me up the rickety stairs past the scantily clad females, I regretted that I could now understand the sordid propositions they purred at him. I almost smacked one who offered to show him what a real female could do, and it bothered me a little just how deep my possessive feelings were.

It was only thanks to his strong arm materializing around my waist that we made it inside without any violence.

A female in a miniscule top that showcased unfairly perfect tits lay sprawled out on a sofa in the front room looking bored, but she perked up when Sin approached.

My fists clenched at the seductive smile she gave him, and another wave of jealousy had my insecurities about my flat chest rearing their head. It calmed a little, though, because his eyes never dropped below her face.

Giving Sin a pouty look when all he did was ask to speak to Yanda, she left the room in a huff without bothering to even acknowledge me.

While she went to go find the Madame, Sin took her spot on the sofa, and I wandered around the parlor, observing their interesting taste in art. A particularly erotic painting of a female servicing two males drew my attention, and I barely heard the soft steps descending the stairs. I turned just as an elegant, middle-aged woman with a hint of gray in her short sandy brown hair reached the bottom step and threw her arms around Sin.

"Dreisin!" she cried out happily, crushing him against her own ample bosom. "I haven't seen you in years. I thought you had forgotten all about me."

I blinked at the two of them embracing. "Dreisin?" I asked, whirling on Sin and switching to English. "Care to explain how you know this lady so well?" I honestly had no issues with sex workers, but I didn't love hearing that Sin had apparently been a frequent flyer at the local brothel. It was just another reminder of how little I actually knew about his past.

The Madame released Sin and faced me, the long skirts of her classy scarlet dress swishing with the motion. Her thin hazel eyes scanned my body, and she smiled.

"And who is this beautiful creature who does not speak our language? Have you brought me a present, Dreisin?"

Sin laughed, though I didn't find her comment that amusing. Before he could speak, I stepped up to her and said in Rivellan, "I'm Rain, and I speak your language fine. Mostly. And I'm not here as a sex worker."

I had to admit the Rivellan word was much prettier than any of the English options. *Melatrice* just sounded a bit more sophisticated than prostitute, even in my annoyed tone.

Sin gestured to each of us and said, "Rain, meet Yanda. Yanda, this is Rain." Then to me, he added, "No need for claws, Fea Remia. Yanda was a good friend of my mother before she died, and she visited our house often. I was never allowed to come here despite my persistent begging when I was young."

Yanda casually slung an arm around Sin's neck. "Your mother always said I was a bad influence on you."

Sin gave her a wide grin. "That's because you kept trying to hire me once I was old enough, saying the females of Civi Obsura deserved just as much attention as the males."

"A statement that is as true today as it was sixty years ago."

They both laughed, and the natural ease with which they interacted had that strange envious feeling bubbling up in the pit of my stomach again. "Uh, Sin," I said, waving my hand in front of his face. "I don't actually have all day."

"Right. Sorry," he said, his expression sobering a little. "Yanda, I was hoping you would be willing to talk to Rain about Leeara. You remember her, don't you?"

At the mention of my mother's name, Yanda's smile faded, and she turned to analyze me. She ran a finger over the spot where my silver hair was starting to grow out at the roots. "Raynella," she whispered, more to herself than me.

"I go by Rain now," I said pointedly before anyone else could take up the Raynella crap.

"I see," she replied quietly. "Come with me, Rain."

Doing my best to dismiss the lingering jealousy because I wanted to learn more about my mom, I followed her up the stairs and down a hall to a tiny room with peeling white paint at the back of the house. It was empty, save for a small bed set beneath a single cracked window, an old brown sofa torn in three spots, and a scratched up dresser with crooked drawers.

Sin plopped onto the sofa while Yanda sat on the bed. I opted for leaning against the broken dresser since I wasn't feeling particularly cuddly at the moment.

Yanda observed me, her shrewd eyes taking in my discomfort. "This room isn't used for entertaining, Raynella. The client spaces are much more decorated, so you are welcome to sit if you'd like."

"That wasn't a concern I had, and please don't call me Raynella," I snapped, wondering if I should find myself a damned name tag. "I'm good right here."

I knew I shouldn't be rude to the person who could tell me more about my mother, but there was just something about the way she looked at me that kept my hackles slightly raised, like she knew something about me that I doubted she was going to share.

"Whatever you prefer," she replied, seemingly unbothered my acidic tone. "This was actually your mother's room, you know. I haven't taken in another stray since her, so little has changed."

I glanced around at the empty space. "That's not saying much."

"No, I suppose not. Your mother had few possessions, and she took most with her to the castle when she left."

My eyes drifted from the busted window down to the musty-looking pink quilt on the bed. "Can't say I'm surprised that she wanted to go."

Ignoring my snarky comment, Yanda scooted back on the bed, crossed her legs, and leaned against the wall. "I loved your mother very much, Rain. I never had children of my own, and she was only three when she arrived at my doorstep. The World Walker who dropped her off said her parents had been murdered, and while she owed them a debt, she could not care for a child. She made me vow to raise Leeara in secret and allow no one to find her. Even as a toddler, your mother was so beautiful, so captivating with her shining silver hair. I knew there was something special about her. Despite my better judgment, I agreed, and it turned out to be the best decision I ever made."

I remained quiet as she continued her story, trying to fight off the wave of emotion from learning that my mother had also grown up an orphan.

"I kept her hidden for over twenty-five years, until one day, a few of the king's guards came here looking for a good time. They caught the barest glimpse of her in the hall, said something about silver hair, and left. When the king arrived hours later, I feared he was there to kill her personally. Instead, he pleaded with her to come to the palace, to live there. I had no idea what he could possibly want with a human, and I tried to tell her that he couldn't be trusted. He was attractive, though, and she saw the chance for a life outside of a tiny bedroom in Civi Obsura. So she took it. A year passed with no word, until she just showed up one night with you in her arms, begging for help. She was so scared that I gave her what she wanted without a second thought, and I never saw her again."

"What did she say when you saw her?" I demanded, stepping away from the dresser. "Do you know why she left the palace?"

"She said only that you were in danger, and she needed the World Walker's help. So I told her what I knew of the Walker's location. I'm sorry, Rain, but I don't know what happened after that."

"What happened?" I shouted, my voice vibrating with anger. "The Walker killed her and dumped me in a different realm. That's what happened. You sent her to her death." My flames burned beneath my skin, growing hotter alongside my anger.

Sin must have sensed they were getting close to erupting because he jumped to his feet and tried to take my face in his hands.

I jerked away and stalked closer to the bed. Closer to the person who got my mother killed.

Yanda didn't look the slightest bit cowed. Her back stiffened, and an air of defiance surrounded her. "That's a lie," she bit out. "Caira would never harm Leeara. In fact, she would come by often to visit with the child to ensure she was safe and healthy. Caira even told me where her home was in case Leeara ever needed help or was in danger. She loved your mother as much as a Walker is capable of love, so no, Rain, Caira did not kill her. Who told you such a thing?"

The fire that had nearly exploded from me dissolved into barely smoldering embers. "My father told me," I answered, realizing how stupid I'd been to blindly accept his version of the story. "He told me the Walker killed my mother just as he arrived to save her."

"Well, Rain," Yanda said, climbing off the bed and stepping closer to me. "Your father is a liar."

Chapter Forty

I moved sluggishly as Sin guided me back toward the main city square in search of a dress. Despite his assurances that he had plenty of Rivellan coin and I could pick out whatever I liked, I couldn't summon any excitement. Maybe it was learning about my father's lies. Maybe it was the unease from spending money on a fancy dress while surrounded by people who could barely feed themselves. Likely it was both.

Either way, I made myself focus long enough to pick out a somewhat plain but still adorable long-sleeved forest green dress with a plunging sweetheart neckline and a baby blue chemise underneath. The silver lacing up the front had the tiniest floral details on it, and a matching ribbon looped around the elbows in case I wanted to wear it with the sleeves gathered up. Not that I would be doing that anytime soon.

I tucked the linen-wrapped dress under my arm as we exited the shop. Holding up a hand to block the bright light, I cursed when I saw both suns high in the sky. "We need to go back to the castle. Now."

Sin frowned. "What's going on?"

"I have a stupid fitting for my ball gown. I was supposed to be back by the afternoon, but I lost track of time."

We raced through the city, and by the time we reached the tunnel entrance, sweat coated my neck and back. Slipping through the small gap in the rock, I stared into the ascending blackness before me. We needed light, and I was too frazzled for Sin's previous method to work.

"Come on," he said, pulling me along into the dark. "You said anger works, yeah? So think about your father. Think about all the lies he's told you. Think about the people of Civi Obsura living in poverty while he sits in a castle made of diamonds."

It was the diamond reminder that did it, and I dropped Sin's hand as my fire sparked to life.

The hike back to the palace took an interminably long time, and Sin had to keep pausing to calm my rising panic. There was no telling what my father might do if he couldn't find me.

I released my grip on my flames as we neared the end of the tunnel, and Sin raised a finger to his lips, instructing me to hold back. I was already far too late, but we couldn't risk exposure, so I waited. And waited. Until eventually, he gave me the all clear.

We raced out of the cavern and into the hallway, pausing only when we knew we were out of earshot. Sin wrapped me up in his arms and pressed a fast yet intense kiss to my lips that left me lightheaded.

"I need to make sure my soldiers are prepared for this evening," he said. "I'll see you at dinner."

I cast him one last longing look, then tore up the stairs.

"Where have you been, Raynella?" my father roared when I burst into my room.

Well, this couldn't be good. Not only were Dey and the seamstress already there, but my father stood in front of the hearth, red-faced and looking like he was about to explode.

He crossed the room and grabbed me roughly by the shoulders. "Do you have any idea how terrified we have all been? You were not in the Sylvarium, nor could we find you anywhere in the castle." He paused to catch his breath, and I could see it wasn't anger driving his intensity but fear. Doubtful it was for me, though. Most likely it was for his plans going awry if something happened to me.

"We thought someone had taken you," he continued ranting. "Or you were lying injured, possibly dead somewhere. Raynella, I..." He registered how tightly he held my arms and loosened his grasp. Taking a step back, he ran his hands smoothly over his brocade gold and silver mantle . "I cannot lose you, Raynella. Where were you? And why is your tunic burnt?"

I took a step away from my father and set the package with my gown on the dresser. "I'm sorry. I was bored in the Sylvarium, so I went to watch Peywyn training in the arena. She was working with an igniservian, and things got a little intense. I caught a couple embers on my tunic. I'm sorry I scared you, but I wanted to see how the elemental magic worked so I would be ready when mine manifested." I dropped my eyes and added in a sad pathetic voice, "If it ever does."

Males were far too easy to manipulate because my father sighed and pulled me into an uncomfortable hug. "It will, Raynella. Give it time."

The feeling of his arms around me caused bile to rise in my throat, and it took everything inside me to endure his touch.

To my relief, he kept the embrace short. "I must go. The other courts will be arriving shortly. You were supposed to be at my side to greet them, but there is no time to prepare you. Carry on with the dress fitting, and I will see you at dinner."

He gave me a peck on the forehead before leaving, and I was proud of myself for not visibly shuddering.

I walked over to the seamstress and said in English, "I'm really sorry I've wasted your time as well. I didn't mean any disrespect to you, and I'm excited to see my dress that you have created." I cast an expectant look at Dey over my shoulder, waiting for him to translate.

He shook his head at me, probably still annoyed I had got him in trouble with my father. Turning to the seamstress, he spoke to her in Rivellan. "She says that she is sorry and would like to see her dress."

I kept my expression neutral as Dey took liberties with my apology.

"She is lucky she is the king's daughter, or I would never accept this insult," the seamstress spat out. "Especially not from a disgusting half-breed."

My teeth clenched together so hard I thought I might crack a tooth, but I just smiled and reached out to take my dress from her.

Ignoring me, the seamstress tossed the gown on the bed. "She will wear the dress as it is made. I do not have time to make alterations now. Is she not aware that I have other outfits to make for the ball?" She slammed the door hard as she left, accentuating her point.

Dey retrieved the gown and held it out for me. "She said the dress should be fine, and no alterations are needed."

I nodded. "Okay," I replied, as if I believed his words completely.

"Would you like to try it on?"

I slipped the dress into the wardrobe. "I'm sure it'll be fine. I was actually hoping for a little privacy. I need to take a shower. It was a bit hot and dusty in the arena."

"Of course." Dey stood up, but instead of leaving, he approached me and placed his hands lightly on my shoulders. "Please do not disappear on me again, Princess. I have never known fear like I did today. If anything were to happen to you..."

Dang. He was either the world's best liar, or he genuinely had been worried for me.

"I'm sorry," I said, and to my surprise, I actually meant it.

Dey left me alone after that, and I immediately dove to the floor to check under the bed. Four tiny little eyes peered back at me, and I sagged in relief. Something glimmered in the dark next to them, and I let out a laugh at the pile of treasure under my bed. Three of my diamond hair pins, a pair of earrings, a hair tie, and the lip gloss from my purse sat in a pile beside the crescia.

"Okay, little thieves," I said laughing. "I see what you do when I'm gone all day. Come on, it's safe to come out now." I left their bounty under the bed and placed the pile of nuts and seeds I'd snagged at breakfast onto the nightstand. Opal made a beeline for the food, but Jenni crawled onto my leg and dug her talons deep into the fleshy part of my thigh.

"Ouch! That's too rough."

"Scared," she said inside my head, all four of her tails swishing angrily.

I ran a hand down her spine, careful to avoid her delicate wings. "I'm sorry Jenni. I'm sure his shouting scared you."

"Scared for Rain."

I gently extricated her talons from the fabric of my leggings and set her on the nightstand by Opal. "You don't need to be scared for me, Jenni. I know my father is awful, but he won't hurt me. He needs me to fulfill the prophecy."

"Jenni protect Rain."

"That's right. I'm safe so long as I have you." I nuzzled the side of her face with my nose.

A loud commotion out in the courtyard pulled my attention away from the sweet moment. Drawing back my curtains, I saw a procession of people making their way into the castle. Diamond Palace guards, dressed in their standard burgundy uniforms with swords at the ready, formed two lines on either side of the courtyard that had been covered with banners to cut down on the intensity of the diamond's glare. A gaggle of courtiers had parked themselves behind the guards, craning their necks to get a good look at the newcomers.

The Gold Court arrived first, their young-looking king a gleaming beacon of bronzed skin covered in gold chains that highlighted the ramentum decorating his arms and chest. Four guards marched in crisp formation behind him, their pristine white tunics and breeches covered with an elaborate gold brocade stitching that put our guard's relatively plain uniforms to shame.

Behind their angelic blond ruler trailed a line of what I assumed to be their competitors for the Games. Two by two, they kept steady pace, each of them outfitted in similar white and gold attire save for the addition of two black sashes accented with golden chainmail crossing their chests.

They all looked so regal with their heads held high, their backs straight, and one hand resting on the golden pommel of their identical swords. They had two females among their competitors, and I was surprised to see one of them with gray hair and wrinkles. Apparently, skilled magic beat out physical prowess.

The Silver Court followed shortly after, and the difference between the two courts was like night and day. While the Gold Court was all shiny golden light, the Silver Court was darkness personified.

Their king cut a terrifying image as he made his way into the castle. He had to be older than my father, with a long gray beard that hung halfway down his chest. The hair on his head was pitch black, though, and I wondered if they had hair dye here. I guess vanity spanned all the universes. He wore a long, sleeveless black and silver robe that hung open in front to show off his ramentum. A nervous-looking guard held the bottom of the garment off the ground, and the king's vicious scowl could give Sin a run for his money.

Tearing my eyes away from their ruler, I scanned the competitors lined up behind him. They also entered two by two, but none were dressed the same. If the Gold Court valued conformity, then the Silver Court valued individuality. And lack of clothing. All of the competitors were clad in scraps of silver and black fabric that showed off far more pale skin than seemed necessary. One female clutching the arm of the male beside her wore little more than a silver chain bikini and a few wisps of black chiffon that hung from her waist. She had the body to pull it off, though, so kudos to her.

Behind them were two of the strangest looking Vitaeans I had ever seen. Both wore translucent, shapeless black frocks that covered their entire bodies from head to toe yet still allowed their skin to show through, revealing their dark undergarments and assortment of thin silver chains wrapped around their legs and arms. A solid black strip of cloth covered their eyes, yet I never once saw their steps falter.

My eyes drifted past that couple to the two males behind them. One was surprisingly scrawny and wore his black robe open at the chest with a pair of black and silver breeches underneath, but it was the male beside him that had me shuddering. He wasn't so much a male as an oversized marble statue brought to life. He wore nothing but a pair of black calf-high boots and tight black shorts that would look obscene even on a beach. His entire body was composed of rippling, overinflated muscle that was far too veiny and bloated to ever be considered attractive. Thick silver chains hung from his neck, and I could hear them clinking all the way from my bedroom. I gasped when he looked toward my window and his lecherous gaze tracked me watching him. He blew me a kiss, and I nearly gagged.

Moving away from the window, I let the curtains fall into place. I would see more than enough of them at dinner tonight.

Chapter Forty-One

I made sure I was showered and dressed before the sisters arrived later that evening. They both wrinkled their noses at my gown choice, then disappeared. When they returned, they had a number of different diamond necklaces, bracelets, and a delicate silver chain with diamond teardrops hanging from it. The latter they looped around my waist. It was actually quite pretty the way it draped off my hips, and I had to admit the jewelry did elevate the look slightly.

Dey arrived shortly after the sisters completed their final touches, a flat black case clutched in his hand. "Your father wanted to be here for this moment, but I am afraid—"

"I know, I know," I said, waving my hand and cutting him off. "Council. Duties. Blah blah blah. I get it. What's in the box?"

His face lit up as he opened the case. "You would not be a proper princess without your tiara."

I stared speechless at the beautiful creation nestled in the velvet burgundy lining. The delicate twisting of silver and diamonds was nothing like my father's ostentatious crown. This was far more understated—a thin band with only a single tier of small oval gems in the front. When my father said a tiara was being made, I had been terrified I would have to endure something akin to his own gaudy crown, but this was perfect.

Dey shifted nervously when I didn't immediately take it from his hands. "Do you like it, Princess? I hope it pleases you."

"It does," I admitted, reaching to take it out of the box.

"Allow me," he said, and I let him weave the ends of the tiara into my hair, surprised to find it weighed practically nothing.

Dey held out an arm, and I reluctantly accepted it as we stepped out into the hall.

I immediately pulled up short when we nearly crashed into Sin waiting outside my door. My heart skipped a beat as I took in his dinner attire. Gone was his standard black tunic, and in its place was a resplendent burgundy jacket secured tightly over his broad chest by a series of diamond buttons with a line of smaller stones stitched along the sleeves. Matching wine-colored breeches with black stitching up the sides and tall black leather boots that hugged his calves completed the look. The outfit, combined with his hair secured tightly at the nape of his neck, made him look regal in a way I had never seen before.

"Dreisin," Dey said stiffly.

"Deylan," Sin acknowledged, then switched to Rivellan knowing full well I could understand him. "King Verren is looking for you to discuss some Silver Court dietary restrictions you didn't relay to the kitchen. I will escort the princess to dinner."

Dey frowned. "I told the kitchen all the necessary requirements."

Sin shrugged. "Perhaps you missed one. I don't know. Simply relaying the message."

Dey looked torn, but I just waited. He was nothing if not predictable and would always rush to the king's side.

"Apologies," he said, turning to me. "I am needed elsewhere. Would it be all right if Dreisin escorted you to dinner? I will join you shortly."

Remembering that I was supposed to dislike Sin, I gave Dey a frustrated look. "I guess." I turned to Sin and glared. "Just keep your distance. You smell awful."

A smirk crept onto Sin's face. "Whatever the princess desires."

Apparently satisfied that he wasn't handing me over to anybody who might be competition, Dey released me and hurried off down the hall.

"You don't smell awful," I whispered, taking Sin's arm. "You smell like heaven."

"And you smell like I want to forget this dinner entirely and spend the night worshipping you in bed."

Heat flared low inside me. "I don't suppose that's an option?"

"Tragically, no. All the competitors are required to be at the dinner. Later, however..." He nipped at my ear. "I would love to see you in nothing but that tiara." His eyes dropped to the delicate silver chain that hung loosely around my hips. "Maybe leave that on as well."

I allowed myself a second to imagine the scene he depicted playing out, but I tripped on the stupid heels I had finally deigned to wear, and it knocked me from my reverie. My grip on Sin's arm was the only thing that saved me from eating palace floor.

"I didn't realize I literally knocked you off your feet," he said smugly.

I scoffed. "Yeah, well, don't let it go to your head."

"It's certainly going to one of my heads," he replied in a voice so low I nearly tripped again.

"You're awful."

"And you love it."

He definitely wasn't wrong, that was for sure.

"So who are the Diamond Court competitors? Anyone I know?" I asked, shifting the topic to something less likely to ruin my panties.

"You know Camden and Ramset, of course."

I was a bit embarrassed by the high-pitched squeak that erupted out of me, but I hadn't seen the twins in days. "Cam and Ram will be there?"

Sin chuckled. "Do I need to be jealous?" he asked, sliding his hand to my low back.

"I don't know," I said, tapping my chin as if deep in thought. "They are pretty attractive. All that smooth, gorgeous brown skin. Now that you mention it..."

We dipped into the stairwell, and Sin pressed me back against the stone wall. Hidden from prying eyes, he leaned in and kissed me roughly, his tongue pressing against my lips. Not a request, but a demand that I open to him.

I did so without hesitation, reveling in the taste of him.

After a second, he pulled back and growled, "Don't make me murder my two best generals, Rain. It's so hard to find skilled warriors these days."

I leaned my back against the wall, threw a hand up to my forehead, and let out an overly dramatic sigh. "Fine. I suppose I'll just have to make do with you."

Sin pressed his body tighter against mine. "You are playing with fire, Rain."

I met his gaze head on. "Then it's a good thing I'm fireproof."

Sin laughed, hearty and unrestrained. It was the most perfect sound I'd ever heard. "You should do that more often," I said, running my thumb over the laugh lines in the corner of his eyes. I hadn't even noticed them, his face was so often a perfectly constructed mask showing no emotion.

"I never had much reason to before you," he replied quietly, his hand sliding down my low back to pull me away from the wall.

We continued toward the formal dining hall at the back of the castle, and Sin told me about the other Diamond Court competitors.

Cam's air partner was a female named Lindyn who Sin suspected Cam also had a small crush on. Ram's fire partner was a young male named Kinyx who had apparently only manifested his magic a few years prior. When I asked why my father would choose someone so inexperienced, Sin only muttered something about Verren wanting to punish Kinyx's father.

I already knew Sin's water partner, Peywyn, but I didn't recognize either terriservian—a mother-daughter duo named Koasha and Jaelin that had served Sin loyally for decades. There was a hint of worry when he spoke about them competing, and I asked why.

"Harpyn," Sin answered, a muscle ticking in his jaw.

"Who or what is a Harpyn?" I asked as we rounded a corner, and the soft hum of conversation started to reach our ears.

Sin clenched his fist where it lay against my back. "Harpyn is the Silver Court terriservian," he gritted out. "He is deadly, unhinged, and utterly without conscience. He and I have... history. He'll go after Koasha and Jaelin to punish me."

I stopped Sin in the hallway and grabbed his arm, forcing him to look at me. "These Games aren't dangerous, are they?" It occurred to me that I never actually asked what would happen tomorrow.

"Yes and no," he said cautiously. "It is against the rules to kill another competitor, and doing so results in immediate disqualification. Beyond that... I wasn't alive for the last Elemental Games, but I've heard they can be brutal."

Worry clutched my chest in a tighter vice than any panic attack ever managed. "You'll be okay though, right? This isn't an 'accidents happen' sort of situation, is it?"

"I love that you're worried about me, Fea Remia, but you don't need to be. I've seen the other aquiservians fight. They are no match for my skills."

I poked his chest. "Pretty cocky there, Sin."

He whispered into my ear, "I told you before, it's not cocky if it's true."

Too soon, we arrived at the formal dining room that was filled with courtiers and competitors. There had to be over fifty people in the room already, and I squeezed Sin's hand to control my breathing.

"I'm right here," he said discreetly while the guard announced our presence. "I'll stay with you for as long as I can, but you're going to need to release me before people start asking questions. You can handle this, Rain. I have faith in you." He squeezed my hand in return, then let it fall to my side.

Right. I could do this. I didn't have to make a speech or anything. All I had to do was smile and nod for a few hours.

Inside the banquet hall, two lengthy tables filled the center of the room. Since nobody was seated yet, Sin pulled me off to the side where I could partially hide behind a thick column. Servants weaved through the crowd handing out glasses of Cevisa, and it took all my willpower not to snag one.

We stood there for a while, waiting for the kings to arrive and begin the dinner. Sin pointed out a few of the other competitors, but the most interesting were the two Silver Court casters that maintained their head to toe black garb.

"What's with the strange outfits?" I asked, gesturing toward them.

He glanced over to the bizarre couple. "The Silver Court is built into the side of a mountain," he explained. "There is a community of people with homes deep underground that live somewhat apart from the rest of the court. It's been said they have their own city down there, and their religion touts that living below ground brings them closer to the Source so their magic is more pure. Centuries of hiding beneath the castle has made them sensitive to any kind of light, so they only ever come out after dark. This is most likely the first time that Tenyn and Tenebra have even seen the sun."

"So they're like vampires?" I asked, finding myself intrigued by this unique subculture of Rivellans. "Cool."

Sin chuckled. "Not quite. They don't drink blood or turn into bats, but they do have the whole pale skin, nightwalker thing down." He paused, considering. "They must be incredibly powerful and want something very badly from their king if they agreed to come here."

"Well now, if it isn't the king's traitorous Cennux."

The gravelly voice floating over my shoulder sounded like the speaker chewed nails and smoked a pack a day. Beside me, Sin stiffened.

We both turned slowly, and I was greeted by the sneering face of the bloated, over-confident prick that had blown me a kiss earlier.

He swallowed an entire flute of Cevisa, then licked his lips at me. "And who is this pretty little princess? Surely you learned your lesson after the last one, Dreisin."

I looked to Sin as if requesting a translation when all I really wanted to do was ask him what the hell this overbearing gym bro was talking about.

Sin didn't even spare me a glance. He snagged a glass from a passing servant and threw it back in one gulp, mimicking Harpyn.

"I'm just a temporary escort," Sin replied in Rivellan, not bothering to include me in this little conversation. "I couldn't care less about her."

"So callous to speak that way in front of a princess," Harpyn said, his eyes sliding leisurely down my body. "Especially one as beautiful as this."

I tucked my hands behind my back to press my nails into the skin of my palms. If I had to act like I was clueless, I at least needed something to distract me from kicking this guy squarely in the balls.

"She doesn't understand Rivellan, Harp," Sin said, angling his body as if the other male didn't even deserve his full attention. "Don't tell me news of Verren's lost daughter didn't make it to your desolate little rock?"

"Oh, I heard all about his little half-human world jumper. I just never imagined she would be so... delicious."

I couldn't help cringing at his words, but he probably took it as a reaction to him fluttering his tongue at me.

"Classy," Sin replied, grabbing another flute.

"Or better yet," Harpyn said, taking a step closer to me. "How about I take her to my room so she can see what it's like to be with someone from the Silver Court. I've never been with a half-human before, but I bet her pussy still tastes as sweet."

I didn't even have a chance to react. One second Harpyn was all up in my space, practically choking me with his disgusting sweaty musk, and the next, he was slammed up against the column with a thin cord of water cutting into his throat. Sin's glass, now empty save for the smear of golden syrup at the bottom, nearly hit the floor, but I reflexively caught it before it shattered and drew unwanted attention in our direction.

The bulky terriservian looked neither upset nor worried about his current predicament. He looked... pleased.

Behind us, I heard a shrill cackle and saw the other Silver Court caster giggling his ass off like a demented hyena.

Sin edged closer to Harpyn, and the cold fury in his eyes twisted something in the pit of my stomach.

"Sin, stop," I said, trying to pull him toward me, though his focus never left the male turning blue in front of him.

"Cennux Dreisin, now is not the time," a smooth yet firm male voice said.

The blond who stepped up to Sin was dressed in the crisp white uniform of the Gold Court, and he strongly reminded me of Dey with his unblemished good looks and charming smile.

"Back off, Vankin. This is between me and him," Sin snarled, and I started to worry he might actually kill the Silver Court asshole.

"You know what happens if you are caught injuring a fellow competitor before the Games," Vankin said. "You're my only real competition, Dreisin. Don't get yourself disqualified." The golden male gave me a pointed look and tilted his head toward Sin.

I placed a hand on Sin's shoulder and said, louder this time, "Sin, stop."

Slowly, so incredibly slowly, Sin turned his head to look at me.

"He's not worth it," I said in English.

I doubted Harpyn had more than a few seconds left, but the grin still hadn't left his face. He didn't even struggle. Unhinged was an understatement.

Something softened in Sin's eyes as he stared at me, and with the slightest twitch of his hand, the water dropped away from Harpyn's neck.

Vankin's hand flicked out, and the falling water reversed course to slip back into Sin's glass. I nodded my thanks to the water caster and pulled Sin away, leaving Harpyn gasping for breath while Vankin tried to see if he was all right. Harpyn just shoved Vankin away from him and blew me another kiss before wandering off.

Once I had Sin away from the others, I whispered furiously, "What the hell was that all about?"

"Nothing," he said, turning away from me, and the small action cut me deeper than any words could.

"Please don't shut me out, Sin. I thought we were past that."

Sin flagged down a servant and snagged a glass of Cevisa, drained it, then followed it up with a second. Then a third.

"So you'd rather stand here and get drunk than talk to me? Thanks, Sin. Way to make a girl feel special." Ice was warmer than the look he gave me, and I felt like I was staring at the old Sin. Closed off, detached, and absent of all affection.

"I told you I had secrets, Rain," he said gruffly.

"Yeah, well, I get a feeling this isn't one you're forced to keep but that you're choosing to keep. Am I wrong?"

His eyes shifted away in confirmation.

"You almost murdered him, Sin."

"He insulted you."

"This wasn't about me, and you know it," I argued. "What did he mean when he said you should have learned your lesson after the last one?"

When he refused to meet my gaze, I grabbed his face and roughly pulled it back to mine. "Tell me," I demanded.

"Don't, Rain. Don't go there. What's between me and Harpyn has nothing to do with you."

"Nothing to do with me?" I released his face and threw up my hands in exasperation. "You know, there's an awful lot about you that supposedly has nothing to do with me, and I'm starting to wonder if maybe you aren't the best person to be making that call. Come find me if you ever decide to let me in."

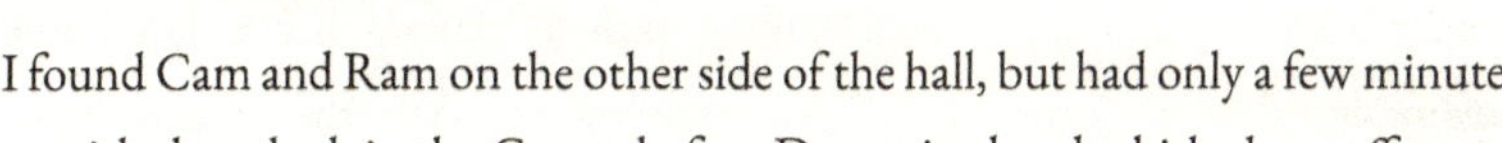

I found Cam and Ram on the other side of the hall, but had only a few minutes to wish them luck in the Games before Dey arrived and whisked me off to my seat near the head of the table.

My father made an elaborate speech in which he introduced me and told everyone about his arduous search and what a joy it was that the lost princess had been returned home. Thankfully, I had to do no more than give a little wave.

He proceeded to drone on about the Games with lots of pomp and circumstance. It started out fairly interesting with him describing the origins of the Games—a chance for the courts to vent aggression so they may live in harmony—and ended with their purpose today. Every hundred years, the courts all came together to discuss the health of all Rivella, deal with any mutual threats, and ensure the thrones were being turned over to the next generation. Apparently when you can live for centuries, it becomes dangerous for one ruler to remain in power too long, so they enacted a law that no king could reign for more than a hundred years. Maybe that's why my father was so desperate for me to separate the lines. His only legitimate heir was trapped in a magical coma.

When his speech descended into swaggering bravado about how proud he was of the Diamond Court casters, I found myself tuning out, and my thoughts drifted back to Sin. I couldn't stop thinking about what Harpyn had said. The only logical conclusion was that Sin had been with a princess or someone of royal standing in the past, but if it was old news, then why did he feel the need to hide it?

My seat at the king's table unfortunately gave me a prime view of him dining amongst the other competitors. He sat beside Peywyn, who spent the entire meal making doe eyes at an olive-skinned Gold Court female named Elona, oblivious to her partner's suffering. I didn't know if it was the alcohol or the altercation with Harpyn, but Sin barely looked up from his meal the whole night.

Dey tried to be a pleasant dinner companion, keeping up the conversation by telling me about some of the other competitors. The Silver Court was notorious for vicious casters that fought dirty. Jacksyn and his oddly devoted partner, Harlix—the bikini clad female—were two of the worst he had heard of and borderline insane on top of it. Thinking back to Harpyn, I wondered how anyone could be worse than him. Their aeriservians, two brothers named Farlix and Forwyn, were the least awful Dey had said, but their egos were so huge they would likely do anything to win.

The Silver Court sounded like it churned out some real gems, and I made a mental note to remove it from my list of places to visit one day.

The Gold Court was better, Dey had said. More honorable and noble for the most part. They held their own qualifiers to determine who would represent their court, though there were rumors Vankin had cheated somehow to ensure his lover, Bartyn, would be the other aquiservian champion.

The Gold Court igniservians were a father-daughter duo named Direff and Sarla. Direff was the Gold Court's Cennux, and Sarla was his second. A tiny flicker of sadness hit me, and I hoped Sarla realized how lucky she was to have such a good relationship with her father.

It was the Gold Court aeriservians I found most intriguing. Both Glorn and Nema were nearly two hundred years old. Glorn had stereotypical old white wizard vibes, while Nema radiated sweet elderly grandma. I didn't know how they could possibly stand up against the skills of the younger casters, but I kind of hoped they did well.

After an hour or so of small talk, my father rose to give his closing speech.

"Tomorrow, the Elemental Games will begin after the King's Council has come to a close. I want to remind all of our guests from the Silver and Gold Courts, as well as my own people, that these Games are meant to foster goodwill and bring us all together as Rivellans. So do remember the rules this evening. There will be no violence before the Games, and no competitor may opt out at this point. You all are committed. Each of our fighters have been assigned a room in the east wing on the third level. Guards from all three courts will be stationed in the hallway to ensure everyone stays in their chambers and has a good night's sleep. Make your courts proud tomorrow. Make all of Rivella proud." He raised his glass. "Honor to Rivella. Honor to the Source."

"Honor to Rivella. Honor to the Source," everyone else intoned with raised classes.

Well, shit. I had no idea where Sin and I stood, but it sounded like I wasn't going to find out tonight.

When the competitors filed out, I allowed Dey to escort me back to my room, my thoughts too focused on Sin to figure out an excuse to avoid him.

"Good night," I said, giving him my best fake smile when we arrived at my door.

"Wait, Princess." He grabbed my elbow before I could fully escape. When I looked down at his grip, he released me.

"What do you want, Dey?" I asked, exhausted from the longest day of faking smiles and playing dumb whenever someone spoke in Rivellan.

He shifted awkwardly, then asked, "Is there something going on between you and Dreisin?"

Well that was the last thing I expected.

I pinched the bridge of my nose. "No, Dey, why would you even ask?"

He gave me a boyish grin. "I am just making sure I do not have any competition."

I pushed through the door into my room. "Well, you can rest easy because there is no competition."

I wasn't lying either. Sin had already won my heart.

"All right, then. Good night, Princess," he said softly. "I will see you tomorrow for the competitor's breakfast."

I shut the door behind me and slumped to the floor, absently petting Jenni and Opal as they happily greeted me. I cursed internally at the reminder of another formal gathering to attend. Tomorrow was the Games, the banquet, the ball, and now we needed to add a formal breakfast? I banged my against the door a couple times.

There was no way I was going to survive it all.

Chapter Forty-Two

The competitor's breakfast was similar to the previous night's dinner save for the absence of the three rulers. Dey told me they were already sequestered away for the Council but would finish in time for the Games. Taking my seat beside him, I wondered what was being said behind those closed doors. Would he tell the other kings about the prophecy? Or would he let it be a great big surprise one day?

I dug into my breakfast, the tight corset of my long-sleeved ruby red dress making it difficult to eat... or breathe. When Kiahna arrived at my door this morning, gown in hand, I realized my father was sending a message, if not a punishment, for my rather understated attire last night.

The competitors were divided by court with Diamond at the head of the table, followed by Gold, then Silver. Peywyn managed to snag a seat next to Elona, who kept throwing shy glances her way, and I was honestly rooting for them. I didn't know how they would make it work being from different courts, but maybe love would find a way.

I risked a glance at Sin, but the sight of his completely disheveled appearance didn't bring me any satisfaction. It was like his very essence had been stripped away, leaving only a shell of the male I knew.

About twenty guards from the various courts arrived a bit later, and Dey told me the competitors were being escorted to the arena for their designated practice time.

As they filed out, I waited to see if Sin would acknowledge me at all.

My heart cracked a little when he didn't.

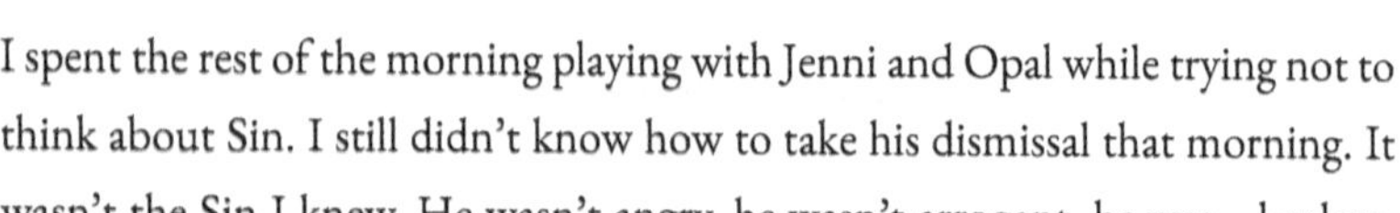

I spent the rest of the morning playing with Jenni and Opal while trying not to think about Sin. I still didn't know how to take his dismissal that morning. It wasn't the Sin I knew. He wasn't angry, he wasn't arrogant, he was... broken. And I couldn't help him if he wouldn't let me in.

I was about to go insane with worry when Dey knocked on my door to inform me the King's Council had ended, and the Games were about to start.

Following him out of the castle, I weaved through a massive throng of people milling around outside the arena. I knew the Elemental Games were a big deal, but I didn't expect to see what was likely the entire population of Civi Adasa funneling into the stadium.

It didn't escape my notice that there wasn't a single imminario among them. Apparently the citizens of Civi Obsura didn't warrant an invite.

There was a palpable atmosphere of excitement as Dey led me down the slick steps toward a cordoned off section at the far end of the arena. About twenty or so individual chairs were set apart from the rest of the bench style seating, and each one was adorned with a plush cushion. My father occupied the centermost seat, with the Gold and Silver kings off to his right. Each one had a guard from their court standing directly behind them, posture stiff and eyes constantly scanning for danger. The rest of the chairs were filled with pompous-looking members of the other court's entourages.

Dey guided me to the spot beside my father, and I was pleased to see Jo seated directly behind me. Since my father was wrapped up in conversation with the other rulers, and Dey had started speaking with a courtier beside him, I rotated so I could see her.

"Rain!" she squealed inside my head. *"You made it!"*

I pushed as much sardonic amusement into my words as I could. *"Yeah, I don't think I had a choice in the matter. I just hope none of my friends get hurt. It wasn't made clear exactly how violent these Games get."*

Jo cocked her head slightly. *"Are you worried about Dreisin?"*

"What? No. I mean, yes, but no more than I'm worried about Cam or Ram."

Jo gave me a knowing smile, and I don't know why I had even bothered lying.

Three loud horn blasts ripped through the frenetic hum of the crowd, and people scrambled to take their seats. A line of Diamond Court soldiers marched down the stadium stairs to the railing that circled the field and spread out in each direction until there was a guard roughly every five feet.

One approached my father and handed him something that resembled a cross between a bullhorn and a conch shell. Once the din of conversation quieted, he lifted the amplifying device and began to speak.

"Welcome, fellow Rivellans, to the Elemental Games. Allow me to introduce your competitors!"

Down in the arena, a line of Diamond Court fighters followed Sin onto the field, while Harpyn led a line of Silver Court competitors from a different entrance, and Vankin was at the head of the Gold Court line. The three groups met in the middle of the field and pivoted to face their kings.

Sin and the rest of the Diamond fighters were dressed in matching burgundy leathers, while the Gold Court wore a similar outfit in white but with a gleaming gold cuirass covering their chest. The Silver Court once again had eschewed conformity, with most of them dressed in outfits much like the ones they arrived in.

Cheers thundered through the crowd as my father announced the names of the fighters from the Diamond Court, each one stepping forward and waving as their name was called. The Gold King took the amplifying device next and announced his competitors, followed by the Silver King.

I scanned the crowds as more raucous applause echoed through the stands. I thought only citizens from Civi Adasa would be present, but a handful of spectators were dressed to support the other courts with all black or all white outfits.

I turned my attention back to the arena floor as the Silver King finished his roll call. Sin looked better than he had that morning, but not by much, and I silently begged him to look up at me. If he was going to risk his life in these archaic battle games, then I wanted him to know I hadn't abandoned him.

But he maintained his rigid posture, never once glancing my way.

My father retrieved the amplifying device from the Silver King and brought it to his mouth. "Before we commence the Games, I have one last announcement to make. It was decided this morning in the King's Council that a change will be made to the rules this year. From now on, the death of a competitor will no longer be grounds for disqualification. While we do not encourage fighters to take the lives of their opponents, they will not be penalized for such actions."

If I didn't have fire in my veins, his words might have frozen my blood. The Diamond and Gold Court competitors looked nervous at this turn of events, shifting and mumbling to each other, while the Silver Court fighters looked positively gleeful. I had a feeling their ruler was behind this somehow, though my father didn't look the slightest bit rattled as he made the declaration.

He waited for the fervent whispers in the crowd to die down before he continued. "I wish all of our fighters the best of luck. May you bring glory to your court. Honor to Rivella. Honor to the Source."

"Honor to Rivella. Honor to the Source," the competitors replied in unison before turning to stride off the field.

"Are you excited, Raynella?" my father asked, taking his seat beside me.

"Um, I'm not sure," I said, remembering I shouldn't know what he had announced. "What did you say that made the crowd so anxious?"

He waved a hand. "Nothing much. Just increasing the stakes a bit. These Games are of tremendous importance, you know."

"Why exactly? I know it's supposed to bring unity or whatever, but it seems like more than that."

He wrinkled his brow at me. "These games are an opportunity for each court to showcase their best fighters. It sends a message to the other courts exactly how powerful we are. And with the magic soon to be restored throughout the land, it is important that we portray the Diamond Court as one of considerable strength. My fighters will not lose, Raynella. They will give their lives before they dishonor our people."

On that rather ominous note, he shifted his attention back to the field below. The sands were barren save for a few large boulders scattered throughout the space, so I assumed the terriservian battle would be first.

My suspicions were confirmed when Harpyn made his way out onto the sands followed by the others. Elona and her Gold Court partner, Lanset, still looked nervous from the earlier revision to the rules, but Harpyn and his partner, Grelkin, exuded sadistic violence as they postured in front of the crowd, flexing and beating on their bare chests.

The clamor of the crowd died to a hushed whisper of anticipation as each combatant took their assigned positions.

I chewed on my nails while I waited for what would hopefully *not* be a bloodbath to begin.

Then the horn bellowed once, and the arena erupted.

One moment, six casters stood spaced apart in a wide circle, and the next, the air was choked by a cloud of dust as rocks ranging in size from pebbles to baseballs pinged and crashed against the walls of the arena. The crowd fell to its first perfect silence of the day while everyone waited for the dust to settle so they could lay eyes on whatever chaos had ensued.

When the field was visible once more, only four combatants remained standing. Off to the far left side, Elona was sprawled on her back, blood leaking from her mouth and pooling on the ground beneath her. The loud wail I heard from below sounded like Peywyn, and I sent out a silent prayer that Elona was just knocked out.

To the right side, Koasha coughed once before falling unconscious, her body draped over the edge of the arena like a ragdoll.

In an instant, a third of the fighters were out of the game. My eyes slid clockwise around the ring, taking in the remaining ones.

Jaelin was building up a swirling cloud of dirt, while Lanset eyed her warily, his right hand clamped tightly to his left arm which hung loosely at his side. Gorge rose in my throat when I realized a shard of bone jutted out from the skin. His healing magic stemmed the flow of blood, but I doubted it would be enough.

On the other side of the arena, Harpyn, in all his Olympian glory, was unabashedly *lounging* on a fucking throne built of stone.

I blinked at him, unable to believe the cocky bastard had taken the time to shape a boulder into a seat, as if the chaos and violence surrounding him was of no concern.

Continuing around the ring, I paused when I noticed Grelkin pulling massive chunks of rock toward himself, molding and shaping them to his body. After a second, he fully disappeared within a squat stone golem, its legs thick as logs with arms hanging nearly to the ground.

In reality, only a few seconds passed as the four remaining casters sized up one another, but time slowed to an agonizing crawl amidst the adrenaline and excitement that permeated the arena. Eyes snapped back and forth from warrior to warrior, each one trying to suss out who would move first.

Lanset made the first strike, lunging forward and swinging his fist in an uppercut motion. A boulder shaped like a demonic ram's head ripped from the ground and flew toward Harpyn.

Completely unruffled, the Silver Court caster put the back of one hand to his mouth, feigning a yawn, while his other hand flicked out. Part of his throne popped off and knocked the stone ram out of the air.

Satisfaction filled me, however, when Harpyn realized his arrogance had caused him to miss the sandstone anaconda that rose up behind him. The snake struck, and coil after coil of serrated shards wrapped about him. His bellows of rage could be heard even over the raucous crowd.

Across the arena, Grelkin's behemoth began to move, loping forward on massive knuckles and stumpy legs. My heart, already pumping with adrenaline, kicked into overtime as I tracked its trajectory toward Jaelin.

The Diamond Court female flowed to one side, the cyclone she created shifting with her as the stone monstrosity crashed by, missing her by mere inches. With each swing of her hands, Jaelin's cloud spun faster, the sand, grit, and rocks condensing into dozens of jagged hailstones. She let out a whooping war cry, and the stones fired rapidly out of the cyclone.

They chewed into the monster's left shoulder and chest, sending fissures through the stone body that threatened to crack the whole thing apart.

Barely phased, the behemoth set his feet and charged Jaelin once more. She dove nimbly to the side, but as Grelkin charged past, his stone arm broke free and flew through the air to smash into Jaelin mid leap. Throughout the arena, cries of terror and blood thirsty shouts of victory rang out in equal measure when her body crashed to the ground with a horrific thud.

Slow and stumbling like a drunkard, the behemoth began stalking toward Jaelin's prone body.

Too afraid to watch, I turned away from that fight in time to see Harpyn burst free from his snake prison. Calmly shaking the dust off, he swirled his left fingers. A stone hand formed out of the remains of his throne and swept Lanset up in a crushing grip.

The Gold Court male struggled for a second, his face turning red, then purple, then blue. He hung his head and held one hand up, his fingers curled into a C shape.

"What is he doing?" I asked Jo.

"He is making the cedo gesture. He yields to the brute."

I waited for Harpyn to drop the wounded fighter, but the stone fist only squeezed tighter.

Lanset's head rocked back, eyes bulging in fear and pain as he choked out, "Cedo! Cedo!"

Harpyn's evil smile grew a little wider, his eyes a little more manic. I watched in stunned horror as blood poured from Lancet's mouth and dribbled through cracks in the stony fingers. His pleas grew weaker as the popping of bone grew louder, until his head lolled limply to one side.

The arena exploded in shouts of anger, anguish, and, to my complete disgust, vicious glee.

Harpyn pivoted on his heel and strode with a brisk yet unhurried pace toward Grelkin and Jaelin while the stone hand crumbled into a pile of rubble, half burying Lanset's broken corpse.

I checked to see if my father shared even an ounce of my revulsion, but he merely watched the fight unfold, not phased in the slightest. He had expected this. They gave the fighters a license to kill knowing full well which ones would abuse it.

As attention across the arena shifted back to Jaelin, a buzz of excitement flitted through the crowd when she struggled to sit up.

Harpyn approached the behemoth from behind and plunged his arm into its back, ripping Grelkin from the stone confines.

"This pretty little thing is all mine," he roared, then tossed his partner to the ground where Grelkin meekly rolled onto his back and lifted a C-shaped hand in the air.

Dragging herself backward, Jaelin slumped against the edge of the arena, one arm wrapped tightly against her middle while her other hand formed into the same yield symbol. Not that it had done Lanset any good against Harpyn's bloodthirstiness.

The brutal Silver Court male stalked over to Jaelin, and at first, it appeared like he might help her up.

I should have known better than to have any altruistic thoughts about Harpyn.

The ground around him rippled as the stone hand crawled forth once more. It scooped Jaelin up, and I closed my eyes, refusing to watch helplessly while Harpyn murdered another person.

"Harpyn!" The loud booming voice cut through my fear, and my eyes snapped open to see the Silver King on his feet, bullhorn conch grasped within his white-knuckled fist. Harpyn hesitated, glancing back at his king who just shook his head.

A collective breath was held by all as Harpyn glared at his ruler before finally flicking his wrist, and the stone hand grasping Jaelin tossed her twenty feet into the stands. Three of the guards positioned around the arena lifted their arms, and her body halted in midair before slowly lowering to the ground.

Harpyn strutted toward the center of the arena and tossed his arms up in victory.

The eruption of cheers from the crowd made me sick, and it fully hit me then exactly how much danger Sin was facing. If the other Silver Court casters were even half as deranged, they would not hesitate to murder him in cold blood and smile while doing it.

I couldn't let that happen. Not when I just found him.

I didn't need to fake my sickly pallor, clammy skin, or shaking body when I turned to my father. "I'm going to be sick. I need to leave for a bit."

He frowned. "Raynella, it is most important that you remain here where everyone can see you. A true Rivellan would support the Games."

I shook my head furiously, fighting the urge to vomit that was all too quickly becoming a viable possibility. "If I don't leave, I'm going to puke in front of the entire Diamond Court."

He assessed my distress, then nodded. "Compose yourself and return with haste. You do not want to miss the rest of the Games."

Actually, that was precisely what I wanted to do, but I gave him a grateful smile and jogged out of the stadium.

Hurrying toward the courtyard that would lead me to the arena's tunnel, I slid to a stop outside the portcullis when Harpyn's cruel voice reached my ears. Ducking behind the wall, I peered around the corner.

And found Harpyn tucked into an alcove, locked in a confrontation with Ram.

"You don't think I forgot, did you?" Harpyn snarled into Ram's face. "What he did? How you helped? I've waited years for my revenge, and I think I'll start with you."

Ram laughed, and it was a bitter sound I couldn't imagine came out of my friend. "Unlike your Silver lackeys, I'm not afraid of you, Harp. And you can't lay a finger on me during the Games."

Harpyn grinned maliciously. "Who's going to stop me? It's just you and me, little firebug. Besides, I don't need to kill you. All I need to do is make sure you don't make it to your battle. Your king will take care of the rest. Seeing him behead his favorite general while Sin and Cam are forced to watch will provide me with years of joy."

Ram's carefree smirk faded, his eyes darting around the courtyard.

"What's wrong?" Harpyn taunted. "No flames around to defend yourself with? Pity. I was hoping for a challenge."

Apparently Ram's boasting that he could pull fire down from the sun was not entirely accurate, because he didn't even defend himself when Harpyn slammed both of his hands together and a massive chunk of the wall above Ram's head exploded, burying my friend under a pile of diamond-studded rocks.

I choked back my sobs, petrified of what the brute would do if he heard me. It nearly killed me to remain hidden in the shadows while Harpyn snapped his fingers, and every boulder and loose diamond merged back into the wall. All that was left was Ram's crushed body, and not a single trace of evidence that might implicate the terriservian.

Harpyn whistled as he strolled out of the courtyard, and if I thought I even stood the slightest chance at surviving, I would have roasted him alive for what he'd done.

Instead, I remained out of sight until he was gone, then raced over to my friend.

Throwing myself to the ground at Ram's side, I breathed a sigh of relief when I saw his chest rise and fall. But his breathing was ragged, and I feared his healing power wouldn't be enough. The rocks had crushed most of his bones, and I barely recognized the bloody, pulpy mess in front of me.

"Ram?" a voice called moments before Cam emerged into the courtyard. "You are not going to miss my battle are you?"

His eyes landed on me, then slid to Ram's broken body. The wail he unleashed as he fell beside his brother chilled me to bone, and I never wanted to hear such anguish again.

My heart broke as tears streamed down Cam's face, and I gathered him into my arms. "It's okay. He's alive. He's going to be fine."

Cam shook in my embrace, violent sobs racking his body. "He cannot fight. If he does not fight, he dies. There is no exception to the rules."

I might not have believed him if I hadn't just witnessed Harpyn murder someone while the rulers sat back and let it happen. I doubted the Gold King would let my father spare his general when he had already lost one of his own.

I was not about to let Ram die, though. Not if I could save him.

I grabbed Cam's face, forcing him to look at me. "Cam, do you trust me?"

Lost to his sorrow, he didn't even acknowledge my words. "Cam!" I shouted, slapping him in the face as hard as I could. "Do you trust me?" I asked again.

His tears slowed as he took in the determination on my face. "Yes, of course, but what does that have to do with—"

"Listen to me. Ram is not going to die today. Do you hear me? I am not losing anyone I care about, and I need your help if we're going to save him."

Normally, I despised hope. It never did anything but disappoint me. Right then, however, I was grateful to see the accursed emotion flicker in Cam's eyes.

"What do I need to do?" he choked out.

"First off, I need you to find Sin and send him out here. And secondly, you can't miss your own battle. So I need you to go out there and fight."

He sniffled, then wiped the tears from his face. "Do you really think you can save him?"

I nodded furiously. "I can, I know I can, but you have to do your part. You have to suck it up and stroll out there with all the confidence of the best aeriservian in Rivella."

"Okay," he said, climbing gingerly to his feet. He headed off toward the tunnel, then paused to look back. "Thank you, Princess. For whatever you are about to do... Thank you."

I gave him a grim but determined smile. I just really hoped Sin was as powerful as he claimed, because I would prefer letting Harpyn murder me to telling Cam that I couldn't save his brother.

Chapter Forty-Three

"Rain!" Sin's voice broke through my wallowing, and I jumped to my feet, rushing into his arms. He stiffened for a second, then pulled me in tighter.

"I'm sorry for everything that happened last night," he murmured.

"None of that matters anymore," I said before he could continue, our argument the furthest thing from my mind. "I need your help."

He released his grip on me. "Cam mentioned that. What's going on?"

Instead of explaining, I took a step back, revealing Ram's body.

Anger seized hold of Sin, and fire flared in his eyes. He took a step toward his general, then stopped. "Who?" The single word held a world of violent promises.

"Harpyn."

Sin's eyes darkened even more. "I thought he might try something, but it wasn't supposed to be Ram. Fucking coward knew he couldn't take me."

"Hey," I said, stepping into his space and drawing his focus back to me. "I know Ram will be executed if he doesn't fight, but he's still alive, and I plan on him staying that way."

Sin knelt by his friend and ran his healing magic over Ram's body. "There's nothing we can do. I can stabilize the worst damage, but not even the best healer could have him in fighting condition by his match."

"I know that, but... Sin, I need you to be truthful with me. How strong are your illusions? Could you affect the entire stadium?"

"Sure," he replied bitterly. "But it wouldn't matter. Illusions aren't real. There's nothing physically there. The first time an opponent struck him, they would realize it was all fake."

"What if there was someone there? Someone you made look like Ram?"

He shook his head. "Even if I was willing to reveal my power to someone, we'd never find another igniservian in time."

I gulped. It was now or never.

"You already have another igniservian, Sin."

His face hardened as my words hit him. "No. Absolutely not. Didn't you see the last battle, Rain? People die in these. I won't help you commit suicide."

"Sin, think about it," I protested. "Their fire can't hurt me. They can blast me all they want, and I won't feel any of it."

His firm expression wavered slightly. "Maybe," he conceded. "But Ram is one of the best igniservians in all of Rivella, and you can't control your flames yet."

"Then I'll go down early on. I'll fake an injury and concede right after the battle begins. Shame is better than death, Sin." I took his hand firmly in mine, letting him feel my resolve. "My whole life I've felt useless. Like a waste of space. But I can do this. I can save him. I just can't do it without you."

Frustration contorted Sin's face as he warred with himself. "If anything happened to you—"

"It won't. I promise. I'll just show up long enough for people to see him, then take a dive."

His shoulder's slumped in resignation. "Okay, but you know this all hinges on me winning my fight right? The fire battle is last. If I die..."

I punched his arm. "Where's the cocky Sin I know? Shouldn't you be telling me how you'll win the whole thing in minutes with one hand tied behind your back?"

Cheers from the stadium echoed through the courtyard, and I panicked that the air battle I hadn't even heard start was already over. "Go," I whispered, pressing my forehead to his. "Have Cam hide Ram somewhere safe for now, then get out there and win this. Prove to me all your swagger and confidence is warranted."

He pressed a quick kiss to my lips. "Whatever the princess desires," he said with a wicked grin, and it was everything I needed to slow my racing heart. My Sin was back.

He scooped Ram's broken body into his arms and was off, racing into the tunnel and hopefully toward a win.

I headed back to the stadium before my father sent someone to search for me, even though I knew I would need another reason to leave again after Sin won.

And Sin was going to win. He was stronger than all of them. I would have surrendered my heart to no less than the fiercest male I'd ever met.

If he could handle me, he could handle anything.

Chapter Forty-Four

My father, Dey, and Jo all gave me concerned looks when I returned. As I sat down, I noticed Cam striding out of the arena.

His ability to win the match while fearing for his brother's life spoke not only to his skill, but to his faith in me. I just hoped I was worthy of it.

Down on the field, the terriservian soldiers finished digging a trench around the edges, and water rushed in to fill it, setting the stage for the next match.

My hands clenched tightly as the aquiservians took their places.

I waited breathlessly for it to begin, sending out a silent prayer to whatever Gods watched over this world to protect Sin.

The horn blared, my heart stopped, and Sin burst into movement, thrusting his arms forward as streams of water leapt to his command. Shifting his body to face the Silver Court male dressed in head to toe black, Sin fired off three rapid punches that sent a trio of watery missiles at Tenyn, who dove into an evasive forward roll then popped to his feet. Sin marched forward, arms pumping, and a dozen lances of water sprang from the trench and hurled themselves at the Silver caster.

Snarling, Tenyn spun away from Sin and slashed his hand through each water spear, dissolving them into nebulous floating blobs.

I held my breath as the watery orbs rocketed away from him, speeding back toward the male who had come to mean everything to me.

With cat-like reflexes, Sin snatched the projectiles from the air, redirected their trajectory, and allowed them to splash harmlessly a dozen yards away.

I let out my breath. He was strong. He could do this.

While Sin gathered more water around him, my eyes flicked briefly over to where Peywyn clashed with Vankin. As much as I despised these battles, I actually cheered a bit when she drew a rope of water out of the canal and wrapped it around Vankin's left wrist, yanking him to his knees.

The male caster slashed his right arm at the rope to cut through the casting, but the water bent to absorb the blow, and Peywyn's foot connected with the side of Vankin's head in a beautiful crescent kick. He slammed face first to the sand, and Peywyn whirled her hand, directing her water rope to leave his wrist and wrap around his throat.

Vankin's eyes bulged as his lungs screamed for oxygen. After a minute, his body fell limp to the ground, and I rose up in my seat to get a better look at the prone male. I knew Peywyn was fierce, but I couldn't imagine her killing in cold blood.

Peywyn released her water, checked her opponent's pulse, then gave him an attaboy slap on the shoulder before she raced off toward Sin's duel.

An anguished shout filled the arena, and every head in the crowd whipped over to where the dark-skinned Bartyn had stalled in his battle with the ultra pale Tenebra, unable to peel his eyes away from Vankin's unconscious body.

Too late, Bartyn noticed what the Silver female was doing, and her leg kicked out, sending a tendril of water to lock around his waist. Before he could defend himself, she flipped into a back handspring, and the water followed suit, flinging Bartyn into the air before slamming him down into the canal behind her. The crowd grew silent as Tenebra lazily twirled her hand, and Bartyn was sucked to the bottom.

A minute passed. Then two.

I screamed inside my head for him to fight back, to do something. This couldn't be happening again.

Except it did happen.

While Vankin lay unconscious on the other side of the arena, the lover he refused to leave behind drowned in less than two feet of water. And nobody did a thing to stop it.

Silence hung thick in the air for only seconds before a body flew across the field, and Tenyn crashed to the ground beside his partner. The fury on Sin's face told me he had seen what Tenebra did.

Closing in on the Silver caster, Sin dove into a forward roll to dodge the spear of water she threw, popped up, and kicked her in the neck so hard I expected to hear a snap.

Tenebra simply rolled with the blow, bouncing to her feet with another agile handspring before she and Sin clashed in hand to hand combat.

Blow for blow, Sin matched her, and soon began pressing her back, advancing forward as she gave up ground.

Just as I thought he might take her down Sin arched his back, crying out as a lance of water thrown by Tenyn collided with his spine. The scream of pain quickly dissolved into choking gasps when he caught a blast from Tenebra full in the face.

"No!" I screamed out as Sin faltered and hit the ground, not caring that Dey and my father whipped their heads in my direction.

I glanced around furiously, searching for Peywyn, only to find her crumpled in the corner of the arena, having taken a hit I didn't even witness.

Sin was on his own, and I could do nothing to quell the icy grip of fear around my heart.

He managed to get back on his feet, but the Silver Court casters pressed their two-to-one advantage, driving him toward the canal with rapid blasts of water. His movements grew sluggish and devolved into sloppy flailing as strikes began landing, eventually knocking him fully into the trench.

Moving in sync, the couple advanced on Sin, spinning their hands in loops and swirls that pulled forth a swell of water. Shifting and writhing, the wave wrapped itself around Sin, lifting him into the air and engulfing him in an azure prison.

My heart stopped beating, and Sin's words echoed through my head.

"I love that you're worried, Fea Remia, but you don't need to be. I've seen the other aquiservians fight. They are no match for my skills."

Tears flowed down my cheeks as the thrashing within the vortex of water began to slow. Sin went agonizingly still, his body forced into a fetal position.

"Sin!" I screamed out, jumping to my feet and racing forward to the edge of the arena. Strong arms wrapped around my waist, pulling me back. Dey grunted as I struggled wildly in his arms, catching him in the gut with a sharp elbow.

I needed to do something. I couldn't just watch Sin die. Flames prickled under my skin, and I prepared myself to torch the Silver Court casters. I didn't care who saw. Sin was not dying today.

Before I could unleash my fury, though, Sin's prison of water began to expand, and a kernel of that damned hope bloomed inside me. The Silver couple backed away, their confident expressions now slack in disbelief.

The crowd watched spellbound as the funnel swelled, doubling in size. Larger and larger it grew, reaching nearly halfway across the arena, and you could hear a pin drop as everyone waited to see what would happen.

Without warning, it burst like a popped balloon, tossing millions of droplets of water into the stands.

The explosion left a hazy cloud obscuring the field, until the mist slowly cleared, revealing an angel of death kneeling in the center. With ethereal grace and perfect control, Sin rose from the sand, his entire being radiating power and malice.

I had never seen anything more beautiful yet terrifying at the same time.

The Silver duo stared at Sin dumbfounded as he lifted his hands and every ounce of water in the canal surged toward him. Thousands of gallons spun into a massive swirling vortex, the water churning and coalescing into the shape of an enormous dragon that loomed up over Sin's back. Two whiplike water tails thrashed while six clawed hands flexed in anticipation.

Sin slammed his palms together, and the dragon lunged, smashing down upon the casters with the roaring fury of a tidal wave. Water flew in every direction, dousing the screaming spectators in the first dozen rows.

After a tense moment, the water ebbed, wicking into the sands and sluicing back into the canal to reveal a lifeless Tenyn and Tenebra suspended in a floating pool.

Without a word, Sin flicked his hand, then turned and stormed out of the arena.

The bubble holding Tenyn and Tenebra collapsed, and the two bodies crashed to the ground.

The entire arena held one collective breath, waiting, but the Silver Court casters didn't move. Didn't breathe. And I couldn't summon any pity for them.

I felt only relief that Sin had won.

Which meant it was my turn.

Chapter Forty-Five

"I'll be right back," I said, ignoring the wary glances Dey was giving me.

"Raynella," my father warned, apparently unwilling to let me disappear a second time.

"I need to go to the bathroom. Seeing all that water… I'll be fast."

He opened his mouth to argue, but I was out of my seat and halfway up the stairs before he could reply.

I raced in the direction of the tunnel, my feet moving faster than I thought capable. When I reached the entrance, I yanked the door open, letting the darkness swallow me whole. Barely registering the flame that surrounded my hand, I dashed toward the arena.

Just as I neared the end of the tunnel, strong hands grabbed my shoulders and pressed me into the wall.

"Are you sure you want to do this?" Sin hissed into my ear.

"I have to," I panted. "I had faith in you, Sin. I need you to have faith in me."

He cupped my face. "No heroics, Rain. When that horn blasts, I want you to take a dive, okay? These igniservians are different. The fire controls them more than any other element. They won't hesitate to go for the kill, so do not give them the chance."

"I won't," I replied firmly. "Where's Cam?"

"He went to hide Ram and heal him as best he could. I didn't tell him about my power, but he knows something is up. I don't think I can keep my illusions a secret from him after this."

"So don't," I said, caressing his face. "You need to let people in, Sin. You can't go through life alone. Cam and Ram care about you, and it kills them that you shut them out. Believe me when I say you can trust them."

He nodded, though his face indicated he didn't agree. "I hope you're right."

I kissed him. "I'm always right."

He barked out a laugh, and his arms tightened around me.

Gasping in his embrace, I struggled to take in a deep inhale with the pressure from my corset squeezing my airway. "I don't suppose you have anything else I can wear?"

Smirking, his eyes drifted up and down my body. "You could always go out there naked. I'd be the only one to know the truth."

"Sin!" I exclaimed, smacking his chest.

"Okay, okay," he conceded. Laughing, he reached down to grab a pile of clothing at his feet. Female fighting leathers. "Peywyn keeps a few extra pairs in the training room. These should fit."

Stripping off my restrictive dress, I held Sin's gaze, blushing a little when his expression grew heated as I stood before him naked. Yanking the leather pants up over my ass, I stifled a giggle when his eyes narrowed at my curves disappearing under the fabric.

"I know what you're thinking, and we don't have time," I said, tugging the tunic over my head while despising myself for being responsible.

"They're still cleaning up the water mess," Sin purred in his sultry voice. "And I can be fast."

"I don't know if you should brag about that," I teased.

He nipped my ear. "You'll pay for that later."

"Promise?"

His wicked grin offered a guarantee, and I nearly abandoned the whole thing just to let Sin have his way with me.

It was only thoughts of Ram's broken body that sobered me up.

"Tonight," I said, leaning in to brush my lips against the column of his neck. "We will get through this. We will get through the banquet. We will get through the damned ball. And once we put this whole nightmare behind us, you can remind me of all the ways Vitaean anatomy is superior to humans."

I cupped him firmly through his fighting leathers, smiling when I felt how hard he was just from my kisses.

He groaned and arched into my hand. "You're killing me, Fea Remia."

"Yeah? Well if I'm such a bad girl, you'll just have to punish me." I rubbed up and down his shaft. "So use the next few hours to figure out all the ways you can make me scream."

His cock twitched, and it took an immense effort to pull my hand off him.

I needed to focus, though, and Sin needed to prepare an illusion. "Use your magic," I said, taking a step back. "Prove just how powerful you are."

A ripple of magic rolled off him, and I held my hand out, watching as my pale skinny arm darkened and filled with thick muscle.

I ran the hand over my chest. I still felt like me, but to anyone looking, I was now my father's famed general.

A call for the igniservians to approach the field rang through the tunnels.

"Go," Sin said. "I'm right behind you. I have to see the people to maintain the illusion, so I'll be in the corner of the arena. If you get worried, just look for me." He kissed me one last time. "You are incredible, Fea Remia. Your bravery, your power. I am in awe of you."

Jogging off into the bright sun with Sin at my back, I told myself that I was ready to meet my fate.

Chapter Forty-Six

I stepped tentatively out onto the sands, the suns' light a warm encouraging caress on my skin. I half expected cries of outrage and challenge, but it seemed Sin's magic had fooled everyone.

A nervous Kinyx arrived shortly after me and took his place on the other side of the flaming barrel.

Focusing my attention on the brazier stirred my own fire inside, and it strained against the leash of my will like a hound scenting blood. Images of Ram's destroyed body filled my mind, and my anger hungered for vengeance. It didn't want to lay down and concede. It wanted to be unleashed.

Soon, I told it, my promise to Sin that I would be good falling to the back of my mind, bowing to the weight of the anger that burned inside me.

The horn blasted, and I was torn from my violent thoughts. Before I could even register the positions of the other fighters, the Gold Court caster, Direff, spun toward Kinyx with viper speed, swinging his hands back and forth. Direff sent dozens of flaming bats flying from the brazier between them to divebomb the younger male.

Kinyx dropped into a low crouch, and the bats slammed into the wall behind him. Long whips of flame crackled around my Diamond partner as he weaved his arms in an intricate pattern, cleaving the second wave of bats Direff sent in his direction.

While Kinyx and Direff locked horns, Jacksyn idly twirled his hand, and a blazing bear-like monstrosity burst out of a flaming barrel to go loping off toward Sarla.

The female didn't even bat an eye at the rushing wave of fury. Streams of fire flowed from her own brazier, forming a pair of massive floating arms, each as thick as a barrel and three feet long. She threw jabs and hooks with her hands, and the flaming fists followed suit, tearing into the ursine construct with ease.

My fire screamed underneath my skin, begging me to stop standing around and do something. I found Sin watching me from near the tunnel, waiting for me to take a dive, but I couldn't do it. I couldn't lay down and surrender after all I'd seen.

I needed to burn.

Scanning the arena, I searched for Harlix.

Across the field, she sank onto her haunches beside a brazier, and to my shock, dipped her hand straight inside. She brought her curled fist out of the flames as if they were no more threatening than a bucket of water and laid a fist-sized ball of fire on the ground. She repeated the action, and each time, her hand came out scorched and smoking, yet her healing powers repaired the damage faster than she was burning. Soon, she had a dozen flaming balls spread about her.

She wiggled her fingers in a shooing motion, and they began scurrying forward like demonic rats.

The horrific yet mesmerizing display was promptly forgotten when Sarla came dashing out of my periphery. The fire raging inside me howled its joyous challenge, drowning out the fearful little voice in the recesses of my mind that begged me to reconsider.

You have no training.

You've never even thrown a punch.

You have no control.

My flames exploded to life along my arms, sheathing them in blazing gauntlets with wickedly sharp talons.

Sarla's arms thrust out as she ran toward me, her fiery fists rocketing ahead of her.

Moving purely on reflex, I flung out my hands, struggling to block strike after strike. Though I felt no burn from the flames, the unrelenting force of her blasts drove my feet skidding across the sand.

Then the glowing hellrats ran underfoot. The craftings swelled and exploded like a half dozen grenades, sending Sarla and me tumbling through the air.

Before either of us even hit the ground, another swarm of hellrats bounded past on their way toward the male combatants.

I cried out a warning to Kinyx as the fiery creature closed in, not even caring if Sin's illusion could mask my feminine voice. The young male snapped his head toward me, registered the incoming balls of fire, then slammed his flame whips to the ground, jettisoning himself backward twenty paces.

Diref was slower to react, though, and the hellrats swept him up in a wave of explosions. He crashed to the ground, his breath choked and ragged.

Sarla screamed, and the unholy sound chilled me to the bone. I didn't know if it was fear for her father, or pain from her scorched limbs as she gathered herself to strike back.

Before either Gold caster could move, Jacksyn appeared out of my periphery, swooped down to scoop up a fresh hellrat, then shoved it into Direff's open mouth.

I couldn't look away, and for an agonizing moment, it felt like time stood still. Every sound faded away save for that one tiny explosion.

When time resumed, bile surged into my throat and blood flecks spattered against my face. I blinked at the remains of Direff, shock immobilizing me while I pleaded with some unknown deity for things to make sense. One minute he was alive and fighting, and the next, there was only a wide smear of blood and gore where his head should have been.

I succumbed to the nausea and lost my lunch all over the sands, relying on Sin's illusion to hide it.

A few yards away, Jacksyn allowed Sarla no time to grieve as he closed the distance between them and rained fire balls the size of pumpkins down on her.

Horrific images of her impending demise filled me, but Sarla's pain didn't trap her as I expected it to.

It fueled her.

Her flaming limbs reformed, blocking and deflecting the incoming missiles. Throwing out a fiery whip that wrapped around Jacksyn's ankle, she pulled him off his feet so her flaming hands could pin his arms to the ground.

A smile tugged at my lips when Jacksyn screamed, his flesh sizzling, but my attention was quickly pulled away to face down an incoming Harlix.

Direff's death fed my rage to the point I could no longer hold back, and flames ripped from my fingertips. I charged her, forcing her to bend fully backward to dodge my claws that swiped at her face.

Straightening back up, she flung a fistful of sand at me, and I shrieked when the dirt blinded me. Stumbling backward, I hit the ground hard, panting and scratching at my face.

Watery sweat swirled from my brow to run across my eyes, rinsing the sand out and leaving only a slight sting.

I glanced over to Sin who dropped his hand and mouthed, "End it."

I wanted to. For him, I really did want to.

But I couldn't. I wasn't the one making decisions anymore. The burning inferno that raged in my soul was in charge, and I couldn't summon the will to fight it. My anger had only flared brighter at the dirty trick Harlix had pulled.

She was no longer interested in me, though. Instead, she raced toward her injured lover.

Sarla continued to burn Jacksyn's unmoving body, so lost in her fury she didn't even notice the flaming python Harlix sent flying her way. Sarla's screams finally broke free when her hair and clothing started to singe and sear away.

Harlix cackled maniacally, showing no signs of mercy as she twisted her hands and wrapped the flaming snake tighter around Sarla.

My rage hit a tipping point, and something inside me snapped. I would not watch Sarla suffer the same fate as her father. Pouncing on Harlix, I grabbed her around the throat, and set my flames free.

They rolled greedily over her body, ripping an agonized scream from her alongside the sounds of her skin sizzling and blackening. Harlix's python instantly dissolved, dropping Sarla's still burning body to the sand as my flames shredded her concentration.

I wanted to help the Gold Court female, but my rage demanded that I hold tight on Harlix, that I continue to burn her until she was nothing more than a pile of charred bones and ash.

Just like Direff.

It was the glimpse of Sin out of the corner of my eye that saved me from doing something I would have later regretted. The look on his face, the deep level of fear he bore for me, was finally enough to crack through the power that overwhelmed me, and I knew I was better than her.

My fingers loosened, and Harlix scrambled away, her healing magic sluggishly mending her burns.

Sagging beneath the weight of my own exhaustion, I glanced over to see Kinyx hunched beside Sarla, patting out the flames.

Too late, I realized I should have known better than to turn my back on Harlix.

Daggers of flame crashed into me from behind, knocking me to the ground, and a wave of fire poured over my skin, warming me like a summer breeze. I stayed down, letting her think she had gotten the best of me.

Raising my hands up, I pretended to fight off the might of her blast. Harlix's flames licked at my arms and without thinking, I sucked them inside of me.

The stolen power coursed through my veins, an almost deliciously cold crackling energy that danced and twined with the heat of my own magic.

Harlix maintained the flaming deluge for nearly half a minute before realizing something had changed. When she let her hands drop limply to her sides, a twisted grin split my lips.

"My turn."

I threw my arms wide and unleashed every ounce of fire inside me.

All the stress and fear of the past few days, all the horrors of what I had witnessed, all the pain of watching my friends suffer. Every raw emotion reinforced the casting as a ring of fire swelled from my chest and exploded out around me.

The flame raced across the field in a rapidly expanding explosion, sending braziers flying and sweeping Harlix from her feet.

Her body whipped end over end before slamming into the arena wall. She fought to get back on her feet, but her limbs gave out, and she collapsed to the hard-packed dirt.

The only thing that moved was her hand as she formed the cedo sign.

I breathed out a sigh of relief, my energy expended and my legs threatening to crumple beneath me.

To my left, boots scraped over the sand as Kinyx shuffled toward me.

The sickened look on his face had me glancing down. I never should have doubted Sin. His illusion was flawless. Blood streamed from Ram's charred skin, his fighting leathers clinging to the wounds in burned tatters.

In the stands, my father leaned forward, steepling his hands under his chin. I couldn't tell if he was hoping we would fight for the claim of victory, or if he was worried he might lose his strongest general if we did.

With all the intimidating presence of a fluffy kitten, Kinyx lifted shaky fists, prepared to fight, and likely die, all for his court.

It made me sick. These people, this world, they all deserved more than they had been given.

They needed to see there was a better way.

I eased myself down to the sands as if too tired to continue. My head drooped, chin to chest, and I held my left hand high, fingers curling into the yield symbol.

Kinyx stood gob smacked while the arena burst into applause and cheers.

Chapter Forty-Seven

Back in the tunnel, Sin helped me hastily brush off the ashes so I could change out of Peywyn's clothing and return to my father. Once I was presentable, he pressed a quick kiss to my forehead, than swatted my ass to get me moving.

Jogging into the courtyard, I cried out when strong arms gripped me, preventing my escape. Imagining Harpyn had returned to inflict more pain, I thrashed and screamed. "Let me go!"

"Princess, stop. It is only me."

Dey's words registered at the same time his applewood smell wafted over me, and I went limp in his arms.

Stepping back, he eyed me cautiously. "Where have you been? We were all worried."

"I, um... I got lost."

His dubious look told me he clearly hadn't swallowed that lie.

"Did you need something?" I asked, covertly wiping an ash smudge from the back of my hand. "Because I should get back inside. I don't want to miss the next fight."

He frowned. "It is already finished. Kinyx was victorious."

"Oh?" I pasted a look of surprise on my face. "Well, I'm glad everyone is okay."

"Indeed." He analyzed my body, likely searching for anything suspicious to call me out on. "Let me escort you to your room," he offered. "The crowds will be exiting, and it would be futile to attempt a return to your seat."

I nodded, letting him take my arm to guide me back into the castle.

When we got to my room, I said goodbye as I tried to close the door gently, but Dey blocked the action with his boot. "Princess, if you went to go find Sin after his match, I would prefer you to be honest with me."

I hid my surprised reaction behind a muffled cough. That's what he thought I was doing? At least it was better than him suspecting I had been in the fight.

"I told you Dey, I just got lost."

He hesitated, then said, "You stood right here last night and told me that Sin was not my competition. Your concern over his wellbeing during the Games might suggest otherwise."

"What do you want from me, Dey?" I asked, heavy with exhaustion. "I'm not saying I have feelings for Sin, but even if I did, why would it matter? I'm going to be gone in a couple weeks, so there's no future here for me with anybody."

The words felt hollow even to my own ears.

"There could be," he insisted. "It breaks my heart you will not even consider it. Consider me."

"Dey..."

"All I ask is that you think about it, Princess. I will be back later this evening to escort you to dinner."

With a small smile, he disappeared down the hallway.

Holy hell.

I looked like a damned princess.

The sisters had spent nearly an hour fussing over my hair and makeup. It was the first time they had pulled out the assortment of little pots filled with powders and paints, and I'd nearly forgotten what a little color could do for my appearance.

Standing in front of the mirror, I couldn't help but sway side to side, watching the dress sparkle and shine as diamonds caught the light. The crescia silk clung to my body, showcasing every newly defined curve. It shimmered with a pearlescent glow, and its softness made velvet seem like burlap in comparison. Tiny diamonds were stitched around the edge of the plunging neckline and down the sides of the bodice, glistening like streams until they reached the flared skirt where they burst into a firework pattern over the front and back of the gown. The front slit went nearly to the top of my thigh, and there was no chiffon or underskirt to hide the long expanse of exposed skin.

For possibly the first time in my life, I felt truly beautiful. There was no voice inside my head telling me that I was too tall or too scrawny or my face was too plain. Instead, I felt sexy, desirable.

Once they deemed me presentable, the sisters took off, and Jenni flew out from under the bed. She made a beeline for my hair, but I ducked at the last second.

Alighting on top of the wardrobe, she glared down at me.

"What's wrong? Don't you think I look pretty?" I couldn't stop myself from giving a little twirl for her.

"Rain stay with Jenni."

I sighed. Not this again. "Jenni, I don't want to argue with you. Dey will be here any minute to take me to dinner."

"No dinner. Rain stay with Jenni." She gave a loud squawk and spit out a tiny stream of fire to augment her command.

"I'm sorry, but I have to leave. I'll be back later this evening." When my words were met with squawks of protest, I decided to opt for bribery. Opening the drawer of my nightstand, I retrieved one of the sharp diamond pins she was so fond of stealing and held it out to her. "Will a present make up for my absence?"

The ball of fire she unleashed made her opinion on that pretty clear, so I jabbed the pin into the long braid that had been twisted into a crown atop my head and walked over to the wardrobe.

I couldn't quite reach her, so I extended my arm as a perch.

She didn't move. *"No dinner. Rain no come back."*

"Jenni," I said, dropping my hand. "I will come back. I always come back. You don't need to worry. I'll bring you a yummy treat, okay?"

The knock on the door pulled me from my negotiations, and I gave her one last apologetic look. "It'll be fine, Jenni. I'll see you soon."

I slipped out of my room, closing the door before Dey could glimpse my cranky crescia.

His formal regalia was quite stunning, and a week ago, I might have drooled at the sight of him in his rich blue jacket and silver embroidered white vest. Diamond buttons ran up either side of the tail coat he left open to showcase the elaborate design of the fitted garment underneath.

Dey was truly the embodiment of Prince Charming, and I couldn't care less.

I barely heard my name announced when we swept into the Grand Hall and the excessive opulence stole my breath away.

Circular tables filled the majority of the room, each one covered with a rich burgundy tablecloth and a dazzling, diamond-encrusted animal statuette. Chandeliers the size of small cars hung from the ceiling, and off to the right side, a twelve piece orchestra played a soft concerto.

What truly ensnared me though, was the beguiling display of magic throughout the hall.

Against each wall, an aquiservian maintained flowing ribbons of water that shifted through startlingly accurate ten-foot-tall renditions of each king and their court's competitors. Igniservians directed flaming bird constructs that flitted about the edges of the hall, while aeriservians kept afloat shimmery clouds of tiny sparkles that danced around the room above the guest's heads. The glittering clouds looked familiar, and I suspected my father was literally throwing diamonds around like confetti.

Sounds of astonishment filtered out from a growing crowd at the center of the grand hall, and curiosity had me tugging Dey toward the commotion. I gasped when I took in the scene. Six terriservians stood around the edge of a raised circular platform roughly twenty feet in diameter, rhythmically swirling their arms. In the center, three marble couples danced and twirled to the music as if they were truly alive. The details in the living statues were exquisite. With smiling faces and silent laughter, they moved in sync with their stone partner, gowns flowing and shifting with each step.

The Elemental Games had showcased combat skills, but this… this was art. For as much as I had dreaded it, I had to admit that the banquet truly was an incredible celebration of the four elements.

Dey led me to a table with a considerably more elaborate centerpiece than all the rest, and I took the seat he directed me toward. Kinyx sat across the table from me, looking adorably nervous yet puffed up with pride. Harpyn occupied the seat beside him, and surprisingly, the brutal terriservian didn't give me his usual nasty grin. Instead, he maintained a death-glare at Cam sitting across from him, probably assuming my friend had something to do with Ram's presence in the Games.

"Cam," I said excitedly. "Come sit next to me."

His eyes swept over my gown, then he gave me a brilliant smile as shifted over to take the seat off to my right while Dey took the spot to my left.

"How's Ram?" I asked.

Worry flickered over Cam's face, replacing his grin with something more subdued. "He is resting. His healing magic is not the best, so he will need some time to recover from the… burns."

"He'll be okay, though? None of his injuries are permanent?"

"No, Princess. He will recover with time." Cam leaned closer and whispered, "I will never be able to repay you for what you did today. My brother and I owe you our lives."

I smiled weakly, uncomfortable under the awe and appreciation in his gaze. Slinging my arm around his neck, I leaned in to give him a side hug. "I'm just glad to hear he'll be on his feet and teasing me again in no time."

Pulling back, I noted the four remaining empty seats around our table. "Who else is joining us besides the kings?" I asked Dey.

He gave me a sidelong glance. "It is a great honor for the champions to dine at the royal table."

Oh. The last seat was for Sin.

I tried to ignore the flutter in my chest and instead focused on chatting with Cam. All around us, everyone could talk of nothing but the Games. Nobody mentioned the deaths, though, as if they could be willed from existence by simply not acknowledging them. Everybody was content to just bury their heads in the sand.

Well, everyone except Vankin.

I heard the Gold Court caster long before I saw him, and when the disheveled male lurched into view, I couldn't help but wonder how many drinks he'd had.

"This is a party, is it not?" he bellowed loudly as he bumped into courtier after courtier. They all turned their noses up, pretending to ignore his outburst.

Ah, polite society. Stay away from taboo subjects and ignore the drunk who had his entire world destroyed in front of a thousand people all in the name of entertainment.

"We are here to have fun, are we not?" he continued, his speech slurring. "Well, I want to have fun! I can be callous and apathetic too." He climbed onto a table and began wildly shaking his limbs. "Let us all dance! Come on, everyone! We should dance and sing and celebrate the complete and utter disregard for Vitaean life. As long as we have our sparkly diamonds and shiny gold bracelets, who cares if the love of my life died?"

He stumbled, and for a second, I thought he might fall off the table entirely.

"Isn't someone going to help him?" I whispered to Cam. Nobody else was even acknowledging Vankin's presence.

Sighing, Cam stood up from the table. Whether he did it for me, or because it was the right thing to do, didn't matter. I was just glad Vankin got some help.

It took Cam almost five minutes to get the belligerent water caster down without hurting himself. It wasn't until Vankin tripped and took a header off the table that Cam put away the kid gloves and sealed the drunk male in a dense cocoon of air.

Cam strode swiftly from the Grand Hall, a struggling Vankin bobbing along behind him.

Remembering Sarla also lost someone during the Games, I searched the room but couldn't find her. I cared very little for the deaths of Tenyn and Tenebra, given what they had done to Bartyn, but I did briefly wonder if Lanset had a family or spouse who might mourn him. How could they even process the news? He left to become a decorated champion and would return in a box.

All thoughts of the deceased competitors dissipated, however, when Sin's entrance was announced, but I forced myself not to react at the sound of his name. It wouldn't help the situation with Dey if I immediately jumped up and ran into Sin's arms like I wanted to.

The intoxicating stormy scent surrounded me long before I heard the rumble of his deep voice.

"Is this seat taken, Princess?"

I turned to look at him, prepared to play it cool, but one glance at Sin made it feel like someone just sucked all the oxygen from the room.

If Dey looked like Prince Charming, then Sin was his dark counterpart. A black brocade jacket with twin rows of silver buttons encased his wide shoulders while tight black breeches stretched over a pair of muscular thighs like a second skin. A pattern of diamond leaves swirled across the vest he wore beneath the jacket, and my fingers itched to trace the exquisite design.

I finally made it up to his face, and my breath hitched. With his slick wet hair looking almost black and his pale green eyes summoning images of a harsh winter forest, he was the epitome of a shadowy prince.

I gulped. Sin reminded me of all the dark little fantasies that lived in the back of my mind, along with some new ones that only he could awaken.

When he smirked at my reaction, the evil little smile promised he would indulge every single naughty request I could think of and some I hadn't. He might be the death of me, but I would die happy.

Sin cleared his throat and spoke again, louder this time. "Is this seat taken, Princess?"

"Um, yes. I mean, no."

His smirk grew, and I knew I would pay for the fluster later.

"Sorry," I stammered. "Yes, you can sit down. No, it's not taken. That's what I meant."

Sin sank into the chair, but his toned ass had barely grazed the cushion before Dey was leaning across me to say, "Actually, that is Cam's seat, Dreisin. Perhaps you could sit beside Harpyn?" The acid in his tone spoke volumes.

Completely unphased, Sin took a sip of Cevisa, then said, "Actually, I believe Cam is currently assisting Vankin with his efforts to vomit on every bush in the garden. I imagine it will be some time before he returns."

Dey grumbled something in response, but a blare of trumpets echoing through the room halted all conversations.

While everyone stood to watch the three kings make their way into the hall, Sin leaned over and whispered in my ear, "You look absolutely stunning in that dress, Fea Remia, but not half as stunning as you're going to look when it hits my bedroom floor."

I blushed and squeezed my thighs together, fighting against the bloom of heat sparked by the guarantee in his eyes.

The kings made their way over to our table, and the dinner ended up being exactly as awful as I expected.

Dey and Sin sniped at each other.

The Silver King made more than one rude comment about my questionable human heritage.

Harpyn sulked the whole time, save for the occasional lewd comment thrown in my direction.

And Cam returned halfway through the meal but spent the entire time pushing food around his plate.

In the end, the only pleasant one was Kinyx, and I had to act like I couldn't understand him.

As the evening progressed, people began abandoning their tables to make their way through the double doors into the attached ballroom. The orchestra had since moved over as well, and a lively melody trickled out from within.

"Care to dance, Princess Raynella?" Sin asked formally.

"I would love to, Cennux Dreisin," I replied, equally as formal, and allowed him to help me out of my seat.

He escorted me into the ballroom, which was little more than a copy of the Grand Hall save for the twelve extravagant floor to ceiling stained glass windows framed with burgundy velvet drapes secured by silver cords. Each window highlighted the crashing waves, the thick fog deepening into hues of red, orange, and purple, and the two suns dipping below the horizon.

I stared at the Rivellans who swept gracefully across the floor, intrigued to see a wide variety of dance styles present. I expected everything to be like some medieval ball out of the movies where everyone magically knew the same dance. Instead, I could see three distinctive types of movement around the room.

The couples that swayed seductively along the outskirts with their hips glued together were likely from the Silver Court, while the Gold Court couples engaged in sweeping motions that mimicked their partner who stood almost a foot away. Which left the Diamond Court dancers twirling across the floor elegantly in a style akin to a waltz.

I would definitely make an ass of myself if I even tried to emulate that dance.

"Don't look so nervous," Sin whispered in my ear. "Just hold on tight."

The rest of the ballroom faded away, and Sin swept me into his arms to glide across the ballroom floor. One by one, the other dancers disappeared as Sin spun an illusion around us. The ceiling vanished next, exposing the clear night sky, followed by the walls dropping away until there was nothing left but Sin and I, dancing along a dock with waves crashing against the shore.

I inhaled deeply, his scent only adding to the realness of the illusion. "Can everyone else see this?" I asked breathlessly.

"No," he said, pulling my gaze to his. "Illusions are created in the mind, and your mind is the only one I'm concerned about. It's just you and me, Fea Remia. I don't want to share this moment with anyone else."

No longer feeling self-conscious, I surrendered myself to him, letting him spin me around underneath the twinkling stars. I laughed when he dipped me, completely forgetting that I wasn't supposed to be smiling at him like a twitter pated schoolgirl. I couldn't summon the will to care, though. I could no more hide my feelings than I could pluck the stars from the sky.

Sin was the other half of my soul, and when he held me, the rest of the world dropped away. Nothing mattered save for me and him and this connection between us.

I would sacrifice everything I had ever known if it meant I could spend an eternity in his arms.

Warm.

Safe.

Loved.

Loved.

So that's what that feeling was. The ache in my heart. The inability to stop thinking about him. The intense pull to seek him out. The feeling that I might die if I couldn't hold him again. The knowledge that in no uncertain terms would I ever feel whole without him.

I loved Sin.

He gazed at me as if I hung the moon, and I wanted to tell him I felt the same. But the words wouldn't come out. I couldn't hand over to him the ability to completely destroy me, because I knew he would in the end.

Not on purpose, of course, but sooner or later, this would all come crashing down around my head. And my chances of recovering from it, from him, were slim to none.

Chapter Forty-Eight

When the song ended, Sin floated me over to the edges and pulled me tight against him. Adopting the Silver Court style, we swayed with the sounds of the music, and I relaxed into him, far more comfortable having abandoned the complicated dance steps.

"When can we leave?" I asked, keeping my voice low.

"I'm fairly certain Verren would have my head if I whisked you away right now," he replied with a small chuckle.

"Hmmm..." I said in mock thoughtfulness. "I might be willing to risk it. The last gamble I took today panned out pretty well."

His arms tightened around my waist. "I thought you were going to die in that arena, Rain. I was prepared to kill every one of them if they took you from me. If you never remind me of that again, it will be too soon."

"I'm sorry I brought it up." Then, needing to see his smile again, I added, "I guess you'll just have to punish me for that too."

A ripple of arousal ran through me when his lips curled up into a feral grin. I could feel my peaked nipples pressing against the thin material of my gown.

"Oh, Fea Remia," he purred. "The things I am going to do to you."

"Promises, promises."

I might have succumbed to the wicked glint in his eye right there on the dance floor, but a throat clearing behind me dispelled the haze of my lust.

"May I cut in?"

Dey's words hit me like a cold shower, but I reluctantly untangled my arms from around Sin's neck, giving him an apologetic look. I thought he might actually kill his friend based on the daggers he was shooting his way, so I hurriedly tugged Dey out to the middle of the floor before dark thoughts became actions.

"I'm not a very good dancer," I told him when he took my hand and slipped an arm around my waist.

He pulled me in close, his applewood smoke smell smothering all traces of Sin's lingering dark ocean scent. "Princess, you could step on my toes a hundred times, and I would still fight every male in here for a second dance."

"You're very good at saying pretty things," I replied, avoiding eye contact.

"The beauty of my words does not negate their truth."

I focused on the dance steps for a bit, unsure what to even say to Dey. He made his intentions very clear, but even without my father's involvement, I just didn't feel anything for him. Apart from a small amount of sadness that our initial friendship may have been nothing more than a carefully constructed deception.

When the song came to an end, I tried to pull out of his arms, but he held me tight against his chest.

"I am not naïve, Rain. I saw the way you looked at Sin. Heard the way you laughed. I do not know when my friend stole your heart, but it seems you have made your choice."

I debated a number of potential explanations, but in the end, I just nodded. I didn't want to hide anymore. I didn't want to pretend that Sin meant nothing to me when in reality he meant everything. Maybe my father would strike back at me for having ruined whatever he was planning with Dey's seduction. Maybe he would abandon his plan altogether and allow me to be happy so long as I fulfilled his damn prophecy. Maybe we could drop all pretenses of him being a caring father and just get to the truth of what he wanted from me.

And maybe I would sprout wings and spend the rest of the night soaring over the ocean.

In reality, I had no idea how my father would react, but I didn't care anymore. Sin was the only person I'd ever felt this way about, and I refused to keep sneaking around if it limited my time with him.

"I see," Dey said, releasing his hold on me.

I turned to walk away but made it only one step before he grabbed my elbow and pulled me back to his side, a spark flaring to life in his eyes.

"Perhaps Dreisin has not told you about his past. Perhaps he has, and you are willing to overlook it. I do know this—he has obviously told you very little about his present because you would not be with him otherwise. He is not a good male, Rain."

And you are?

I bit my tongue to keep the words from escaping.

"I care about you," Dey continued. "More than you know. And I have no intention of giving up. We could be happy here together. I am the king's Foster, and you are his daughter. Our lives have been intertwined before you were even born. Do you not see the poetry of it all? We belong together, here in the palace. This," he gestured around himself, "...all of this could be yours. Ours. Eventually you will learn the truth about him, and when you do, I will be there to pick up the pieces of your broken heart. If you can trust nothing else, at least trust that I will always be here for you."

It was a beautiful speech. A beautiful dream. It just wasn't *my* dream.

"Dey..." I began, and he must have read on my face what I was about to say because he quickly spoke over me.

"Just think about it, Princess. Promise me you will really think about giving us a chance. If you still want to leave in the end, I cannot force you to stay, but I truly believe you would be remiss not to at least consider it."

He dropped my arm and strode briskly out of the ballroom.

I should have been relieved that I didn't have to hide anymore, but I couldn't shake the tiny hint of doubt that bloomed in the pit of my stomach.

He has obviously told you very little about his present because you would not be with him otherwise.

How much did I really know about Sin?

"Where are we going?" I asked Sin later that evening when he dragged me from the ballroom. After Dey left, I'd suffered through maybe ten more dances with random courtiers and competitors while my father regarded me intently from his throne at the back of the ballroom.

"I just need to get you alone for a minute," he said, rushing me down a darkened hallway toward the back stairs. "Just one minute. Maybe five. Then we can go back. You have no idea the torture it is to watch you dance with those other males. I adore Kinyx, but if his hand dropped any lower, I would have been honor bound to snap it off."

I laughed at Sin's faux bloodthirstiness, knowing full well he would never harm the young male.

Sin pulled me up the winding staircase at the back of the castle, but I only made it a few steps before I stumbled in my heels. In a flash, he had one arm behind my back and the other under my knees.

I fell into his arms, and a high-pitched squeal slipped out, echoing along the stairwell as Sin charged up the steps. "You know I can walk," I said through the high-pitched giggles that sounded strange coming from my mouth.

"Of course you can. But do you really think I would pass up any opportunity to hold you in my arms?"

He pushed the door open, and a cool night breeze washed over my face as we emerged near the rear parapet of the main keep. "It gets harder and harder to let go of you," he confessed, setting me on my feet. "There might come a day when I'm no longer able to."

I rose onto my tiptoes, kissed him sweetly, and whispered, "I know the feeling." Pulling out of his arms, I turned to take in the view. "It's beautiful," I gasped, the full visual hitting me.

My previous trips to the roof had always been at the front of the castle, but here at the very back, I could step up to the edge of the parapet and see nothing but the sea. No bustling courtyard. No city lights. Only crashing waves and a thick, dark fog.

The rooftop space was expansive, and it was so freeing to be out in the open air, away from the stuffy rooms of the palace. I took a deep breath in, and when I let it out, a tremendous weight sloughed from my shoulders.

Looking down at the thousand foot drop to the jagged rocks below, I envied the waves that crashed against them. How they slammed into the sharp stones, broke into a million pieces, and slowly reformed, only to do it over and over again. They were unrelenting, those waves. Able to withstand repeated abuse, yet they always found their way back to themselves.

Sin's arms slid around my waist as he came up behind me. "Your mother used to do that exact same thing," he said.

"What thing?"

"Exhale the weight of the world the second she got up here. This is where we would chat most nights. It was her favorite spot because she couldn't see the city. I think she wanted nothing more than to put Civi Obsura behind her." He paused. "It was rough for her to be a human in this world that harbors so much hatred for them. Even here at the castle, everyone treated her like a walking disease. Like something to fear. None of Verren's orders to treat her with respect were heeded. I'm sure you saw a bit of that warm welcome yourself."

I had, and I was even half-Vitaean. What my mother went through must have been awful.

I twisted around in his arms, wanting to see his face even more than the ocean. He was like my own portable sea. My personal source of calm and happiness.

He regarded me with so much love in his eyes that I couldn't help but feel like I didn't deserve it. Sin loved the same way that he fought—with his entire being—and I wanted to be worthy of him.

"Sin..." I began, struggling with the urge to tell him how I felt.

He put a finger on my lips before I could say anything. "Look up, Fea Remia." His tone, gentle yet commanding, sent my gaze skyward without hesitation.

Sin's illusion earlier had been nearly perfect, but when compared to the real thing… The blues and purples of faraway galaxies gleamed in the darkness, surrounded by trillions of shining stars that humbled any who would dare gaze upon them for too long.

There was no pollution here. No big cities to dim their brilliance. The small flickers of lamplight from Civi Adasa could do nothing to impede the magnificence of the celestial tapestry that unfurled above me.

Painstakingly, I lowered my eyes to meet Sin's. "Can we stay here?" I asked with a vulnerability I didn't recognize. "I don't want to go back."

"I don't want to take you back," he said, securing me tighter against his chest. "I could spend hours watching you watch the night sky. The way your face lights up. The way your lips part slightly in awe and you forget to breathe at times. The way you slow your blinking as if you fear closing your eyes for even a second. You are so beautiful, Rain. And it breaks my heart that you don't see yourself the way I see you." He claimed my mouth, and I gave myself over to the tender kiss.

There was no pulsing heat or flood of desire. There was no urge to rip his clothing off. As he cupped the back of my neck gently, I felt only his love. His ocean-deep, unending love for me that went way past the physical into something that made me uncomfortable.

I could handle sex and desire. I could show him that I loved him with my body. What he was giving me, though, was so much deeper, and I didn't know how to reciprocate.

Maybe I wasn't capable of loving him the way he loved me—completely and utterly without reservation or hesitation. Or maybe I was just too scared to.

I pulled away from the kiss and turned to lean out over the parapet. I needed the soothing calm of the breaking waves while I sorted through my emotions.

"What's wrong?" he asked.

"Nothing," I whispered. "And everything."

He came up beside me and captured my chin so I was forced to look at him. The worry in his eyes cracked something in my heart, seeing this imposing warrior brought down by his love for someone like me.

"Talk to me, Rain."

"That's just it," I choked out as the weight of reality came flooding into me. "I don't know what to say to you, Sin. Everything over the past week has been so much. Too much. Seven days ago, I was an emotionally stunted cashier at a Taco Hut in New Jersey with little to no chance to ever be anything more than that. Now, I'm a princess in a different realm with a manipulative long lost father, and I'm supposed to fix this broken world because I also happen to be the prophesied savior. Oh, and I have fucking magic!" I shot a spark of flame up into the night to accentuate my frustration.

I probably sounded hysterical by this point, but it needed to come out. Everything I'd tried to dismiss needed to finally come out.

"And then there's you, Sin. Do you even understand what you mean to me? I gave up on finding someone to love a long time ago. Wrote it off as yet another thing that was not in the cards for me. And I was fine with that. It was safer and easier, and I had accepted it. Then you came along and pulverized every fucking brick of the wall I built around my heart. It hurts, Sin. It hurts to be away from you, but it hurts even more to be with you because I know it won't last. How am I supposed to just go back to my life before you?" I pulled away from him, rubbing at my chest and the ache that only seemed to grow as I spoke. "But you know what the worst part is? I can't be that person for you. I don't know how to love you the way you love me. The way you deserve. I'm broken, Sin. I'm just... broken."

I couldn't stop the tears flooding down my cheeks, and for the first time, I didn't even try to. Only around him could I let myself be weak and vulnerable without fearing judgment.

Sin tugged me away from the wall and tucked a stray hair behind my ear. He looked at me, *looked into me*, and said, "You are not broken, Rain. You never were. Not to me. I have been a ghost for over forty years, drifting through life without living. You brought me back. I don't need a prophecy to tell me that you're the savior. You've been my savior since the first moment I saw you. You say that you can't love me the way I deserve? The truth is I don't deserve even a piece of your love, but I will take anything you give me and consider it paradise. You don't need to change. Not for me. I love everything about you, and I will continue to do so until my last breath." He cupped my face, his thumbs brushing away my tears. "You are it for me, Rain. From now until the last star in the sky winks out, you are it for me."

His lips descended on mine, and I could feel the full weight of his words behind the kiss, every ounce of his love for me, so I met it with my own. With everything I was capable of.

Perfectly imperfect. That's what he was to me. And maybe, that's what I was to him.

"Oh, my dear Raynella. I had so hoped Deylan was mistaken."

A basso voice cut through the still night air, and I jerked away from Sin.

My father stood in the doorway, watching us with a mixture of sadness and disappointment.

I wiped my hands down the front of my dress, uncertain as to why I was suddenly so nervous. I'd decided not to hide my relationship with Sin anymore, so my father was bound to find out sooner or later. There was something about the way he looked at me, though. As if finding out that I cared for Sin was in some way a great betrayal that hurt him personally.

"Father," I said stiffly. There were so many lies between us that I could barely remember how I was supposed to act around him.

"Dreisin, leave us please. I need to speak with my daughter," he said in Rivellan.

"No," I cut in, also in Rivellan. "Whatever you want to say to Sin, you can say to me. I don't keep secrets from him."

My father raised a single eyebrow at how smoothly I spoke his language. "You may not keep secrets from him, but it seems you have kept quite a few from me. What else have you been hiding, sweet daughter of mine?"

Anger rose up in me at his words, and I could feel the sparks coming to life underneath my skin. I took a step toward him, balling my fists at my sides.

"Are you kidding right now? You want to talk about secrets? You want to get it all out in the open? Fine. Why don't you tell me why you ordered Dey to seduce me?"

Something like genuine shock appeared on my father's face. And maybe, just maybe, a tiny bit embarrassment.

"My reasons for requesting that Deylan spend a substantial amount of time in your company are my own."

"Right," I said dryly. "Because you want to know everything I'm keeping from you but have no desire to share whatever twisted machinations have been cooking inside your head. How about we try this, then? Why don't you tell me what really happened with my mother, huh? I know the Walker didn't kill her. I want to know the truth."

"You truly wish to know what happened to your mother?" he asked, his face hard and unyielding.

"I do."

"Then perhaps you should ask the male standing beside you."

Chapter Forty-Nine

Threads of icy fear wound through my veins as I stared at Sin. My father was lying. He had to be. Sin knew how badly I wanted to find out what happened to my mother. He would have never withheld it from me. Never.

Except the look on his face told me I couldn't be more wrong.

"Rain," he said, taking a step toward me.

Wobbling in my heels, I backed away from him. "No," I said, shaking my head as my heart cracked open in my chest. "Don't touch me. You lied to me. You brought me to see her friend, and the whole time you knew the truth. You stood here and told me you loved me! Was that all a lie too, Sin?"

"Don't ever say that," he argued. "I told you there were things I wasn't able to reveal to you. If I could have, I would have. You need to believe me, Rain."

I wanted to, but I just couldn't. Not anymore. Corym had worked around his compulsion, which meant it was possible to overcome.

Sin simply hadn't wanted to tell me the truth.

I whirled on my father. "I want to know. I want you to tell me what happened that night."

His eyes shuttered, and when he opened them, he said, "How about I show you?"

One second I was on the top of the castle, and the next, I was standing on the edge of the clearing in a dark forest, watching a scene unfold before me.

The expression on Sin's face told me this was most definitely not his illusion.

My father stepped up beside me. "I haven't been entirely honest with you about my abilities, Raynella. And for that I do apologize. This is my true power." He gestured at the illusion around us. "Please bear with me as the event has been pieced together from the memories of my soldiers, but *this* is what happened to your mother. This is the truth you want so badly to know."

Standing at the edges of the illusion, I watched a contingent of the king's guards enter the dimly lit clearing and halt, taking up defensive stances as they surrounded a woman with long silver hair. She was tall and slender and very much like me in every way. Except for the eyes. Those I had gotten from my father.

I wanted to pause the scene so I could just look at my mom. Study her and commit every nuance to memory. Time was never that kind to me, though.

My heart plummeted when an illusion version of Sin stepped out from behind his guards and drew his sword.

"Bring the child, Leeara, and let us return to the palace," he said. "Let us put this unpleasantness behind us."

"I will never go with you," she hissed. "Do you honestly think me to be so naïve? Do you think I didn't hear all of you talking? I know what will happen to her, and I will not allow it."

"Leeara, there is nothing you can do," Sin stated plainly, stepping closer and placing the tip of his sword at her chest.

I had to fight the urge to spring forward. To stop him. To help her. But it was only an illusion, and there was nothing I could do.

"This was always to be your fate," he continued. "And hers. There is no use fighting it."

A flash of light drew my attention from my mother, and behind her, I saw a middle-aged woman with auburn hair chanting softly, arms raised high. Her fingertips sparked with magic, and there was something painfully familiar about her.

My mother's voice drew me back to the unfolding drama.

"I don't believe in fate," she said firmly.

I cried out in horror when she thrust her body forward, impaling herself on Sin's sword.

"No!" I screamed, racing forward to grab her, but my father's arms locked around my waist, pulling me away from the images that refused to pause so I could grieve.

When I finally stopped fighting, he lowered me to the ground, and I sat there sobbing, watching the thick red streams of blood spill from my mother's chest.

The illusion of Sin let out a pained cry, and my mother slumped forward onto the sword still held between them. He pulled the weapon from her chest, agony contorting his face as she fell to the ground.

Her eyes focused on something, and I followed her gaze back to the other side of the clearing.

The older female, a World Walker I assumed, raised her arm and slashed a hand through the air, ripping a hole through the very fabric of existence.

Staring into the portal, I recognized the orphanage that had been my home as a child. I spent so many afternoons sitting on those worn steps, watching other children laugh and play, wishing that I could be like them. Above the door, the familiar brown sign appeared almost new.

Saint Philomena's Orphanage
A Caring Home for Abandoned Young Girls

I hated that sign. Not because it called us abandoned. There were no misconceptions about that. We knew what we were. No, what I hated was the word caring. Not a soul inside that building ever cared for me or Jenn or any of the young girls that came and went. The nuns were harsh and cruel, and staying there was just as bad, if not worse, than the foster homes. The only difference was that I didn't have any scars from the nuns. Well, not physical ones anyway.

Shoving the memories back into the vault of my mind, I looked back over at my mother. She stared into the portal with dead eyes, a smile frozen on her lips.

“Stop her,” illusory Sin shouted. “Grab the child!”

Guards raced toward the Walker, but they were too slow.

She scooped up a small bundle of cloth at her feet, then disappeared through the rift, sealing it behind her.

I recognized it—that gray blanket. I had clung to it so many nights as a child while I dreamed about what my mother would be like.

Tears streamed down my face for a second time in less than an hour, and I choked back another sob when the illusion of Sin returned to my mother’s corpse. I didn’t even recognize him as he knelt down beside her. There was not even a hint of the male I loved.

I had been played for a fool.

“Take her body,” the illusory Sin commanded his guards as he ran a hand reverently over my mother’s pale face. “He will want to know why we failed in our mission.”

The illusion faded away, and the last thing I saw was Sin marching off into the dark forest.

Chapter Fifty

I didn't bother looking at Sin. There was nothing he could do or say that would ever make me trust him again. He chased down my mother, forced her to take her own life to escape him, then lied about it. All my love for him vanished the moment I watched her take her final breath.

He was just the puppet, though. Even I could recognize that.

I wanted the master pulling the strings.

I yanked free of my father's grasp and whirled around, letting him see every ounce of rage that burned behind my eyes.

"What did you do?!" I screamed in his face, shoving him backward. "What did she overhear that sent her fleeing from the palace in the middle of the night? What could have been so bad that she would kill herself rather than see me brought back to you?"

My fire came roaring up from the place it slumbered inside me and burst forth, wreathing my hands in flames. The flickering shadows that whipped across my father's face underscored the stark terror painted there.

"Tell me!" I shouted, advancing on him while my flames pulsed brighter with each jagged breath.

I didn't control the fire.

I was the fire.

And my father was about to learn that firsthand.

"Rain, you need to stop!" Sin called from behind me.

Stop? I wasn't going to stop. I was going to make every single one of them pay.

I whirled around, thrust my hand out, and a fireball larger than my head rocketed toward Sin.

He dove to the side, but not fast enough. The flaming orb splashed across his hip, spinning him off balance and slamming him into the parapet. I didn't even wince as his head cracked against the stone and he fell still.

Good. I didn't need any more interruptions.

Turning back around, I faced the male trembling against the castle wall.

"Raynella?" he asked in a tiny, horrified voice.

"My. Name. Is. RAIN!"

Wings of fire exploded from my back, unfurling and stretching out behind me, the furious blaze driving away all the shadows and their secrets within. My rage fueled the flames, and they grew and spread until I didn't have just wings, but an entire cascading river of fire over my skin that engulfed me completely. A phoenix, born from the ashes of my pathetic life to never again bow at the whims of others.

The crescia silk flashed away to become nothing more than embers on the wind. I built a new dress from my flames, letting them curve and coil around my body until I had a gown of living fire that highlighted the harsh beauty of my ramentum.

Stalking toward my father, I let him see everything I had kept hidden—my magic, my fire, and most importantly, the anger burning inside me that I had to suppress my entire life.

"Don't act out Rain, or you'll be punished."

"No one will adopt you with that temper, Rain."

"If you sass me one more time, Rain, you're going back to the orphanage."

"Nobody will ever love an angry little girl, Rain."

Angry little girl.

Angry little girl.

The admonishment echoed through my brain. My anxiety disorder manifested out of a childhood spent hiding who I really was. Hiding my hatred and frustration at the unfairness that was my shitty life. I buried it deep, so deep that most of the time I could pretend it wasn't there.

Not anymore.

I was finally the person I was always meant to be.

I was wrath and rage. I was violence personified.

Planting my hands on my father's bare chest, I let him feel every bit of my fury. The flames burned hotter as he screamed, and I reveled in the sound.

He was the reason I grew up in poverty.

He was the reason I had been abused and scarred.

He was the reason my mother was dead.

My hands slammed down onto his chest, and layers of skin and muscle melted beneath my touch.

"Why?!" I screamed. "Why did she run? What did she overhear?"

I let up on the pressure, allowing his magic to struggle in its attempt to repair the scorched section of his body.

"Tell me," I hissed, crouching down beside him.

"The truth," he whispered through clenched teeth. "She learned the truth."

I leaned even closer, allowing my flaming wings to curl around me so they snapped and popped in his face. "And what is the truth?" I snarled, not even recognizing my own voice. "What did my mother learn?"

"She learned... she learned that you won't survive it," he confessed, his voice a pathetic whimper as my flames continued to lick at his skin. "There was a part of the prophecy I kept hidden. It says that when you go to pull the ley lines apart, it will take all of your magic to restore them. It will drain you completely and... it will kill you, Raynella. That is why your mother took you and fled."

I reeled back as if I had been slapped in the face.

I was robbed of a mother who cared about me enough to sacrifice her life for my own.

Because of my father, I had been denied a lifetime of warm hugs. A lifetime of bedtime stories. A lifetime of comforting words when I was sad and encouragement when I was nervous.

I had been denied a lifetime of *love.*

I plunged my hands back into my father's chest, letting my fire devour his flesh. I would hold his beating heart in my hands and watch it turn to ash.

He struggled against my grip, but it only made me press harder. I let his screams wash over me, delighting in his anguish. Finally, he would know what it felt like to suffer.

A wave of cold water crashed over my head, and I cried out as the deluge swept me across the rooftop and tossed me into the wall.

Sin stood with his back to the ocean, his hands upturned, and a massive wave suspended behind him.

"I can't let you do this, Rain. I can't let you kill him. There's still so much that you don't understand."

"I understand enough!" I bellowed, jumping to my feet. The cool night breeze on my wet skin reminded me that I had torched my clothing, so I called to my fire, trying desperately to force my flames back to life. Sparks flickered but only smoldered against my soaked and shivering skin. "You told me she was your friend!"

He flinched, a dark cloud rolling over his face. "She was."

"Liar! She was running from you. You could have let her go, but instead you stood there and watched her die. You did nothing. Nothing!"

I almost felt bad for Sin. The heartache on his face was fiercely evident, and instinct told me he wasn't actually lying about caring for my mom. Unfortunately, my instincts had betrayed me far too often to ever listen to them again.

I tracked Sin out of the corner of my eye while I stalked toward my blistered and charred father, my nudity the farthest thing from my mind.

"Are you going to kill me now, Sin? It's the only way you'll stop me."

"This isn't you, Rain," he argued. "You're letting the magic rule your emotions. You can't control them both at once. You need to let go of the fire."

"I don't think so," I snapped, my voice bitter and harsh. Willing my flames back to life, I smiled when they answered my call, slithering into place across my skin once more.

Kneeling in front of my father, I noted his labored breathing that indicated he didn't have much time left. Maybe if he got to a healer, he could be saved, but I had no intentions of letting that happen.

He needed to pay for what he'd done. What he'd stolen from me.

Despite all my rage, some small voice that lingered in the recesses of my mind screamed at me to listen to Sin. It begged me to stop, shouting that this wasn't me.

I slammed the door shut on that little voice.

"Rain!" Sin thundered from behind me.

I paused to glance over my shoulder.

He swirled his hand, gathering water above his head.

Before he could unleash his magic on me again, I shot a blast of fire across the roof. He dropped into a crouch to avoid the flaming projectile, and his grip on the water faltered.

With Sin's magic temporarily out of reach, I turned back to my father.

"Raynella," he wheezed out. "There is so much I wish I could tell you."

"I don't care," I hissed. I knew enough. Swirling my flames around my palms, I thrust them back down on his chest.

No screams of pain reached my ears though, as cool hands coated in water settled over mine, snuffing out the flames before they could tear into flesh.

Sin leaned in close to me, ignoring the spots where his clothes and exposed skin began to smolder. "Please, Rain," he whispered. "You trusted me once. Trust me again. Don't do this."

I yanked my hands out from under his and urged the fire back to life, but a thin layer of his water magic covered my skin once more like silken gloves.

"You won't let me kill him?" I asked, staring into eyes that once captivated me.

"I'm sorry," he replied. "But I can't let you do that."

I nodded as if agreeing with him. "I'm sorry too, Sin, because no one tells me what to do anymore."

In one smooth movement, I yanked the sharp six-inch hairpin from my braid and plunged it into my father's pulsing jugular.

His body seized, and blood spilled from his mouth. Thrashing against the wall, he reached up to pull the pin out, but it was too late. His pathetic magic might have healed his ruined chest, but it wasn't enough to save him from the gushing hole in his neck.

Choking on his own blood, he coughed out, "I love you, Raynella. From the moment I first held you in my arms, I loved you. And I failed you. I am so sorry that I was not stronger. Whatever happens next... please... don't... blame... yourself."

Then he was gone.

Chapter Fifty-One

"Well, I must say," a snide voice crooned from the doorway. "That was quite entertaining."

I looked up from where I knelt at my father's corpse.

A stocky male on the tail end of middle age with close-cropped black hair emerged from the dark of the stairwell. His sneer oozed arrogance, and I would have dismissed him as nothing more than a courtier who wondered upstairs if it wasn't for his eyes.

Pale blue with gold-ringed irises.

My father's eyes.

My eyes.

"And you are?" I asked warily. He didn't seem to be the slightest bit bothered that my father's blood coated my hands, and flames covered the rest of me.

"Do you not recognize me, Raynella?" he asked, sliding a step closer. His eyes scanned my body, taking in my fiery dress, then dismissing my power as if it was no concern to him.

There was something about him that felt familiar, but I couldn't put my finger on it. "I've never seen you before." As I spoke the words, it dawned on me that the male in front of me was speaking English.

The confidence with which he sauntered toward us set me on edge. The king was dead at my feet, and this male seemed completely unbothered or even surprised.

The stranger halted two steps shy of me, and I rose to my feet with Sin by my side, my anger with him temporarily delayed while I assessed the potential new threat.

"Belarius," the male said simply. "My name is Belarius. And you do know me, Raynella."

I scoffed. "That's not possible. My grandfather is a sweet older male. I met him a few days ago."

Had it really only been a few days? It felt like a lifetime ago.

The sneer on his face grew wider, the dreadful smile stretching ear to ear.

"Tell me, Raynella," he said smugly. "What exactly do you recall about your conversation with your dear old grandpa?"

Thinking back to the day I followed a random yummy smell into a small study, I pictured my grandfather: frail, gray hair, and a face full of wrinkles.

"He was older, very old. And kind," I said defiantly.

"No, Raynella. Tell me what you spoke about."

I hesitated, racking my brain. "We had a nice chat. It was nice."

"Specifics, Raynella," he pressed. "What specifically did you talk about? Name one thing. Just one."

Sweat began to bead on my forehead, and I struggled to maintain my grip on the flames that coated my naked body. "I... we... It was nice." I searched for snippets of our interaction, but the details were fuzzy, slipping from my mental fingers before they could solidify. "There was... food, I think. He gave me his meal, and he was... nice. So nice." My knees shook under the strain, and I unconsciously placed a hand on Sin's shoulder for support.

"Stop it," he pleaded with Belarius. "Just let us go. We can leave, and you'll never see us again. We won't tell anyone."

Why was Sin begging? Sin didn't beg. And why did my head hurt so bad?

"I am afraid that was never an option, Dreisin. For her anyway." Belarius took another step closer to me, secured my gaze with his piercing blue eyes and said, "Remember."

My head exploded as the memory of our first meeting came rushing back in, false memories overlapping real ones, and I struggled to separate them.

"Hello?" I called out, pushing the door open.

"Come in, Raynella," a smooth male voice answered in English.

I stepped into the small room, and my eyes scanned the furnishings before I noticed a male seated in a large cushy chair with a plate of food near him. He appeared to be pushing fifty based on the creases around his eyes, but his short hair was still a strong shade of black. What caught my attention the most, though, were his eyes. I would recognize that pale blue color anywhere, and the golden sunburst around the pupil just confirmed it—whoever this guy was, we were definitely related.

He gestured to the chair beside him, and I sat down, staring at his plate of food with thinly-veiled desire.

"I am sure the kitchen will make you something should you wish, Raynella, but please do refrain from ogling my lunch." He took a bite and chewed it deliberately as he evaluated me.

"Sorry," I mumbled, embarrassed. "I didn't realize how hungry I was until I smelled this from the next hallway over."

The male frowned and settled back into the chair, watching me with disappointment in his eyes. "You are Vitaean, Raynella. Our senses are somewhat heightened when compared to those of humans. Have you learned nothing in your time here?"

I sank into myself a little. He wasn't wrong. I hadn't learned anything. If I was half-Vitaean, then I really needed to figure out exactly what that meant. I would ask Dey the next time I saw him. Whatever it took, I would get a straight answer about who and what I was exactly.

"So how do you know English?" I asked, wiping a slight bit of drool from the corner of my mouth. I was so hungry it was killing me.

I saw him cringe slightly at the action, so I quickly folded my hands in my lap.

"The same way the others do. Corym gave me the knowledge," he replied dismissively.

"Oh," I said, my face wrinkling in confusion. "I was told I already met everyone who knew my language."

"Ah, yes, well, I took it upon myself to make the request of Corym shortly after you arrived," he said, drumming his fingers on the arm of the chair. "Naturally, I wanted to be able to understand everything you said. You are very important to my plans, Raynella. I would not allow something so simple as a language barrier to derail them."

"Oh, um, what plans, exactly? Are you talking about the ley lines?"

"Something like that. Not that you need to know."

Okay, this conversation wasn't going the way I would have hoped.

I leaned back in my chair. "So, I'm guessing you're like my grandpa, then? The eyes kind of gave it away."

"So observant you are, Raynella," he replied, sarcasm dripping from his words. "And yes, I am your father's sire. I have actually been looking forward to meeting you."

"Uh, yeah. Likewise," I said, a bit subdued. "So what do I call you? Grandpa? Grandfather? Gramps?"

"You may call me Belarius," he replied harshly, as if the idea of me calling him Gramps was highly insulting.

"Belarius it is, then. So how come I haven't seen you before today?" I asked, trying to shift the conversation in a direction that might remove his annoyed expression.

"It is necessary that I remain in the shadows. For now, anyway."

"Oh," I said, unsure how else to respond. "So if you're Verren's father, and he's over a hundred does that mean you're like two hundred or...?"

His condescending laugh sent a shiver down my spine. "Oh my, you really do know nothing of Vitaeans."

I frowned. "You know, you don't have to be so rude. This is all kind of new to me."

So much for having a nice old grandfather.

I stood and moved toward the door. "I'll leave you to your meal, I guess."

He rose from his own chair, and when I turned back around he was only a foot away, his eyes searching mine.

"Well, this was enlightening," he said. "I was beginning to worry that you might become a problem like your mother was, but you really are little more than an ignorant human. How sad for you. To know so little. You are the perfect puppet, Raynella. You will do everything I need you to, and you will believe the entire time that you are making your own decisions."

I opened my mouth to ask who the hell he thought he was to speak to me like that, but he cut me off.

Capturing my eyes with his intense gaze, he commanded, "Be quiet, Raynella. When you think back on this conversation, you will only remember that you had a nice chat with a doddering old fool. Nothing more. Now go. I do not wish to look at you any longer."

I gave him a wide smile, then left, feeling lighter than I had in a while. It was nice to have a grandfather, someone who liked me for me. I wasn't the savior with him, I was just his granddaughter.

It was all so... nice.

I gaped at the male standing before me. Belarius, my grandfather. The man behind the curtain.

Oh, God.

Sin had tried to warn me as best he could, but I never saw it. I was so convinced it was all my father.

"You're the one compelling everyone," I said slowly as everything clicked into place—why my father was so hot and cold, one minute loving and caring, and the next manipulative and vindictive.

"Oh, look. Perhaps you are not as feebleminded as I thought," Belarius taunted.

My mind fought with the knowledge, turning it over like a rubix cube, trying to understand it all. "But why not just compel me to do whatever you wanted?" I asked. "Why did you have to hurt everyone else?"

"Compulsion on humans is tricky," he admitted. "Too much and they, well, they crack under the pressure. Being half-human, I assumed you could handle one or two instances, but I could not risk anything more. I have no use for a vegetable. I must confess, though, I have also enjoyed the game—nudging people in just the right direction to get you where I wanted without too much suspicion." He smoothed his hair back in an arrogant gesture. "It is an artform, truly."

At the mention of other people, I briefly glanced over at Sin, noting the drops of water that flecked up from the rooftop to coalesce around his wrist. I snapped my focus back to Belarius, but it was too late.

His eyes tracked mine, catching the planned attack.

In a flash, Sin thrust his arm out, and the water formed into a noose that he whipped toward Belarius' neck.

Not even the greatest aquiservian in Rivella could be faster than the sound of words, though.

His entire body froze in place when Belarius barked, "Halt."

Sin halted, his magic recoiling back around his wrist.

"Drop the water."

The water sloughed away and pooled at Sin's feet.

"Now be a good lad, and go stand by the back wall until I say otherwise. I am having a conversation with my granddaughter, and could do without these interruptions."

Sin marched robotically across the roof to stand as still as a statue by the castle parapet—all of his passion and intensity stuffed deep behind the obedient facade.

"How are you doing all of this?" I demanded once I was able to tear my eyes away from my ensnared lover. "I thought compulsion was forbidden?"

Belarius' lip curled up in a nasty grin. "Of course it is, but I was blessed with a weak father who could not bring himself to kill his only son. It was quite easy to hide, you know. Nobody questions the king's powers, after all. Look how easily my son managed to fool you."

My hands curled into tight fists at my side. "That's not fair. How could I even tell his magic was an illusion?"

The laugh Belarius let out made my skin crawl.

"That is not all he fooled you with. Look again, Raynella."

The last thing I wanted to do was turn my attention away from him, but I couldn't stop my eyes from wondering back to the bloody, charred body at my feet. Most of his chest was little more than ash and burnt tissue, but there... on the edges. The ramentum that had covered his chest were gone, and that which remained barely reached his shoulders.

"Secunnario," I said quietly. Even his ramentum were an illusion.

"And a weak one at that," Belarius sneered, disgust lacing his voice. "Do you have any idea how embarrassing it was for me when he never manifested his third power? And his healing magic? Pitiful. Since his only real skill was illusion, I decided that I would use it to my advantage. Clearly he would never carry on my powerful legacy, so when my time came to abdicate the throne... well, let us say I took measures to sustain my good works. I have always been around, Raynella, hidden from sight by the veil of Verren's illusions. Whispering instructions in my son's ear. He was so weak-willed that controlling him took next to no effort at all."

He knelt in front of my father's body, shaking his head. "Did you know he allowed the plague to spread? Allowed his own family to succumb to it when all he needed to do was kill every human. A simple solution really."

Belarius plucked a garish ring with the Diamond Court crest from Verren's hand, slid it onto his own finger, and stood up. "He would not do it, though. It was the only compulsion he ever managed to successfully fight off. I thought perhaps I could break him down over time, but then Leeara came along."

The disdain in Belarius' tone when he spoke of his son was nothing compared to the venom for my mother. It was all I could do to reel in my anger and not blast him off the roof. The flames of my dress flickered, and I could feel my fire begging to be unleashed. But if Sin was no match for his compulsion, what could I do?

"I spent decades searching for the silver-haired female to fulfill the prophecy," Belarius continued casually, as if all this was merely a mild disruption to his evening. "I had hoped you would be my daughter so I could mold you from birth to do exactly what I needed. Imagine my surprise when it was my son who found your mother. And imagine my horror when he fell in love with her. A human." He spat the word as if he were talking about something truly vile and disgusting.

"Your father begged me to abandon the prophecy because he could not stand to let his precious baby girl die for my agenda. Pathetic, really. To place an infant above the future of his kingdom. Annoyingly, I did not realize until too late that your mother had been listening at the door. Nasty trait, eavesdropping. So very human."

Talons sprouted from my fingers, curling into sharp spikes of white hot flame. "That was the conversation that made her flee," I growled. "You ordered Sin to chase her into the woods, and you're the reason she's dead."

"When I learned she had disappeared with you, of course I immediately sent my best assassin to retrieve her. Surely Sin has told you about all he has done for me over the years?" Belarius smiled maliciously, absently picking at a bit of dirt under his fingernail as if he hadn't just dropped a huge bomb. "Did you know your father tried to stop me from compelling Sin that night? He failed, naturally, but oh how he fought, his love for you and your mother was so great. Such a shame you murdered him in cold blood."

His accusation hit me like a sledgehammer to the chest, knocking the breath from my lungs.

I *murdered* him.

I *murdered* my father.

Every hint of the fire I had so painstakingly summoned vanished in an instant, and I dropped to my knees, ignoring the pain when they smashed into the hard stone.

I focused on my father's body then, really seeing what I had done. The blood congealing around the pin I had stabbed into his neck. The bits of his skin that flaked and blew away on the wind. The blackened bit of sternum that showed through the burnt mess of flesh and gore.

I had done that. I had plunged my flaming hands into his chest because I wanted him to suffer like my mother suffered. And his last words to me were that he loved me.

He was innocent, and I tortured him to death.

I was the real monster.

My fire tried to flare to life around me once more, but my anger was smothered under the torment of what I'd done. I was an empty vessel, lacking fuel for my rage. The only thing that poured into me now was despair.

My mother sacrificed herself for nothing.

My father was dead at my hand.

I viciously attacked Sin, the only male I might have ever loved because I wasn't smart enough to see that he had been compelled.

I had nothing and no one left. Nobody was coming to save me. Not this time.

I collapsed forward, lying naked on the cold stone. Deeper and deeper, I sank into the abyss of my pain. It surrounded me. Burrowed into my very soul, and I didn't even try to fight back because I deserved it.

I deserved all of it.

The poverty growing up. The abuse, physical and emotional. The anxiety attacks that prevented me from ever becoming anything more than a fast food cashier.

It slammed into me—this knowledge that I was a complete waste of space in this universe or any other. I was born for the sole purpose of dying to fulfill a prophecy. My death was all I had to offer.

When I felt like I could sink no lower, when the depths of my suffering could go no further, something caressed my mind.

It was gentle at first—a light questioning touch, asking for permission to enter. I had nothing left to lose, so I opened myself up and let it flood into me.

Power. Magic.

It didn't burn this time—the manifestation. Didn't consume me the way the fire had. It just coated my mind and body in a soothing harmony, nestling under my skin like a sleeping cat's soft purr.

My mental power.

I instantly knew what it did, as if it had always been a part of me, waiting to be awoken.

I knew now what I was capable of.

I would not be controlled and compelled like a puppet. I was Rain Motherfucking Solis. I survived more in my twenty-five years than any person should have to endure in a lifetime, and I was still here.

Rising to my feet, I summoned back all the rage and fury I thought I had lost. My flames exploded across my skin and out my back in a flash of brilliant red-gold light. A slight prickling on my arms drew my attention, and I watched as elegant new black and purple swirls weaved themselves into the edges of my ramentum, spreading across my skin from my elbows up to my shoulders.

Then I faced the male responsible for nearly every bad thing that ever happened to me.

And I smiled.

He chuckled in response. "Oh, Raynella. What exactly do you think you can do against me?"

"You're about to find out," I growled as my flaming talons burst out once more, demanding that I rake and claw his flesh. I would tear him apart for what he did to my family.

"You do not understand, do you?" he said smugly, locking onto my eyes. With a rich voice full of bravado, he commanded, "Drop your fire."

The flames flared brighter, and my smile morphed into something that felt almost evil.

His eyes flicked around, confused, before he focused on me once more. "Stop where you are."

I took a step closer.

He backed up, fear finally sparking to life on his once smug face. He furrowed his brow and said, louder this time, "Raynella, you will release your fire and stand quietly without moving."

"What was it you said?" I asked mockingly, "Oh right. You do not understand, do you?" I lifted one flaming hand to my face and made a show of inspecting my fiery talons, letting him see in my eyes exactly what I was going to do to him. "You don't control me anymore, Gramps."

His eyes grew even wider. "You're a vitiate," he breathed out with equal parts horror and awe.

"If that means I'm immune to mental powers, then yes, I do believe I am a vitiate. Looks like this ignorant human is more than you expected."

His fear morphed into anger before sliding into something worse—arrogance. "You are forgetting one thing, Raynella. You may be a vitiate, but Dreisin is not."

Inhaling sharply, I shot a look over to Sin still standing by the wall, completely unmoving, fully entrapped by the compulsion.

"Dreisin," Belarius called out. "Climb up onto the parapet."

To my horror, Sin obeyed.

Gasping, I lunged forward when he teetered slightly before catching his balance.

"What are you doing?" I demanded. "You have no reason to hurt him."

"I have every reason to hurt him!" Belarius snarled. "Do you have any idea how much effort I put into constructing my perfect plan for you? How many compulsions I put into place? Dey seducing you so love would make you compliant to anything I had him ask. Camden and Ramset taking you into Civi Adasa with that damn shroud on to an area where I knew some of the more fanatical court members would be. Your father holding off saving you until the brink of death as I assumed a vicious beating would keep you inside the castle. Corym witholding the language so you would never learn anything I didn't want you to learn. And Josira, well, she was the lynchpin."

A sickening feeling settled into the pit of my stomach.

"I compelled her to become your friend and report to me everything she observed. Do you see the truth now, Raynella? I have been moving the pieces around the board since before you were even born. The only thing I never saw coming was your love for him." He jerked his chin at Sin. "He ruined everything. Every one of my carefully laid out plans was destroyed because he did everything in his power to fight my compulsion and help you." Belarius moved leisurely over toward Sin. "Remove your jacket and vest," he ordered.

Sin complied, mindlessly removing his clothing, and it killed me to see him so helpless.

Belarius twirled his finger. "Now turn around."

With stilted movements, Sin rotated in place, giving us a perfect view of his scarred back and the faintest hints of black ramentum beginning to reappear.

"I always suspected, you know," Belarius said, turning back to me. "My abilities didn't work on him quite as well as they should. I only just realized that it was his concealed illusion power mucking things up. Two mental casters with the same ability tend to cancel each other out, so he saw right through the veil of Verren's illusion. Every time I gave Sin an order, I compelled him to forget about me, but then he would see me whispering in Verren's ear, and I imagine he realized things were more than they seemed. If he had been a little stronger, he might have been able to break my compulsion all together." Belarius glanced back to Sin, a wicked smile spreading across his face. "But I don't think he entirely wanted to, did you, Dreisin? You didn't want her to know about all the awful things you've done."

"It wasn't his fault," I said, the love I felt for Sin flooding back into my heart. "You forced him to do all of it."

Belarius let out a sinister chuckle. "You know nothing, Raynella. You have no idea what he is capable of. His powerful magic isn't the only reason I've kept him around this long, but I find myself in need of a new plan now that things have changed. My son served his final purpose well enough, getting the other kings alone in a room with me, so I don't even mind that you killed him. Saves me the effort. You, however, are still very much pivotal to my end goal."

I struggled to wrap my brain around Belarius' words. "Why do you even want me to restore the ley lines? I can't imagine you actually want to see the people of Rivella have access to their magic again."

He chuckled, and the hideous sound sent a cold, ominous feeling creeping down my back. "Now when did I ever say I wanted you to restore the lines?"

I blinked. "What else could you possibly need from me?"

"You didn't think I was going to tell you everything, did you? I have plans for the Onyx Palace, but you don't don't need to worry about that. Right now, all I want is for you to do exactly as I say." He swept his hand toward Sin, and a gust of air magic lifted him from the edge of the wall to hold him out over the thousand-foot drop.

"No!" I screamed, rushing toward him.

"Stop right there," Belarius ordered, "or I will let Dreisin fall."

Fear locked my feet in place even as every cell in my body itched to run toward the male I couldn't lose. Not when we'd finally found each other.

"Don't hurt him," I begged, staring into Sin's sorrow-filled eyes. There was such resignation in them, as if he knew he wouldn't survive this.

All he ever did was love me and try to help me as best he could despite the compulsion. Telling me to visit the Laneum at night which led to finding Corym and receiving the language. Taking me to Yanda to learn the truth about my mother. Telling me to look for the man behind the curtain. He did it all to prevent this from happening, and I had treated him like he was no better than the monster in front of me.

I wouldn't let him die.

"I'll do whatever you want," I said quietly. "Just don't hurt him."

"Now there's a good girl. Let us start by dropping your flames."

It killed me to obey, but I pulled every bit of my fire back inside me, save for thin strips around my breasts and waist. I would not stand naked in front of him. I didn't have much left, but I had my dignity.

He frowned slightly at the remaining flames, likely judging whether or not they might be a threat. Ultimately, he let it go. "Now I would like you to go over to the stairwell and scream for help. Loudly, please. Let the guards at the base of the stairs know the king has been murdered. That should bring them running."

I grit my teeth and, for a brief second, I wondered if I could be fast enough to save Sin.

"Do not bother, Raynella," Belarius chided as if reading my mind. "Should you attack me, my concentration might lapse. I would hate for Dreisin here to meet an untimely end. Now do as I say."

Seeing no other option, I walked over to the stairwell, took a few steps down, and shouted loudly in Rivellan, "HELP! PLEASE HELP! THE KING IS DEAD!" I kept up the litany until I heard the clomping of boots echoing up the stairs.

My throat raw from screaming, I walked back over to Belarius. "I did what you asked. Now let him go."

The smile he gave me was positively gleeful, and my heart ceased beating.

"Whatever the princess desires."

He flicked his wrist.

It was just the slightest little motion. Inconsequential, really. Barely noticeable. And yet it was all he needed to rip my universe apart.

My eyes connected with Sin's as the cage of air holding him vanished.

"I love you," he mouthed.

I lunged forward, but there was nothing I could do.

Sin didn't even scream as he plummeted a thousand feet to his death at the hands of jagged rocks and an unforgiving sea.

Chapter Fifty-Two

Everything that happened after that was little more than a blur. It felt like I was moving through gelatin. Like the world around me couldn't possibly be the real world. Like I couldn't possibly still be alive when Sin was dead.

The door burst open, and three pairs of scuffed black leather boots entered my field of vision.

"She murdered your king," Belarius shouted. "Take her to the Sonaria immediately."

Rough hands hauled me to my feet, but I didn't struggle in the slightest.

"What is going on?" Dey demanded, appearing behind the guards.

"Raynella has murdered King Verren with her secret magic," Belarius stated calmly.

I could feel the compulsion in the air as if my own magic despised even being in the vicinity of it. It felt oily and alien against my skin.

"You are the interim ruler now. It is very important that you do exactly as I say," he continued. "She is still needed to fulfill the prophecy, so she cannot be harmed." He paused. "Harmed much, anyway. Have the guards seal her in the Sonaria so she cannot use her fire magic to kill you too. We will decide how to proceed with her later."

"Aquiservians," Dey barked sharply. "Do not let her summon any flames. Lock her in the Sonaria. Nobody is to speak with her until I allow it."

I almost laughed at his order to restrain me. Every bit of fight I had inside me died alongside Sin. They could torture me for all I cared. Nothing could feel worse than this.

A layer of cold water slid over my entire body save for my nose and eyes, compliments of the guards that glared at me like I was filth.

Dey approached me, his eyes sweeping over my arms and the ramentum I had worked so hard to hide.

"What did you do, Rain?" he asked, his voice tight with anger

I had no answer for him, so he called for the guards to take me away.

There was only pain in the Sonaria. Unrelenting darkness and misery. I didn't even look up as they slammed the heavy metal door shut, locking me in the all-encompassing blackness of the windowless cell.

Only when the fenite forcefully ripped the power from my veins did I finally succumb to the agony that had descended upon me. Violent screams filled the tiny space, a symphony of torment that lasted until my lungs had no breath left to fuel my suffering. It felt like someone had torn my body open and dug around inside to find every last ounce of magic that permeated my cells, burning away the only strength I might have clung to.

When the last drop of magic faded, death took up residence inside me. A cold feeling of emptiness like my soul had been extracted alongside my power, and now there was only pain. Neverending pain.

I had only the abyss as a companion, so I gave myself over to it.

Chapter Fifty-Three

"Rain?"

The soft voice cut through the fog of grief and fatigue, pulling me back into myself.

"Jenni?" I croaked out, my throat still hoarse. I recognized my crescia's voice, but it sounded different somehow. Older.

"Rain is in trouble."

"How can I even hear you," I asked, still fighting the grogginess. "My magic is gone."

"Jenni belongs to Rain. Jenni does not belong to the Source."

Her stilted, childlike cadence was slightly more mature, and I found myself missing the innocent sound of my sweet little crescia in my head.

"Rain needs to escape."

I slumped against the wall of the Sonaria. I could barely move let alone escape.

"There's nothing I can do," I said hopelessly.

"Jenni can help. Rain is vitiate. Rain can break compulsion."

I laughed bitterly as another wave of pain crested and washed over me. Maybe she wasn't aware of what had happened. "I don't think that's going to change anything. The damage is done. Belarius doesn't need to compel me."

"Rain will listen!"

Her tone was so forceful it almost distracted me from the pain. Almost.

"Jenni will bring Dey. Rain will free Dey. Dey will help Rain and Jenni escape."

My face sagged. I hated to crush her little baby crescia dreams. "I don't know how to use my powers to nullify someone else's compulsion. Bringing Dey here won't accomplish anything."

"Rain will trust Jenni. Rain will trust herself. Be ready. Dey comes soon."

I wanted to allow myself to hope. To have faith like she did. To believe that maybe Jenni could do something, anything, to save me.

Hope was the eternally elusive emotion, though, and nothing was ever going to change that.

I let myself fall back asleep. The only hope I could muster was the hope that maybe I would dream of Sin.

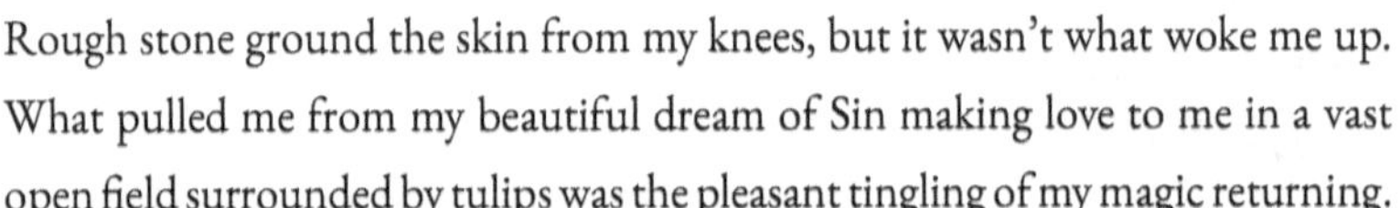

Rough stone ground the skin from my knees, but it wasn't what woke me up. What pulled me from my beautiful dream of Sin making love to me in a vast open field surrounded by tulips was the pleasant tingling of my magic returning. The warmth of my fire and the coolness of my mental ability melding together in a soothing balm for my soul.

I wrenched my eyes open. Two guards dragged me through the halls of the dungeons, each with an arm hooked under my shoulders. Someone had dressed me, but I barely registered the feel of the rough burlap on my skin.

I was out of the Sonaria.

They hadn't taken me far, I realized when they roughly tossed me into a regular cell down the hall from the fenite prison. My head cracked against the hard floor, and I absently rubbed the spot of the impending bruise.

The door to the cell swung shut as the guards marched away, and Dey stepped into view, kneeling to look me in the eye. Any affection he previously held for me had been wiped away by Belarius, leaving only hard resolve on his face.

"You owe me answers," he seethed.

I opened my mouth to tell him that I would be happy to explain whatever he wanted, but my ability for speech dried up when a creature flew down and hunched beside him.

"Jenni?" I gasped. She was exactly as I last saw her save for one rather significant change. She was bigger. Much bigger. Nearly the size of a fat rabbit. Twelve hours ago, she could fit in my palm and now... "What happened to you?" I asked.

"Rain gets stronger. Jenni gets stronger."

A small little chitter echoed through my cell as Opal crawled up Jenni's back to sit on her head. She chirped at me once, and I couldn't help but crack a tiny smile. At least she was still the same.

"You have a lot of explaining to do," Dey snarled. "Start with why you killed your father, and end with when you manifested your magic. And don't leave out how you have a crescia that can speak inside my head."

My eyes darted from Jenni back to Dey. "She spoke to you?"

And here I thought I was special.

Dey ran a hand through his hair, but the boyish gesture did nothing to soften his features. "I thought I was going insane at first, but she wouldn't leave me alone. She kept saying 'Rain has answers. Rain will help.' So why don't you tell me, King Killer, do you have answers for me?"

His eyes clouded with disdain and hatred, and I needed to make him see the truth. I just didn't know how.

I reached a hand out, thinking skin contact might augment my new ability that still hadn't fully returned, but he jerked away.

"I can't tell you, Dey," I huffed out. "You would never believe me. I can only help you to see the truth. You'll just have to trust me."

"Why would I ever trust you?" he scoffed.

I looked into his eyes, letting him see the real vulnerability in my own. "Please, Dey," I whispered, reaching for him again.

This time he allowed my fingers to land on his arm, and I focused my will on the concepts of clarity and truth. When I started to feel the tingling sensation rise up, I released my power into him. In a flash of lightning, my mind connected with Dey's, and my magic penetrated all the hidden crevices of his brain, seeking out and destroying every hint of compulsion, burning it all away.

Dey's body seized up, his eyes rolled back, and he slumped bonelessly to the ground. For far too long, he simply lay there, unmoving.

Just as panic began to rise inside me, he stirred and sat up, his wide eyes seeking out my own. He looked at me differently then, his expression innocent and afraid, like a child who just learned a terrible truth about the universe, but didn't know how to process it.

"Rain..."

I could see the apology forming on his lips, so I stopped him. "Later," I said, hastily. "Can you get me out of here?"

He nodded absently, his motions stilted and clumsy as he stood up.

How long had Belarius been compelling him? How many years of compulsion were just wiped clean?

A key clicked in the lock, and Dey helped me to my feet.

"Rain," he began again, this time more forceful. "There is so much inside my head that I do not understand right now, but I need to tell you one thing. If only one."

Leaning heavily against his shoulder, I looked up into his sorrowful amber eyes. "What is it, Dey?"

He ran a hand down my sweaty face, and a small river of warmth snaked through my body, healing the cuts and bruises I'd barely noticed were there. "It was real for me," he whispered after a long moment. "I know you believe it was all the compulsion, but... it was real for me. I just need you to know that."

I had no response for him, not one that he wanted to hear anyway, so I dipped my head in acknowledgement and pushed off his shoulder to hobble out of the cell. I was still weak, but I could mostly move on my own.

"There's a tunnel," I coughed out. "To the left of the Laneum. It will take us out of the castle."

Dey asked no questions, only helped me up the stairs.

To both of our surprise, Cam appeared at the top, a shocked expression on his face. "Princess? Dey? What is happening?"

"Long story," I replied wearily. "What are you doing here?"

"I heard from my soldiers that you were locked away, and... I was coming to rescue you."

The swell of emotion I felt from his words—the reminder that I wasn't entirely alone in this world—would have broken me if I let it. Instead, I shoved it down deep and gave him a quick hug. "We have to get out of here," I said. "My grandfather, Belarius, has everyone compelled to obey him. I don't know what he's planning, but it involves the other kings. It's bad, Cam."

His eyes darted between me and Dey. "But Ram is still in the infirmary..."

"We'll come back for him," I declared. "We'll come back for him and Jo and everyone else. I promise." As I spoke, I knew it was more than just words. It was a vow. Belarius wouldn't hurt anyone else I cared about.

Cam nodded and followed us down the hall toward the pools.

"What about Sin?" he asked Dey hesitantly.

My heart stopped at the sound of Sin's name, but I fought back the flood of pain that nearly dropped me to my knees.

"Sin's dead," I answered, my voice harsh and cold. My heart had been dashed against the same rocks that stole my love from me, and now I had nothing left to offer but retribution.

Lifting a hand, I watched as my fingers began to smolder, and small wisps of fire flickered at the tips, my claws returned to me once more.

Whatever it took, I would have my revenge.

For my mother.

For Sin.

About the author

T. M. Kirk writes paranormal rom-coms and romantasy books filled with spice, banter, and side characters that love to steal the show. Originally from Alaska, she is a rolling stone, eternally searching for that perfect place to call home. Currently residing in California with her partner and two fur babies, her days are spent riding her motorcycle, traveling to new places, and creating fantasy and paranormal worlds as a much needed escape from reality.

www.ingramcontent.com/pod-product-compliance
Lightning Source LLC
Chambersburg PA
CBHW021123260626
47169CB00005B/1422

* 9 7 9 8 9 9 2 0 7 8 1 0 7 *